Other Simeon Grist Mysteries by
Timothy Hallinan
from Avon Books

INCINERATOR

THE MAN WITH NO TIME

A SIMEON GRIST MYSTERY

TIMOTHY HALLINAN

AVON BOOKS ◆ NEW YORK

AVON BOOKS
A division of
The Hearst Corporation
1350 Avenue of the Americas
New York, New York 10019

Published in hardcover by William Morrow and Company, Inc.; for information address Permissions Department, William Morrow and Company, Inc., 1350 Avenue of the Americas, New York, New York 10019.

First Avon Books Printing: May 1995

AVON TRADEMARK REG. U.S. PAT. OFF. AND IN OTHER COUNTRIES, MARCA REGISTRADA, HECHO EN U.S.A.

Printed in the U.S.A.

RA   10   9   8   7   6   5   4   3   2   1

For two American families,
the Aguayos and the Choys

For two American families,
the Aguayos and the Choys

Acknowledgments

This book was written largely in Thailand. The wonderful staff members at the Tawana Ramanda Hotel, Bangkok; the Royal Garden Resort, Hua Hin; and the Phi Phi International on Phi Phi Island kept the book on track and its writer off the streets and off the beach.

Many men and women, both Chinese and non-Chinese, in Los Angeles, Bangkok, Taipei, and Hong Kong found time to talk with me while I was gathering material. I'd especially like to thank Alex Cheung, G.C., A.B.D., Tippawan Phoosri, S. Li, and H. Datoon. Others wished to conceal even their initials. Thanks to them as well.

The links among the Chinese make up a network
that covers the globe.

—GONTRAN DE PONCINS
From a Chinese City

PART 1

THE DOG

The dog is a creature that keeps watch and is skillful in its selection of men. On this account the ancients on all their festive occasions of eating and drinking employed it.

—KHAN HSAING-TAO

1

___

Another Saturday Night

Horace Chan had pointy little eyebrows like upside-down Vs. If they'd met over his nose, they would have formed a perfect M, and the M would have stood for Maybe. For years I'd been watching Horace make a bet and then hedge it, as reflexively as the rest of us inhale after we exhale, and now I was watching him hedge the biggest bet of his life: the one he'd made when he got married.

This was serious, because Horace was almost my brother-in-law. And even worse: He was one of the very small group of people whom I love. So why was I watching him nuzzle some stranger dressed in a little something that could have been sewn from the cellophane torn from four packs of Marlboros?

"She like you," Horace's Uncle Lo observed sagely.

Horace snickered. Horace had an unappealing snicker under the best circumstances, and these weren't they. I tried to kick him under the table.

My kick missed and struck Uncle Lo in the shin.

"Sorry," I said. Uncle Lo was the guest of honor, the reason I was watching Horace punch holes in his marriage.

Uncle Lo didn't seem surprised that I'd kicked him. He was maybe seventy years old, and looked like nothing had surprised him since his seventeenth birthday. His face, generously seamed by gravity and time, had probably been under absolute control since his whiskers sprouted. Control over facial expressions was something people apparently learned early in Mainland China.

"You have hiccups?" he asked. For the tenth time that evening, I asked myself why I didn't like him. I was *supposed* to like him. After all, Uncle Lo was the Chan family hero. And the Chan family included Eleanor Chan, my longtime ex-girlfriend and the person I loved most in the world. I corrected my aim and tried to kick Horace—Eleanor's equivocal brother—again, and missed everyone.

"Getting late, Horace," I said, resorting to a less physical form of communication.

"I love you," the girl to my right said promptly, wrapping her arms around my neck. "No shit."

"That's very promising," I slurred, perhaps denying the line the points it deserved for sheer novelty. How many beers had I *drunk*, anyway?

"Promise her anything," Uncle Lo said, leaning toward me as though we shared a confidence.

No points for him, either, as far as I was concerned. There was a candle on the table, shielded in a rippled red glass, and it splashed his face from beneath with a malevolent light. To my intoxicated Anglo eyes—even after years of seeing my future in Eleanor's Chinese eyes—Uncle Lo, looming over the candle, still looked like a lot of racial stereotypes—mostly of a host of villains in black-and-white movies. The effect was heightened by a black eye that reminded me of the circle surrounding the eye of the mutt in the "Our Gang" comedies, except that there was nothing comic about it. Of course, the stereotypes might have been suggested by our surroundings, a mostly-Chinese hostess bar somewhere in the Asian colony known as Los Angeles. But bar or no bar, Uncle Lo didn't look like a hero. A pirate, maybe, but not a hero.

The hero glanced at his watch for the eighth or ninth time. "Telephone?" he asked. The girl to my right said, "In the back," and stuck her tongue into my ear.

"Yeesh," I said, swabbing it with my little finger.

We all watched him go, thin and only slightly stooped, against the background of the bar, prematurely tinsel-festooned for Christmas. The other booths were jammed full of Chinese males in three-piece suits and young Asian women in outfits of varying degrees of transparency. A dead Christmas tree twinkled depressively in a corner.

"He's only been here twenty-four hours," I said to Horace. "Who could he know?" I looked at my little finger. It was wet. "And where'd he get the shiner?"

"Somethin wrong with you ear?" asked the girl to my right.

"It's the humidity," I said, striving for pleasant. "Listen, Horace—"

"Taste funny, too," said the girl to my right. She'd told me her name was Ning when we sat down, and I saw no reason to doubt her. Whether she loved me was another question. I wiped my finger on my shirt.

"Want a Q-Tip?" Horace asked, producing one from a vest pocket. Horace made a practice of carrying one of everything, up to and including small articles of furniture, in his pockets. Another sign of irresolution. Why be prepared only for the library just because you've decided to go to the library? You might change your mind and wind up on a freighter bound for Kuala Lumpur. I could have traveled the world for a year on the contents of Horace's pockets.

I didn't want a Q-Tip, but Ning had already grasped it and inserted it into my ear. I yanked back as though she'd poked me with a cattle prod, and the girl sitting next to Horace joined Ning in a hearty laugh. The laugh settled it: Both women were Thai. Nobody but a Thai can laugh that heartily without breaking a rib.

Horace managed an economical Chinese chortle, and Ning put the dry end of the Q-Tip in her mouth and bounced it up and down. Horace, who didn't smoke, produced a lighter from somewhere and extended it, and Ning waggled it up and down between her teeth and said, "Peetah. Peetah, Peetah, Peetah."

"Bette Davis never said that," I observed.

Ning gave me what the Thais call "small eyes." It's not a friendly expression. "You no fun," she said. "Him," she added, indicating Horace, "him fun."

"He's also married," I said, looking at the girl sitting next to Horace. "In fact," I said, stretching a point, "we're all married."

"You *taste* married," Ning said, sliding away from me.

The girl next to Horace responded to the bulletin by twining her arms around his neck and saying, "Married. *Pah.*"

"Who married?" The lady whom the management had assigned to Uncle Lo slid into the booth. She was a few years older than Ning, and maybe a decade older than Horace's girl, and she was mistakenly trying to make up for added years by subtracting clothes. With less on than the average whelk, she succeeded only in looking like she'd somehow managed to reclaim her baby fat. Her name came to me out of the fumes: Lek, Thai for "little."

"Everyone in the world," I said, a bit wildly, noticing that my glass was empty again. "Me, him, and the other him." Ning picked up my empty glass and waved it in the direction of the bar.

"More," she called. Actually, "Mo-ah."

"No," I said. The bartender sang out something cheerful and untranslatably Asian, then began to pour.

"Married?" Lek shrugged. "If he not married, why he's here? Man who's not married don't need bar. Not married, got plenty girl."

I rubbed my face, which seemed to have gone numb with a wooden, absolute numbness that suggested the onset of some exotic neurological disease. So I wasn't drunk. I was only dying. "We don't need girls," I said.

All three girls responded with merry Thai laughter, the Mormon Tabernacle Choir on nitrous oxide. As the hilarity crested, a beer was slapped down in front of me, and a young Chinese-looking woman seated herself at an electric piano and began an energetic phonetic rendition of "Jingle Bells." People sang along in various languages.

"We're leaving," I said to Horace, trying and failing to stand up. "Pansy's waiting for you." Pansy was Horace's wife and the mother of their twins, and as far as I was concerned an immediate candidate for sainthood.

"Pansy," Uncle Lo said dismissively, standing above us again. "Who cares?"

He'd sounded a lot fonder of Pansy at Horace's house, and now his tone caught Horace's attention. Horace looked up at him, wide-eyed.

"I do," I said. This time I managed to get to my feet, and I was relieved to see Horace stand up, too.

"Gotta hit the toilet," Horace said, edging out of the booth.

"Good luck," Lek said cheerfully, and we all watched Horace weave his way toward the plumbing, as though it were part of the floor show.

Uncle Lo sat down next to me, closer than I would have liked. He smelled like the old clothes at the bottom of the hamper.

"The check," I said, leaning away.

Lek pouted politely and then floated in the direction of the bar. The electric piano gurgled out the opening chords of Elvis's "Blue Christmas."

"You detective boy," Uncle Lo said, surprising me. When I'd been told the family hero was in town, I hadn't known he'd been told what I did for a living.

"Yeah," I said, worrying about Pansy and the twins. "Detective boy."

"Hah," Uncle Lo said, as though I'd admitted personally eating most of the members of the Donner Party. "Some Chinese not like detective."

"And some detectives don't like some Chinese," I said, draining my newly full glass without thinking about it.

Uncle Lo put his hand on my arm and squeezed. I lowered my head—which seemed to take a *lot* of time—to check it out. His index finger was scraped raw, its nail split vertically to the quick. It must have hurt him to squeeze my arm, but nothing showed in his face. "What you think about me?"

"I think you've got a terrific black eye. And I think Horace should be home with his wife."

Uncle Lo sank his fingers more deeply into my arm, and I watched the skin beneath the nail go white, except for the livid line of red beneath the split. It had to hurt like hell. Then he smiled a cheese-yellow crescent that defied the pain and stood. He didn't wobble this time. "We go home then."

"Swell," Horace said, materializing next to the table. He'd splashed his pants, leaving a pattern that suggested an archipelago of uninhabited islands adrift in a khaki sea. "The urinal moved," he said.

The girls laughed again, dutifully this time, and Horace settled the tab, added a big tip, and led us out through the door in an imprecise conga line. Horace and I had lost the ability to identify either of our feet as right or left, but Uncle Lo walked with the kind of precision that would have qualified him to lead the Long March. Once we were squeezed into the front seat of Horace's little Honda—the backseat was taken up with the twins' stuff—Uncle Lo leaned against my shoulder and went promptly to sleep.

"I gather the dog tried to bite you," I said conversationally, but he'd departed the conversation zone.

Horace was far too drunk for L.A. on a Saturday night, but the luck that had deserted him in the men's room rejoined us in the car. He swerved away from oncoming headlights once or twice and said *"Wheeee"* too often to reassure the faint of heart, but eventually we pulled up behind the apartment house that he and Pansy and the twins rented from his and Eleanor's mother. Pansy stood silhouetted in the light from the door as Uncle Lo revived against my shoulder and gave the world a survivor's squint.

"So," I said as Uncle Lo and I climbed carefully out of the car beneath Pansy's sober gaze. "Who'd you call in the bar?"

"Always detective," Lo said. He held up the wrist bearing the watch he'd kept checking. "I look my watch, and all wrong. So I call Time."

I started toward my car before the question struck me: "Why didn't you ask one of us what time it was?"

"Detective boy," he said dismissively, "Good night."

I thought about it all the way home.

2

Dim Sum and Then Some

As much as I loved Eleanor Chan, my hangover was making it difficult to like her.

"He saved my *life*," Eleanor said, grabbing my arm with surprisingly strong fingers.

"This seems to be a family trait," I said, pushing her hand aside. Then I hung onto her wrist. The room had developed an alarming tilt.

We hadn't been seated yet. Horace, Pansy, the two kids, and Uncle Lo were late meeting us, and the competition for tables at the Empress Pavilion was too fierce to allow us to do anything but mill around hopelessly, clutching our paper numbers and praying that the rest of the group showed up before our number was called. The entire Chinese population of Los Angeles proper, which is to say all but the more recent Mandarin-speaking arrivals who had laid claim to Monterey Park, showed up at the Empress Pavilion for *dim sum* on Sundays. Every single one of them was talking. For all the myth of the inscrutable Orient, the Chinese are the most demonstrative people on earth.

"Well, he *did*," Eleanor said, raising her voice over the din. Like many Chinese, she seemed perfectly at ease packed shoulder to thigh with strangers. "He carried me, literally carried me, more than two hundred miles across China on his shoulders with my pregnant mother following behind dressed as a peasant. When we hit the water he tied my hands around his neck and swam toward Hong Kong with my mother paddling along behind."

We hadn't actually talked about this in detail before. "Lo did that?"

She turned away, scanning the crowd for latecomers. "The harbor was full of police boats. He bought them off, somehow. Three or four times we saw the spotlights skipping over the water. Once a light stopped just above our heads and someone yelled something in Cantonese. I thought we were dead."

"What did he yell?" I just can't help asking questions.

"Who knows? I was just a little kid. But whatever it was, and whatever Uncle Lo called back, the boat turned around without picking us up and moved away from us, and Uncle Lo told us to follow the boat, and half an hour later another boat picked us up and we were in Hong Kong."

"He must be very resourceful," I said.

She gave me Full Glare. "You make it sound like an accusation. If he *hadn't* been resourceful, I'd still be in China."

"I'm grateful," I said, meaning it. My headache approached tumor magnitude. "But there's still something wrong with him. Whose brother is he? Your mother's or your father's?"

"Neither," she said. She looked at my big doleful white man's face, mistook my grimace of pain for a pang of conscience, and lifted herself up to kiss my cheek. She'd always been forgiving, and I'd often taken advantage of it. "Uncle is a term of respect. For years, I thanked Uncle Lo in my prayers every night for what he did for my family. If he hadn't, there wouldn't have been any family."

Now we were on familiar ground. Eleanor's family
had been landowners, a fatal mistake when the Chinese
government made one of its Great Leaps forward. Her
father, a university professor, had spent eighteen hours
kneeling on broken glass and reciting his sins to illiterate
Red Guards. Then he'd been sent to prison in Manchu-
ria, and when the prison officials realized he was going
to die, they released him so they wouldn't have to bother
with the body. Somehow he got himself home and im-
pregnated his wife with Horace as a final gesture toward
life. That finished, he'd turned his face to the wall and
let life go. That was in 1959. Eleanor was two.

Like many men of his class, he'd been an intellectual,
which made him doubly guilty. He'd written a long
scholarly treatise about Cao Xueqin's *The Dream of the
Red Chamber*, the novel that Eleanor and I loved best
in the world. It had brought us together at UCLA, me
in Literature, she on loan from Oriental Studies. Both of
us had been transfixed by the tale that set forth the problems of Bao-Yu, the pampered and neurotically sensitive
rich boy, and his two beautiful female cousins, the ethe-
rèal Dai-Yu and the earthy Bao-Chai—a vanishing *Gone
with the Wind* way of life painted unexpectedly on a
Chinese canvas like the frilly blue tragedy of the Willow
Pattern.

"So, Uncle Whoever," I said as the room listed in
the other direction. "Uncle Duplicitous who doesn't like
Pansy."

Eleanor's eyes narrowed, never a good sign. "*Simeon.*" Then she heard what I'd said. "What do you
mean, he doesn't—"

A hand landed heavily enough on my shoulder to
make my teeth crack together, and I turned to see Horace
grinning lividly at me. He was an especially drab shade
of olive and perspiring freely, and there were flushed
blotches under his eyes. Over his shoulder, Pansy gazed
cheerfully at me through her square spectacles. Com-
passion surged over me. "Nice imitation of military

camouflage, Horace," I said, throwing an arm gently over his shoulders. "How are you, Pansy?"

"We are fine," Pansy said as she always did, meaning the family. Pansy's ego could have floated in a fairy's tear. She was wearing jeans and a sweatshirt that said OHIO U, and her inevitable high heels. Something was missing.

"Four-ninety-one," said the woman at the cash register.

"Here," Eleanor called urgently, waving a slender arm. She grabbed my sleeve and yanked at me, and Horace came along in my wake, grunting unhealthily as he bumped against me. Pansy, who couldn't see his face, put a possessive hand against the small of his back and beamed affectionately at his neck. "Horace isn't hungry," she said to me.

"I'll bet he isn't," I said as Eleanor pulled us along. Horace burped discreetly, and the burp reminded me of what was missing. "Where are Julia and Eadweard?" I asked. I hadn't seen Pansy without the twins since the day they were born.

"Home," Pansy said. In the absence of the twins three cameras hung around her neck, vestigial organs from an earlier life in which she'd wanted to be a photographer. Marriage and the twins had recast her, in the Chinese tradition, as wife, mommy, and daughter-in-law to Eleanor and Horace's remarkably difficult mother. Until that moment in the Empress Pavilion, the only mementos of her earlier calling had been the twins' names, which were bestowed in honor of Julia Cameron and Eadweard—pronounced "Edward"—Muybridge, two of the seminal figures in photography, and the abandoned cameras hanging high on the walls of the apartment where the children couldn't reach them.

"You're kidding," I said. The jade-green dining room of the Empress Pavilion yawned open around us. An infinitesimal Chinese waitress in a black skirt and white blouse was leading our wagon train toward an empty corner table. "Who's taking care of the twins?"

"Uncle Lo," Horace said, succeeding at speech against all odds.

"He didn't come?" I asked stupidly, craning my neck around to look past Pansy. "But this was supposed to be in his honor."

"He decided to stay home," Horace said enviously. "Said he'd had too much to drink last night."

"Also, jet-lagged," Pansy said, translating her Fukienese dialect as she went. "He has some kind problem with time."

"We're here." Eleanor said. An empty table for four blocked our way, and Eleanor began to organize. "You there, Simeon. Me, here. Horace, across from me, and Pansy—"

"Just minute," Pansy said, circling the table and doing things to lenses. "Sit, Horace, please. Sit, everybody."

We sat. Pansy took enough pictures to fill the Spiegel catalog and then seated herself, her face gleaming with exertion and good humor. I hadn't seen her look so happy since Horace had brought her home from Singapore, where they'd met. At that time her conversation had been full of Edward Weston, Robert Capa, Duane Michaels, and Cindy Sherman, photographers who had made a difference. She'd said "I'm fine" when asked, instead of "We're fine." Now she said "we" all the time, and the names in her conversation were Horace, Eadweard, Julia, and Mommy, and the cameras had been left to hang on the walls.

"It's, um, noisy," Horace offered, surveying the room with ill-concealed loathing. As always, he clutched his knife and fork, the Empress Pavilion's sole concession to *gwailo*s—non-Chinese—straight up in his fists, like a baby. A very large, very belligerent baby.

"Poor Horace throw up this morning," Pansy contributed. "I don't know why." Her face was innocence personified.

"Maybe it was the motion of the earth," I said nastily. I made a whirlpool in the air with my hands. "You know, it spins and spins and spins . . ."

Horace waved my hands away pleadingly. "I want another planet," he said. "One that isn't noisy. One that doesn't spin." He fanned himself with his right hand. His upper lip was slick with sweat. "What was Uncle Lo drinking?"

I tried to recall, but my memory seemed to be wrapped in opaque white cotton. "Not much, whatever it was. He said he was hung over?"

The first *dim sum* cart appeared, an aluminum two-decker filled with balloons of white pastry, pushed by an angular Chinese man in a too-short white jacket above impossibly narrow black trousers. He rocked the cart back and forth as though the dumplings were infants about to cry.

"If he's hung over, it's because he's not used to drinking," Eleanor said a trifle severely, giving 90 percent of her attention to the *dim sum*. "He's a Responsible Human Being." Eleanor was good at speaking in capital letters.

"I gather Bravo didn't think so highly of him," I said, watching her choose something white and vaguely spherical for me. Bravo Corrigan was the dog I'd loaned to Horace and Pansy so the kids could have something to torment. Big, genetically generic, raffish, and fiercely territorial, Bravo was Topanga Canyon's canine free spirit, taking up residence with anyone who would put out a bowl of something to his liking. "Tried to bite him, didn't he?"

"Bravo only like the twins," Pansy said, swallowing first, as always. Pansy's manners were brilliant.

"He's wonderful with them," Eleanor acknowledged as she flagged another cart pusher. "He sleeps in their room. He follows them all over the apartment. He lets them ride on him and try to tie his ears into knots."

"They call him 'Papa,' " Pansy said, laughing. "Horace get *so* mad."

Horace was staring balefully at the steamed buns on his plate as though he was afraid they might start square dancing. "I can understand their confusion," I said.

"Eat, poor Horace," Pansy said, helpful as ever. "Make you strong."

"I don't want to be strong," Horace said sullenly. "I want to be sensitive."

"The new Horace," Eleanor cooed. "Remember all the new Nixons? Did I tell you," she said to me, "that my mother's coming out to see Uncle Lo?"

"Good lord," I said. "Turning her back on the bright lights of Las Vegas?"

"And the new one, too," Eleanor said.

I poked whatever she'd served me. "That's right, there's a new one, isn't there?"

"A plumber. Actually, a plumbing contractor." Eleanor put something that was almost certainly a chicken's foot on Horace's plate. Horace recoiled discreetly and looked out the window. "She wouldn't have a mere plumber."

"Should be good for her grouting," I said. Mrs. Chan, now working on husband number four, was an energy demon whom I'd frequently seen scouring the grouting between her kitchen tiles with a toothbrush and a bottle of Clorox. Her fingers looked like she soaked them in lye, but her grouting was immaculate.

"What's his name?" I asked Horace, trying to bring him back into the room.

"She calls him Stinky," Horace said. "I think it's a nickname."

"I certainly hope so. Rich, huh?"

Horace shrugged experimentally. His head stayed on. "Who knows? He's Chinese."

"Mom says he's lazy," Eleanor ventured. "But from Mom's perspective, who isn't?"

Horace, often the cynosure of his mother's wrath at

his inability to hold down more than two jobs at the same time, let out a sigh that fluttered his napkin, and Pansy put her hand gently over his. Horace retracted his hand, leaving Pansy looking down at empty tablecloth. I wondered, and not for the first time, whether something was going wrong between them.

"What's your mom say about Uncle Lo?" I asked. "She must be thrilled."

"Well, she's coming. Sometime today."

"*Today*?" Pansy said, knocking over, and catching, a glass of water.

"What time?" Horace demanded, alert at last.

"Three." Eleanor lifted a hand. "Horace, I told you on the phone last night—"

"Who remembers last night?" Horace snapped.

"The pictures," Pansy said. She licked her upper lip and then wiped it with a pale forefinger.

"Blinking baby Jesus," Horace said. He stood up. "We gotta get home."

"I'm not hungry anyway," I said truthfully. "What pictures?"

Pansy, frantically hanging cameras around her neck, said, "Just pictures."

"We haven't paid," Eleanor pointed out. She seemed privately amused at something.

I got up and dropped thirty dollars onto the table. "Take that off last night," I said to Horace, "and let's go."

"What's *your* hurry?" Eleanor asked.

"I want to see those pictures," I said.

"It's Pansy's rogues' gallery," Eleanor said as Horace, thirty feet in front of us, passed a truck on a blind curve. There was an indignant raspberry from the horn of an oncoming car, and a bright red Ultra-Nondescript hurtled past us, hugging the curb. The driver was facing backward and screaming out the window.

"Remember when you could tell cars apart?" I asked.

"Sweet little Pansy? A rogues' gallery? Who are the rogues?"

"Everybody," Eleanor said. "Pansy's been wicked with her camera. But it's mostly Mom."

"Ah," I said, closing my eyes as I passed the truck. When I opened them, we were still alive. "Ergo, the rush."

"Pansy's always been the perfect Chinese daughter-in-law," Eleanor explained cheerily. " 'Yes, Mother, no, Mother. Of course you can cut the children's hair, Mother. Why should I have anything to say about how my children look?' And all the while, she had the cameras dangling all over the house. And good for her."

This was surprising. Eleanor had escaped her mother's massive gravitational field approximately ten minutes after she entered college, but she'd always seemed to expect filial piety from Horace and Pansy. After all, it was traditionally the responsibility of the eldest son to take care of the parents. And Horace had come through. Until Mrs. Chan had moved to Las Vegas, only eighteen months earlier, she'd exercised absolute dominion over the small apartment in which all the Chans except Eleanor lived, and which Mrs. Chan owned. It had always seemed to me the most claustrophobic possible living arrangement; there was literally no room for disagreement. Not that Mrs. Chan, then between husbands and lacking a sinkhole for her supernatural energy, would have tolerated disagreement even if they'd all been rattling around in the Taj Mahal.

"So what's wrong between Horace and Pansy?"

I could feel Eleanor's glance. "Who says anything's wrong?"

"Eleanor," I said, "either I'm a member of the family or I'm not. They're not the same. Something's wrong."

"I don't know," Eleanor said unconvincingly.

Well, I thought I knew. I could smell Ning's perfume coming out of my pores.

"I can understand if he's frustrated," Eleanor said,

capitulating. "Mom is the boss, and Pansy knows it, which is pretty hard on his ego. And Pansy's pregnancy was, well, difficult, you know? They couldn't make love for months and months."

"They can now," I offered, and then I thought about it. "Can't they?"

"Pansy says they don't." People, even private people like Pansy, volunteered things to Eleanor. "I was there one night with the kids, and Horace hadn't been home for hours. She was setting the table for dinner, way too late to expect Horace to eat anything, and all of a sudden she fell to the floor and started to cry. She missed a chair on the way down. So I sat next to her, and the next thing I knew, she opened up. Yikes, of all the things I didn't want to know. She thinks he's got a girlfriend."

"I doubt that," I said, joining the Brotherhood of Guilty Males as we coasted up the driveway of Mrs. Chan's apartment building. Horace and Pansy were climbing out of their car, Horace shouting at Pansy in Cantonese until she silenced him with something sharper in tone and further north in dialect. Over the squabble I could hear Bravo barking a manic welcome, but the barking sounded muffled. Pansy threw some phrase that was all elbows and edges over her shoulder as she climbed the steep exterior stairway leading to the back door of the apartment. Then, turning face forward again, she stopped climbing, so suddenly that Horace, running on momentum and alcohol fumes, stumbled into her back. Pansy had to throw out a hand and grasp the banister to keep from toppling back on him, but the gesture was nothing but muscle. She was completely focused on the landing at the top of the stairs.

The rickety wooden child-restraining gate that Horace had installed to keep Julia and Eadweard from the first, and potentially last, fall of their lives was hanging open. Pansy snapped something that was clearly a question, and Bravo suddenly loosed a volley of barking that was more frantic and deep-chested than simple welcome.

The gate was always kept closed. It was the last thing Pansy checked every night and the first thing she re-checked in the morning. She took the stairs two at a time, cameras banging against her body and each other, and bolted through the open back door. Horace trudged resignedly up behind her, and Eleanor pushed past me, her face grim and tight, a mask of muscle.

Then Pansy screamed. It was a virtuoso, three-octave shrill. A diva's scream, breaking at the top of the scale and shivering its way down again. Eleanor and I got through the door just in time to see Pansy, hands pressed against her cheeks, fill her lungs all the way to her knees and start a new one.

Horace had reached her by then, hoisting her like a sack of rice and carrying her backward. Following, I saw the kitchen.

It had been trashed: utensils spilled glittering onto the floor, flour dumped everywhere, the first snowfall after the bomb. Bravo thundered away somewhere near.

The hallway took me past the kitchen and into the combination dining and living room. The table lay on its top, legs sticking up into the air as stiff as a dead cow's. Upholstered chairs had been slit open and evis-cerated. The rugs had been pulled aside. Pictures, in-cluding some from Pansy's rogues' gallery, had been torn from the walls and trampled. The family shrine had been bent and smashed, and a hole had been kicked in the wall below the mantel on which it stood.

Horace deposited Pansy on a sofa that looked like it had vomited its intestines and headed off toward the bedrooms, and I followed, leaving Eleanor to try to take Pansy in hand. Horace was already in the twins' room by the time I hit the hallway behind him. I could see that one of the beds was lying on its side.

"*Shit*," he said, and the door to the hall closet buck-led outward and then snapped back, held by a childproof external bolt five feet from the floor. I slid the bolt, and Bravo rocketed out between my legs, hitting me so hard that the door slammed shut again. I was turning away to join Horace, who was shouting something to Pansy from the twins' room, when I saw the piece of paper tacked to the door.

It said: THEYRE OKAY. DONT DO NOTHING.

The sign drew my eyes back toward the door. I opened it and saw a surprisingly large and very dead Chinese man. He had a small mustache and wide empty eyes. He was no one I knew.

From the driveway, far below, I heard Bravo loose a long, bereaved howl.

3

Table Talk

The dead man's gaze gripped me. Even when I looked away I could sense it tugging at me as I shifted from foot to foot, feeling like a boat on a short rope. I forced myself to take a big enough step backward to break the strand. Free, I stood irresolute for a long moment, looking at nothing, and then I closed the door and followed the sounds of grief back into the living room.

Pansy lay facedown on the erupting sofa, her body shivering under spasms of sobs that threatened to break her into pieces. Eleanor was massaging her rhythmically, stroking upward from the base of Pansy's spine in long, steady motions, as regular as the waves on a good beach. She was softly singing what sounded like a Chinese lullaby.

Horace was still yelping and swearing in the nursery. Eleanor looked at me and then through me, indicating that there wasn't much I could do to help with Pansy, so I turned around and went to join him. Halfway there, I realized I was operating on automatic pilot: Head aimlessly for the living room, get bumped from the living room, head for the bedroom. Running on physics, not feelings or intellect, bouncing off other people's emotions like a human pachinko ball. I wasn't feeling anything yet.

The nursery was hurricane country. It looked like one of those amusement-park houses where the furniture is on the walls in one room and on the ceiling in the next. Horace sat in the center of the floor holding on to a quilt Pansy had made for the two children when they slept in one crib. His other hand was screwed into a fist and pressed against the bridge of his nose. He was bent forward so far his forehead almost touched the floor. I sat next to him and wrapped my arm around his shoulders, and he straightened and turned in to me and wept, his face pressed tight against my chest and his shoulders shaking convulsively. I looked down at him from what seemed like quite a distance.

"We'll get them back," I said, focusing on plans. Plans seemed like the thing. "We'll call the cops. I've got a friend on the cops, you know? And we'll go after Uncle Lo ourselves."

"Sure," Horace said, drawing back and wiping his nose on a corner of the quilt. "And we'll kill the kids playing cowboy." He listened to the echo for a moment. "Uncle Lo? Uncle Lo didn't do this."

"Why not? I mean, he was the only one here."

"Why would he?"

"I don't know," I said.

He spread his fingers wide and curled them inward, looking for something to strangle. "I wish he had. I wish I knew it was Lo. At least we could *talk* to—"

"Horace. He set it up. Sent you guys out for *dim sum* and stayed home like he couldn't face it, when we both know he was the only sober one last night."

"Huh," Horace scoffed. He glanced down at the quilt in his hand and tossed it onto one of the beds, where it dangled disconsolately from a wooden leg like an abandoned battle flag.

"Okay, if it wasn't Uncle Lo, who was it?"

"Whoever took him away," Horace said, after swallowing twice. "Whoever came and got him."

That stopped me, and I said, "Oh." There was, after all, a dead man in the closet. Still, I *knew* Lo had faked his hangover so he could be alone in the house.

Horace plowed on. "Why would he save our family and then do, do—this?"

"Right," I said, filling the silence.

"And anyway," Horace said, "why would he tear the place apart?"

"Maybe he was looking for something."

"Like what? I've lived in this apartment most of my life. I know everything that's in it. There's *nothing* in it."

"Horace. Lo didn't know there was nothing in the apartment. He needed something, so he tossed it. And when he didn't find it, then he took the twins so he could demand whatever it was later."

Horace looked around as though he expected to see what Lo had missed. His nose was running, and his long hair, usually sprayed and combed forward to hide his balding scalp, was standing straight up. Without realizing what I was doing, I put out a hand and smoothed it. "However," I said, "I have to tell you that someone else *was* here."

"Who?" Horace barely cared.

"He's still here," I said. "In the closet. We've got a dead guy."

It took a second for the words to cut through to him. Then he blinked heavily and said, "No."

"Can you look at him?"

"Oh, sure," he said. "Look at a dead guy. In my house." He blew out a quart of air. "Let's get it over with."

The dead guy was still there, still folded neatly into his corner. He was in his middle thirties, maybe, wearing corduroy trousers, a Hawaiian shirt, and a shoulder holster that nestled incongruously among the printed palms and flamingos. "Know him?" I asked.

"Just another Chinese to me." Horace turned away from me. "I need to talk to Pansy." I followed him down the hall. He walked without lifting his feet, like an old man whose slippers were too big for him.

Pansy had turned over onto her back, and Eleanor was rubbing her temples as Pansy sent up skyrockets of Chinese. Eleanor stopped looking into her eyes just long enough to say to me, "Pansy wants the back door locked."

"Why?" I said. "We should be calling—"

"Lock the door, please, Simeon," Eleanor said. She put enough weight in the words to catch my attention.

Okay, Pansy wanted the door locked. I went to lock the door. The important thing right now was to make Pansy feel she had some control over something. So I closed the door, listening to desperate new commands from behind me, and as I tried to lock it, the knob turned in my hand and the door flew open and smacked me in the center of the forehead.

The blow wasn't that strong, but it was unexpected. It propelled me backward into the hallway. My hip hit the little table that held the telephone, and my legs tangled around each other, and as I fell I saw two children come in.

Well, they *looked* like children. They were tiny and delicate and black-haired and Asian, and they both had big, oily-looking, black semiautomatics.

"Up," the one in front said, gesturing skyward with a repeater that looked like it could uproot a live oak at half a mile. The other one eased past him, plenty of room in the hall for two people their size, and followed the barrel of his gun into the living room. I heard a sharp yelp in yet another language I didn't speak, and Pansy's commands ceased.

"Up," Number One said again. He was no more than five feet and a few inches tall, handsome in a diminutive way, and he was dressed in black jeans and a black T-shirt. A cascade of expensively curly black hair tumbled over his forehead. Tony Curtis, 1953. Watching his trigger finger as I climbed to my feet, I saw the initials *FF* tattooed blue on his right hand.

"I'm up," I said. "Where do you want my hands?"

"On your head." I complied, and he grinned. It wasn't an encouraging grin. "Carrying?" he asked.

"No." My stupid little gun was down in my stupid car.

"Turn around. Forehead against the wall, legs wide, hands behind your neck, elbows back." I saw him grin again as I turned.

"Good," he said behind me, patting me down. "Behave or I'm shooting you *here*"—he tapped a spot at the base of my spine. "No more marathon man," he said. "No more knowing when you're going to go to the toilet."

His English wasn't actually accented; it was lilted, syllables tilted upward at the end of the words, so that "knowing" became "know*ing*." "And now," he said, "turn around slowly, toward in there, and go say hi to everybody else."

"Okey-doke," I said, sounding braver than I felt. I completed the distance to the living/dining room and followed directions. "Hi," I said.

Pansy, Horace, and Eleanor were huddled together on the exploded couch, staring at Number Two or, more likely, his gun. I hate guns, but most of all I hate guns and nervousness. Rattlers are calm before they kill you; after all, they're just doing what millions of years of natural selection have thoughtfully equipped them to do. But killing, for a person who's not a really advanced psychopath, is light-years from routine. Most of the people who kill other people are *very* nervous. This kid, whose ears looked wider than his shoulders, wider than Dumbo's, was ready to jump out of his skin.

"This is all a mistake," I said, trying to sound as calm, as dull, as a psychiatrist. "You guys are in the wrong place."

"No," Handsome said behind me. "*You* in the wrong place."

Dumbo-Ears, also small, even thinner and shorter than the other, also dressed all in black, with a coil of rope hanging at his waist, eased the safety off with a tiny *click* that almost blew my eardrums out. His hands were shaking. He had a protruding Adam's apple that made him look like he'd swallowed a thumb, and it did a quick dive as he swallowed.

"This is silly," I said, hearing my voice crack. "These people just came home and found their children missing. Look at this place. Do you think we did this?"

"Where's Lo?" Handsome said behind me, establishing himself as the dominant personality. He didn't slip his safety off because it was already off.

"We don't know," Eleanor said in a steady voice. "He was here when we left."

Dumbo-Ears looked quickly at Handsome. It wasn't a look my insurance agent would have appreciated. "What you think?" he snapped.

"Slowly," Handsome said. Actually, he said "Sa-*low*ly." He tapped my shoulder with the barrel of his gun. "Children missing?"

"Yes," I said, scared enough to volunteer information. "Two. Twins."

"How old?"

"Four," I said.

"Who's mommy?" Handsome asked.

"I am," Eleanor said, before Pansy could speak. Her face was paper-white.

"And daddy?" That was Handsome again.

"Here," Horace said.

"Then this is the deal," Handsome said calmly. "We shoot mommy if daddy won't tell us where Lo is." My sweat glands suddenly let go, a cascade down my sides.

"Get up, Mommy," Handsome said to Eleanor. "Get up and go to the wall."

Eleanor stood, slowly and gracefully, smiling regretfully at Handsome, as though he were a child whose intelligence she'd overestimated. She went to the wall at the long side of the room and put a steadying hand on the mantel over the false fireplace, where the family shrine had been. I'd never loved her so much. "Should I face you," she asked, "or turn away?"

"Up to you," Handsome said with a shrug.

"Then I'll face you," Eleanor said. "That way, you'll remember me."

She turned to face him fully and put her hands behind her, offering him her heart, her lungs, her stomach, all the places that couldn't be fixed.

"Where's Lo?" Handsome asked again.

"I don't know," Horace said. "Honest to God—"

"We shoot mommy in the knees first," Handsome said. "Then in the elbows. That's four. Number five is for keeps."

Dumbo-Ears looked startled. "Aaahhh," he said. It might have been a protest.

"He's not here," Horace said hoarsely.

"Left knee," Handsome said, lowering the gun that was pointed at Eleanor.

"Wait," Pansy shrilled. "I mommy, not her. She only—"

Dumbo-Ears looked from Eleanor to her, and Handsome took a step forward so that he was beside me, and raised the gun. I shifted my weight, ready to slam him with my shoulder, and then there was a shuffling sound behind us and a sharp *crack*, and Handsome hurtled past, hitting me as he fell. A tornado followed him.

"*Badboy,*" Mrs. Chan bellowed, battering Handsome again with the wooden handles of her umbrellas, two of them, carried against the certainty that it would rain double-hard wherever she was. "Badboy, badboy, badboy."

I went for Dumbo-Ears's throat and gun arm and got an elbow around them, jerking my arm upward to point the barrel of his gun at the ceiling. It went off twice, showering Horace and Pansy with plaster, at the precise moments that Mrs. Chan's umbrellas struck Handsome, the sound making the blows seem supernaturally hard. Handsome, realizing that his assailant was a woman in her sixties, rose to one knee and brought the gun to bear on her, just as Horace launched himself off the couch and knocked him to the floor on his side. The two of them sprawled there, and Dumbo-Ears freed himself from my grasp with surprisingly wiry arms and brought the gun around into my face.

I was backing away, trying to outrun the bullet, when something brown and compact flew snarling through the air and attached itself to Dumbo-Ears's right shoulder. Flailing at Bravo, he let the gun sag, and I grabbed it and swung it to the right, hearing a little pop as his finger, caught in the trigger guard, was dislocated.

"*That's it*," I screamed, reversing the gun and pulling the trigger and spraying the walls with high-velocity slugs. The noise got everyone's attention. Mrs. Chan stopped biting Handsome's thigh, and Handsome looked up from the tangle just long enough to let Horace seize the gun in his hands. Horace turned it around and pointed it at Handsome's chest. The kid went limp, lying on his back and panting. Bravo, growling low in his throat, backed off and then sat.

"My hero," Eleanor said to me. Or maybe to Bravo. Then her knees went, and she toppled onto the couch.

No one else spoke for a moment. We were all panting. Dumbo-Ears was clutching his dislocated finger and making a rasping sound. "Now what?" Horace said. The gun in his hands was shaking violently.

"Call the cops."

"No." He looked over at Pansy, who had her eyes closed. "Not yet."

"You're nuts, Horace." No reaction. I looked at Eleanor, who refused to meet my gaze. My own knees were beginning to shake. "Okay, it's your house. But let's at least secure these twerps so we can talk. Eleanor, unroll the dining-room rug."

As she went to do it, Mrs. Chan registered the state of the apartment. "*Aiya*," she said mournfully. Then, a small, round woman in a loose-fitting quilted silk jacket and slacks, she started straightening things.

"Horace, tell your mother she can clean up as much as she wants, but not to get anywhere near either of these guys. Also, you might want to keep her away from the closet."

Horace said something in Cantonese, and Mrs. Chan glared at the two black-clad children and then puttered off to the kitchen. "Sonoma*gun*," I heard her say.

"It's unrolled," Eleanor said from the dining room. She was standing on an Oriental rug, about six by eight. "What's in the closet?"

"It's a surprise. You, Junior," I said to Handsome. "Over there. Horace, you make sure that this guy and his ears stay put. If he blinks, shoot him."

"Sure," Horace said. The gun aimed at Dumbo-Ears was steady.

Eleanor backed away as Handsome reached the rug. "Lie down," I told him. "Right there, on the edge. Put your hands in your pockets, real deep, as far as they'll go. I want your elbows straight."

He lay down on the short edge of the carpet, his head a couple of inches above the corner. His face was a mask of indifference.

"Roll over once," I said. He did. "Eleanor, I want you to lift the edge of the rug and put it over him. Stand at his waist. Good. Now tuck the rug under him and roll him forward with both hands. Junior, don't move *anything*, understand? Don't even nod your head."

Eleanor got down on her knees and rolled the boy away from her, then looked up at me. "Keep going," I said. "I want the whole rug wrapped around him."

By the time she was finished, Handsome was encased in a tight cylinder of rug that ended at his nose. He let his expressionless eyes bore into mine.

"Sit on his chest," I told Eleanor. "If you feel him

moving his arms, get up and tell me and we'll see if this war machine he was toting will go through four or five layers of Persian carpet.''

"Astrakhan," Eleanor murmured, sitting on the boy.

"What about this one?" Horace asked.

"Well," I said, "we could wiggle his finger around a little."

The kid backed away on his elbows, gabbling at me, until his head hit the wall. Then he grabbed his finger again.

"Okay," I said. "He's the baby, even if his ears are all grown up. He's going to get special treatment. Go turn the table over."

"The table?" Horace asked.

"You know, where you eat dinner?"

Horace nodded. "The table."

I trained the gun on Dumbo-Ears while Horace, grunting with effort, put the heavy table upright. "How long is that thing?" I asked.

"About six feet," Horace said.

"Great. Get the baby's rope. Baby, put your hands behind your head and keep them there."

Horace fumbled through the coil of rope hanging from the boy's waist and worked it through the belt loop on his jeans. Then he did it again. By the time he had the entire rope free it seemed to have taken hours. He stood up and backed away from the kid, the rope dangling from his hands.

"Okay, Baby," I said to Dumbo-Ears, "go over and get on the table. On your back."

The boy grumbled, but he did as he was told and lay there, looking up at the ceiling, still clutching his right index finger in the palm of his left.

"What did you say?" I demanded. Sitting on the rolled-up rug, Eleanor was looking at me as though she'd never seen me before.

"*Baby*," he said scornfully.

"And you are a baby, too, even if you're a mean-spirited, murderous little shitheel of a baby. Pull yourself down so the table hits you at your knees. I want your legs dangling over the edge.''

Still muttering, still grasping one hand in the other, the boy scooted down the length of the table on his back.

"This stuff isn't real strong," Horace said, testing the rope.

"Well, the little jerk doesn't weigh much. It should be fine. Get a knife, would you? You're going to need to cut it.''

Horace went into the kitchen, asked his mother a question, and came out with a big serrated bread knife in his hand. I could hear drawers banging in the kitchen, percussion for a cantata of Cantonese complaint.

"Okay," I said to Horace. "Now wrap the rope around his left leg and the left table leg. Start at the knee and go all the way down. Don't be thrifty or gentle. I want it tight." Two minutes later Number Two's calves were tied to the legs of the table.

"And now?" Horace asked.

"Now we put the table on end so that the little fucker is upside down. You'll have to stand on the legs so it doesn't tip forward.''

Horace dragged the table around so the boy's head was facing me and then tilted the other end upward. The boy let out a shriek, but Horace kept upending the table until Dumbo-Ears was dangling, head toward the floor, arms hanging down. His face immediately filled with blood. A vein throbbed in the side of his neck.

"Comfortable?" I asked him. "I hope not, because you're going to be there a long time.''

"How long?" Eleanor asked, the softy.

"Until he sings 'Humpty Dumpty'," I said. "In two languages." I put the gun down next to the couch, where Horace had left the other one. Pansy scrabbled away from it and then closed her eyes again, her knees drawn up and her arms wrapped around her own shoulders, presenting the smallest possible area to the room.

Eleanor shifted her weight on the rolled-up carpet. "What are you going to do to him, Simeon?"

"Well, first, I'm going to let him hang there until he starts to get spots in front of his eyes. Then I'm going to play kickball with the spots." I touched the toe of my boot to his big right ear for emphasis. "This is called the Torture of One Foot," I explained.

"You *can't*," Eleanor said.

"Get his wrists, Horace," I said. "Grab them tight. Try to hurt his finger if you can, but don't get careless. He's going to want his hands back very badly in a moment."

"Got them," Horace said from behind the table.

"Well, keep them," I said. "He's stronger than he looks, and he's going to start jerking around." The boy watched me wide-eyed as I lifted my foot and swung my boot back and forth, limbering up my knee. "Holding tight, Horace?" I asked. "Here goes."

"No," Pansy said. "No. No. No." Eleanor and I turned to look at her, sitting on the couch with her knees under her and her hands clutched into fists. Her big square glasses were on crooked.

"They not take the children," she said. She pointed her chin at the boy hanging upside down. "This is a baby."

"Kick the little swine," Horace said behind the table.

I tapped the boy's forehead with my boot and thought about it. "Okay," I said to Pansy, "since he's a baby, we'll try a baby's torture." He was just young enough that it might work. I turned back to him and spread my hands wide. "This one is called the Torture of a Thousand Fingers."

"But Simeon . . ." Eleanor began.

"Shhh," I said. "I want to hear him scream."

I curled my fingers and passed them up and down both sides of the boy's narrow torso until my fingertips were dug into the spaces between his ribs. The boy was rigid, breathing sharply and shallowly, watching me like a dog watches a snake.

"Who's Lo to you?" I said. "Why do you want him?"

"He your boyfriend," the boy whispered venomously.

"I really hate to do this," I said. Then I dug my fingers in and began to scrabble them up and down his ribs.

He convulsed and started shrieking with laughter, trying desperately to wrench his hands free. I left the ribs and started in on his armpits, and his laughter soared heavenward and dissolved into coughing. I went for the ribs again, for a good minute, and then backed away and watched him weep and cough.

"Who's Lo?" I said, when he'd regained control of himself.

"Don't know," he gasped.

I thought about the tattoo on Number One's fist. "What's FF mean?"

"Don't know."

A swelling started to build in my chest as though someone were blowing a bubble that encased my lungs, a hot bubble that almost closed my throat. I grinned at him, feeling my face straining into the Mask of Comedy, and forced my voice past the bubble. "Here's your problem," I said, straining against the gravel in my throat. "You're upside down. You're salivating, but it's hard to swallow. You're going to laugh so hard you have to inhale, and when you do, sooner or later, you're going to breathe spit. Then you're going to cough and try to breathe again, but I'm still going to be tickling you. If it gets bad enough, you could swallow your tongue. How does that sound?"

He spat at me.

"You'll have more saliva in a minute," I said, "but no point waiting." I looked at my watch to give myself time to calm down, but it didn't work. I attacked him with my fingers, gouging his ribs, his underarms, and his abdomen, and I kept checking my watch as though I cared how long it lasted. Gouge and check, gouge and check, and I kept at it for a full two minutes as he shuddered and trembled and coughed and shrieked, until the noise brought Mrs. Chan in from the kitchen to watch, fascinated.

When I saw her, I stopped and backed away, ashamed. The boy's face was covered in tears and spit and snot, and the convulsions went on for at least twenty seconds.

"Who's Lo?" I asked again, breathing almost as hard as he was. "Who sent you to get him?"

"Don't know." He swung his head, upside down, from side to side. His eyes were beads of hate, so intense they looked like they might pop out of his head and roll across the floor at me to bite my feet.

"Kick him," Horace said again.

A wave of revulsion swept over me. I glanced at Eleanor, and caught her staring at me as though I'd just emerged from the kitchen drain. I aimed all the fear I felt at the kid. "Back to Plan A, then. Do girls like you? I should think they would. You're a good-looking kid. It's a shame I'm going to have to kick your face in."

I stepped up to him and lifted my right foot. My left knee was rubber.

"He doesn't know," Handsome said, muffled in his rug. "He doesn't know anything."

"But you do," I said, finding someone new to hate. "And he'll remember that you let me kick his face in."

Nothing.

I hauled back my foot and kicked hard. My boot thudded into the table, half an inch from the kid's extraordinary right ear, and he screeched in a satisfying fashion and then glared back up at me. Even upside down, his face was poison.

"Lo's this old man," Handsome said sullenly. "Mainland Chinese. He do something wrong, and we came to get him."

"What did he do?" I could barely get the words past the bubble.

"They didn't tell us," Handsome said.

"You're going to punch his ticket, and you don't even know what he did? What a guy."

"They pay us," Handsome said. Dumbo-Ears was still fixated on my foot. "They don't have to tell us." It sounded like the truth.

My pulse, a jackhammer in my ears, was slowing. "You were just supposed to kill him. Not ask him any questions or take him with you."

"What I said."

"Then why the rope?"

He opened his mouth and then closed it again.

"You were supposed to take him, weren't you?" The mouth was a tight, straight line. "Where were you supposed to take him?"

The boy looked up at the ceiling for a long moment. Then he said, "Go ahead. Kick him in the face."

I grabbed a breath. Time to change tack. "Who sent you?"

"You don't want to know," Handsome said.

"Horace," I said, fighting an overwhelming desire to go to sleep, "tell your mother to go into the kitchen. Hang on to Junior here."

Feeling old, hung over, and bone weary, I slogged to the closet and grabbed the dead Chinese man beneath his tropically decorated arms. Something sticky clung to my hands as I pulled him out of the closet. His rubber-heeled shoes squealed like the door to the Inner Sanctum, but there was nothing I could do about it, and the three little pigs chased me all the way into the living room as I dragged him.

"Oh, no," Eleanor said hopelessly.

"One of yours?" I asked Handsome, letting the head and shoulders sag to the floor. I could see the entry wound now, under the left nipple. My right hand was covered in blood. Neither of the Asian kids replied.

"This," I said to Eleanor, "is why we're calling the cops."

"No," the two little gunmen said in unison.

"Well, that's interesting," I said. "You want to tell me why?"

Handsome said something sharp in Chinese, and everybody went still. More Chinese followed, fast and shrill, and Horace stepped quickly out from behind the table, which began to topple forward on top of Dumbo-Ears. I caught it with one arm and held it, hoping it looked easier than it felt.

"Quit, Simeon," Horace said. "Quit right now."

Eleanor stood up. "It's finished," she said. "You've done enough."

"Like hell I have. The twins—"

"These guys don't know anything about the twins," Horace said. "They're after Uncle Lo."

"And there's Mr. Snappy Dresser here," I said, and then Horace's words registered. "Why? Why are they after Lo?"

Horace looked at Pansy and then at the floor. "Chinese business," he said, sounding ashamed of himself.

"Well, that's wonderful," I said. I pointed at the dead man, Dumbo-Ears, and Handsome. "And these are Chinese business, too?"

"Yes," Horace said, very softly, avoiding my eyes.

"Great." I took a breath. "And what do we do with these assholes?"

"We let them go," he said. "If we don't we're all dead."

The bubble started to swell again. "How about one little kick?"

"No." That was Eleanor.

"Just unwrap them and send them home to mommy," I said. "They tried to kill us. Somebody *did* kill this guy who thought he was in Hawaii."

"They know they made a mistake," Horace said. "They won't come back." He closed his eyes.

"Okay," I said, giving up. "I'm finished." I let go of the table and stepped back, and it crashed to the floor with Dumbo-Ears underneath it. He made a sound somewhere between a groan and a sigh, and then went silent.

I crouched down in front of Handsome, who scowled up at me. "These people just lost their children," I said to him, "and they don't know why. Do you?"

"Lo's crazy," Handsome said sullenly.

"I thought you didn't know him."

"I know about him."

"Where would he take them?"

"Simeon," Eleanor said peremptorily.

"Hey," Handsome said, "you find Lo, you tell us."

"Right," I said, straightening. "Well, I'm the one who gave your friend the hard time. These folks didn't do anything. My name is Simeon Grist, and I live at Thirteen twenty-one Topanga Skyline Drive. You got a problem about what happened here today, you come and look me up. Not them. You touch them, and I promise I'll cut your little heart out and give it to the dog. Got it?"

"Thirteen twenty-one Topanga Skyline Drive," Handsome said. Eleanor looked at me and almost smiled. Thirteen twenty-one, the house two down the hill from mine, had burned four years earlier.

"You'll leave them alone," I said.

"It was a mistake," Horace said hollowly. There was so little blood in his face that I had the impression a finger pressed against his cheek would have left a dimple.

"Yeah, yeah." I got up and retrieved the two semis. "You want these, you come and get them from me," I told Handsome.

"Deal," Handsome said through very narrow eyes.

Dumbo-Ears had a bloody nose and a scraped forehead from hitting the floor face first, but he didn't make a sound as Horace snipped the rope away from his legs. The look he leveled at me, though, was worth serious thought. Two minutes later they were gone, toting the body between them wrapped in an old blanket.

Mrs. Chan had been released from the kitchen to scour the living room. She picked up a photograph and turned it over to see herself asleep in her favorite chair with her mouth wide open. Her English was almost nonexistent, and she still didn't know her grandchildren were missing.

"*Aiya,*" she said, turning the photograph accusingly toward Pansy. "*Aiya, aiya.*"

Pansy took a step back, but her mouth was unyielding. Mrs. Chan tore the photo into little pieces and threw them at her. Pansy started shrilling and running around the room, grabbing picture after picture until she had both hands full, and thrust them in Mrs. Chan's face like a bouquet of deadly nightshade. Now it was Mrs. Chan's turn to back up, blinking very rapidly, and Horace stepped between them and said something to his mother.

The scene went to freeze-frame, the three of them standing there like actors waiting in the wings, and then Mrs. Chan wailed and held out her arms and Pansy fell into them, sobbing and gulping air. Horace put his arms around both of them and led them into his and Pansy's room, talking to his mother all the while. I sat on the couch and patted Bravo, shaking violently and hoping I could get it under control before Horace and Pansy and Eleanor finished shoving furniture around in the bedroom.

When I was absolutely certain they were all too busy to hear me, I stopped fighting the bubble and went outside and threw up.

4

Q & A

"There are two possible scenarios," I said ten minutes later. I'd rinsed my mouth half a dozen times.

Horace and Eleanor were sitting side by side on the exploded couch, which had been covered with a bedsheet. Horace's eyes were vague and his face pinched, white lines framing the corners of his mouth, and he systematically tugged at his thinning hair with his right hand, yanking the occasional loose strand free. Eleanor had put her arms around him and pressed her cheek against his shoulder. From time to time she reached up to stop his hand, but he'd be at it again a few minutes later.

It was another family trait. I'd seen Eleanor do the same thing when she was worried. Early in our relationship I'd reached up to stop *her* hand.

"Either Lo set up the lunch so he could search the place and took the twins when he was interrupted," I said, talking to keep myself from slapping Horace's wrist, "or else Uncle Lo set up the lunch for some *other* reason that required him to be alone here, like maybe to meet someone, and then something went wrong and whoever he met took both him and the twins after *they* searched the place. Either way, Lo set it up.''

Nothing. Horace, I suddenly realized, was looking at the TV. It wasn't on. "And either way," I said, "Uncle Lo killed the guy in the closet."

Eleanor took Horace's right wrist as it climbed scalpward and held it. Then she kissed him on the cheek.

"Except," I said, wondering if he'd try with the left, "if the other guys took Lo and the twins, why were those kids here? So Lo killed the guy in the closet and got away with the twins, and the kids came here to do some damage control."

"What are you saying, Simeon?" Eleanor asked. She was still holding Horace's wrist.

"I'm saying we call the cops."

"Can't do it," Horace said, immovable as a fireplug.

"Well, you can't just sit here and get older."

He used his left to pluck a strand. "Sometimes holding still is the wisest choice."

"Don't sound so Chinese, Horace. Murder and kidnapping are what the police are *for*." Pansy moaned in the bedroom, and I heard Mrs. Chan whisper something urgent, a sound as taut as a rope snapping.

"No Chinese remarks, Simeon," Eleanor said severely. She had herself under control, except that the hand that wasn't thrown around Horace's shoulders was balled into a white-knuckled fist. She rolled the fist back and forth, knuckle over knuckle, across the bedsheet as she talked. "This is a Chinese situation."

I felt like I'd just walked through a pane of glass I hadn't known was there. *"Chinese?"* I asked. "What about Julia and Eadweard? They're babies. They don't even know they're Chinese." Horace made a noise like a hiccup, his eyes still fixed on the blank screen.

"What good will it do Julia and Eadweard to lose their entire family?" Eleanor asked. "Anyway, we don't think the twins are in danger."

That made me sit back. "Who's 'we'?"

"Uncle Lo will take care of them," Eleanor said.

"I really *seriously* don't understand," I said.

"He's our benefactor," Horace said automatically. "Even if he did take Julia and Eadweard, he took them because he needs something. He took them to make sure he'd get it. That's all." It was the longest speech he'd made since we got home.

"He's in danger, obviously," Eleanor said. "He's running away from something. Maybe he thinks that having Julia and Eadweard will protect him."

"From what?"

"We don't know," Eleanor said, after waiting for Horace to respond.

"Our little buggers," I said, "would shoot right through the kids to get dear old Uncle Lo."

"They won't," Eleanor said, sounding a touch shaky about it. "They promised."

I looked at her as I listened again to what she'd said. I thought I knew her, *had* thought I knew her for years, but now she was like a face on an exotic stamp, small and far away and foreign. "They *promised*?" I finally asked.

"In Cantonese," she said, "as they left. They said if we'd tell them when we found Uncle Lo, they'd make sure the kids got home."

It sounded like a wan hope at best, but it wasn't one I was going to contradict. "And how are we going to find Uncle Lo?"

"We're not," Horace said. "He's going to come to us."

There were a million possible questions, and all of them seemed wrong; all of them seemed like they'd rip Horace apart. I chose the least harmful. "What does he want?"

"God knows," Horace said.

"Does your mother?"

Horace tore his eyes from the television, and he and Eleanor exchanged glances. "Perhaps," she said.

"Let's ask her."

"No," brother and sister said in unison.

"Well, for Christ's sake," I said, suddenly angry, "why not?"

"*We'll* ask her," Eleanor said quietly. "Not you, we. You want to do something, Simeon, and we're grateful to you for it." Horace reached over and patted my knee, awkwardly but feelingly. "But we can't let you. Those guys who were here? The one you tickled already wants to kill you. You cost him a lot of face. You should have just gone ahead and kicked him."

"You know me," I said, deciding not to remind her that she'd been horrified at the idea. "Could I kick someone in the head?"

"He'd hate you less if you had. But he's not going to go after you unless you do something. And they'll kill all four of us, and then come after you, the minute they learn you're trying to do something. Anything. And they would learn. You just have to believe that."

"If all I did was talk to the cops, how would they know?"

"They'd know if the cops did anything in the Chinese community after you talked to them. Anything at all."

"Where *are* we?" I demanded. "Albania?"

"We're in China," Eleanor said. "Right now, we're in China."

"This is Willis Street," I said stubbornly.

"No," she said. "Three or four hours ago, this was Willis Street, Los Angeles. Now it's China. Something Chinese happened here. Whatever happens next will be Chinese, too."

I looked at her with longing. "You're as Chinese as I am."

"Three or four hours ago, that was true. Now it isn't."

I sat there, trying to control my giveaway Occidental face and waiting for all my immediate responses to line up in an orderly fashion. Then I eliminated all of them and said something else, something that might let me into the game.

"Chinese or not Chinese, maybe I can help you without doing anything."

"Yeah?" Horace asked skeptically.

"I know how to ask questions. I can ask *you* questions. Only you and Horace. And maybe those questions will help you get a better picture of whatever the hell is going on. I won't act on the answers, I promise. But maybe they'll help you when it's time for you to stop holding still and make decisions."

"Decisions," Horace said vaguely.

"What do you do when the phone rings?" I asked. "Let's say it's Uncle Lo, and he's got a deal. You've got to know as much as you can. I don't know anything, which makes me the perfect person to ask the questions. I promise, I swear on whatever you want, that I won't do anything with the answers. They're for you. They're to help you think of things you might not think of otherwise, because otherwise will be too late. And you know how Edmund Burke defined Hell? It's the truth, recognized too late." Well, maybe it hadn't been Edmund Burke.

They looked at each other again, brother and sister united against a world that included me. It was a new wrinkle in our relationships. I sat there feeling like a visitor from Internal Revenue. I wanted to hug them both and then knock their heads together.

"Go," Horace said when they'd finished their silent conference.

I went, taking refuge in reason. "Hypothesis one: Uncle Lo came here from Hong Kong. Did you pick him up at the airport?"

"No." Horace looked surprised by the question.

"Did anyone you know pick him up?"

"No." That was Eleanor.

"Did he phone first?"

"He knocked on the door," she said.

"When?"

She glanced at Horace, who had gone very still. "About nine on Friday. Nine at night, I mean." She looked at me, and faltered, then swallowed and went on. "I'm always here for dinner on Friday, you know."

I had a question ready, but her words choked it off. Friday was Eleanor's happiest night, the night Horace and Pansy shared the twins with her, and she'd arranged her working schedule to accommodate it, and also—I privately believed—to make it more difficult for them to cancel. Six days a week she wrote at home in Venice; on Fridays, she drove early in the morning to the big downtown library and did research there until it was time for her to drive to Willis Street for dinner. No one could call her to change the plan. Once, when we were both drunk, Horace had suggested that Eleanor loved the twins as much as she did because she and I had never had any. I'd pushed the idea away in self-defense.

"So you were eating," I finally suggested.

"We'd just finished," Eleanor said. "You know Pansy, she was in the kitchen slogging around in soapy water. Horace was introducing himself to his fourth beer, and Bravo and I were carrying the twins around on our backs." Bravo, curled beneath the uprighted dining-room table, thumped his tail at the sound of his name.

"Bravo and you?" I asked, seeing the picture.

"He can't carry them both," she said defensively. I ached to hold her.

"So the doorbell rang."

"He knocked," she said. She saw the look in my eyes and almost smiled. "He was at the back door."

"How'd he get the address?"

"He had a letter Mom wrote him six or seven years ago. He showed it to me. There was an address, but we'd changed our phone number."

"Did you see his airline ticket?"

"Oh, come on."

"But he told you he'd just landed from Hong Kong."

"That's what he said." She was sounding impatient.

"Did he go down to pay a taxi or anything?"

"Um," she said, looking at Horace again. "No. No, he didn't."

"So if he came in a cab, he paid the cab off, and he sent it away before he climbed the steps leading to a seven-year-old address."

Horace liberated another strand of hair and let it whiffle its way to the floor. We all watched it all the way down. Eleanor's hand was in her hair, a prelude to pulling.

"So, he could have come from Hong Kong or from Stockton," I said. "No way to tell. Eleanor, lay off your hair, okay?"

"Yikes," she said, pulling her hand away and tucking it under her.

"Okay. We don't know where he came from." I cleared my throat. "Hypothesis two: It *was* Uncle Lo who took the twins, instead of someone else. What's gone that belongs to them?"

Horace blinked. "Good question," he said, getting to his feet and plodding toward the bedroom, like a man walking uphill.

Eleanor waited until he was gone and put her hand in mine. "Don't try to understand," she said.

Her hand was warm and smooth and familiar in mine. I moved over to sit next to her, and she leaned against me and breathed on my neck. I knew she didn't mean anything by it; she was just breathing. She breathed a couple more times, and I bathed in her warmth.

"Four sets of clothes," Horace said, returning, "for each of them. And Julia's duck and Eadweard's clown ball."

Eleanor straightened. "Their favorites," she said. She looked reassured at the news.

"Did he see the twins play with them?" I wanted her back against me.

"That's all they play with," Eleanor said, blinking very fast.

"Hypothesis three," I said, raising my voice to distract her."Uncle Lo wasn't really Uncle Lo."

Eleanor passed a hand over her eyes and stared at me. "Of course he was."

"What did he say when you opened the door?"

"He said, 'Mei-Yu.' "

I must have looked blank, because she said, "That's my name, remember?"

"You recognized him?"

"I was a little girl when I saw him last. It was more than twenty years ago. Of course I didn't recognize him."

"So he told you who he was. He said, 'I'm Uncle Lo,' or something."

"Yes. And showed me the letter from Mom. He called Mom by her first name, too, Ah-Ling, and he asked about Horace, calling him Ah-Cho." She recited the Chinese names like magic words, and they had been; they'd been the spoken charms that opened the door.

The letter. "And you let him in."

"First I hugged him, then I started crying. Then I shouted for Ah—for Horace, I mean—and then I let him in."

"And then Bravo tried to eat him."

"I forgot," she said. "Bravo barked before he knocked on the door. Yes, Bravo went for him. Uncle Lo looked like he was going to faint."

"Did you doubt at all that he was who he said he was?"

"Not then," Eleanor said. She sighed. "I still don't, to tell you the truth. He knew everything, how we got out, and what our names were. He talked about the escape for hours, it seemed like. We were all so *happy*, Simeon. And he had that letter from Mom."

The letter was the big problem. "Did you read it?"

"No." She wiped her nose.

"Well, did it look like her handwriting?"

"Simeon, it was in Chinese. All Chinese writing looks alike to me."

"When did you call your mother?"

"Right away, but she wasn't home. I told her machine to call me instead of Horace because I knew the kids would be asleep."

"So she never talked to him."

"He was so *warm*," she said suddenly. "I mean, we were *all* crying. He held me like a daddy and cried and laughed. He knew everything about us."

I took a breath. "Did he know about the twins?"

"He even knew their names. He joked about Eadweard's."

"The twins are four," I pointed out.

A car passed us on the street below, stitching a seam of noise into the fabric of the night. Eleanor put both hands on Horace's forearm but kept her eyes fixed on me. "I see," she said tonelessly.

I wanted to put my arms around her and tell her everything would be fine, but I didn't believe that it would. "He used the return address on a seven-year-old letter."

"Maybe Mom wrote him more recently." She was looking at me but talking to Horace.

"Ask her," I said.

"Yes," Eleanor said, not doing anything. "Right." Then she let out a deep breath, stood, and left the room.

"What did *you* think, Horace? Did you have any doubt?"

"I'm not sure I do now," he said. "If that wasn't Uncle Lo, it was Laurence Olivier."

As long as Eleanor was out of earshot, I decided to try a sneak play. "Why won't you let me do anything?"

"Those kids with the guns," he said. "They're not on their own."

"Who are they with?"

He shook his head.

"She didn't," Eleanor said faintly from the doorway.

She was leaning against the doorjamb. "In fact, she's not sure she remembers writing him seven years ago."

"*Wah*," Horace said, abandoning hope.

"But you know Mom," Eleanor added unconvincingly.

Horace knotted his hands behind his neck and rotated his head with a noise like someone stepping on a wineglass, and Eleanor pushed herself away from the wall and sat beside him and began to knead his shoulders.

"And, of course, your mother never saw him."

"Of course not," Eleanor said, concentrating on Horace's shoulders.

"Pansy," Horace blurted, pushing her hands aside.

"What about Pan—oh, good Lord." Eleanor got up and hurried back into the hallway.

Two minutes later Mrs. Chan was seated on the couch, flipping through a thin stack of Polaroids. She looked longest at the fifth, then took it between thumb and forefinger and brought it up to her eyes. It was a close-up of a laughing man with a seamed face, a lot of gold teeth, and a puffy black eye.

She held the picture up to Horace accusingly.

"Lo," she said.

5
—

Hypothetical Vietnamese

The very next day, Monday, I broke my promise.

"Vietnamese," Hammond said smugly. "Those kids have to be Vietnamese." I'd spent the night dreaming without sleeping, thrashing around on my bed like a gaffed fish, tangling myself in the sheets, and trying not to look at the pictures projected on the insides of my eyelids: Eleanor finding the house I now lived in, Eleanor making the curtains that still hung on the walls, Eleanor's face when she'd learned I was having an affair, Eleanor's straight, slim back going down the drive-way on the day she'd moved out. Eleanor with the kids. Pansy, the trusting bride from Singapore, luminous with pride after the doctor had told her she was carrying twins. Horace, that same day, being transparently modest about the strength of his loins.

Eleanor with the kids again, the three of them tumbling and laughing in an early-morning room splashed with sunlight and bright dust. Eleanor and the kids she hadn't had.

At five I'd given up on sleep and taken an early shower. I was jogging the perimeter of the UCLA campus by seven, trying to run off a load of guilt that was way too heavy to carry, and by nine, after a second shower in the men's gym, I'd used my stacks privileges at the University's Powell Library to pull out everything I could find about Chinese crime, and especially about Chinese crime in America. Maybe I could *work* the guilt off.

There was a whole lot more than I'd thought there would be.

Nine cups of coffee and three hundred pages later, it was three in the afternoon, and I was jittering in a chair at Parker Center, laying a line of carefully worked out bullshit on Al Hammond.

As always, Hammond was a lot bigger than he needed to be and, as always, he looked mean enough to eat kittens. In front of cats. He always intimidated me, in spite of the fact that most of the time, Hammond was my friend. I'd chosen him from a roomful of cops at a Hollywood cop bar called the Red Dog when I'd decided to be a detective, as opposed to a university professor. At the time I had put years into preparing to be a university professor and only weeks into being a detective, but those weeks were quality time, as people seem to like to say these days. A good friend of Eleanor's, a quiet Taiwanese girl named Jennie Chu, had been tossed onto the sidewalk from the roof of one of the UCLA dorms. Jennie had been dead on arrival, and Eleanor had been alive in my bed when someone had called to give her the news. Since the UCLA cops and the LAPD didn't seem all that interested, I'd helped Eleanor through her grieving process by finding the cocaine dealer who'd used Jennie to practice the vertical shot put. His mistake: He couldn't tell Asians apart. I'd happily broken both of his elbows, learning something sort of thrillingly unpleasant about myself in the process, and delivered him to the police. At that point I had more superfluous degrees than a Fahrenheit thermometer, the result of having stayed in college for what seemed like decades because I couldn't think of anything to do.

After Jennie, I had something to do.

"Why Vietnamese?" I asked. We were in a long room full of sickly fluorescent light and scarred wooden desks. Other detectives talked on phones or slogged on big heavy cop feet toward the coffee. I'd passed on the coffee.

"Why are you here?" Hammond countered. He was a cop to his bitten fingernails.

"This is purely hypothetical, Al," I said, retreating toward the bullshit.

"And it has nothing to do with Eleanor," Al said with ponderous irony.

"Eleanor who?" I asked, crossing my arms to emphasize the scholarly patches on my jacket. The lapels spread to reveal the aging Megadeth T-shirt beneath, and I tugged them closed. Hammond, like most cops, thought heavy metal was the musical equivalent of assault and battery. "I've decided to finish an old sociology thesis on urban crime. Asians are tops in their high school classes, tops in the graduation lists of lots of universities. Where are they in urban crime?"

"Tops," Hammond said promptly. "They're fucking with the Mafia like no one ever has. Ninety percent of the heroin brought into America today—" He stopped and lifted a hand half the size of Moby Dick. "You're actually sitting there and looking right at me and telling me this is for a paper?"

"The professor is named Mamie Liu," I improvised, stalling. So far I'd met Chinese-Americans named Eleanor, Horace, Pansy, Eadweard, and Julia (as well as Homer, Ruby, and Maxine), and I'd worked up considerable curiosity about the American names Chinese parents chose. "What do you think, Al?" I asked. "Why do Chinese choose names like Mamie?"

"You want to ask someone on the Asian Task Force?"

"No," I said, too quickly.

His grin turned wolfish. "Yeah? Why not?"

"Because it's only hypothetical. I don't want to waste their time. Is that straight about the heroin?"

"You bet." He shifted his weight in his chair, settling in to be the expert. "The old French Connection through Marseilles, which the Mafia ran, was shut down years ago. Now the stuff moves from Burma through Bangkok and Hong Kong, and the Chinese run it."

"All Chinese?"

"One hundred percent. Ethnic Chinese in Burma, Thailand, and Laos."

Hammond's stomach rumbled. It sounded like an automobile accident.

"Who runs it here?" I asked.

Hammond looked hungry. "Like I said—"

"No, I mean who specifically? Who among the Chinese? The tongs?"

Hammond sat up. "You know about the tongs?"

"A little." I'd also read about triads, village associations, and name societies.

"Like what?"

"The tongs started in San Francisco in the middle of the last century as protective associations," I said, dredging my caffeinated memory. "The Chinese were very unpopular in those days. They made the mistake of working cheap. Occasionally they were shot for sport. The cops didn't care what went on in Chinatown as long as no white people got hurt, so the tongs stepped in and kept order. Also helped people in trouble, arbitrated disputes, paid for funerals if somebody died broke."

"So far, okay," Hammond said grudgingly.

"Chinese try not to die broke," I said. "They come from a culture where starvation is the common denominator. Still, it's hard to make it into a visible tax bracket when you're working for half the minimum wage. But the Chinese work at it anyway. There are people working in Chinatown at three dollars an hour who save sixty, seventy percent of their salaries. And the tongs, today's tongs, I mean, help them keep their heads far enough above ground so that they can still open their mouths to eat.''

"You've been doing research," Hammond said accusingly.

"For the paper. But there are lots of things I don't know. Like when the tongs got crooked."

He gave me a long glance. "Right at the beginning." He looked a little uncomfortable. "The U.S. immigration laws were pretty raw then. Chinese men weren't allowed to bring their wives in with them. The idea being that they were supposed to come, build the railroad, light the fuses in the mines, do the laundry, and go home again."

"The ones who got blown to pieces were allowed to stay?" I asked. "And how do you know this stuff?"

"Interracial sensitivity meetings," he said. "Three hours a week, when I have the time to go, which isn't exactly often. Also, the Asian crime situation is so out of hand that everybody's trying to be an expert." He settled back, forcing a tiny scream of pain from his chair, and tried to remember where he was. "So anyway, you had a Chinatown full of bachelors. Classic economics. Demand creates supply."

"And the tongs," I volunteered, recalling a detail that had caught my attention at the library, "brought in slave girls."

"I hate to say it," Hammond said, "but that's a phrase with real interest value. Slave girls."

"But against the law," I said virtuously.

"Well, the law," Hammond said. "The law never works where sex is concerned, you know? Ask the guys in Vice." He chewed on that for a second. "Slave girls. The tong leaders didn't see the crime in it. It was just business. Brothels in China were no big deal. Lots of the girls wound up as third or fourth wives."

"Third or fourth wives?"

"God," Hammond said acerbically. "Imagine four

wives." He was in the middle of a vehemently acrimonious divorce.

"So there are tongs in every American city now?" I asked. I already thought I knew the answer, but I needed verification.

"Yeah. Except they're all the same tongs. The tongs, most of them anyway, are national. Hell, they're international. They've got branches in Hong Kong and on the mainland, and especially in Taiwan."

"Why 'especially'?"

"We don't have an extradition treaty with Taiwan," Hammond said. "And I'm hungry."

"I promised you a meal," I said. "So why don't you guys bust the tongs? That's what the Asian Task Force is for, right?"

He shook his big, badly barbered head. Hammond's hair always looked like it had been cut with a can opener. "We can't get inside. Can't even tap a wire and listen in. You know how many dialects there are in China?"

"No."

"So guess."

I tried to remember anything Eleanor might have said and failed. "Fifty," I ventured.

Hammond tried to grin, but the grin was nothing but a mechanical muscle-pull at the corners of his mouth. "A couple thousand."

"Jesus." His stomach growled again. "What do you want to eat, Al?"

He glanced around the big ugly room. "Something expensive and far from here."

"Steak? The Pacific Dining Car?"

"Fine," he said, underplaying it. Hammond would have chewed his way through a yard of concrete to eat a steak.

"Why are the kids Vietnamese?" The Vietnamese hadn't been mentioned in the books I'd read.

"The kids in the Vietnamese gangs are the enforcers.

They're the ones who scare people shitless when they're late with their loan payments. They're the ones who pour Krazy Glue into the locks of the jewelry stores when the owner won't pay protection. They're the ones who break the elbows and slice the faces and pull the triggers. Hell, they've lost their country and their culture, and they're starting to forget their language. There are still lots of great Vietnamese kids, or so I hear. But, all in all, the bad ones are just about the meanest, scariest, deadliest little motherfuckers going.''

"Great," I said. "That's absolutely great." I had a big molten ball of lead in my gut.

"And behind the tongs," Hammond said, watching me, "are the *real* bad guys. The triads. The triads are the real Chinese Mafia."

"I don't want to hear about it," I said, giving up. "It's just a paper."

"Yeah," Hammond said, laying it on thick. "It's just a paper."

Two hours later Hammond and I stood on a downtown sidewalk while a couple of Asian parking attendants hiked toward Mexico to get our cars. He'd had three glasses of red wine to wash down two pounds of raw steak, and he was at the point where we were two buddies, not cop and non-cop.

"Is this about Eleanor?" he demanded. "And don't shit me." In his present embittered state, Eleanor was at the top of a very short list of women whom Hammond was willing to tolerate.

"No," I said, shivering. It had turned cold while we ate. "It's something a relative of hers might have gotten into."

He gave me a couple of eyes that were smaller than raisins and he screwed up his mouth until he looked like Roy Rogers's mummy.

"Do you think Roy Rogers was mummified?" I asked him.

He didn't even look interested. "Might be. Any ass-hole who could stuff a horse. And look at Disney, he became a Creamsicle."

"They made Lenin into a coffee table."

"Which relative?" he asked, without a pause.

"Just some uncle. Listen, Al, about all this. I'd rather you didn't talk about it with anyone, okay?"

"I'd be embarrassed to," Hammond said. He burped french-fried onions and waved it away, toward me. "I'm supposed to be a cop."

"I'll call you if it gets any closer to home," I said, but he was looking over my shoulder and chewing at the left corner of his mouth.

"Hey," he said, and then he stopped. He put one hand in his pocket and took it out again, then put it back. "Hey, look, did I tell you I'm seeing someone?" He stared off at the horizon, avoiding my eyes, and a slow flush began at his jawline and climbed upward like the mercury or whatever it is in a thermometer.

"That's great." His blush deepened. "I think."

He shook his big blunt head. "She's on the job," he said, and then stalled again.

"Really," I said, just to keep the afternoon moving. "Does she rank you?"

"I may be stupid," Hammond said, "but I ain't no masochist."

"What's she like?"

"It's what she's *not* like. She's not like Hazel." Hazel was Hammond's soon-to-be-ex. I'd never met Hazel; Hammond and I hung out mainly in male-bonding areas like bars and places where someone either just had been, or was immediately likely to be, killed. Since I didn't know Hazel, the statement wasn't particularly informative.

"In what way," I asked, "is she not like Hazel?"

He shifted his focus to a spot a foot above my head. "She's Hispanic," he said.

"Oh-ho," I said. I waited until the pressure in my

chest subsided and I was absolutely certain I wasn't going to laugh, and then said, "Bit of a change in the routine." Although he generally behaved himself, Hammond's feelings toward people of color were not likely to attract the official attention of the Vatican after he passed on. "Well, well," I offered. Hammond was still waiting for the moon to rise. "I'd like to meet her, Al."

"You will," he said as one of the attendants pulled up in the car. "Maybe tomorrow night. Look whose car came first," he said, tilting his chin discreetly toward the attendant, who immediately looked very interested. Chinese people point with their chins. "Looks like you pay for the parking."

"You know, Al," I said. "You should really attend more of those interracial sensitivity sessions."

"Can't," he said. "I'm giving all my time to the homosexual empathy hours." He opened the door of the sedan and slid heavily in. The car sagged with a certain mechanical irony. "By the way," he called, "Roy Rogers is alive."

My first stop was Horace's, where I picked up Bravo. I'd called from UCLA and volunteered to get him out from underfoot, not saying what I really felt: that he was a living reminder of the twins. Eleanor, who'd answered the phone, hadn't said it either, but she'd been a little too bright about what a good idea it was.

Horace opened the door, looking like someone who'd just bungee-jumped off the Eiffel Tower tied to a shoelace: hair on end, pouches of flesh beneath the eyes, a broken pencil dangling from his mouth like a dead yellow cigarette. One corner of his shirt collar poked a dimple in his left earlobe.

"Oh, yeah," he said by way of greeting. "Bravo's here somewhere."

"How are you?"

"Awake," he said. "Alive."

"Eleanor here?" Bravo bounded out and, seeing me, started to bark.

"No, she's, I don't know. Shut up, Bravo."

"Pansy asleep?"

"Not now," Horace said sourly, looking down at Bravo.

"I'll get him out of here."

"Good idea. I'll call you if anything happens." Horace closed the door on Bravo's rear end, and I stood on the porch, rebuffed. With Bravo at my heels, I went down the stairs and got in the car, feeling walled out.

Despite all the ups and downs Eleanor and I had endured, this was something new. We'd been friends briefly and then lovers for years, first in various student hovels around UCLA, and then in the awful little shack Eleanor found for us in Topanga Canyon, a tilting, rickety, three-room tribute to threepenny nails and wishful thinking, with nothing to recommend it except the best view in Southern California. I'd been accepted by Horace as a drinking partner almost at once. Mrs. Chan, who, after almost thirty years in the States, still considered all non-Chinese to be foreign devils, was a bit more difficult. It took months before she stopped calling Eleanor every forty-eight hours to harangue her about pure blood. Eventually she invited me home for the sole purpose of feeding me things she was sure no Westerner could eat. Over the course of ten or twelve dinners I swallowed steamed sea cucumber, the eyes and cheeks of fish, a veritable Fannie Farmer Assortment of entrails. I got it all down, nodded, smiled, asked for more. Most of it was delicious, although I have to admit the fish eyes later rolled uninvited into my dreams, goggled at me in threes, and waved at me with tiny white gloves.

I completed my trial by fire one evening when Mrs. Chan uncovered a dish of brown, dense, grainless meat surrounded by some kind of fungus and proudly announced that it was dog. It was too much.

"Does it have a name?" I'd asked Eleanor.

"Spot," Eleanor said, catching a smile from Horace. "Dick and Jane are out combing the streets for him now.'' There were just the four of us at the table; Pansy was still living, undreamed-of, in Singapore. Husband Number Two had skillfully fled the scene after only seven months.

Mrs. Chan said something to me in Chinese, gave me a thousand-watt smile, and cut off a great whacking piece. It made a slapping noise as it hit the plate.

''I wonder whether it could do tricks,'' I said, feeling my stomach shrink away to nothing and threaten to invert itself.

''Ihavetosaythisveryfast,'' Horace said, looking at Eleanor but talking to me, ''thisisreallyvenison.''

Eleanor nodded at Horace and smiled. Their mother looked suspiciously from son to daughter and back again, and Eleanor held up her plate like a good little daughter. A couple of minutes later, we all dug into Bambi. When we finished, I was a member of the family.

Months later Mrs. Chan clarified matters by admitting over yet another meal that she'd consulted a fortune-teller on the morning of the Bambi Banquet, and that the soothsayer had peered into my future and seen a golden shower. Horace, who was translating, stopped suddenly, looked down, and scratched his nose, and Eleanor remarked that it was a good thing her mother didn't understand American slang.

''If she did,'' she'd said, ''God only knows what you'd be eating.''

And I'd been a guest of honor at Horace and Pansy's wedding and at the twins' hundred-day party, and welcome always in the cramped apartment that Mrs. Chan ruled. I'd seen Husband Number Three abandon ship in haste after his wife, having already gone to all the nearby barber shops to pick up hair clippings for her backyard compost heap, dragged a comb through his brush and found several long blond hairs. There had been a scene. There was always a scene.

I wasn't used to scenes. My family didn't have them.

We loved each other politely and fought with silence. No one in my family ever threatened a relative with a meat cleaver or kicked a hole in a door. We touched each other's clothing, not each other's skin. I found that I liked scenes. I liked getting the anger out and over with, the spontaneous upwellings of love, the unpredictable eddies from some deep, lovingly familial current.

Horace's roomful of broken computers and applications for jobs he never intended to take. The encyclopedic, uncataloged knowledge of wholly unrelated facts that he unveiled in long, rambling lists. Pansy's cameras and quiet wit and shy, blinding smile. The big round heads and sweet, unblinking eyes of the twins. The sheer variety of Mrs. Chan's husbands. Everything about Eleanor. I'd isolated myself in years of study, wondering where I was going and who I was going there with. I woke up next to Eleanor one morning, sometime after the death of Jennie Chu, and thought I'd figured it out at last.

Bravo sat bolt upright in the backseat, indulging the conceit that he was in a limo and I was the chauffeur. I reached back to pet him, and he dodged my hand, discouraging familiarity from a mere driver, and I pointed the car south toward Wilshire.

It had all held together until Topanga. As long as Eleanor and I moved from temporary dwelling to temporary dwelling, a couple of nomads setting up and striking our tents, we were inseparable.

Maybe it was something about the idea of a house. I said I wanted it, and I thought I did. I said I looked forward to the prospect of more time together without friends and acquaintances to bother us. After months in the house, after she'd finished her first book and sent it off and I'd earned some money as an investigator, we began to talk, loosely and theoretically but earnestly, about marriage. I immediately had an affair.

And then another and another. They were meaningless, joyless, mechanical, purely technical violations of faith. She found out about one and forgave me. Later she forgave me again. Then she received simultaneously an advance for book number two and the news of affair number three, and she stopped forgiving me and moved out, into the little house in Venice in which she still lived.

Once separated we became close again and remained close, closer to each other than we were to anyone else in the world, and then the twins came along. We both loved the twins and they drew us closer, until her publisher, a New Age entrepreneur named Burt, took her to bed. Or maybe Eleanor took him to bed. It didn't help matters that I thought he was a vulgar, pretentious clown. Even then, though, I still had the family to love. I could still share in their lives.

But now they'd become Chinese, and they'd built a wall around their crisis that only a Chinese could pass through. I didn't have the password.

As I drove I asked myself whether my feelings were hurt and answered the question untruthfully in the negative. What was burning a hole in my stomach, I persuaded myself, was that they had done so much for me—they'd opened my life emotionally, they'd given me their love without asking themselves whether I was worth it—and here was an opportunity for me to do something for them, something I was reasonably good at, and my help was being refused.

I wanted desperately to see Eleanor.

Colored Christmas bulbs gleamed and winked in the gathering November dusk, framing the houses of the impatient. We picked up a little drizzle halfway to Santa Monica, not really rain but low fog sliding in from the ocean. Bravo put his head out the back window and let the wind pin his ears back, and I fought the temptation to do the same as the windshield slowly went from transparent to translucent to opaque. "Maybe you'd like to drive," I said to him as I pulled over on Santa Monica

Boulevard and got out to wipe the glass. He barked.

"You've been watching too much TV," I grumbled, climbing back in. "It isn't funny there, and it's not funny here." He maintained a dignified silence until we turned south onto Ocean, when his ears went up straight.

"Well, aren't you the navigational genius," I said. Normally I didn't go to see Eleanor unannounced—especially since Burt emerged from the ether—but under the circumstances I figured it would be all right. Anyway, Burt was in New York. Bravo whined, and his tail thumped against the seat as I made the right onto Windswept Court and pulled up in front of Eleanor's house. As I came to a stop he put both front paws against the window and panted loudly.

"Slow down," I said. "Do you see her car?" He turned his muzzle over his shoulder to look at me. "Do you see a light in the window?" His tail whapped the seat back. "God, what a stupid dog," I said, feeling desolate. "Anybody can tell she's not here."

He looked away and made a hunching motion with his hind legs, ready to jump out of the car.

"Hold it," I said, putting my hand on his rump. "We'll go up and check, but you've got to get out of the car like a gentleman."

I opened my door, and he scrambled over the seat back and across my lap and out, waiting for me by running short, impatient circles in the driveway. I climbed out with exaggerated slowness, and the moment I had both feet on the driveway, he charged up the sidewalk to the front door. I joined him and rang the bell three times, as much for me as for him.

"See?" I said, trying to sound happy about it. "Nobody home."

We got back into the car together, both disappointed. He lay down on the backseat, dispirited, with his ears flat. "I know," I said. "I love her, too." We made the long slow drive to Topanga in silence.

The fog had preceded us. Topanga Skyline was

blocked by a police car parked lengthwise across the street, its flashers firing red and blue into the mist.

"You can't get up," the cop said. "Fire equipment."

"I live there." I showed him my driver's license.

He shrugged. He had small, uninterested eyes and nostrils you could have saved quarters in. "Back it up. Go somewhere else."

I started to say something snarky and then remembered that I still had the Vietnamese kids' semiautomatics in the trunk. "Thank you, Officer," I said. "Always nice to talk with a servant of the people."

I took Alice around the back way, up an unpaved fire road and then down again until it struck Burson, which in turn intersected Topanga Skyline at the top of its arc. We were above the fog here, and I could see it brimming silver like a ballet lake below us, cradled in the cup created by the sides of the hills. It wasn't hard to imagine the ghosts of plesiosaurs paddling through it.

I parked Alice at the foot of the steep, rutted, unpaved driveway, and Bravo charged up it ahead of me. I huffed up at my own speed, toting the two guns, and joined him at the house. He was too busy sniffing to notice me until he heard the door open, and then he barreled past me and went to sit in his cave under the table that holds my computer. I put the little warriors' semis away the way I put most things away, which is by dropping them behind the largest object in sight. In this case, it was the couch. I made a note to take a look one of these days and see what else was back there. When I got the courage.

We are creatures of habit, and my habit when I get home is to go out on the deck in front of my living room and look at the best view in Southern California. I was anticipating a placid vista of pale mist and dark mountains. What I saw made me swear out loud and brought Bravo out to stand next to me and stare down through the darkness at 1321, on fire for the second time in four years.

PART II

MIGRATING STARLINGS

G. Kramer of the Max Planck Institute in Germany noted that when migration time arrived, starlings tended to take off at a certain angle with respect to the position of the sun. If the apparent position of the sun was changed by mirrors, the migrating starlings tended to take off in a direction which had the same angle relative to the sun's position in the mirror . . .

—GEZA SZAMOSI
The Twin Dimensions:
Inventing Time and Space

6

Guardian Angels

She finally emerged from the bar a little after two-thirty
in the morning, looking smaller and chubbier than she
had inside. I waited in the shadow of a van and watched
her come, dressed in pressed jeans, white sneakers, a T-
shirt, and a white unzipped windbreaker, the sleeves
pushed halfway up her forearms. Her shoulder-length
hair looked like she'd wet it and then combed it with
her fingers. She'd turned the collar up against the drizzle. She was humming.

The name of the bar, according to the scrawl of darkened neon tubing across its front window, was BEHIND
THE FAN. I'd missed that last time I was here. It shared
a tiny mall with a Korean liquor store and a laundry.
Both were closed and dark. At this hour, there was virtually no traffic behind me on Western Avenue. Being
there again brought Uncle Lo to mind, and I found that
I couldn't really remember his face as a whole. It had
disintegrated in my memory into a collection of Identikit
options: a mass of downward-sloping wrinkles set off by
a black eye, high, sloping cheekbones, a mouthful of
gold teeth.

I let her get well past me before I stepped into the light and called her.

"Lek," I said.

She wheeled immediately, the heel of her sneaker making a faint squeal against the asphalt, and her hand came up out of her little purse with a white canister in it. She extended her arm to its full length and pointed the can at my face. Bracelets jingled on her wrist. "Stop there," she said.

I stopped. "Mace?"

"You bet," she said. "Put you away good, too. What's your problem?" Her English in the bar had been heavily accented. She'd left most of the accent inside.

"I was here on Saturday night," I said. "With two Chinese guys, one young and one old, remember?"

"So what?" The hand with the mace didn't shake at all. I hadn't paid much attention to her in the bar, but now I was struck by the size of her eyes. They seemed to take up half her face, and their whites were as clear as porcelain under the streetlight. "I didn't ask you who you were, I asked what your problem was."

I slowly held my hands up, palms toward her, two feet apart. Gave her my Harmless Smile, just a big Boy Scout looking for a good deed. "Nothing up my sleeve," I said. "I want to talk for a minute."

"I get paid to talk," she said tersely.

"And you sound different when you do."

She made a small raspberry sound. "Oh, shooah," she said, "everybody like pidgin, *na*? Make everybody feel same-same Rambo, got too-big gun."

I couldn't help it. I laughed. Her face darkened, but then her Thai good nature carried the moment and her teeth gleamed, sudden and white in her face.

"Well, it's the truth," she said. "You think the guy wants to know that his little piece of sweet-and-sour has a day job translating English news for the local Thai paper? Will he tip her more if he knows she went to school longer than he did?"

"You have a degree?"

"I have two from Thailand, in English. Ning's a nurse, three-quarter time." She turned her head slightly to one side, regarding me. "I remember you now. You're the one who was no fun."

"You can put down the mace, then," I said.

"No way," she said, "but I'll change hands and lean on my car. My arm's getting tired and my feet hurt." She backed up against a gleaming little white Toyota that was parked facing out. The mace went from the right to the left hand. Her chin lifted a quarter of an inch, a prompt for me to talk. "So?"

"I want to ask you about the old man."

"Lo," she said.

I nodded, faintly surprised that she remembered him.

"Funny old guy. Still likes the girls, maybe too much. Like a dog sniffing, but funny about it. Some old guys never seem to run out, you know?"

"Lucky him," I said. "Some of us run out almost immediately. You were with him when he made his phone call."

"No." She raked damp hair back from her forehead with her right hand, and her eyes suddenly seemed even larger. "I was in the toilet, trying to look younger."

"Could you hear him?"

I got the sidelong gaze again. "I liked him," she said.

I spread my hands in what I hoped was an international gesture of reason. "I don't want to do him any harm. I just want to know who he called."

"Why?" It was thick with skepticism.

"I can't tell you."

"Go away." She started to back around the Toyota, mace still pointed at my face. "Go to the end of the parking lot and stay there until I've driven away."

"Wait," I said. "Um, wait, look here, I'll put my driver's license and my business card and whatever else you want right here on the hood, and then I'll back off and you come and check it out. Would I do that if I was going to hurt him?'' I slipped my wallet out of my shirt pocket and started to pull pieces out of it. "Oh, hell, look at the whole thing."

The wallet landed with a hollow thump on the Toyota's hood as I backed away, my hands in plain view again. Lek waited until I was a good ten feet off before she came and flipped through it one-handed.

"Okay," she said at last. She'd read everything in it and compared my face under the lamplight with the photo on my driver's license twice. "I'd take your check."

"Anything happens to Lo, the cops talk to you and you can send them straight to me."

"I said I liked him. I said I thought he was a funny old man. I didn't say I thought he was a good old man."

"No," I said, "he's not a good old man."

She pushed her lower lip out and then drew it back in again. Then she lowered the mace and dropped it into her purse. "In fact, I think he's probably a pretty terrible old man. I don't think he told the truth once all evening. And he was jumpy, always looking at his watch like he heard it ticking all the time."

"Did he speak English or Chinese on the phone?"

"I still don't know why you're asking."

"He did something to someone I love."

She weighed it. "A girl?"

"The people I love are mostly girls."

Her teeth caught the light again, and she chuckled. "I didn't think you were a lady-boy."

"As you said, he's a pretty terrible old man."

"Fun, though." Lek sighed at the injustice of it all, and then made up her mind or, more likely, her heart. "Spoke mostly English, a little Cantonese when he ran out of words. Only talked a few seconds. He called a lady, said he'd come for his things the next day. '*Dim sum* time,' he said."

Sure. *Dim sum* time made sense. The rest of it didn't.

"His things? Are you sure?" Eleanor had said he'd brought a canvas suitcase.

She did the thing with the lip again, dropped the long eyelids briefly and then shook her head. "No," she said. "The *rest* of his things."

"Do you think she was a Chinese lady?"

She fished in her purse while she considered the question, and pulled out a ring of keys that would have slipped easily over her ankle. "Don't know. If she's Chinese, she didn't speak his dialect and she's married to an Anglo. He called her Mrs. Summerson."

A bubble of air forced its way through my lips, surprising both of us.

"You know her?" Lek asked, looking startled at the sound.

"I know her," I said. And I did, and there was no way in the world I could talk to her without Eleanor's permission. If Lo was the Chan family's guardian angel, Esther Summerson was their household god.

I even knew where she lived. I'd been there twice, most recently after the twins' hundred-day party. Mrs. Esther Summerson occupied a perfectly restored 1918 Craftsman's Bungalow, set back at least fifty feet from the sidewalk on an idyllic one-way lane called Jacaranda Street. The house was dark now, sleeping under ivy and dormant climbing roses, just visible beneath arbors that had dangled sweet, dusky clusters of grapes only two months before. By daylight, the whole thing looked like the scenes they'd painted on the labels of orange crates in the twenties.

With Alice parked two streets to the west, I toted a large Styrofoam container of coffee up Jacaranda Street and found myself a dark little piece of curb between two parked cars almost directly across from Mrs. Summerson's. I couldn't talk to her, but nobody had said I couldn't look at her house.

My watch said 3:20 when I sat down to look at Mrs.

Summerson's house. The Styrofoam quart of coffee said DONUT DEELITE. I needed the coffee more than I needed the watch; I'd gone to bed for a couple of hours after the firemen finished putting out 1321 and then gotten up to go meet Lek, and every time I closed my eyes I saw little bitty fireworks.

The coffee was so extraordinarily awful that it held my attention for almost an hour. Since nothing whatsoever was happening in front of me, I had ample time and attention to devote to analyzing the components of its taste. Foremost among them seemed to be wet dog hair, softened and modulated by a hint of aluminum and a reedy note of newsprint, the entire rich and complex bouquet culminating in a strong finish of industrial-strength benzine. In mitigation, it had enough caffeine to set an army of water buffalo doing the hokey-pokey.

Lek, I thought. Thai. Lek and Ning and Lala, all of them thousands of miles from rice paddies and gilded temple spires and easy smiles. The Chans, Chinese. The tongs. The Vietnamese kids. All of them here now, part of a city that has more Koreans than anyplace outside Korea, more Cambodians and Thais than anyplace outside Cambodia and Thailand, more Japanese than anyplace outside Japan. Hell, we have more Canadians than Vancouver. A hundred languages, literally, are spoken in the public schools. All these people, Filipinos and Armenians, Turks and Guatemalans and Salvadorans, migrating over the lines and the empty blue spaces on the maps to create whole communities in a big ugly basin where the dominant gas is carbon monoxide and the dominant currency is disappointment. Mass movements, mass migrations, to get here.

And what was here?

Immigration. Im-*migration*. In my caffeine-saturated state, the word broke apart easily. I was composing an ode to immigration and my knees were taking turns jiggling up and down by the time the day was born rosy-fingered through the haze in the eastern sky, and a light went on upstairs in Mrs. Summerson's house.

The light beckoned to me. I looked around. No one in the street. No one watching from the windows of the other houses, or at least no one I could see. I got up and stretched and ambled across the street, just your average wired guy out strolling at the crack of dawn, and then I ducked under the arbors and ran, half bent over, to the wall of the house that faced the street, positioning myself against a section of clapboard between two large windows.

I heard singing, and the window to my left lit up. Growing in front of it was some sort of bush that someone who knew something about bushes could probably have identified. With the low arbors behind me I felt secure from the street, so I sidled like a good moth toward the light and waited behind the bush, peering through the gossamer or crinoline or whatever it was for all to be revealed.

What was revealed, eventually, was a woman in her late seventies having tea with her breakfast. I learned a new way to break and eat a soft-boiled egg, and I learned that Mrs. Summerson used linen napkins even when she ate alone and that she refolded them neatly to present a clean surface each time she touched one to her lips, which was often, and in general I learned that my standards of gentility were precariously low. Abandoning the light, I left her to her protein and checked every window I could see through and found the rooms on the other side empty. No lamps came on anywhere else in the house. If Mrs. Summerson was secretly playing host to Uncle Lo or to several thousand tong members, they were apparently breakfasting in the rooms upstairs. In the dark.

The orange rim of the sun was barging its way over the horizon by the time I arrived at the Chan apartment and found all the lights blazing away. I went up the stairs two at a time to try to burn off a little of the caffeine and walked into bedlam.

Pansy was on her knees in the corner, directly below the cross that Mrs. Chan, who took no chances where religion was concerned, had hung next to the family's Taoist shrine. Horace was pacing the rug around the dining-room table in precise rectangles, changing direction every time he reached the chair at the head of the table. He was holding his wristwatch in his hand. Eleanor was pouring coffee onto her wrist, missing a cup on top of the television set by inches, staring at me.

"How—but how did you know?" she sputtered.

"Know what?"

The coffee hit her foot, and she looked down. "Lord," she said, without force, "look at that. He's called, Simeon. He called about twenty minutes ago."

"What did he say?"

"Just said hold tight, he'd call back." She picked up the cup and poured into it, rattling it badly against the spout of the coffeepot, and extended it to me.

"Thanks anyway," I said, feeling something hot rise in the back of my throat.

She nodded absently and started to look at her watch. She was holding the cup in the hand that had the watch on it, so I reached out and took the cup before she dumped coffee all over her stomach. Since I had it, I drank some.

"What time, what time?" Pansy demanded, getting up from her place of worship. Her pillow had pressed her hair flat on the left side of her head, and her cheeks were flaming red. She'd buttoned her blouse crooked.

"Five-eighteen," Horace said, reversing direction around the table. He looked like one of the wooden soldiers in *The Nutcracker*. "Five-nineteen," he corrected himself, staring at the watch in his hand as he marched. He walked into a chair and knocked it over.

The phone rang.

Everybody stopped dead.

"Simeon," Eleanor said. "The extension in the bedroom. Horace, you take this one. Pick up, both of you, at the end of the third ring." Pansy stood absolutely still in the middle of the room, hands clasped in front of her stomach like an old-fashioned opera singer about to embark on the big aria.

The bedroom was a mess, blankets thrown to the floor and clothes spilling out of the closet. I unplugged the cord leading into the handset, lifted the handset, and plugged the cord back in at the end of the third ring.

"Hello," Horace said.

"I'm Lo," Uncle Lo said. Then he said something in Chinese.

Horace responded. Since I couldn't follow the words, I listened to the other sounds coming through the earpiece: a horn, something that might have been a motorcycle, birds. A pay phone, then.

"—okay?" Uncle Lo said at the end of a long string of tonal monosyllables.

"MacArthur Park," Horace said, sounding like he was about to have a coughing fit. "Alvarado entrance."

"Walk two hundred steps," Uncle Lo said in English.

"Okay," Horace said. "Two hundred."

"Look left." Then Uncle Lo asked a question in Cantonese.

"All of us," Horace said, "and Simeon, Eleanor's boyfriend. You met—"

"I remember. Okay, okay. No problem. Come now." He hung up.

Ninety seconds later we were at the bottom of the stairs, piling into Alice. Pansy rocked back and forth in the backseat, repeating something under her breath.

"What is it?" I asked. "What did he say?"

"Says he wants to show us he's serious," Horace said. He was sallow and there were circles under his eyes as definite as the rings left by a wet glass. His hair stuck up wildly on the back of his head.

"Whatever that means," Eleanor murmured. She had

her arms wrapped tightly around herself as though she were very cold.

"It means, it means, that he's going to ask us for, for whatever he wants, and he wants to prove, you know," Horace said a little feverishly. He peered through the windshield at the brightening sky as we cruised east toward the park. "Prove he means it," he finished. He swallowed with a sound like someone pulling a cork.

"What did he say the first time he called?"

"He say, good morning," Pansy said unexpectedly.

"She answered the phone," Horace said. "She's answered every single phone since . . ."

"He say, can we go somewhere," Pansy continued. "I say, sure. He say, call back." She subsided. A moment later I heard her say it all again, very quietly. Then she said it again.

"Left," Horace said. "Left."

"He knows, Horace," Eleanor said.

"Then he can just do it." Horace's voice went up. "You don't have to correct me."

"Sorry," Eleanor said, and everyone fell silent.

"He say, call back," Pansy repeated for the fourth time, and then she began to weep, a little stifled sound that went *put-put-put*, like a child's imitation of an engine. With Pansy's sobs powering us, we arrived at MacArthur Park.

The sun was still slipping up, but a low ridge of cloud had eased its way east, cutting off the top of the bright circle. With the circle's bottom edge still below the horizon, the day was momentarily lighted by a deep orange strip. The trees had that peculiar luminescent lividity they sometimes assume before heavy rain.

The light revealed the park as brown and dirty. Bums slumbered beneath newspaper blankets at its edge, too smart to risk being caught farther inside. The dead grass was littered with bottles and crumpled paper.

An asphalt path led from the Alvarado entrance into the park. Horace began counting at the first step, and the path led us down a short hill, through a copse of bushes, and to a gate. Eleanor had Pansy by the arm.

"Two hundred," Horace said. He looked left at some tall oleanders.

Horace had short legs. I ran a couple of yards forward, to the edge of the oleanders, and stopped. No one else moved.

Then I said, "Pansy. Horace." I wasn't sure I trusted my voice.

They all came up behind me and stopped. Eleanor drew in her breath, and it caught and broke, and Pansy let out a small flat high sound like the whistle from a steam kettle and ran past me to the swing where Julia sat, her left wrist tied to the rope of the swing by a bright pink gift ribbon.

Eleanor's reaction was the Chinese one.

"He kept the boy," she said.

7

The Lord's Servant

The room was full of babies, and they all had numbers written on their wrists. Some of them wore colored ribbons around their throats, trailing enormous floppy bows over their shoulders. Those babies were not crying. The other babies had lengths of string around their necks, dirty pieces of string tied in rotting knots, and they were crying desperately. A very thin, stooped woman in a conical straw rice-paddy hat like the ones we used to see on the newsreels from Vietnam moved from one crying baby to another, spooning something white and thick into their mouths. As they sat up and sucked at the spoon the strings around their throats blossomed into bows, and when the bows became big enough they pulled the babies over onto their sides. Now the other babies were beginning to cry, their colored ribbons dwindling into dirty string, but the thin woman ignored them and shuffled in her rope sandals to the wall.

There was a big round orange button on the wall. I hadn't seen it before. The thin woman pushed it, and the wall slid upward to reveal a broad, steep chute. She pointed to a handle below the chute and gestured for me to pull it. When I did, dozens of new babies cascaded down the chute and into the room. The old woman raised her head to look at me, and beneath the conical straw hat I saw she had a black eye.

"Simeon," Eleanor said.

I rolled over and came face-to-face with a cerise bear, one of the twins' menagerie. "What time is it?" I asked. The couch was too short for me, and my legs were stiff from having slept with them drawn up.

"Eleven. I've fixed some *juk*."

"Any word?" My feet hit the floor sooner than I ex-'pected them to, jarring me all the way to my teeth.

"Shhh," Eleanor said reprovingly. "Pansy and Julia are asleep."

I eyed the couch, a world-class collection of lumps. "How do you sleep here?"

"You managed," she said, smiling at me.

"But you're delicate," I said. "The slightest wrinkle in the sheet—"

She pulled my nose between her thumb and forefinger. "Oh, bananas. I sleep like a horse and you know it. Come and eat something."

I got up. The floor only heaved twice beneath me. Horace was sitting at the dining-room table eating *juk*, rice gruel, from a bowl. He'd combed his remaining hair with water, making him look like a farmhand visiting the big city.

"Morning again," I said. "How long has it been?"

"A little more than five hours."

"Let's figure he was somewhere close by when we got Julia," I said, sitting. My back cracked. "He'd just called, so we know he was near MacArthur Park at five-thirty. What's he doing now?"

"Who knows?" Horace said. In spite of the slicked-down hair, he looked much better, five years younger than he had when we left for the park. He'd gotten one child back, and his faith in Uncle Lo had been vindicated, after a fashion. "He'll call when he's ready."

"Maybe the question is, *where* is he now?" Horace

gave me an interested glance, and it suddenly struck me that I hadn't seen him alone with Pansy since the kids disappeared. He'd always been with Eleanor and me, consigning Pansy to other rooms. "Maybe he needs this time to get from here to somewhere else." I looked around. "Speaking of where, where's your mother?"

"Pansy packed her off," Eleanor said, coming into the room with a bowl in her hands. "Mom was driving her wild. Tears, accusations, nattering." She put down the bowl, sat next to me, and pushed her fingers through my hair, coming it back. "About four yesterday afternoon she told Mom to get out of here and go home."

I dropped the spoon into my *juk*. "Your mother's house," I said.

"Sure, her house," Horace said crankily. "Where else—"

"That's where he's going," I said.

Eleanor sat up. "Whatever it was he wanted, he didn't find it here." She looked at me, but she was thinking about something else. "Should we call her?" she asked Horace.

"Why?" Horace said. "He doesn't know where she lives."

"Actually," I said after thinking about it for a moment, "he probably does."

"How would he?" That was Horace.

"How'd he know about the twins?" Eleanor asked him rhetorically.

"I know who told him about the twins," I said. "Who told him everything except ancient history, in fact."

"Who?" Eleanor had a hand on my arm.

I pointed across the room at the cross on the wall. She followed with her eyes and then gave a small gasp.

"Mrs. Summerson?"

Even in his distracted state that caught Horace's ear. "Mrs. *Summerson*?" he asked.

The phone rang, breaking through the silence like a dentist's drill.

"No games this time," I said. "Just answer it."

Horace went to the phone, blew a deep breath out through tight lips, and picked it up. "Hello?"

Eleanor's fingers tightened on my arm.

"Hello, Lo," Horace said. He looked over at Eleanor and their eyes held. Horace nodded twice and rattled off something in Chinese. I caught "Ah-Ma," or mother, several times, and Horace shifted his gaze to me and lifted his eyebrows. "Okay, okay," Horace said and then listened. "Yeah, okay. Yes. Bye-bye." He pushed down the buttons on top of the telephone and said, a little grudgingly, "Good, Simeon."

"Mom's," Eleanor said.

"He wants the place empty by noon. He wants it to stay empty until five this evening. He wants all Mom's stuff put out in plain sight."

"Not just another pretty face," Eleanor said, making circles with her fingertips on the back of my hand. She hadn't done that in years.

"Can you reach them?" I asked to mask my confusion.

"They're home right now," Horace said, starting to push buttons.

"How do you know?"

"Uncle Lo says both cars are there." He finished dialing and waited.

"Uncle Lo's very careful," Eleanor said. "It's a good thing he doesn't really mean to harm us."

"I don't know about you," I said, hanging on to her fingers, "but I'd gladly throw him out of the helicopter for what he's done already."

Horace started talking. He encountered some resistance, raised his voice, remembered that Pansy was asleep and lowered it again, and began to gesture with his right hand. He rolled his eyes and looked at Eleanor. "Her purse, too, right?" he asked.

"Of course," Eleanor said. "And her wallet, and all the money in it."

Horace returned to the fray, using his right hand to drive home points and, occasionally, to wave inarticulately in the direction of heaven. When he hung up he looked as tired as he had the first time I'd seen him that morning.

"She could tie a knot in a tree," he said. "Nothing is simple. Should she leave her purse? Should she call the neighborhood security guard? Should she send the plumber out and hide in a closet? How do we know someone else won't come along and rob the house? Everything has to be turned inside out, held up to the light, weighed in the hand, bitten, and once all *that* adds up, it's time to argue about it. When I was growing up I thought everyone was like that. I thought that was how people figured things out. When I went to junior high school it took me most of the class period to answer the first question on my first multiple-choice test. I was looking for the trick, the double-cross, the sucker punch. Jesus, no wonder I've lost my hair. I failed the written part of the driver's exam four times because I was too busy searching for the hook to answer the questions. It's a miracle I can drive today." He fell heavily into his chair.

"She's had a lot of trick questions," Eleanor said levelly, although I knew she agreed with him absolutely.

Horace shook his head from side to side. "Oh, sure, sure. Bad luck all the way. Treachery on every hand. And after Daddy died she managed to get out of China and wind up in America with two grown kids and two grandkids, one of whom is a boy, and she owns property all over the place, more safety-deposit boxes than I've got dresser drawers, and she's finally got a plumber of her own. She hasn't exactly ended up like Auntie Shih, has she?"

"Okay, Horace." Eleanor glanced at me. "Auntie Shih got her back broken during the Cultural Revolution," she said. "Some ham-fisted farmer was helping her with self-criticism and didn't know how strong he was."

"They're going to clear out?" I asked Horace.

"They're probably gone already," Horace said tightly, "What the hell does he want?"

I looked at my watch and yawned. "Nothing to do till five," I said.

Eleanor reached over and put her hand politely over my mouth. "Yes, there is." She got up and stretched. "Clear your plates, please. I'm tired of servitude."

"What's to do?" I asked her, knowing what she was going to say.

"Well, Uncle Lo's in Las Vegas. Let's go talk to Mrs. Summerson."

"Yes, who is it?" she said, peering pale blue at us through glasses that were not only thick but dusty.

"It's Eleanor Chan." Eleanor pulled me forward. "And a friend."

"Eleanor, dear," Mrs. Summerson said, fumbling with the lock on the screen door. "What a treat to see you, not that I can really see you, I'm afraid. How are the children?"

"The children," Eleanor said, momentarily thrown. She absolutely *cannot* tell a lie without preparation.

"Your little boy and girl," Mrs. Summerson said, all blue eyes though the lenses. "Twins, aren't they?"

"The twins, yes," Eleanor said, "well, no, they're not mine. They're my sister-in-law's."

Mrs. Summerson peered at her for a moment as though she'd forgotten what she was going to say next, but then her face cleared. "Of course," she said, "you're their aunt, aren't you? I vow, I'm losing my mind completely." She waved a hand in front of her face, dispelling the fumes of confusion. "And look at me, keeping you standing here on the step like a pair of orphans. Please, come in, come in."

She opened the door and then turned away from us and led us into the dim hallway, which smelled simultaneously of old sachet and cooking oil. As she retreated I heard her say, "*Pansy* is the mother, of course. Whatever is the matter with you?"

Mrs. Summerson was as tall as I was and had better posture. Her hair was white and cut bluntly, in a way that brought to mind the Chinese rice-bowl haircut. There was, in all, something indefinably Chinese about her in spite of her height and her big hands and fair skin and ice-blue eyes, something Asian in the way she held herself and in the way she walked, as though she were living in a climate much hotter than that of Southern California, and energy were something to be conserved. I could almost hear sandals slapping, and for a moment I remembered the old woman in my dream, the old woman with Lo's face.

". . . the parlor," Mrs. Summerson was saying. "Right there, dear, to the right, you remember. Tea in a twinkling." Eleanor and I went through a wide archway into the parlor, and Mrs. Summerson padded off toward the kitchen, saying to herself, "How *nice* this is."

"She's gotten old," Eleanor said wistfully, looking around the familiar room. We could have been in Canton. Chinese artwork was everywhere: fine old watercolors of clouds and mountains and bamboo and horses hung on the walls. Ivories and bronzes, smooth with touching, nestled close on shelves. The Three Ancients, ceramic and brightly colored, stood close together like gossiping old men, offering their blessings on the house. Above the fireplace hung a large black-and-white photograph of a plain wooden building set into a level, dusty field. The horizon was featureless. Lined up in identical uniforms in front of the building, which I had been told was a missionary school, were perhaps seventy Chinese children. They stared patiently into the camera, not hiding behind the photographic smile of the West. In the lower right-hand corner of the photograph, in white ink, was a date: January 10, 1942.

Next to the photograph was a framed embroidered sampler that said MY HANDS ARE FOR MY FELLOW MAN. MY HEART IS FOR GOD. Stitched below these lines were four lines of Chinese that, Eleanor had explained to me on the day of the twins' hundred-day party, meant the same thing. She'd spoken as an expert, since she'd done the embroidery when she was eight years old.

Eleanor had once lived in this house.

"I am a servant of the Lord," Mrs. Summerson sang from the kitchen. "His wishes I attend." Her voice was low and resonant, and it carried well. It had carried through churches and schools all over the face of China for almost twenty-five years.

Eleanor was staring at the sampler as though it were several miles away. Then she let her gaze wander over the room and down to the carpet. She listened to Mrs. Summerson sing, her eyes downcast, eight years old again and abandoned in Los Angeles.

"How long since you were here?" I asked.

"Same as you," she said to the carpet. "Um, no. You've been here more recently." She went to the sampler and straightened it. Then she untucked her shirt and ran it over the surfaces of some of the carved objects. She picked up a little ceramic statue of Christ, robed in incongruously bright Chinese gold and red, and blew on it. "She really can't see," she said. "This place was never dusty."

"No help?"

"Mrs. Summerson doesn't believe in help."

"Well," I said, "she's got the Lord."

"You've got it backward." She put the little Jesus down and went to the large photograph of the children and drew her sleeve across the glass. "Mrs. Summerson is the Lord's servant."

"We're all the Lord's servants," Mrs. Summerson said. "If only we knew it." She pushed a jangling three-wheeler tea table into the room, lifting the back edge to roll it in front of her, and I hurried around to take it from her although she looked strong enough to carry it one-handed. She regarded me in a kindly fashion through the magnified eyes that made her glasses look like a dime-store joke. "So," she said as I positioned the table in front of the small rosewood sofa, "this is your young man."

"What a *sweet* thing for you to say," Eleanor cooed. "Especially about an old codger like Simeon."

"He looks young enough to me, dear," Mrs. Summerson said, smoothing her big hands on the front of her skirt. "Young and vigorous. Lots of good hard work in him."

"And that's where it'll stay," Eleanor said. "Inside him."

"The way you young people talk." Mrs. Summerson bent forward and peered at the tea table to see whether she'd forgotten anything. "Jam, sugar, rolls, cream—do you take cream or milk, dear?—well, never mind, we have both, lemon, butter. The tea is Darjeeling. Please sit down. When I was married my husband and I never bantered back and forth like that. Of course, we were serious people. Too serious, I dare say. Still, it was a good life." She sat at one end of the sofa, tucking her skirt under her legs. "You remember Dr. Summerson, don't you, Eleanor?"

"No," Eleanor said, trying not to look surprised. "He was gone when I moved in." She sat next to her.

"Honestly," Mrs. Summerson said, waving her hand in front of her face again. "It's not enough I can't see what's in front of me, now half the time I can't remember what's behind me. It's like living by flashlight, and the little circle of light keeps getting smaller. Dr. Summerson passed on," she said to me, "two years before Eleanor's mother—how is your mother, Eleanor?—took Horace up to Sacramento to open that what-was-it?"

"She's fine," Eleanor said, smiling at her. "It was a grocery store."

"Grocery store," Mrs. Summerson said simultaneously, then tapped her temple. "Not completely gone yet. I told them it wouldn't work," she said to me. "Sacramento had too many Chinese, I said, and the people up there couldn't tell them from the Japanese and there was still bad feeling about the Japanese in some places. Not as bad as in China, of course. If the Americans had suffered Japanese atrocities the way the Chinese did, I doubt there'd be a Jap left in America. We'd have run them into the sea." She cleared the tension from her throat, a ladylike *ahem*. "They're your brother's twins, aren't they?"

"Yes, Mrs. Summerson," Eleanor said, sounding like a little girl.

"Nice boy. More common sense than you have, but you've got the poetry." She regarded the framed sampler. "Did you know, Mr. um . . ."

"Grist," I said.

"Did you know, Mr. Grist, that Eleanor tried to change that saying when she embroidered it in Chinese?"

Eleanor suddenly looked very uncomfortable.

"No," I said. "Did she now?"

"She certainly did. She wanted to put in a whole new line. After MY HANDS ARE FOR MY FELLOW MAN, she wanted to write, MY HEART IS FOR MY FELLOW CHILD. MY SOUL IS FOR GOD. And only eight years old. Isn't that something?"

Eleanor was scarlet. "It certainly is," I said.

Mrs. Summerson clinked her teaspoon against her saucer. "And she used to call it 'Christ Must.' "

"Mrs. Summerson," Eleanor began urgently.

"Because Christmas was the one day each year when you *must* believe in Christ." She sat back triumphantly. "Isn't that wicked?"

"Tea, Simeon?" Eleanor asked between her teeth.

"You little pagan," I said. "I'd be afraid to take tea from your hands."

"But I'm forgetting my duties," Mrs. Summerson said hastily. "Please. Let me pour." Her hands trembled slightly as she lifted the pot. Aside from a plain gold wedding band she wore no jewelry. Eleanor's eyes followed the big hands with an expression I couldn't quite read.

"Someone was just talking to me about you," she said, passing Eleanor a cup and saucer with a wedge of lemon. "Who was it?"

"Uncle Lo," Eleanor said conversationally, as though we'd been talking about him for hours.

"Oh, of course. Poor man." She shook her head gravely. "I suppose he came and saw you?"

"Last Friday." Eleanor sipped her tea and waited.

"Dreadful thing. Mugged, right there on the streets of Chinatown. It's getting so no place is safe any more. I've been thinking of putting in new locks."

"It's a good thing he wasn't really hurt," Eleanor said neutrally.

"Well, his pride was hurt. And there was that eye, of course. Not very distinguished-looking, I must say. He's always been such a self-reliant man. I suppose he's getting older, too."

"I wasn't aware that you'd kept in touch with him," Eleanor said. "I knew you and he knew each other in China, of course."

Mrs. Summerson moved things around on the tea cart in a way that, in a less godly person, might have suggested a stall for time. "He popped up about a year after your mother and brother came back from Sacramento," she said to the dish of lemon slices. "You must have been eleven. Just knocked on the door one fine morning with some lovely ivory for me. That was when there were still elephants, of course. We simply went back to the same work," Mrs. Summerson said, putting down her tea untouched. "Exactly as we did with you and your mother. Mr. Lo got them out of China and Dr. Summerson and I got them into America. They'd just eased up on the Chinese quotas, and it was easier than it had ever been to get visas and passports. I only wish Dr. Summerson could have lived to see it. It would have gratified his soul.''

"So Uncle Lo brought out people after us." Eleanor was clearly surprised at the news, and not entirely pleased. She actually sounded jealous.

"A few."

"From where?"

Mrs. Summerson pursed her lips. "Mostly Fujian," she said. "It's on the coast, so it's a little easier. And then, too, the people are mostly fishermen, so there are lots of boats around."

"Well, I'll be darned," Eleanor said.

"How many times have you seen him since?" I asked.

"Two or three. He came every five or six years or so, so make it three. Three times in the last twenty years. Of course, the Chinese government put a stop to all that in the eighties, and I haven't heard from him now in, well, let's see, five years.''

"You never told us about this." Eleanor managed not to make it an accusation, although her feelings were plainly hurt.

"It never came up, my dear."

I put down my own cup. "What did he say about the mugging?"

"Oh, he was in a terrible state. Mad enough to spit. Said he'd been jumped right on the street."

"What did they take?"

"Everything. His money, even his cigarettes. I gave him some money, of course, and let him stay here. I let him buy his own cigarettes.''

"What day did he arrive?"

"Well, he was here three nights and he left on shopping day, which is Friday, so it must have been Tuesday, mustn't it? Tuesday, Wednesday, Thursday night, and gone on Friday morning."

"Did he come back?"

She glanced up at me and then looked at the ceiling. Then she looked back down at the cup in her hand. Her back was rigid. "No," she said, an Asian quarter-tone higher. She was a terrible liar.

I let it pass. "Who beat him up?"

"Thugs. One of those gangs. Everyone's in a gang these days, it seems."

"Did he say what he was doing in America?"

She relaxed. "Just visiting," Mrs. Summerson said. "More lemon?"

In the car, Eleanor wrapped her fingers around my upper arm and rested her head on my shoulder. "There was a time when I loved that lady more than my own mother," she said. "She was everything I wanted to be."

"Meaning?" We were most of the way back to the apartment, and it was still only three-thirty.

"Generous, good-hearted, self-sufficient, and white. All the white kids in school were calling me names then. Ching-chong. Wang-wang. And I'd go home, and she'd be white, too, even if she did speak better Cantonese than I did. Horace and Mommy were in Sacramento, and I felt like the only Oriental in the world."

"Poor prickly little Ching-chong." I was thinking about Mrs. Summerson's lie. Lek had heard Lo say, "*Dim sum* time."

"I outgrew it," she said. She rubbed her forehead against my shoulder. "I'm sleepy."

Her forehead felt good. "Me, too."

"You've been great through all this. Very steadying."

"It's not over yet." Mr. Manly speaking.

"It's going to be all right. I'm not going to ask you how you found out about Mrs. Summerson. You made a promise, and I know you didn't break it."

"Of course not," I said with the quick indignation of the guilty.

"I may have to kiss you on the neck."

"The ear," I said.

"What have you got to bargain with?"

"I didn't have to go anywhere near Chinatown to find out about Mrs. Summerson."

"What a man," she said. "The ear it is."

As she reached her face up to me I hit the bump at the bottom of Horace and Pansy's driveway. Alice took a good bounce, and I leaned down and got her on the lips.

She settled back, looking satisfied. "That's cheating," she said.

"Bugger cheating, as the British would say." I coasted Alice to a stop and looked up at the apartment. "Bet you a big one they're all asleep," I said.

"What happens if you lose?"

"Then *you* have to give *me* a big one."

"I am completely indifferent," she said, "to the outcome of this bet."

We closed the car doors softly and went quietly up the stairs. I eased the door open and let Eleanor in. The apartment was silent. At the end of the hallway, Eleanor stopped and said, "Oh."

Over her shoulder, I saw Horace and Pansy lying on the couch, their arms and legs in a knot. Pansy was facing us, and her eyes flew open at the sound of Eleanor's voice, and Horace jerked around spasmodically and then fell off the couch. Both of them were blushing furiously, but Horace just rolled all the way over and came up on his knees facing us with his hands outstretched, looking like Al Jolson.

"Eadweard's at Mom's," he said. Pansy sat up, her face crimson, smiling like a fool.

"Already?" Eleanor looked at her watch. "But it's—"

"You know Mom. She drove by every fifteen

minutes. He was only in there an hour. The third time she went by, his car was gone. She went in and found Eadweard sitting on the living-room floor.''

Eleanor ran to him and kissed him and then kissed Pansy. Pansy let out a kind of strangled giggle, and Eleanor backed off. ''She's bringing him down?''

''No,'' Pansy said firmly and happily, putting one hand to her forehead as though she had a fever. ''We take a plane, six o'clock.''

Eleanor surveyed the two of them. Horace's shirt was held closed by only one button, and his hair was sticking up again. ''I think we old folks ought to leave these two kids alone,'' she said, turning to me. Her delight made her look ten years old.

''I'll take you on a double date.''

''That sounds half as good as a single.''

''It's already set,'' I said. ''Want to come?''

''Sure,'' she said. ''We've got celebrating to do. Let me change my clothes. What are we doing, anyway?''

''Dinner.''

''That's very informative. Dressy or not?''

''Not.''

''What else is new?'' Eleanor said.

''Horace,'' I asked, ''what did he take?''

Horace looked at Eleanor and then at me, and then he tucked his shirt in. ''That's the funny part,'' he said. ''He didn't take anything.''

8

Card Tricks

The double date turned out to be a fivesome.

"This is Sonia de Anza," Hammond said proudly across the table. Then he forced a smile that looked like it weighed ten pounds and added, "And this is her brother, Orlando."

Seated, Sonia de Anza was as tall as Hammond and a lot better-looking. She was dark-haired, straight-nosed, square-jawed, and striking, with oddly yellowish eyes, the longest real lashes I'd ever seen, and delicately flaring nostrils that made me think of perfume. Orlando was Sonia as a boy of seventeen, with the same features metamorphosed, as though seen through water: The square jaw added definition to her face while the fringe of lashes softened his. Even a member of another species could have seen at once that they were brother and sister. Hammond and Sonia were dressed casually, Hammond in a red muscleman's polo shirt and Sonia in a pale lavender blouse that made her skin look darkly creamy, but Orlando was decked out in an IBM-issue white shirt with a badly ironed collar and a narrow black patent-leather tie. He glanced once at my aging Megadeth T-shirt and then looked politely away.

We all mumbled pleasant preliminaries at each other, and Eleanor and I let go of each other's hands long enough to sit down. I immediately grabbed her hand back. The restaurant was Hammond's choice, one of those vestigial time capsules from the fifties where you sit in red leather booths and eat red meat, and women with red lipstick drink Manhattans with red cherries and blow smoke rings. A big Christmas tree blinked and shimmered in the foyer, dropping needles on dummy presents and scenting the air with pine. I felt like all I'd done in the past three days was eat meat. The sleepless nights were playing tricks with my sense of time, making the lunch with Hammond seem only hours ago. Lo was as two-dimensional as a figure in a frieze.

"Al says you should have been a cop," Sonia de Anza said at once. Her voice was low and throaty, softer than her face had led me to expect.

"I did not," Hammond said huffily. "I said he *thought* like a cop."

"Gee, Al," I said, "almost thanks for the compliment."

"What does a cop think like?" Orlando asked. He made it sound like a trick question.

"Like a snowplow," Hammond said, fearsomely avuncular. "We bull our way through the fluff until we hit something hard."

"How disappointing." Orlando offered kindly old Uncle Al the cold shoulder. "I'd hoped cops thought like Porfiry in *Crime and Punishment*."

Hammond threw him a sour glance and then looked at Sonia. "Orlando's gifted."

"He'll graduate from USC next year," Sonia said, a little apologetically. "He'll only be seventeen." She patted his hand. "But he's still being a little fart. He knows what cops think like. They think like me." He opened his mouth, and she said hurriedly, "Like I."

Eleanor nodded toward Orlando, and said to Sonia,

"He's very beautiful," and Orlando went redder than the leather in the booth.

"Well, you know what they say about appearances," Sonia said, clearly pleased.

"Thinking like a cop," Hammond offered, hoisting a menu bigger than The Little House on the Prairie, "how are your hypothetical Vietnamese kids?"

Eleanor withdrew her hand and very slowly turned to look at me.

"Real discreet, Al," I said, my ears burning.

"Lookit, Sonia. Now they're *both* blushing." Hammond made a show of fanning me with the menu. "Anyway, Sonia already knows about it. She's the only one I've told."

"You don't get your kiss back," I said to Eleanor. "I didn't get Mrs. S. from him."

"Mrs. S.?" Hammond's ears went up the way Bravo's do when I mention food.

"Are you Chinese?" Orlando asked Eleanor, as though no one were talking.

"If I'm not," Eleanor said, "my mother has gravely misled me."

He leaned toward her. "How old are you?" Sonia looked alarmed.

"Far, far, too old, but thanks."

"Have you got a sister?"

"Orlando!" his sister said. Hammond, looking at me, slowly crossed his eyes.

"No," Eleanor said seriously. "But surely, you shouldn't have any trouble—"

"I'm too young for them," Orlando said with surprising bitterness. "Girls at school are what, nineteen, twenty? I'm sixteen. I can't even *drive*." For the first time he sounded like a teenager.

"I see," Eleanor said. "That's a problem."

"As long as we're talking hypothetically, Al . . ." I began.

"Do you know anybody?" Orlando asked Eleanor.

"I'm thinking," Eleanor said.

"Let's assume a hypothetical kidnapper," I said. "Let's assume he steals a kid or two, or even just takes something precious—"

"She doesn't have to be Chinese," Orlando said helpfully.

"That's enough, Orlando," Sonia said, very much the older sister.

"But it would help if she could drive," Orlando finished very quickly. Then he looked down at his plate and began to pick at the cuticle of his left thumb.

"What does he want, your kidnapper?" Sonia asked me.

"He doesn't say. Just demands that a house be left empty and unguarded for a certain number of hours and that everything of any value be sort of piled in the middle of the living room. And the person who owns the house comes home at the appointed time and the kid is right there, and nothing's missing."

"Something must be missing," Hammond said. "Did they check carefully?"

"Oh, yes," Eleanor said, "this person would have checked very carefully."

Hammond looked from her to me as the silence yawned around us. "You guys are sharing a hypothetical life, huh?"

"We have been for years," Eleanor said.

"It was a card trick," Sonia suggested. "He asked them to pile up everything valuable just to distract them and then, uh . . ."

"Took something worth nothing?" Hammond challenged.

"This is thinking like a cop?" Orlando asked. He didn't sound awestruck.

"He risked a lot to take this kid or these kids or whatever it was," I said. "If it was a kid, he even transported it over state lines."

"Hey, hey," Orlando said, snapping his fingers, "maybe he *left* something."

We all looked at him.

"Sure," he said. "Maybe the whole thing was for him to get inside when no one was there and *leave* something. He never wanted to take anything at all. He just told them to put the stuff out because—"

"That's pretty good," Hammond said grudgingly.

"Alternative," Orlando said promptly. "What he took doesn't have any value at all except to him. It wasn't even with the stuff they put out. That's why he had them put the important stuff out, so they'd look there instead of anywhere else. Like Sonia said, a card trick. It's something so unimportant that it won't be missed, but it's important to him."

"I may have a girl for you after all," Eleanor said.

"That's the direction I've been leaning toward," I said to Sonia. "Something that seems to be worthless."

"Nothing is worthless to my mother," Eleanor said, and then stopped. "Oh, good lord," she said. She wrapped her right hand into a fist and pretended to try to force it into her mouth.

"Just some relative, huh?" Hammond said accusingly.

"Case closed, Al. All over, and at no cost to the taxpayers."

"A kid was transported across state lines?" Sonia demanded.

"What do you think about Emily Liang?" Eleanor asked me.

"Nice little girl. Plays the piano, doesn't she? Wears a lot of pink?"

"I mean, for Orlando."

Orlando pulled the center out of a piece of bread and rolled it up between his palms, the picture of adolescent nonchalance.

"Nah," I said, "she's too nice for Orlando." He gave me a startled glance.

"What do you mean, it's over?" Hammond's shoulders loomed toward me.

"The kids are home. Nothing valuable is missing. It was all a . . . a—"

"A family misunderstanding," Eleanor finished for me.

A big pill made out of bread hit me on the ear. "How could she be too nice for me?" Orlando said.

"What a question," his sister scoffed. "Have you got a brother, uh, Eleanor?"

"Do I ever," Eleanor said.

"And you seem so calm," Sonia said.

"How many conversations we got here?" Hammond asked. "I feel like I've got jet lag."

It reminded me of Uncle Lo, and it seemed like safe territory. "Just what exactly is jet lag?"

"It's a displacement of the circadian rhythms," Orlando said, getting it out of the way so he could return to his main theme. "How could she be too—"

"Circadian," I said. "Pretty word. Sounds like Shakespeare, the seacoast of Circadia."

"What I really don't like," Orlando announced to the world at large, "is when someone asks a question and doesn't listen to the answer."

"Circadian," Eleanor interposed, "*circa dies*, literally 'about a day.' A rhythm that repeats approximately every twenty-four hours."

"An internal rhythm," Orlando said sulkily.

"Like sleeping?" Hammond asked.

"You have hundreds of them," Eleanor said. "Your digestive system, your basal metabolism, body temperature, endocrine glands, brain waves. All cyclic, all set to a period of about twenty-four hours. When you change time zones—" she glanced at me, realizing what I was thinking—"you, um, you have to readjust all those little clocks to local time."

"What do you think?" I asked her. We'd already

more or less settled it, but nothing seemed to be settled about Lo.

She shook her head. "I don't know. I didn't know then and I don't know now. He was tired, that's for sure."

"I'm tired, too." I yawned again. "That doesn't mean I just flew in from Hong Kong."

"Who just flew in from Hong Kong?" Hammond asked.

"Circadian rhythms persist for a long time, even where there's no sunlight," Orlando contributed, more to thwart Hammond, I thought, than for any other reason. "People living in deep caves for months still function in twenty-four hour cycles. Astronauts in space, same thing."

"Orlando is interested in time," Sonia said, a bit wearily.

"Who isn't?" Orlando demanded.

"Can we have a show of hands?" Hammond asked.

"Time is everything," Orlando said, warming to his subject, "and we don't know doodly about it. We haven't got words for it, even; we recycle the words we use about space. 'The near future' and 'the distant past.' Like I just said, 'a long time.' Time isn't like space in any way, but we use the same words. Space goes on in all directions. If time moves at all, it moves in only one direction."

"Time moves in only one direction?" Orlando had jogged Eleanor's metaphysical funnybone.

"Maybe it doesn't move at all," he said, looking mysterious. "But if it does, it moves in only one direction."

"Says who?" Eleanor asked.

"Says atomic decay, for one thing." Orlando sounded positive.

"I thought time was cyclic," I said.

"You would," Orlando said coolly. "Stone age."

"Most of the people in the world believe in cyclic time," Eleanor volunteered.

"Most of the world," Orlando said dismissively, "believes in reincarnation, too. That doesn't make it anything except a remnant of a primitive worldview."

"Yow," Hammond said. "Listen to the boy. Am I the only one who's hungry?"

"You don't believe in reincarnation?" Eleanor was on the fence about it.

"I'd say the mix is a bit rich in former Egyptian princesses," Orlando said. "There couldn't have been that many Egyptian princesses. How come nobody was a dung-beetle farmer, that's what I'd like to know."

"Dung sounds great," Hammond announced, "but I'm having steak."

"You had steak yesterday, Al." I thought for a moment. "*Was* it yesterday?"

"Time is a cycle. What about you, Sonia?"

"Surf and turf," Sonia said. "And something white and dry."

"I want to eat something with a head," Eleanor said. "I'm feeling fifties. Maybe a steak, like Al's. How can you be so sure about reincarnation?"

"Because it's cyclic. Cyclic time doesn't happen in nature." Orlando closed his menu. "I'd like pork chops."

"It doesn't happen in nature, huh? Tell me about the year," Sonia said.

"A perfect example."

"For whose side?" Eleanor put an oar in.

"Prime rib," I said. I hadn't even realized a waiter was present until I felt him behind me. He was as tall and thin and melancholy as Ichabod Crane, and he had a small hole in the elbow of his red jacket.

"Anything for starters?" he asked mournfully.

"Salad all around," Hammond said, assuming command. "Bring all the dressings you got."

"For my side, of course," Orlando said. "Every year is absolutely different."

"And wine?" the waiter asked.

"A jug of each color," Hammond said impatiently. "Can't you see we're debating the nature of the universe?"

"Let me know if you figure it out," the waiter said, turning away.

"Spring, summer, fall, winter," Sonia said, counting each off on a finger. "You remember a year when they came in a different order?"

"And garlic bread," Hammond called after the waiter.

"Oh, sure," Orlando said. "And day and night, high tide-slash-low tide, waking-slash-sleeping, the phases of the moon, the apparent motions of the planets and stars, the solstices, circadian rhythms—I mean, give me a *break*. Local phenomena, card tricks. So the planet circles a star. So it rotates. Mercury doesn't. On Mercury, it's the same day all year. A Mercurian's circadian rhythms would last forever. So what? We have a day every twenty-four hours, but it's never the same day."

"I told you he was bright." Sonia didn't sound entirely happy about it.

"And why do you care about this so much?" I asked.

"It just pisses me off. Our brains are the most complicated things in the universe, and we don't use them. We understand time intuitively in ways we don't even consider." He picked up the salt shaker and threw it at me.

It was a pretty quick snap. I caught the shaker left-handed, and salt poured over my forearm. "Great," I said. "And I've been trying to cut down."

"You just performed dozens of complicated calculations about time and space," Orlando said. "You estimated the thing's velocity and trajectory, and you timed it to the split second. Your brain told your arm where to go and then interpreted the information from the nerves in your hand to let you know that you'd caught it, and then you made a joke. Not much of a joke, of course, but you were busy. You can do all that literally without thinking about it, but you and lots of other people persist in thinking that time is like a . . . a clothes dryer or something, just going around and around in easy, predictable, stupid little patterns.''

"I could have done without the 'of course,' " I said as the waiter put two carafes of wine on the table and gestured for a black-coated acolyte to set the green salads. He watched critically, dismissed the acolyte, bent forward from the waist in military fashion, placed Sonia's more exactly in the center of her place mat, and retreated, a puffy little blister of white shirtsleeve protruding through the hole in his jacket.

"Watch him go," Orlando said. "What do you see?"

"What do you mean, what do I see? I see the waiter heading for the bar."

"What you *see*," Orlando corrected me, "is a man with his back to you, moving his legs and getting smaller. You know what it is because you're *time-binding*—you think of the waiter as a more or less permanent object in space and time, and you put together the different pictures you see every moment to conclude he's leaving. Otherwise you might think he's one man getting smaller and smaller, or a succession of men, each smaller than the other. Same thing when you listen to music: You hear a succession of pitches over a period of time and you put them together into a melody. Listen to something moving in the dark, and you know it's the same thing although you can't see it. It's called *time-binding*. Even birds can do it. Migrating starlings take off when their clocks tell them to, and stop when they get there, the same place every year. And they use, birds use, time-binding. Starlings can fix on a permanent object, like the rising sun, and use it as a reference point for takeoff every morning, even though they haven't seen it for twenty-four hours. Obscure the sun and show them its reflection, and they'll take off in the wrong—''

''Here's a man getting bigger,'' Hammond interrupted, grating pepper over his salad and offering the mill to Sonia.

The maître d' leaned in and addressed Eleanor. ''Miss Chan?''

''Good guess,'' Eleanor said.

''You have a phone call.''

''Where are we,'' Hammond asked heaven, ''the Polo Lounge?''

''I left the number on my answering machine.'' Eleanor smoothed a hand over my shoulder, but not before I'd asked her to give my regards to Burt. She grabbed a lock of my hair and yanked it as she followed the maître d'.

''Burt, huh?'' Hammond grunted, shoveling a bale of romaine lettuce into his mouth. ''Talk about permanent objects.''

''The reptilian brain, on the other hand,'' Orlando continued as though no one had interrupted, ''can't really time-bind. Its prey has to be the right shape, the right size, and moving. Surround a frog with dead flies, and it'll starve to death.''

''And that's enough,'' Sonia commanded. ''No more flies, no more dung. We've been very patient.''

Orlando started to say something, then closed his mouth so sharply I could hear his teeth crack together. He prodded at his salad with a forefinger, the picture of a man looking for dead flies.

''Do you really think,'' Sonia asked, softening, ''that Eleanor might introduce him to someone?''

On cue, Eleanor beckoned to me from across the room. Even at that distance I could see that something was wrong.

''I'll ask her,'' I said, getting up.

''Collar the waiter while you're up,'' Hammond said. ''No Russian dressing?''

"Getting smaller now," I said as I left the table. Orlando fixed me with a poisonous look.

The Christmas tree twinkled hyperactively at me, silhouetting Eleanor in its prism of light. She grabbed my wrist and led me toward the phone, out of sight of the table. The receiver dangled by its coiled cord, and she picked it up and gave it a shake, as though there were someone unpleasant inside it.

"I don't know whether to laugh or cry," she said, hanging it up. "I wish I'd been born an orphan."

"What is it?"

"It's Horace," she said. "The jerk. He's left Pansy and the kids in Vegas and gone after Uncle Lo."

9

Hill Street O

My room in the TraveLodge on Hill Street was mercifully lacking in Christmas cheer. No dying tree, no cards lining the mantel. For that matter, no mantel. I'd checked the window for a glimpse of festivity and found myself looking at a concrete wall two feet away. After my first night on the street, I'd found the dour little room a relief from the faux-Oriental facades of Chinatown, sparkling with lights and ringing with scratchily amplified carols, as though a missionary had seized control of a small Asian country and decreed a cure for his homesickness.

Tossed over the sagging princess-sized bed a stained lemon-yellow spread struggled for chromatic dominance with a carpet the color of decayed teeth, an irregularly mottled brown over which you could have changed the oil in a car without leaving a noticeable stain. I'd dropped my keys on it the second evening I was there and spent ten minutes on my hands and knees trying to find them by touch. They didn't move or jingle, so I didn't get a chance to practice my time-binding.

This was my fourth evening, which made it Sunday night. One week since I'd stared at Lo over the red candle.

One wall framed a door and a mirror, below which were a narrow Formica counter and a curved plastic chair. The chair and counter had seceded from the color wars and assumed a sort of spit-gray neutrality. The decor was completed by a simulated wood dresser shoved up against the wall with the pictureless window in it. Above the dresser a bent nail supported an impossibly vivid laser-generated photo of two kittens in a basket. That was it, except for two more doors, one leading to the tiny closet and the other to a bathroom where the grouting was in serious need of attention.

Sitting becalmed on the lemony pouf of the bed, I tried to convince myself that I knew what I was doing. I knew I was putting on my Reeboks because my feet would hurt later if I didn't, but long-term goals were conspicuous by their absence. I didn't really think I would turn a corner and bump into Horace, or that my two murderous Vietnamese kids would wave cheerfully at me from across a room. But the kids had come from Chinatown and Uncle Lo had been assaulted in Chinatown—or so he'd told Mrs. Summerson. Or so Mrs. Summerson had *said* he'd told her. Still, Eleanor had been sure that Horace was in Chinatown, and more than anything in the world right then, I needed to find Horace. I needed to find him for Eleanor and Pansy, and I needed to find him for me. So I'd sentenced myself to wandering aimlessly around Chinatown morning and night, working my way through Horace's known haunts, and enduring the TraveLodge so I could get an early start.

After three nights of merciless Cantonese meals—*lop sop*, Eleanor called it, dismal imitation Chinese food the restaurant help would never eat themselves—and after wearing down the tread on my Reeboks tracking kids who, on closer inspection, looked like visitors from the Valley, I'd come to one firm conclusion. I'd concluded that I'd eat at McDonald's.

Only in a city as horizontal as Los Angeles would Hill Street be called Hill Street. Most of it is as level as a billiard table, four lanes of flat black asphalt distinguished from a million other L.A. streets only by the two-story, Chinese-cheesy architecture that crowds it on either side, replacements for the original buildings, slapped together in 1938 by the ephemeral architects of Paramount Pictures as a gift to the Anglo city's fantasy life. The development had been so romantically and persuasively unauthentic that scenes from *The Good Earth* had been shot there before the whole *mishegas* burned to the ground. The canned-Cantonese frippery that replaced it was no less unauthentic but much less glamorous, sets for a movie starring Victor Mature, with someone like Veronica Lake playing the Chinese girl he loves, all shorthand Asian Mystery and inscrutable proverbs, pidgin English, horsehair wigs, and rubber eyelids. The wigs were in plentiful evidence, re-Orienting the Western mannequins modeling Chinese robes in the shop windows. The eyelids, the ones on the street, that is, seemed to be real.

Of course, not all of them these days belonged to Chinese. Hill Street, its two parallel streets, and the web of cross streets, alleys, and walkways that connected them were relics of what had at least been a real Chinese neighborhood all those years ago. Now the Asian presence in Los Angeles was more complex, a confused stew of people with nothing in common but tonal languages. The Chinese and Japanese had been joined by the refugees from wars in Vietnam, Cambodia, and Laos. Add the ambitious economic opportunists from Korea and Indonesia and Thailand to the mix, and you had the diverse population that the Anglo newspapers lumped together as "the Asian community."

Grumbling loudly enough to draw stares, I angled across Hill and into a little pedestrian walkway between shops, on the way to my car and a Quarter Pounder with Cheese. I didn't make it.

My car, Alice, was in view, gleaming horsefly-blue under a streetlamp thirty yards away, when the girl screamed. She was tiny and Asian, and she burst from an alley twenty feet ahead of me and to the right, and then an arm snaked out and grabbed her down jacket at the neck and jerked her back in. I heard the *squeeee* as her rubber-soled tennis shoes left the pavement, and then another scream, higher and more urgent than the first.

Well, so it wasn't a time for reflection. I wrapped my fist around my car keys so that the points protruded between my knuckles, and sprinted after her. Fist-first, keys raking the air, I rounded the corner and dove head-first into sucker heaven.

Something hard and heavy landed on the back of my neck, coming from the left, and the whisper it made as it parted the air gave me just enough warning to launch myself off the balls of my feet, subtracting my forward velocity from its momentum, and it struck my neck and folded my left ear forward and pasted it to my head like the flap on a glued envelope, pushing me forward and off my feet. I felt hot blood pour down my neck as I landed on my stomach, and the girl giggled.

Scuffle of shoes behind me. If the girl hadn't giggled I might have been dead then and there, but the giggle galvanized me and I rolled to the right, away from the shoes and into some wooden packing crates. They folded themselves noisily down over me, and whatever had hit me on the neck swooped down again and pounded them into confetti. The feet I'd heard were right next to me and had ankles attached to them, and I drove the points of the keys into the left ankle, trying for the little bones that you can separate but never quite put together again. One of the keys went all the way home.

The giggle was lost in a yowl, and the ankle I'd hit disappeared from view. I rolled farther under the scraps of wood and put both hands against the bottom of a crate and heaved a big piece of it in the direction of the vanishing ankle. Then I stood up, new blood heating my face and neck, and a fist hurtled toward my eyes. Orlando's claims for the miracles of the mind notwithstanding, I failed to calculate the fist's trajectory and velocity properly, and it treated me briefly to a new and gaudily unattractive version of the star-spangled banner. Still, the mind had sufficient time and electricity to suggest that the proper course of action would be to fall down and play almost-dead, and the broken slats of the crate folded themselves cozily over me like a masochist's bed of splinters, and I ignored the shard that had put a second hole in my right ear and lay still. I smelled fish, an odor seeping up from the wood uninvited, like someone else's memory.

"Motherfucker," panted a familiar voice.

"Is he dead?" That was the girl. She sounded winded.

"Not half," said the kid I'd treated to the Torture of a Thousand Fingers. "But second half is easy."

Hands grasped my Reeboks and groped their way up my ankles. The other kid, the one with the ruined ankle, was whimpering. Okay, one down, for the moment. I let Dumbo-Ears pull me out into the alley, grunting with the effort.

"He's fast," said the girl.

"He's through," said Dumbo-Ears.

"Fuck you," said the corpse, and I brought my left leg up between the kid's thighs and hit him right on his personal share of the Vietnamese genetic destiny.

Dumbo-Ears said something that sounded like *scummmpff* and folded forward, landing conveniently, if heavily, on top of me. I threw him in the general direction of the girl and pulled myself to my knees, a lot more slowly than I would have liked. My hands were so far away that I seemed to be communicating with them by telephone.

He slammed into the girl. I listened with satisfaction as the two of them struck the pavement and then, with a Herculean effort, I got my feet under me. I looked up for a point of reference that might keep me from falling on my face, and focused on the barrel of a small revolver.

"You wouldn't dare," I said.

The other kid, the good-looking one, cocked the gun with a click, a welcome sound. A revolver takes two clicks. Immediately after the first, I rolled to the right, thrusting my feet forward and tangling his damaged ankle between mine. He fell sideways, and the shot gouged concrete with a resonant *spang* that bounced back and forth between the walls of the alley like a berserk Ping-Pong ball. I found myself standing over him and raised one leg and sank it into the pit of his stomach.

"Ooof," he said, lifting his knees to shrink his diaphragm, trying to catch his breath. With another shot at a set of genetic jewels presenting itself, I drove my foot into his crotch.

It worked again. He squealed in soprano, curling himself away from me. He was painfully thin, and I did my best to shatter his ribs, bringing a Reebok-soled foot down on his solar plexus.

I was winning. And if I wasn't, who was around to contradict me? I fumbled my way to my feet, fighting for breath, and sighted an angel.

"That's my baby," the angel said. As I'd thought at first, she couldn't have been more than fifteen. Her left hand came up and leveled a gun, a new gun, in the very specific direction of my brain. "You can't hurt my baby."

"Honey," I said, "I was only trying—"

"You hurt him," she said. She cocked it. She was too far away to reach. I heard the first click and then the second, and I kissed it all good-bye. Eleanor would know that I'd tried. The eyes in the absurdly young face narrowed, and I watched the knuckles circling the trigger go white. Someone else's life flashed before my eyes, the life of some poor, dumb fool who had missed all his chances, who had turned his back on the love that might have saved him, redeemed him. Chances rejected, love denied, lifelines refused. What the hell; it was my life after all.

"Drop it," said a new voice, a voice I'd never heard before. "Drop it, fish sauce."

She turned away from me, toward the entrance of the alley, her mouth an open, vulnerable O. A large number of Chinese men, seven or eight of them, stood there. Most of them had guns. All the guns were pointed at the angel.

"Gone," she said, dropping it.

"Jesus," I said fervently to them as they advanced. "Thanks."

"Forget it," the nearest of them said. He had a semi in his hand, and he leaned down to pick up my keys. Then he smiled at me and took a step in my direction.

The last thing I remember from the alley was the barrel of the semi hitting me on the temple. Whatever I landed on seemed very soft.

Across the room, the girl was chained to a concrete pillar.

So was I.

To be exact, we were both handcuffed, and the chain connecting the cuffs had been passed behind metallic electrical conduits that terminated at the tops of boxy outlets about six feet from the ground. That put my hands directly behind my head, but the girl's arms were stretched straight up and her feet pointed downward balletically. She was even shorter than I'd thought. Her eyes were closed, but her lips were moving silently, and she was conscious. Other outlets sprouted from similar pillars studded throughout the room. The room, which was quite large, was windowless and rich in pillars. A basement, maybe, supporting the weight of the building above it. The dirty cement floor was cluttered with desks and pallid beneath a thin wash of fluorescent light. On each desk was a sewing machine, and each of them was plugged into one of the boxes on a pillar. Cartons of unfinished garments, sleeves and collars and whatever comes between them, squatted next to the desks. A sweatshop. Chinese men were yanking the plugs from the outlets and shoving the desks and cartons aside to clear a space in the center of the floor, an action that struck me as sinister for some reason that might have been related to the fact that I was, after all, chained to a goddamn pillar.

My head felt like leftover gristle, and my neck felt like it had been flayed. It was difficult to focus my eyes; things kept getting watery. Dried blood pasted my shirt to my neck and shoulder. Whoever my rescuers were, they'd been forceful about things. No one had been worried about diplomacy. On the other hand, I was alive.

I wasn't sure why, but then I wasn't sure about much of anything.

"He's awake." One of the men said, giving me what he probably thought was a hard stare from the middle of the room. He was thin and round-shouldered, wearing a short-sleeved white shirt tucked into pleated, shiny-kneed slacks that he belted about six inches below his armpits. He came toward me, loafers flopping lazily on his feet, and one of the other men, the one who had clouted me with the gun, said something short and sharp in Cantonese. The natty dresser laughed, showing me a partial set of third-world teeth, and stopped about eight feet from me. Too far away to kick.

"Head hurt?" he asked, cocking his head to one side and giving me a diagnostic survey.

"No," I lied.

"It will," he said.

This got a big laugh from two of the men on the floor. There were six of them, counting the guy with his belt loops in his armpits and his pockets at his nipples. So a couple were missing, probably in the back room torturing puppies.

"Do a lot of sewing?" I asked him.

He looked absently around the room. "That's funny," he said soberly. Then he stepped forward, lifted a leg, turned quickly, bent at the waist and swung a shoe into my ribs.

It took my feet right out from under me, and the cuffs took a bite out of my wrists as I dangled there, fighting back a sudden upsurge of vomit. As I tried to get my feet working again, he knotted his fingers together and swiped both hands, arms fully extended, across my face. The blow drove my head back and into a corner of the electrical box, and I saw a brief explosion of light and my legs went slack again.

"Now does it hurt?" he asked.

"Bruce Lee," I said. I'd bitten my tongue hard, and my mouth tasted hot and salty. "Everybody thinks he's Bruce Lee these days."

"Bruce Lee is dead," he said informatively.

"That's the trouble with impressionists," I said, finding my feet at last. "They never take it far enough."

One of the other men, a mild, even scholarly-looking specimen several inches shorter than the one who'd hit me, laughed and loosed a volley of Chinese. I recognized "Bruce Lee," and then the translator laughed again and the other men joined in.

It didn't sit well with Highpockets. His eyes narrowed, and his long upper lip raised to reveal those teeth. His hand went to an elevated pocket and came out with a knife. He flicked it downward and a very bright blade appeared, and he angled away to my right, out of reach of my feet.

The other men watched fascinated. Highpockets was behind me now, breathing shallowly and fast, and I could smell garlic and beer and the odor of my own fear. Something brushed past my hair, and the edge of the knife came to rest at the top of my injured right ear, at the spot where it joins my head. He began to press down.

"No," the translator said. Then he said something in Chinese.

The knife was lifted, and Highpockets came around

me, staying clear of my feet, and grinned at me. "Hero," he said. "Mr. Hero."

He turned his back on me and crossed the room to the girl. Her eyes were wide open now, watching him come. He stopped beside her, turned to give me a mocking look, and grasped her chin with his left hand. With his right he drew the knife down her smooth cheek.

She made a muffled, whimpering sound, and a line of red appeared. It began below her left eye and ended below the corner of her mouth. The blood coursed down her throat and dripped onto her jacket.

"What about it, Mr. Hero?" Highpockets asked. He released her chin and crossed behind the pillar to reappear on her right side. He grabbed her chin again, and now she began to cry. "Got anything funny to say?"

"Please," I said.

"Pretty little fish sauce, isn't she?" he said, raising the knife again.

"Please," I said again. "Please don't." The girl sobbed hopelessly without moving, frozen into immobility by the point of the knife.

"*Please*," he mimicked, forcing his voice into a soprano squeal. "Oh, *please* don't."

"That's right," someone said. "Don't."

Highpockets jumped back as though the girl had given him a shock. The knife dangled impotently at his side.

The man who had come into the room was short, maybe five-six, but wide as a door frame. He wore a meticulously cut suit in an improbable shade of powder blue that didn't mask the huge muscles at the tops of his shoulders, muscles that seemed to crowd his ears. He was clean-shaven and blandly pleasant-looking, with thinning black hair combed straight back, a little too long at the back of his neck. Something gleamed at one corner of his wide, straight mouth. Two semifinalists from the Mr. Chinese Universe contest stood possessively behind him. They would have been identical except that one of them had two eyebrows and the other had one, a straight line of hair that joined over his nose like a furrow of corn.

"We will speak English," the man in blue said in a mild voice. "To be polite." Then he pointed at Highpockets and said, "Ying. Cut yourself."

Highpockets looked at his friends on the floor, but no one moved. Most of them seemed to be fascinated by the unfinished garments in the cartons at their feet. One of them actually picked up a sleeve and gave it an experimental stretch.

Highpockets swallowed and then looked an appeal at the man in blue. The man in blue took whatever it was out of his mouth and lifted his eyebrows expectantly. Highpockets immediately put the blade against his own face and sliced downward. Blood flowed.

"Face the girl," the man in the blue said. Highpockets did as told, bleeding face to bleeding face.

"You may spit on him," the man in the blue suit said. The girl spat on him.

"Ying," the man in the blue suit said. "Take one of those pieces of cloth and clean her face."

Highpockets—or Ying, I guessed—took a sleeve or something from a carton and mopped her face with it.

"Press it against the cut to stop the bleeding," the man in the blue suit said. His eyes were calm, almost uninterested.

Ying did as told, very gently. Blood from his own cut stained his white shirt. The man in blue turned to face me.

"It's always wise," he said, "to demonstrate control at the outset. People think it's easy to be the bad guy. They don't take into account the kind of help you have to hire. Does your head hurt?"

"Yes," I said this time.

"Good," he said, nodding. "There's no reason you should escape Scotch-free."

"Scot-free," I said without thinking.

His eyebrows went up and he smiled. "Thank you,"

he said. "Idioms give me some trouble. So many of them make no sense. The first time someone said 'How do you do' to me, I asked him how I did what." He paused.

"How about that?" I said, since he obviously expected me to say something.

"You are in the way," he said, apparently fascinated by the sound of the words. "Is that what you say, 'in the way'?"

Was he kidding? "That's what we say."

"I thought so. It's not your fault, exactly. Or, rather, it is, because you are a persistent soul. But it's not your fault that the Confucian ethic is breaking down."

"Glad to hear it," I said, not having the faintest idea what he was talking about.

"Everywhere you look," he said, "old values are failing. Your country is certainly not immune."

"I guess not."

"Look at the work ethic," he said, settling in for a chat. "Americans used to like to work. Now they're as lazy as fleas on a dog." He raised his eyebrows inquiringly.

"That's a new one to me," I said.

"'As lazy as fleas on a dog'?" he asked. "This is not something you say?"

"Well, it's not something I say."

"The flea," he said quite seriously, thinking things through, "is not an industrious animal."

"Hungry, though," I said, equally seriously.

"Hungry?" He put the thing back in his mouth, and I saw it was a gold toothpick. "'As hungry as fleas on a dog,' perhaps?"

"Perhaps."

"That may be the trouble with Americans. They're not hungry anymore." He seemed to be waiting for applause.

"I think that's something we're proud of."

"Ah, yes, but it takes the edge off." He smiled in

triumph at the idiom, the gold toothpick protruding from one corner of his smile. Something gurgled.

"Excuse me," he said, the model of politeness. He pulled one lapel of his suit aside to display a holster, and my stomach did a sudden flipflop. The holster gurgled again, and he pulled a cellular telephone from it, turning away from me as he did so. Highpockets— Ying—watched him, his shirt soaked with blood, not daring to remove the cloth from the girl's face. The girl seemed to be concentrating on something taking place in the Andromeda Galaxy.

"Yes?" Mr. Blue demanded. He listened for a moment, and then snapped his fingers, twice. One of the Mr. Universe contestants, the one with the single eyebrow, leaped forward, pad and pen in hand. He handed them to the boss and turned submissively away, offering a back as broad as the Mississippi Delta as a writing surface.

"Yes, yes," Mr. Blue said into the phone. Then he said, "San Pedro," and followed it with a couple of very fast paragraphs in Chinese, but it didn't sound like Cantonese. He took the phone from his ear and punched a button, turning back to me and holding out the pad and pen in one smooth gesture. Mr. Universe took them, and Mr. Blue holstered the phone.

"You understand Mandarin?" he demanded.

"No."

He snapped something at me, watching me closely, and then flung a few syllables at his bodyguards. They started to move toward me, and Mr. Blue gave me the big calm eye for a moment and then snapped his fingers. The muscle twins froze.

"I told them to remove and eat your liver."

"I'd rather they didn't," I said, hoping my knees didn't decide to fold again.

"So I see. And I see you didn't understand when I said it." He gave me a forgiving smile. "I am Charlie Wah," he announced. "You see, I tell you my name.

Do you know anything about Charlie Wah?''

"I'm learning."

He laughed softly, a precisely measured and tightly controlled little ha-ha-ha, and then stopped, cutting the laugh off in mid-ha. "Well," he said, "that's probably good. I would like you to tell me everything you know."

I tried to think of something I could tell him, and failed. "I don't know much of anything."

Charlie Wah smiled at me, one reasonable man to another. "And yet you are here."

I said, "I was looking for Little Tokyo."

"Please," he said, "don't mess with my head."

"That's a little dated," I said.

He nodded. "And what would you say?"

"I don't—" I began.

"Would you say 'Help'?" Charlie Wah snapped, stepping closer. The two bodybuilders came with him in perfect lockstep. "Would you say 'Oh, don't' if Ying here was told to cut your nose off? You can live without your nose, but many veins supply it and a lot of blood would be involved. And then, of course, you wouldn't be exactly a fashion model when it was over."

"I don't know anything," I said, on the edge of pleading. "It's true."

"Let me be the judge of that. Just tell me why you're here. Start at the beginning, please. Everything you know."

"I know that my girlfriend's uncle showed up unexpectedly—"

Charlie Wah held up a finger. "Lo."

"Lo. And he kidnapped my girlfriend's niece and nephew and then returned them without taking anything."

He pulled the gold toothpick from his mouth. "Without taking anything from where?"

"From my girlfriend's brother's house."

"In Los Angeles." He was watching me very closely.

"And Las Vegas," I added quickly. "Her mother lives in Las Vegas."

Charlie Wah nodded, one short jerk of the smooth chin. "What was he looking for?"

"I have no idea."

"And this is why you're here? To ask him what he was looking for?"

"Sort of."

He smiled. It didn't raise the temperature any. "Pardon?"

"I'm curious," I said. "That's my job, to be curious."

"Yes. You're a detective. It says so in your wallet. But not a policeman."

"Not," I said. "Not a policeman."

"Lo must have taken something," Charlie Wah said persuasively.

"That's what I thought, too. But they say not."

"Where is your girlfriend's father?"

"Dead."

"Chinese?"

"Yes."

Charlie Wah thought for a moment. "Of Lo's age?"

"Yes. I think they were friends."

"In China."

"I guess so."

"But he came here before he died. The father."

"No. He died in China."

Charlie Wah looked at me for a very long time. "Think about your nose," he said at last.

"He died in China. The Cultural Revolution got him."

"You have no doubt about that."

"It's one of the first things my girlfriend ever told me."

"And when was this?"

"Years ago." My nose was beginning to itch.

"Years ago," Charlie Wah repeated. "How old was your girlfriend then?"

"You mean when she told me?"

"No," he said impatiently. "When her father died."

"Two," I said.

"Nothing was taken," Charlie Wah said. He sounded puzzled.

"Not that I know. Not from either house."

"How odd," Charlie Wah said distantly. Then he called something out without turning around. I heard "Lo" twice, and one of the men left the room. Charlie Wah drew in the corners of his mouth and stared at the floor for a moment, and then looked up at me.

"You are remarkably lucky," he said.

I immediately felt better. "Well, whoopee."

"Yes, whoopee. If you were Chinese, you'd be dead. Instead, you're going to live to be an old man and have many grandchildren."

"I can't wait."

"Unless you get in Charlie Wah's way again. If you do that, you'll be as dead as any Chinese. And we're going to persuade you not to get in Charlie Wah's way again. We're going to kill two birds with one stone. Ying," he said without turning his head, "her bleeding has stopped by now."

"Yes, Ah-Wah," Ying said, stepping back.

"Bring in her friends."

Ying hurried off like a good little wounded soldier. He still hadn't mopped the blood from his own face.

"She's pretty, as Ying said." Charlie Wah sounded faintly regretful. "But trash. All Vietnamese are trash."

"Whatever," I said. He needed response to keep his rhythm going.

"Still, trash has its uses. In the old days, before things started to break down, you could use trash without worrying about it."

"You can't touch pitch," I said, "without being defiled."

"Yes?" he said. "What is that?"

"I think it's the Bible."

"And the meaning. Pitch is something in baseball, isn't it?"

"It's like tar, dirt. But sticky."

"Dirt sticks to your fingers," he said.

"Exactly."

"Bingo," he said. Then he smiled again. "English is an exhilarating language."

"Glad you like it."

"Shakespeare," he said irrelevantly.

"Cao Xueqin," I said.

He looked startled. "*Red Chamber*," he said. "You know it?"

"It's my favorite book."

"You"—he paused for a moment—"you are pulling my leg."

I couldn't help it. I laughed.

His face darkened, but then he smiled. "Who do you like," he asked, "Bao-Chai or Dai-Yu?" It wasn't an idle question; it was a pop quiz.

"Bao-Chai," I said. "Dai-Yu cries too much."

Behind him, three beefy Chinese pulled the Vietnamese boys into the room. They'd been stripped to the waist. Two of the men carried long machetes.

"She cries always," Charlie Wah said, relaxing slightly, "but such sentiment."

"Coughs a lot, too," I said, watching the two boys. The one with the Dumbo ears looked terrified.

"She was dying," Charlie Wah said. "Don't you think that's sad?"

"Death is always sad."

He saw me looking past him and turned to regard the boys. "But sometimes necessary."

"Oh, Jesus," I said.

"Jesus?" Charlie Wah asked, swiveling back to me. "My least favorite god."

10
—

Pas de Deux

"In the good days," Charlie Wah was proclaiming from one end of the room, "we had respect. We had natural order." He paused, and the mild-looking translator who'd gotten the laugh at Ying's expense turned it into Chinese. Charlie had one hand in the pocket of his blue, double-pleated suit trousers, jingling enough change to choke a parking meter. He liked making speeches.

The girl sagged drunkenly against her pillar. The cut on her cheek had scabbed into a rusty thread, border-straight. I'd decided to kill Ying if I got a chance.

The boys had been stood back to back in the center of the floor.

"The man who enjoyed respect was the oldest man," Charlie Wah said comfortably. "As it should be. The wisest man, the grandfather, the one richest in experience. This was Chinese. This was proper and right. This was Confucian."

One of the Vietnamese boys, the handsome one, snickered. The man nearest him slapped him in the face, not hard enough to hurt but hard enough to snap his head around. Hard enough to humiliate.

The boy looked straight forward, his cheek scarlet.

Dumbo-Ears blinked rapidly, as though he'd been the one who'd been hit. He looked childishly small, childishly young.

"Now the man who gets respect is the man with the gun," Charlie Wah continued, shaking his head sadly. Fluorescent light gleamed on his high forehead, and change clinked and jingled. "He can be a thug, he can be the most stupid man in the room, but if he has the gun he becomes the leader. Why is this?

"Is it because we are in America?" He paused rhetorically as his words of wisdom were translated. "Not really. We see the same thing these days in Hong Kong and Taiwan. America has no corner"—he turned toward me and smiled—" 'no corner'?"

I nodded.

"No corner on thugs," he said proudly. Then he bypassed the translator and rendered the idiom into Chinese for the benefit of the thugs present before returning to English. "Now we have the two-week millionaires, the men who sell the heroin. Slime." He turned to regard the two boys, his eyes flat and black. "And now we have the Vietnamese."

The baby with the Dumbo ears took a quick look at Charlie Wah and clamped his eyes shut.

"We need the Vietnamese in America." Charlie sounded regretful. "There are things no Chinese man should be asked to do. But the old values are being broken down, and in America the Vietnamese are the hard end of the battering ram."

He paused and then smiled. "Just so no one makes a mistake, my sons," he added jocularly, "I am the man with the gun at the moment." On cue, the two Mr. Chinese Universe contestants displayed short, ugly automatics. Charlie Wah beamed at them paternally. "The Vietnamese," he said, picking up the thread and stowing the smile belowdecks. "We use them when we have to, and we pay them well, but they are trash and they act like trash. We could kill them, of course, just as we could kill this *gwailo*, but would it be smart? No." He seemed to like answering his own questions even more than he liked speechmaking. "We need the Vietnamese, and killing a *gwailo* brings the police." He lifted a finger and said sententiously, "Killing a *gwailo* always brings the police. We do not need the police."

This sentiment, translated by the mild-looking little guy, brought a murmur of consent. Only Ying seemed unhappy. His eyes flicked to mine and then looked away. I was sorry to see that he'd stopped bleeding.

"So we will send a message," Charlie Wah said. "One of these boys will take it to the Vietnamese, and the *gwailo* will write it in his daybook."

"Diary," I said.

"And he will not be back." He looked at me inquiringly.

"Absolutely," I said absolutely.

"It would be very easy to kill you," he said, a man considering a purely technical challenge. "We could, for example, strip away the covering from the wires above your head and plug in a sewing machine and turn it on. The handcuffs would be a very good. . . ." He looked up at the ceiling as though the word he sought was likely to be printed there, like a drunk actor's prompt.

"Conductor," I said, just to move things along.

"Or we could simply shoot you," Charlie Wah said impatiently. He'd had his English corrected enough for one evening. Ying brightened and made a clucking noise.

Charlie scowled at him. "But, as I say, it would bring the police. Still . . ." He looked at me, and I decided it would be an extremely good idea to shut up.

One of the Mr. Chinese Universe finalists trained his gun on me.

In the darkness, as they used to say on the old *Fugitive* TV show, fate moved its heavy hand. Dumbo-Ears decided to go for the exit.

His boot came down on the instep of the Chinese man

closest to him, and the man made a surprisingly musical sound, raised his foot, grabbed it with both hands, and demonstrated an energetic new variant on the hop, skip, and jump. He was still in the hop phase when Dumbo-Ears, five steps away, stopped cold and sucked in his bare midsection to keep the point of a machete from finding a way through it to his backbone. The other end of the machete was in the hands of the guy who'd introduced the side of my head to the barrel of his gun with such memorable results.

"Ssshh*aaaaah*," Dumbo-Ears said, sinking to his knees. Then he burst into tears.

The mood in the room changed, as though atomized blood had been sprayed into the air vents. Men shuffled their feet and sniffed it.

"Swine," Charlie Wah said meditatively. "And cowardly swine at that."

"He's just a kid," I said.

Charlie Wah let go of his change, reached up to his mouth, and took out his gold toothpick. Then he pointed the sharp end of the toothpick in the direction of his left eye and poked it. Message received.

"Kill them all," Ying said, encouraged by Charlie's dumb show.

"You," said Charlie, spacing the words for effect, "are too stupid to be Chinese." It got translated, and a few of the men laughed. Ying's eyes got very small, and he aimed them straight at me. I was losing friends fast.

"Put him back," Charlie Wah instructed the goon with the machete, and the goon hauled the kid with the unfortunate ears to his feet and dragged him across the room until he was standing behind his friend again. The handsome one put a hand back and grasped Dumbo-Ears' wrist, and the two of them held hands, standing back to back as Dumbo-Ears fought to control his sobs. The girl against the pillar did something with her breath that could have been a cough but probably wasn't.

"You brought this upon yourselves," Charlie Wah

said sententiously. "You were given an address and told to wait outside. All you had to do was fetch Lo if he came out, and come back and tell us if he did not. This you did not do. Instead, when only one of our men came out and Lo escaped into the neighborhood, you terrorized a Chinese family and then tried to kill a *gwailo*. You got personal, and there is nothing more stupid, nothing more *Vietnamese*, than getting personal." Then he said something in Chinese, very fast indeed.

A lot happened.

Most of the men converged on the Vietnamese boys. One of the men carrying a machete, the one who'd clobbered me, forced the knife into the hand of the kid with the Dumbo ears. The machete's mate, identical from my perspective, was urged upon the handsome one. The others forced the two boys apart by six or eight paces and then turned them so they were facing each other. The boys stood there, machete points dragging the floor, like mechanical soldiers that hadn't been wound up.

"One of you will live through this," Charlie Wah said. He was having a great time. "The one who does will let his friends know what becomes of—what's the idiom?"

I wasn't having any of it. The girl against the pillar stared at Charlie Wah as though she hoped her eyes could burn holes through him.

"Bad little boys," the handsome one said. "And screw you."

"A brave one," Charlie Wah said, sounding regretful. "Unusual in a Vietnamese. Still, you will do it. Because if you don't—" He raised a hand.

The room was full of guns. All of them were pointed at the Vietnamese boys.

"—you'll both die," Charlie Wah said. "And we'll let little Miss Vietnam carry the message. Or, better still, we'll kill her first and then flip a coin to decide which one of you we should kill. Not as much fun, of course, and if we do it that way only one little fish sauce gets to go out and play. One instead of two. In fact," he said, jingling the coins again, "maybe that's best."

"Kill me," the girl said, her face twisted. "You fat pig."

Charlie Wah gave her an understanding gaze. "I'm not really very fat," he said, "but you can be excused an inappropriate figure of speech, under the circumstances. This must be a stressful time for you." He strolled over to her, change ringing like church bells, and touched her face, the side that hadn't been cut. "Maybe we can find a way to make it more interesting. Who would like to fuck her before she dies?"

"You first," the girl said defiantly. "If you think you can."

Charlie Wah put his finger on the tip of her small nose and dragged it upward, distending her nostrils and pushing deep wrinkles into the bridge. The girl bit at him ineffectually, and the cut on her face opened up again.

"Not so pretty this way, is she?" he asked. "Still, she'll do in this light. I'll have to decline your offer, my dear. No way to be sure exactly what a Vietnamese *has*."

"We fight," Dumbo-Ears said. "You leave her alone."

"Of course we'll leave her alone." Charlie Wah let go of the girl's nose so suddenly that her head snapped forward. "This isn't personal. The idea is to discourage the rest of you from showing initiative when it isn't called for. Initiative is a fine thing in its place, but it's always touchy trying to figure out what its place is. Clear away, sons. Give them room."

The sons backed off, looking disappointed. Now it was the handsome one who seemed adrift, the machete weighing his arm down. The boys stood in the center of a wide, flat concrete circle. Here and there on the floor threads sparkled, remnants shorn from minimum-wage garments.

Dumbo-Ears raised his machete. One of the men

cheered derisively, earning a place on my must-kill list.

Dumbo-Ears struck a slow, sweeping blow that the handsome kid parried easily. Sparks flew off the knives. The handsome kid backed off, shaking his head, and Dumbo-Ears aimed a quick swipe at it, a swipe that would have cleaved a stone. The force of the missed blow swung him all the way around, and for a split second he stood with his back completely turned to his opponent.

Laughter.

The handsome kid backed away, saying something in Viet-namese.

When Dumbo-Ears turned around, he was weeping again. With his eyes closed he advanced and sliced the air with his machete. Its tip made a red line across Handsome's brown chest.

Dumbo-Ears had decided to live.

Now he was off balance, the weight of the machete dragging him down, and Handsome was backing away, staring down at his own sudden blood. Their feet scraped on the concrete, and their breath rasped like fingernails on silk. Dumbo-Ears recovered his balance, still sobbing, and swung the knife again, and this time it split the air above Handsome's skull, and Handsome raised his knife to stop it and then brought the knife down reflexively and cut Dumbo-Ears shallowly from sternum to navel, a diagonal slash that broke the fine brown skin, parted it, and let the red blood escape into the air. It splattered among the remnants, bright red berries in a drab Christmas wreath. Handsome looked startled.

The girl screamed a confusion of words.

"They're only playing," Charlie Wah complained in English.

But one of them wasn't.

Dumbo-Ears took his knife in both hands and swung it horizontally waist high with a grunt of effort, and Handsome jumped back and just avoided being cut in half at the navel. He stumbled into one of the goons, and the goon grabbed his shoulders and threw him back, into the point of the other boy's upraised knife, which passed through the skin over his right deltoid muscle. Handsome emitted a shrill sound and dropped to his knees, the knife slipping out again, and blood pulsed out of the wound and drenched his chest and stomach.

But the other boy was coming after him now, slicing downward at his head, and Handsome got the machete up in time to parry the blow and then scrambled back between the thugs' legs and out of reach. The men laughed and backed away, and Charlie Wah, laughing too, said, "Give them room."

The men backed up, widening the circle, and then one of them yelled something sharp and surprised, and Handsome burst into the circle from a new direction, behind Dumbo-Ears, and the machete split the air coming down and cut a flap of red meat from Dumbo-Ears's left arm.

The men applauded.

Dumbo-Ears backed away, staring in disbelief at his arm, and Handsome brought the knife up this time, sharp edge pointed toward the ceiling, in a swipe that missed everything but the point of Dumbo-Ears's chin and the tip of his nose. There was, as Charlie Wah had surmised there would be, a lot of blood.

Now both boys were screaming, not words, just raw red noise, and Dumbo-Ears was running forward at Handsome in a move so devoid of grace and lethal meaning, so obviously planless, that the men laughed again. Handsome retreated quickly, knife pointing up at a forty-five degree angle, at the ready, methodically seeking an opening, and it was obvious to me that Dumbo-Ears would be dead the moment he found it.

And then the harmless-looking little man who'd translated my joke stepped out of the group and stuck out a foot, and Handsome went down on his back, and Dumbo-Ears lunged forward and down and pierced him through the chest, falling over him in his eagerness to drive the knife all the way through and into the floor. His momentum carried him forward and he somersaulted over his friend, losing his grasp on the knife, but the knife wasn't going anywhere. Its handle pointed at the ceiling, the blade held in place by the bone of the other boy's sternum.

Handsome put both hands against the blade of the knife and pulled, either ignoring or not feeling the sharpened edge cutting into his palms. He tugged once and then again, more slowly this time, and then he gargled his own blood and his left hand fell away and landed on the concrete with a slap like a dead fish. He gazed at the ceiling, looking like Charlie Wah seeking an idiom.

"That wasn't fair," Charlie Wah said mildly. "Someone check the rule book."

The one who'd tripped the boy translated, and it got a big laugh.

Dumbo-Ears pulled himself to his elbows and turned to look at his friend. Then an anguished wail burst from him, a bright, burnished bubble of sound, and he crawled over and wrapped his arms around Handsome's head.

"Hit him," Charlie Wah said. "Not too hard."

The translator leaned over and struck the boy sharply at the base of the skull, and Dumbo-Ears looked up, puzzled by the impact, and then slumped across Handsome's chest. Handsome didn't move.

"How long?" Charlie Wah said impatiently.

"Maybe a couple of hours," the translator said. He was slender and balding, and cooler than old coffee. "He'll be out of here long before the morning crew arrives."

Charlie Wah nodded in satisfaction. "Don't bother cleaning up," he said. "They have to be found somewhere." He turned to me. "Just so you know we're not kidding," he said. Then he snapped his fingers twice. "Ying. Kill her."

Ying approached the girl, knife in hand. He waved it in front of her face once, just trying for a little fun, a little reaction, and he got it. She spat at him again.

"Quickly," Charlie Wah said, and Ying raised the knife and grinned and cut the girl's throat. Her feet kicked out, mimicking a folk dance, and Ying stepped back to avoid the blood.

Charlie Wah came over to me. "Open your mouth," he said calmly. I did as I was told, and he put something small and cold into it. "The key to your cuffs," he continued. "You should be able to work your hands around and spit the key into your right hand so you can use it to set yourself free. This should pose no problem to a resourceful man like you. Once you are free, leave. The stairs will lead you to Hill Street. Go home. Get a new girlfriend. Stop thinking about Chinese matters. Do you understand?"

I nodded. I couldn't have spoken if my life depended on it.

"I like to think I have a certain flair for these things," Charlie Wah said. "I will exert it to the fullest if I have to kill you. But I won't have to kill you, will I?"

I lowered my gaze. Blood roared in my ears.

He smiled. "I didn't think so," he said. Then he patted me on the arm and said, "It's been nice discussing English with you." The translator got another laugh.

On his way out, Ying gave me a mean little jellyfish sting of a glance and snapped out the lights.

I waited at least half an hour, partly to regain my strength and partly to make sure they'd really left. I was fully appreciative of Charlie Wah's flair.

As he'd predicted, it was relatively easy to get the cuffs undone. I simply followed the scenario he'd outlined, found the keyhole, and listened to the snap. It was a musical sound.

I would have left there and then if my legs had worked, but luckily for me they didn't. I had to sit on the floor in the dark and flex them for a few minutes before I could trust them to bear my weight, and by then

I knew that I had to take something with me.

First I felt my way to the light switch and snapped it on, waiting as the fluorescents flickered into a chalky glow. Then I checked the girl and Handsome and found both of them cooling rapidly. I touched my pants pockets and discovered my car keys right where they should have been.

Charlie Wah knew his man. I'd been properly cowed. I was a sensible man, no threat. It was a perfectly reasonable scenario: I'd unlock my cuffs like a scared puppy chewing through his leash and drive home with my tail between my legs, and Dumbo-Ears would wake up around five in the company of a couple of dead friends and head for a hole to nurse his wounds before the police came and gave him a new set of problems. And he'd carry the news to the members of his gang, and there wouldn't be any unwanted displays of initiative for a while. Why take us anywhere? The soldiers might be spotted as they dropped the living and the dead into alleys and ashcans. Let the dead be discovered where they died, the living having sensibly scattered.

But I wasn't feeling reasonable.

It's so easy to exercise the power of life and death. It doesn't take courage, it doesn't take skill, it doesn't take Confucian virtue. It does, however, take something very special to promise someone she'll live and then break the promise, and what it takes is something that should be eliminated on sight.

So I climbed the stairs and made sure the door could be opened and then went back down again and onto the killing floor, where I ransacked the boxes of garments until I found a jacket with sleeves that would cover a torn arm, and I got Dumbo-Ears to his feet by wrapping the good arm around my shoulders and dragged him up the stairs and took him home. To Topanga.

11

Pas de Un

Thank God I'd just bought Saran Wrap.

It was past five by the time I'd hauled him up the steep, rutted driveway and into the house, Bravo growling at him with each step, and he was still dead weight. Charlie Wah's martial-arts expert had underestimated the effect of his rabbit punch. As I propped Dumbo-Ears upright on the couch, I was hoping it was only an underestimate. He'd be a bigger problem dead than alive.

Ransacking my haphazard kitchen for the Saran Wrap, I did an emotional inventory for pity and found none. Except for the arrival of Mrs. Chan and her two umbrellas, he might now be a multiple murderer and Eleanor, Horace, Pansy, and I might be murderees.

On the other hand, I'd recently found someone I hated more, and that meant the kid got a shiny new uniform and number—a spot on the home team.

In my line of work you tend to get hurt a lot. I had two bottles of Bactine and an old scrip for antibiotics in the medicine cabinet, and after I'd dropped the Saran Wrap on the couch, I went to the bathroom and fished out the pills. I dabbed Bactine onto the long, shallow scratch on his chest and the nicks on his chin and nose, postponing the hard part. When I'd assured myself that the minor cuts wouldn't give him any trouble, I held my breath and poured quite a lot of the Bactine into the flap of skin and muscle below his left shoulder. Then, silently reciting the alphabet to distract myself from the task at hand, I moved the flap around to distribute the Bactine and wrapped the upper arm with Saran Wrap. I tried to leave some room for air at the apex of the wound.

Hauling him more or less upright, I pulled his arms behind him and wound a spiral of Saran Wrap first around his right wrist and then around his left. Finally I sheathed both wrists tightly together, mummy-fashion, with about twelve feet of crisscrossed Saran Wrap. Pulling off his boots, I took the handcuffs Charlie Wah had thoughtfully left me and snapped them tight around his delicate ankles and laid him sideways and folded his knees so I could pass a short, twisted Saran Wrap rope between the chain connecting the cuffs and the Saran Wrap that linked his wrists. Every time I moved him, Bravo growled a warning low in his throat.

After I got a couple of Ampicillin and a few aspirin down his throat, I laid him down on the couch on his side, injured shoulder up, covered him with a spare blanket, and then, in the tradition of good homemakers everywhere, I tidied up before going to bed. I made a mental note to buy more Saran Wrap in the morning. It's so useful.

I hadn't slept in what seemed like months, and this night proved to be no exception. I'd given the kid my last two aspirins, I hurt in places I hadn't known possessed nerve endings, and Bravo kept trying to set up camp on my extra pillow. Until this evening I'd been operating on fear that something might happen to Horace, but now I found that the fear had been shouldered aside by rage. The rage centered itself busily in my chest like the old fifties version of the atom, lots of little hornets zipping circles around a walnut. Each of the hornets was a separate rage: rage at the memory of the girl's slashed and terrified face, rage at the fact that Charlie Wah was still alive somewhere in the world, rage that I hadn't snapped the pillar like Samson and eviscerated Charlie and his fractured idioms with a transitive verb or a piece of broken concrete. The girl closed her eyes as the blood flowed from her cheek. The little translator stuck out his foot, and the boy fell again, over and over, like a loop of film.

I'd been a detective for almost five years now, and I'd learned that my parents' clean and comfortable world, so absolute when I was a child, was actually something that existed inside a bubble only while the real world was too busy to burst it and let the horror in. Still, I'd never built up resistance to horror as naked as this. Every time I saw the girl's eyes close, I thought, *she could have been Eleanor.*

The last time I looked at the clock, it said six-forty-five. At seven-twenty, the kid revealed yet another character flaw by snapping awake, with a yell, no less.

Just what I needed: an early riser.

I wrapped a towel around my middle and went into the living room. My neck ached, my sliced ear burned, and each of my joints was competing to register a complaint of its own. He was sitting up, wearing his black trousers and his Saran Wrap, and looking a little woozy. It had gotten cold during the night, so I let him stew while I threw some kindling into the wood-burner that serves as the house's only heat source and got a fire going. Duty fulfilled, I turned my attention to my patient.

"How you feeling?" I asked, trying for bright.

He glared at me, swore in Vietnamese, and slammed his back against the couch. I didn't have to understand Vietnamese to know he wasn't wishing me many grandchildren. The winter sun was just starting to beat against the east-facing windows, and as the kid thrashed, the couch threw motes of dust that danced mockingly in the air. Presumably there were always motes of dust doing the latest steps at that hour, but I was rarely privileged to see them. It was going to be a long day.

"Let's look at that arm," I said, adopting the first-person plural of nurses everywhere. He jerked away at my touch, and Florence Nightingale did a fast fade. "Hold still or I'll pull your tongue out," I snarled. "I'm going to look at your arm." I looked at his arm.

His arm looked terrible.

It looked ragged and red and rotten and infected. It looked like something I couldn't look at very long. I did what men have done for centuries when faced with something too revolting to stomach. I called a woman.

"Holy smoke, Simeon," Eleanor said from the couch less than an hour later, "this looks terrible."

"I know," I said, staring out the window. "Do something about it."

Even with a stop at an all-night market to pick up more Bactine and Saran Wrap, she had arrived from her place in Venice only fifty minutes after I'd awakened her with my call. She'd always been a woman who could get dressed fast.

"He needs a doctor," she observed.

"He's not going to get one. I told you on the phone how it happened. I was there. If we call a doctor, the doctor will call the police, and I'll probably be in jail as an accessory to several murders."

She ignored the reproach. "That's an ugly cut. I think he's got a fever. How do you know he won't die?"

"Come here," I said. "Into the kitchen." She continued to peer at the wound, and I said, "Now."

She followed me around the single corner that shielded my kitchen from the sight of those in the living room. It was a pitiful privacy, but it was all we were going to get.

"Listen," I hissed, "it's Horace who's out there chasing these guys, Sir Galahad in his tinfoil armor, and he has *no idea*—"

"What if the boy dies?"

"He's not going to die. It's his *arm*, for Christ's sake. People get it in the arm all the time and live. Don't you watch TV?"

"Infection," she said loudly. From the living room the boy shouted something.

"Shut up," I yelled. "Listen," I said to Eleanor, "if I really think he's in trouble I'll push him out of the car in front of Santa Monica Emergency. In the meantime, he's my way in."

She closed her eyes. "Into what?" she asked at last.

"Into whatever Horace is stalking. Remember Horace?"

"Horace." Her eyes were still tightly closed. "Poor dumb Horace. This is how he's going to make everything up to Pansy, you know."

"Pansy's not going to be happy if he's dead," I said, "and these people have a flair for killing. That's a direct quote."

She turned to look out the kitchen window at a mountainside waking up to the sun. "I'll need soap," she said. I turned to the sink to get it. "And water," she added.

"Thank you," I said nastily, unloading my anger on her as I had so many times. "I never would have thought of that."

Dumbo-Ears was sitting upright on the couch, the Saran Wrap rope connecting his ankles and his wrists cut, courtesy of Eleanor the Merciful. After cleaning and disinfecting the shoulder and swabbing the other cuts and scratches, muttering generalities about man's inhumanity to man, she'd gone down to the Fernwood Market to buy a jug of Excedrin and three bottles of red wine. Only after she'd returned, loaded down with wine and unsolicited opinions about someone who'd drink it under such circumstances, did I get to take the shower I wanted so desperately and check out my ear. It looked like something belatedly snatched from a document shredder, but it would stay on. She'd dabbed it dispassionately with Bactine and left again, but not without a concerned backward glance at her homicidal little patient. Talk about wasted motion.

"Pay attention," I said as he scowled up at me. All the lines on his face went down, and I thought briefly of those frowning faces kids draw that turn into smiling faces when you turn them upside down. "You there?" His eyes narrowed, which I took to mean that he was listening. "Okay, here it is. I really don't care if you die. But the way I figure it, we've got the same enemy."

"Go hell," he said.

"Up to you." I fought down the urge to throw him through the window. "The two who were killed. What were they to you?"

His mouth tightened and relaxed and then tightened again. I figured he was going to spit, and I stepped back. But he surprised me.

"What?" he said.

I replayed what I'd said and found what I thought was the problem. *What were they to you*? So, unlike Charlie Wah, he wasn't a student of idiom. "Your friend?" I probed. "Your girlfriend?" He said nothing, just looked at me as though he was trying to figure out where we'd met before.

"Relatives?" I asked.

The mouth worked again, and I kept my distance, but all he did was repeat, "Go hell."

"Fine," I said, advancing on him. "Be a hardass." Idioms be damned. I leaned over and punched him lightly on the arm that Eleanor had so meticulously unwrapped and washed and Bactined and rewrapped.

The scream would probably have pleased Torquemada, but it made me feel like shit. He fell sideways onto the couch, blubbering in the language of his mother and father and his vanquished country, and I stood over him trying to see a murderer and seeing instead a frightened seventeen-year-old.

"That's just the beginning," I said, but my voice lacked conviction even in my ears. I heard Hammond's voice, saying something about the Vietnamese kids having lost everything. If they had anything left it was dignity, and I knew I couldn't take his.

"Don't you want to get Charlie Wah?" I asked, still leaning over him.

At the sound of Charlie Wah's name the blubbering turned into real weeping: choking, shuddering, gut-deep sobs that overpowered his will, that came from a place inside him where the will was a distant rumor. I silently went into the bedroom and closed the door to leave him alone with his grief.

When I woke up, aching like a hit-and-run victim, and remembered that I'd forgotten to take any aspirin, it was getting dark. I'd slept nine hours, and there was no sound from the living room.

He was out cold on the couch, his mouth partly open, snoring as delicately as a girl. A little more hair, I thought, and a little less ears, and he'd make quite a passable girl. I poked the fire and added some paper and wood, and waited until the coals did their incendiary work. Older than the Parthenon, I limped into the kitchen, turned on the light over the sink, ran some water, and took four Excedrins, gagging as they went down. Then I poured a glass of milk to protect my stomach from the acid and trudged heavily back into the living room to entertain my guest.

Once I'd flipped on my one and only floor lamp, the wound looked a little better, despite my shameful and inept attempt at torture: The edges weren't quite so red, and nothing unwholesome seemed to be seeping from them. I tugged the Saran Wrap down to let the wound breathe, and he made a little sound of protest and then sank back into sleep. He looked even younger asleep. It was very hard to hate him, but I was determined to try.

The music for hatred is Wagner. I put *Parsifal* on the CD player, cranked it up, and went to open all three bottles of wine.

The opening chords had already whacked the kid awake by the time I returned, bearing a tray containing a bottle and two crystal glasses Eleanor had given me for use on special occasions. Well, this was special, if not in the precise sense she'd intended.

"Drink?" I asked.

"No," he said sullenly, refusing to look at me.

"It wasn't really a question," I said, pouring. It had a promising color.

"I need toilet," he said.

"God," I said, putting down the bottle and glass, "I thought you'd never ask."

I lifted him to his feet and helped him hop into the bathroom. "You'll have to sit," I said, undoing his pants and yanking them down, "and I'll have to leave the door open. Problem?"

"Yes," he said.

"Then hold onto it," I said. He lapsed back into angry Vietnamese, but he sat. Listening to the splash of water on porcelain, I went into the bedroom and got the gun I usually keep in Alice's dash compartment.

When I came back with the gun shoved into a pocket, he was trying to stand. I pulled him to his feet and reversed the process with his pants. The fly took some attention, which is why I was off guard when he tried to kick me.

A knee struck my thigh, but he'd forgotten that his ankles were cuffed together, and the force of his kick pulled his other ankle up and he tilted backward and fell. Adrenaline, prompted by the vision of his head striking the toilet, kicked in, and I managed to straighten up and grab him before the collision took place. He was already pitching away from me, and I felt my back emit a murmur of protest, followed by a shout of pain. I strained against it and kept him upright somehow, but by the time we had both stabilized I was mad again.

"Try it again," I said, my face inches from his. "Try it again, and I swear I'll take your fucking arm off. *This* arm," I said, tugging at the wrist below the sliced shoulder.

He sighed, in a fashion that might have been described in the nineteenth century as "melting," and folded like a marionette whose strings had been sliced. He'd fainted.

Disgusted with myself, I towed him back into the living room and lowered him gently to the couch. Air, pushing itself out of his midsection, made a popping little motorboat sound between his lips.

"Party time," I said. I put the gun on the table in plain sight, poured an ounce of wine into a glass, and tossed it into his face.

Accompanied by a crash of Wagnerian *Sturm und Drang*, his eyes snapped open. They were glazed and vague, and I knew, as he tried to get to his feet, that he had no idea where he was. I stepped back to let the handcuffs around his ankles remind him, but Bravo pushed past me, making a sound like an idling tractor, and the sheer malignancy of the dog's gaze got the kid's attention. His eyes widened and focused on Bravo's face, about eight inches from his own, and he froze.

"He remembers you," I said.

The kid said nothing, but he kept his eyes on Bravo. "If I tell him to kill, he'll take your throat out," I lied. Bravo didn't know the command for "sit." "Understand?"

He nodded, still staring into what he probably thought was the face of death. Bravo chose that moment to let his tongue loll out in a grin, so I stepped on a paw, and he looked up at me. "Bravo," I said sternly, "if he moves, kill him." I growled at Bravo, and Bravo growled back. It was his one trick.

"Not me, you idiot," I said, "him." I snapped my fingers in front of the kid's bare chest, and Bravo swung his head around, back into the kid's face. He was still growling.

"Drink?" I asked the kid again. I held up a glass and poured some wine into it and held it out to him. Bravo, momentarily diverted from guard duty by the possibility of refreshment, followed the glass with his eyes.

The kid nodded, never taking his eyes off the dog.

"We'll take a little medicine at the same time," I said, lapsing once again into Nursese. I sat on the table in front of the couch and measured out two more Ampicillin and a couple of Excedrin. "Open," I said.

"Nuh-uh," the kid said, staring at the pills as though they were hemlock. He was more afraid of them than he was of Bravo.

"Look," I said, putting one of each into my mouth and washing it down with what turned out to be a very nice red wine. This was getting to be a lot of Excedrin. "Medicine. For your arm." I gestured toward his arm and he shrank from me, making me feel like Klaus Barbie. "Make you strong," I said hurriedly. "Fix your arm." I rubbed my own shoulder with the hand holding the pills and then flexed it. The kid's eyes went to my mouth.

"Swallow," he said, with a hollow note of command.

I poured some more wine into my mouth, swallowed extravagantly, and opened wide to show him that the pills were gone. The second gulp of wine hit my stomach like a hot, wet towel and spread out, radiating upward toward my chest. "Now you," I said. I dropped the two pills into his mouth; he gave me a dark, sour look as he tasted the aspirin.

"Drink this," I said, holding out the glass, which was empty. "Whoops," I said, "sit tight."

"What?" he asked, a little furrily, as I poured.

"Just stay there," I said, resolving on the abolition of idioms forevermore. "Here." I held the wineglass to his lips and he took a suspicious sip and stopped. He washed it around inside his mouth and then drank the rest.

"Good boy," I said. "Listen, I can't keep saying 'good boy' to you. It confuses the dog. What's your name?"

He looked down at my chest and pursed his lips, and I growled at Bravo, who responded with something that sounded like the overture to the Lisbon Earthquake. It even cut through *Parsifal*.

"Tran," the boy said quickly.

"Okay, Tran." I pulled the glass back and refilled it. "I've got the dog and I've got the gun and you've got a bad cut on your shoulder. And you tried to kill some people I love not so long ago—"

"Not kill," he said. "Only frighten."

"Spare me the embarrassment. And then you tried to kill me. Twice." I drank half the wine.

"Only beat up," he said. He squirmed to find a more comfortable position and failed. "You tickled me."

"And you set a house on fire," I said, letting him finish the glass.

"Not yours," he said, the soul of reason. "We came to beat you up but the house was burned down. I got mad, burned it the rest of the way."

"If you had come to this one, you'd have tried to kill me."

"No. Beat up only."

"I'll take that on faith," I said, "but only because nothing depends on it." I poured again and decided to skip a turn. "Drink up." He took the wine easily this time, and why not? It was better than he deserved.

Bravo sat happily on my foot, watching the wineglass again, and I prodded him up onto all threatening fours. "This is the deal—sorry, forget that. Here's what's going to happen. Do you understand me?"

"Understand," he said, sounding insulted.

"I need to know that you do. Understand, I mean." I watched him closely as I poured another glass, remembering, a little late, that I'd brought two into the room. I drank and said, "I'm going to take care of your cut, okay? I'm going to keep you here for a few days and the nice lady you wanted to kill, frighten, whatever, is going to come around once in a while and give you medicine until you're better, and you and I are going to talk." I poured again.

"Talk what?" he asked suspiciously.

"Talk everything." It was catching. "You're going to tell me why you wanted Uncle Lo, and who those Chinese are, and what they're doing, and all sorts of stuff."

"Stuff," he said shortly, and I wasn't sure whether it was a request for clarification or a command, but I passed on aggressiveness and put the glass to his lips and let him drink again.

"Stuff," I said equably, "like, first, who's Lo and why were you sent to get him?"

"Don't know," he said. Then he looked at the wineglass and said, "Good."

"Glad you like it. More?" He nodded, more enthusiastically than before, but this time I drank a full one myself before I gave him another couple of ounces. The Grand Inquisitor at work, pitiless and perhaps slightly drunk.

"Where were we?" I said. "Uncle Lo, and don't tell me you don't know."

His mouth went wide and negative. "Don't. They said get him. They said if he came out from apartment, get him."

"Why did they send you to get him? Why not send Chinese?"

The mouth curled scornfully. "Two Chinese they sent. Only one got out."

"Lo killed the other one?"

He shrugged. "Must be. Only one got out."

"So you were supposed to be backup?"

He nodded.

"And they didn't tell you who he was or why they wanted him?" Some epicurean judge inside was telling me that this was a *very* nice wine.

"Why?" he asked, eyeing the glass in a fair imitation of Bravo, who had managed to sit on my foot again. His weight felt good, so I let the bum sprawl.

"Why what?" I asked, getting confused.

"Why tell us? If they don't tell us, we don't know."

There was a certain unassailable logic in that. It was what he'd said before, under the Torture of a Thousand Fingers. "You didn't know who he was, but you were going to kill him."

He shrugged, as well as someone can who's sheathed in Saran Wrap. "Only get him. If he come out. Kill him if we have to, sure. If he try to kill us."

"Or if he was getting away," I suggested. He hesitated and licked his lips, and I poured a little wine down his throat.

"Sure," he said, after he'd swallowed, "kill him. No problem." There was something elaborately casual about the words. They sounded like make-believe.

"Have you killed a lot of people?" I asked. I was thinking about how he'd laughed when I tickled him.

"Very many," he said gruffly.

I let it pass. "You were supposed to get him if he came out. Why'd you go in?"

He blinked. "Uh," he said.

"Could you be more specific?"

He tried a smile. "Mistake."

"It sure was."

"We run out of gas," the hitman said, dropping the smile and looking embarrassed. "Gas thing on my car broken. So, late, almost half hour. We don't know who's in, who's out. Think maybe Lo's there."

It was too stupid to be a lie. At seventeen, I'd *always* run out of gas.

"One more time," I said, "who was Lo?"

He looked into the middle distance, and oak popped

in the fireplace. The boy started at the sound and then tried to hide the movement by turning it into a shiver. Something furtive and intelligent came into his eyes, and I involuntarily caught my breath as words formed themselves on his tongue. Here it came, the big news flash. He looked at the wine again, and then at me. He licked his lips.

"Water chaser?" he asked.

I heard myself laugh, and I heard Bravo's tail thump against the floor, and I said again to Bravo, "Kill him if he moves," and then I laughed again and went to the kitchen for a glass of water.

Two hours later I was sitting next to him on the couch, and he was leaning against me in a friendly fashion. I'd undone the cuffs around his feet and slightly loosened the Saran Wrap connecting his wrists, and we were well into the third bottle. I'd learned that he was, in fact, seventeen, that the name of his gang was the Flying Fists, and that his parents were long divorced, his father gone God knew where. I'd learned that he lived—whenever he was home—with his mother, who worked as a cashier in a Vietnamese restaurant in Westminster, about forty miles south of L.A. He'd learned all about the relationship between Eleanor and me, and he'd agreed that nothing was harder than being a bad man who has somehow come into possession of a good woman. A grand and malicious joke. He'd also taken another Ampicillin, to make up for the one I'd eaten, and another Excedrin, and he was, both literally and figuratively, feeling no pain.

"Why join the gang?" I asked again. I was propping him up and pouring the seven hundredth glass of wine, and Bravo was snoring under the table and chasing phantoms from the ankles down. He'd had a little dog-dose himself, out of the extra glass.

"If you don't join one gang, two gangs try to take money. If you join a gang, only one." He grinned at me, looking suddenly shy. "Better odds," he said.

"Fine. Why work for the Chinese?"

The grin vanished. "More money," he said as though it were painfully obvious. "Chinese have all the money, same in Vietnam. Chinese *always* have all the money."

"Where does the money come from?" The words were no more precise than my mental processes, but he understood them.

"Chinese," he said with an odd mixture of admiration and scorn, "sweat money."

Eleanor, as far as I could remember, didn't seem to sweat at all. There was no question, though, that she was tight with a buck. I wasn't. It was one of the things we'd fought about.

"But where does it come from?" I put the glass to his lips and wondered briefly why I seemed to be doing all the talking. "The money, the Chinese money, I mean. Those men, for example."

His eyes went opaque. "Don't know." He looked around the room, seeming to notice it for the first time. His eyes fell on the loudspeakers, almost as tall as he was, bounty from a case on which I'd actually had a client. "Music, please. Rock and roll?"

"Music," I said, sighing. It was getting late. I tilted him upright and got up—not quite as stiffly as before, lubricated by the wine—and put on a CD by the Kinks, not his vintage, but fuck him. If he wanted Ice-T, he could escape.

"Old fart stuff," he said after the opening guitar riff, wrinkling his nose.

"That's because I'm an old fart," I said, draining the glass. "And you're a young one."

"Young fart," he said, grinning again as I settled back onto the couch and rested a foot on Bravo's shoulder. "Funny man."

"Back to business," I said, drinking again. "How did they find you when they needed you?"

He shook his head dismissively. "Guy came around."

"Around where?"

"School," he said. "More, please."

"School," I said, pouring. I was dealing with a drunk baby. "Names."

"Wine first," he said, looking cunning. I put the glass to his lips, and he gulped it down.

"Charlie Wah," he said immediately after swallowing. "Charlie Fucking Wah."

"Who is he?"

"Taiwan king shit. Big man. Back and forth, yo-yo, yo-yo, Taiwan to America."

I leaned forward. I was getting some content at last. "They're from Taiwan, then."

"Shit floats," he said. "They float here from Taiwan."

"Why? What are they doing?"

The smooth features froze tight. "Don't know." He looked into my eyes. "True. Don't know."

"Well, what do they ask you to do?"

"Dangerous stuff. Stuff they afraid to do. Frighten people, beat them up. Pick up stuff and deliver it."

"Drugs." It was a guess.

"No. Charlie Wah doesn't like dope."

"What, then?"

"Don't know." He inhaled and then blew out through his lips. "Lying to you. Money. Always wrapped up, all taped up in a bag or in a briefcase, but money."

I was feeling dubious. "They trust you to pick up money?"

"Oh, sure," he said. "With about twenty Chinese watching. Cars in front, cars in back. Everybody with guns, everybody except us. Sure, they trust us."

"Where did you pick up the money?" Ray and Dave Davies were singing in trademark octaves, Dave taking the top.

"San Pedro." Charlie had said "San Pedro" into the phone.

"And took it where?"

"Chinatown."

"Always the same place in San Pedro?" I drank, feeling flushed and excited, and heard myself humming to the Kinks.

"Three or four places."

I put the glass to his lips again and tilted it. "And in Chinatown."

"Sometimes one place, sometimes not."

"Where's the one place?"

"Granger Street. A white man."

I stopped humming. "Name?"

"Don't know."

"What kind of white man?"

"Sloppy man, big stomach, wet lips. He pays us sometimes. Lawyer," he added.

I drank, unaware at first that I was doing it. If my hand hadn't been shaking with excitement I might not have noticed it at all.

"Chinatown," he continued. "American lawyer in Chinatown. Rice freak."

My turn not to catch the idiom. "Rice freak?"

"Chinese girls," Tran said. "Likes Chinese girls. Office full of Chinese girls. Bigtime kung-fu asshole. White clothes, big feet, big nose. Nose bigger than his feet." He chuckled briefly and then hiccupped twice. He was very drunk. "Bigtime bignose kung-fu asshole. White-eyes, eyes very like water. Wine, please."

"Can you take me there?" I asked, pouring.

"Does the Pope," he asked rhetorically, "cross the road to shit in the woods?" Good question. I gave him the glass. He slurped ambitiously. "Pluto and Bluto," he said. "They the guys with the muscle bumps hanging onto Charlie Wah. Eat steroids all the time. Go really batshit once in a while."

"Anybody else?" I had to close one eye to keep him in focus, and I had a feeling I should have been taking notes.

Tran looked at me blearily. "Little one, wears his pants high? Ying. Think he's king shit, big Snake Triad guy. He the one Lo didn't kill. Zowie, you know zo-wie?''

"Which one is Zowie?" It sounded like an improbable name for a Chinese.

"No, *zowie*," he protested. "Like, zowie, good wine.''

"Sure is." I held the bottle up to the floor lamp. "About half dead.''

"Me, too," Tran said, laughing. It was the first time I'd heard him laugh, except under torture. It was a very young and very innocent laugh.

"You'll be okay," I said, "youth being wasted on the young, and all.''

"Pardon?''

"Nothing. What does the Snake Triad do for its money?''

"Don't know," he said for what felt like the hundredth time. "Why tell me? But big money. Even for us. To bring Lo, one thousand. Five hundred for me and five hundred for . . .'' He faltered.

"For your friend," I said.

He started to nod and then put his head on my shoulder instead. He was trembling violently. I heard him fight for a breath. It fought him all the way in.

I patted his shoulder, feeling big and useless. "We'll get them.''

"They *killed* her," he said. "And I stabbed him," he cried, suddenly pulling himself away from me. It was quite a feat, considering that his hands were bound behind him and he was drunk.

"No one knows what he will do until the time comes." I sounded like Charlie Wah.

"She my cousin," he said, and I shut up, completely and profoundly. For a moment I thought he was going to start weeping again, but instead he shook his head and said, "Wine.''

"No problem," I said, but pouring it without spilling took all the concentration I had. "You made a choice,"

I said, "between your cousin and your friend."

He swallowed air twice. "Brother," he said.

"Shit," I said, gaping down into a yawning gulf of tragedy. I hadn't meant to say it. I drank the glass he'd asked for.

"Yes," he said fiercely, displacing his grief, "shit. Shit triad."

"I need names," I urged. "You want them dead."

He turned an unlined face to me. Up close, he looked younger than seventeen. "I can kill them." It sounded like a new clause in the Boy Scout pledge.

"You can kill one or two, maybe. I can get them all." I almost believed it. "The ones I can't kill, I can put in jail."

"Taiwan," he said bitterly, "you can put them in jail in Taiwan?"

"Give me names," I said. If I couldn't get them all, I could die trying.

"Names," Tran said mechanically. "Chinese guy. Peter Lau."

"Who's he?"

"Newspaper writer. Drink, please."

I looked at his wine-red face. "I really think it would be better—"

"You want to know about Peter Lau?" He opened his mouth, and I poured and extended the glass.

"Chinatown newspaper," he said, when he'd finished. "Not with them, against them. They told us to frighten him, not one time. Two times. But we couldn't find him. He writes about them. He *used* to write about them," he corrected himself, "but we couldn't find him." He giggled.

"What's funny?" I asked.

"We found him, both times. But he paid us more than they paid us."

"How much?" It wasn't what I needed to know, but I wanted to keep him talking.

"Five hundred. He used to write about them but they

make big noise at the newspaper and talk about burn it down, and he got fired. We find him and he give us six hundred to say we didn't.''

Five hundred bucks, and he wrote about them, and Lo was worth a thousand. I lose certain abilities when I drink, but subtraction isn't one of them. ''Where did you find Peter Lau?'' I asked.

''Never same place, but always some coffee shop. Monterey Park. Moves around. Scared all the time.''

''And he paid you.''

''Scared to death,'' Tran said, forcing a smile. ''Six hundred just to go away.''

''Anyone else?'' He looked at the glass and opened his mouth, a fish seeking the bait, and I gave it to him.

''Also old lady,'' he said when he'd drained it.

''Old lady,'' I said neutrally.

''Old Jesus lady. Jesusloveyou, Jesusloveyou, come-tojesus.''

''Summerson,'' I said, feeling like someone had just punched me in the face.

''Excuse me,'' Tran said politely, turning his face back to mine. ''Okay I throw up?''

I guided him to the toilet and, when he'd finished voiding his insides, back to the couch. He was singing along with Ray Davies, syllables only, not a recognizable word per line. ''Listen,'' I said after he'd settled himself, ''you're not going to go anywhere, are you?''

''Where?'' he asked dreamily.

''Right,'' I said. ''Nowhere. Because even if you walk out of here you'll be lost in the middle of the Santa Monica Mountains. It's miles to L.A. And you've got a hole in your shoulder and Saran Wrap around your arms—well, do you understand?''

He nodded and wiped his chin across his shoulder.

''Go to sleep, Tran,'' I said, tucking the spare blanket around him. I picked up my gun and the cuffs, and he mumbled something and closed his eyes, and I went into the bedroom and folded down the remaining blanket and closed my own. It was pretty late, and I was pretty drunk.

Bravo came in and made the usual nuisance of himself, and I shoved him aside and tried to force my eyelids down again, and then I heard the sobbing. I decided to ignore it. Ten or fifteen minutes later I decided not to ignore it.

Mumbling to myself about nothing in particular, I grabbed my blanket and went into the living room and propped Tran up again so I could sit next to him. Then I threw the blanket over both of us and sagged to the left, with Tran leaning on me. Bravo joined us, on top of Tran, and Tran cried all of us to sleep.

12

—

Crash Landing

I woke up with a spacious red headache, and I woke up alone.

My initial reaction—pure reflex, embarked on even before I'd begun to explore the margins of my headache—was to feel blindly around for Bravo. For some time now I'd been entering each day nasally, via Bravo's bravura pong, and my nose knew immediately that something was missing. It took me a few excruciatingly queasy moments and a couple of blind gropes with my right hand to discover that more than Bravo was missing.

"Holy shit," I groaned. A memory bloomed, horribly bright through the red murk: I had unwrapped Tran. Since there appeared, under the circumstances, to be no reason ever to open my eyes again, I rolled over onto my side and resolved to sleep forever. Death sounded appealing. Better, at any rate, than facing Eleanor, or even myself, and admitting that I'd let the kid get away. With Horace still out there, no less.

Something said, "Ping."

It did not engage my attention. A ping could have been anything, any kind of mocking reminder from the land of the living: a moth against a windowscreen, for example, or the tags on Bravo's collar, wherever the hell Bravo might be. I consigned all pings to hell and concentrated on the details of a comfortable death. I waited patiently for it to come, to spread its anesthetic wings around my head. It kept its distance. A comfortable death, it seemed, would require effort. I'd have to cure my headache first.

Something said, "Burra-burra-burra."

I cranked one eyelid open and looked at the cracked leather covering my couch. If I'd achieved paradise, I'd apparently taken my couch with me. I'd imagined paradise before, full of willing, lissome houris, but I hadn't imagined them on my couch. Paradise seemed a lot cheaper with my couch in it.

Someone said, "Wheeee." Not something, but someone.

"Left wing up," the voice said, and I recognized words I had spoken myself while I was still alive.

"Throttle back," croaked a rusty hinge that I recognized as me. "Not so fast."

"Quiet," the other voice commanded. "Working it out."

"Fine," I said to the back of the couch. "I'm dead anyway."

"Landing, me," the other voice said unsympathetically. "Die later."

"Then get the goddamn left wing up and throttle back."

"Yeah, yeah, yeah," the other voice said. I closed my eyes. Then it said, "*Shit*."

"You crashed," I said, disappointed that the exit from life wasn't more clearly marked. What if there was a fire?

"I totally eat it." The tone was apologetic.

"Do you think," I asked, trying not to plead, "that you can find the Excedrin?"

"Already took three," Tran said. "Water?"

"Good idea," I said, reconciling myself to the thin

and tepid gruel of life. "You can walk okay?"

"You took them off, remember?" Tran said over the splash of running water. "I got no place to walk, that's the problem."

"That's *your* problem," I said primly.

"You should learn to throw up," he said, sounding closer. "Me, I throw up." A tentacle touched my arm, and I rolled blindly toward it and opened my eyes to see a hand that looked larger than Australia, with a couple of pills in it.

"Five," I suggested.

"Sa*low*ly," he said. "Two first." He extended a glass of water in the other hand.

I gulped them down, closed my eyes again, and slid down a long greased chute into queasiness. I had no indication that we were no longer alone until I heard Eleanor's voice saying, "What's wrong with this picture?"

"We're alternating," I said. "Tomorrow I take care of him."

"Well, who should I look at first?"

"Him," I said, without turning over to face her. "There's nothing that can be done for me."

Something clinked. "All three bottles," she said accusingly. "Did you get this boy drunk?"

Tran laughed, a light, merry, truly merciless little laugh.

The bottles hit the paper bag in the kitchen that serves as a garbage can. "Sit down," Eleanor said. She sounded sympathetic.

"I haven't got that much energy," I said.

"Not you, you sot. *You*." The chair in front of my computer—the computer on which Tran had just totaled an electronic airplane—creaked. Saran Wrap rustled. "Well, well," Eleanor said approvingly, "this is much better."

"He's seventeen," I said bitterly.

Tran said, "Ouch." It momentarily cheered me.

"Shhh. Have you had coffee?" she asked.

"Yes," Tran said.

"Thanks a lot," I said.

"You know where it is," Eleanor said.

"I know exactly where it is," I told the back of the couch, "and I know I can't possibly get there."

"Sit tight, sweetie," Eleanor said to the little murderer. "Let me get the old sot some coffee."

"I finish it," Tran said, without a tinge of guilt.

"That's all right. He needs some special coffee. We make it with uranium." Extremely familiar puttering sounds came from the kitchen. If I'd died, I found myself thinking, I would never have heard those sounds again. A little butterfly, or, more likely, a cabbage moth, spread its wings in my soul.

Two and a half hours later, I was sitting in a blindingly bright coffee shop in Monterey Park, watching the most nervous man I'd ever seen in my life. Peter Lau was definitely not enjoying his middle forties. He was tall, almost six feet, and unhealthily thin, with the jaundice-yellow face of a drinker whose liver is moments away from retirement. Wary eyes swept the restaurant from above dark circles that looked like they'd been planted with a punch press. He'd checked me out twice, but he hadn't seen Tran, who'd retreated strategically into the men's room.

Across an expanse of scalp that began three inches above his eyes, Lau had meticulously pasted twenty six foot-long hairs, left to right, to form a clever little hair hat. The vanity behind this hopeless pretense was echoed in his clothing, which was stylish in a way that had nothing to do with style, like someone who'd once heard a description of the well-dressed man on the radio but had never actually seen one: color-coordinated tie and handkerchief, both in a large check; striped shirt; blazer nipped too sharply at the waist; wide gray slacks; white shoes. The gold rings on his index fingers, like the rings under his eyes, were a matching set.

We'd visited five coffee shops before we found one with a window table that had a RESERVED sign on it. Tran had led me to a table and we'd had more coffee, not as bracing as Eleanor's, but strong enough to keep the floor level. After a few minutes, one of the Chinese waitresses had started to set the reserved table: a carafe of coffee, a couple of pieces of toast.

"Here goes," Tran said, and did his fade. Thirty seconds later, Peter Lau jittered in with three briefcases, looking like something that had been run over by the Doodah Parade. He'd sat down as though he were afraid his knees would snap, and gone immediately to work on the latches of the first briefcase. After nine or ten false starts he worried the snaps into submission and pulled out a laptop computer, which he opened and put dead center in front of him. The next case yielded, after a prolonged struggle, a cellular telephone and a miniaturized fax machine. Case number three, which probably contained his secretary, he placed on the seat next to him.

Only then, floating office in place, did he take any sustenance: He lit a cigarette, cupping his shaking hands around a cheap plastic lighter as though he were in a full-force gale. Smoke streaming from his nostrils, he carefully poured coffee onto the table near his cup and then gave up and handed the trembling carafe to the waitress, who doled out something less than half a cup. When he lifted it, I could see why; his hand was so unsteady that I would have taken equal odds on his dropping it, spilling the coffee on his shirt, or knocking out a tooth with the rim of the cup.

It was the tooth. I was standing over him by the time the cup reached his mouth, and when he saw me the crack of porcelain on enamel was enough to bring my own coffee halfway back up into the light.

"Whawhawha?" Peter Lau said, looking around

wildly. He seemed to have forgotten already where the exit was.

"Relax," I said, sitting opposite him and trying to look reassuring and urbane, rather than green and sticky and reeking of Bordeaux. "I just want to talk to you."

"This table . . ." he said, "this table, ah . . ." Words failed him, and he snatched up the RESERVED sign and brandished it in my face.

"I only need a few minutes," I said, looking at him more closely. He was wringing wet.

"No talking," he said jerkily. He started to put the RESERVED sign into his shirt pocket, found it wouldn't fit, and tucked it under the lapel of his jacket. "I don't talk. I never talk. Ask anybody."

I leaned in and took an inconspicuous sniff. Alcohol fumes roiled off him. If I had the mother of all hangovers, Peter Lau had all four of its grandparents.

"I need some help," I said, reaching over to extricate the sign and put it back on the table.

"I don't help." He started the catechism. "I never help. Ask—" He broke off and stared past me, looking like one of those little rubber dolls whose eyes pop out of their head when you squeeze them.

"He's with me," I said, feeling very sorry for Peter Lau.

"Hey, Peter," Tran said, dropping a hand onto my shoulder.

"Mr. Lau," I corrected him.

"How you doing, Mr. Lau?" Tran amended.

Lau wrenched his gaze from Tran to me, and his brain might as well have been a blackboard: *The kid is back, but this time they've sent someone with him and he can't be bought off.* Sweat beaded on his forehead, and the points on his collar had begun to curl up. "You're from Tiffle," he finally said. It was more a gasp than a question.

"*That's* the name," Tran said happily, slipping into the booth beside me. "White guy. Tiffle." He was swimming in one of my shirts, looking very small and brown.

I knocked my leg into Tran's. "Why would Tiffle send me?" I asked.

"I don't know," Lau said jerkily. "I'm not writing—"

"They threatened you," I said.

"This little monster," Peter Lau said, peering around for help. Literally everyone in the place looked away, finding the answers to long-held questions on the walls or in the middle of their plates. "This little *beast* and his—his—"

"Mr. Lau." He jumped slightly. "Mr. Lau, I'm on your side."

"I don't have a side," he said quickly, "and if you're on it, why's *he* here?"

"Tiffle and the Snakes," I said, and this time Lau positively leaped. His fingers, frantic for something to do, scrabbled lightly over the keys of his laptop. "They killed his brother and cousin. They kidnapped," I added, stretching the truth some, "the children of some friends of mine."

"My stars," he said, and I realized he had a faint British accent. Hong Kong.

"I'm going to reach into my pocket and bring out a card," I said. "Don't be alarmed." His eyes followed my hand as though it were the first one he'd ever seen, and stayed on it even after I'd dropped the card, right in the middle of the coffee he'd spilled.

"Sorry," I said. "I'm in worse shape than you are."

"I severely doubt that," Lau said, picking up the card and wiping it with a napkin. He had to read it twice, closing his eyes between passes. "So what?" he said at last. "Anybody can print a card. You should see some of mine."

"Tran," I said, "would you please ask the waitress to bring us some coffee?"

"Oh, sure," Tran said. "Make me very happy, be of

service." He was gone, and Lau never took his eyes off him.

"The other one is really dead?" he asked when Tran was out of earshot.

"I saw it," I said.

"I won't ask how," he said, sitting back slightly. "But I need to ask *you* some things."

"How do I know," he asked, his voice notching up half an octave, "that Tiffle didn't send you to see if I'd talk to you? Hmmm?"

"You don't. Look, Mr. Lau, I'm a private detective. I'm in the phone book. I have a terrible red-wine hangover."

His eyes narrowed sympathetically. "Did you mix it?"

"No, but I drank enough so that it doesn't matter. Do you want," I asked, "to go on living like this?"

"It's a perfectly good method," he said. "I bought dozens of these things." He pointed to the RESERVED card. "I just call the restaurant I want to be in, and they set up for me."

"It's a little public," I said.

He almost smiled. "That's the point."

"And I have to say that it wasn't very hard to find you."

"Yes," he said thoughtfully, "there is that. But you didn't kill me."

"I don't *want* to kill you."

"So you say." His eyes went back to Tran.

"If you like, I'll ask him to wait in the car."

"That would be peachy," he said. "In fact, why don't you ask him to drive the car to New York?"

"Coffee, boss," Tran said, setting the cups down. Then he turned to Peter Lau and folded his hands together over his chest, looking penitent. "Mr. Lau," he said. "Sorry. Please forgive me, you." He bowed very low. Every eye in the restaurant followed him.

"Bloody little—" Lau began. Then he pulled himself

up short and blinked twice. "I have to absorb this," he said. "Come back tomorrow."

"Not possible. I want to hot-wire the Snakes, and I haven't got the time."

"Ho-ho," Peter Lau said politely. "You're going to undo the Snake Triad?" He clinked together the rings on his index fingers, waiting for something persuasive.

"Mr. Lau," I said. "This is the situation. I want to help someone I love. With your help, I might be able to be a genuine pain in the ass to the Snakes. Without your help, they'll probably catch me. And if they do, Mr. Lau, if they catch me because you didn't help me, I'm going to tell them you told me everything you know."

"Oh," Peter Lau said, blinking again. "You mean you'll lie about it."

"That's what I mean." Tran was looking at me admiringly.

"Love is a terrible motive for doing something vile," Lau said after a moment's reflection.

"And I'm sorry about it. I'm sure you're a nice man and a good journalist and all that. But you're just not as important to me as they are."

"That's bald," he said. "And you're only one man."

Tran waved at him, palm downward, fingers curling in. "Remember me?" he said. He sat beside me.

"You're murderous," Lau said, "but I don't know that you're smart." Tran took it in silence.

"What'll it be?" I asked.

Lau sighed. "What do you know?"

I told him about the kidnapping and about Charlie Wah. When I mentioned Wah's name, Lau looked very much like a man who desperately needs the bathroom. "So Wah's the Taiwanese boss, right?"

Lau nodded and wiped his upper lip with a finger.

"And Tiffle?"

"Tiffle's a lawyer." He closed his eyes, like someone about to go over Niagara Falls in a teacup. "He's the Anglo front, when they need one. Legal chores. He launders a little money." He fiddled with his cup, clinking it against the saucer, and the waitress Tran had been flirting with hurried over to half fill it. He waited until she was out of earshot before he said, "Tiffle's *very* unpleasant."

"Money from what?" I asked. "And why, specifically, a lawyer?"

Lau measured me with his eyes. "I thought you said you knew something."

"I didn't say I knew everything."

"You don't know anything at all."

"But you're going to tell me." He sat absolutely still, looking out the window as if he hoped the U.S. Cavalry was about to gallop into the parking lot. "Is it drugs?" I prompted. "Prostitution? Gambling? Extortion?"

"No," he said. "It's bigger than that."

"Bigger than drugs?"

He reached up and passed both hands over his scalp, knocking his heavily sprayed hair turban askew, and then reached back and laced his fingers together behind his neck. With a sigh that seemed to have its roots in centuries of finely honed malaise, he arched his neck back against his hands. Vertebrae popped.

"You have to understand the Chinese," he said, turning his head slowly from side to side. "They're always ready to go somewhere, to follow something that might lead them to a lifetime of regular eating. They followed the Red Eyebrows in the first century, the Boxers in this one, Sun Yat-sen and Chiang Kai-shek, then Mao on the Long March. Millions of Chinese, *hundreds* of millions of Chinese, have literally nothing to lose. They accept the first emperors, they overthrow the emperors, they set up a republic, they overthrow the republic and accept communism, they embrace capitalism. They follow the light someone holds up, a light suspended over a full bowl of rice. When the light goes out and they lose their direction, they starve for a while in the dark. When someone shines a new light in their eyes, they follow it again. They've followed the greatest assortment of scoundrels ever produced by a single country in all of history." He sighed once more, even more heavily. "Of course, part of the problem is that we've had more history than everyone else put together."

"They're following Charlie," I said, realizing that the back of my neck was beginning to tingle, although I didn't fully know why. "Charlie's got the light now?"

"Charlie's part of the Snake organization is specialized," Lau said as carefully as if he'd learned the words phonetically. "They, ah, they effect migrations."

"Migrations," I said, my hangover suddenly over. Orlando's migrating starlings swarmed into view, diving and swooping hungrily through a confusion of light-seeking moths.

Peter Lau turned away from the parking lot, bathed in sweat. No help was at hand. He started to say something and then stopped.

"The Snakes," I said, sitting there surrounded by immigrants who had all gotten here somehow, and wondering why it had taken me so long to figure it out. "The Snakes deal in people."

"The Snakes," Peter Lau said, "deal in slaves."

PART III

THE SUN IN A MIRROR

—

A very few migrating creatures seem to guide themselves by following the lines of the earth's magnetic field, perhaps sensitized to its alignment by magnetized particles they have swallowed. Since the planet's magnetic field has reversed itself several times in the past, the theorist can only wonder whether these purely physical events have caused wholesale biological exterminations as entire species lost their way over the surface of the earth.

—MARTIN FIELDING
Natural Navigation

13

Sojourners

"Eleven million dollars," Peter Lau said, "every two weeks."

We'd followed him to a new restaurant, and the air, or something, had done him good. His eyes were steadier, his voice less susceptible to sudden spikes of nervous energy. The front of his shirt had dried out. He even smiled occasionally, like someone picking up radio jokes on his fillings. He was drinking lemonade without spilling it into his lap.

At my suggestion, Tran had taken up watch in the parking lot, conserving a Coke and eating ice cream and peering through Alice's dirty windows for a sight of the enemy. In his absence, Lau had grown more expansive.

"Eleven million dollars," I said. It was a nice thing to say.

"That's just on this coast." He narrowed his eyes, either in speculation or in defense against the light. "Another five, maybe, on the East. Let's make it sixteen million dollars every two weeks, so that's about four hundred and sixteen million dollars a year." He put down the lemonade and clinked the rings together. "Tax free."

"All under Charlie Wah?" Four hundred and sixteen million dollars didn't seem real.

"Charlie Wah runs the West Coast only. East Coast is Johnny King."

"King?"

Lau smiled, for perhaps the third time. He'd wanted me to ask. "Koh, actually," he said. "His first name, obviously, isn't really Johnny, either." Now that he'd decided to talk, he was making a good story out of it, Chinese-style.

"Johnny King," I said. "Charlie Wah. They sound like movie gangsters."

"Very good," Lau purred. "Hollywood has a lot to answer for." He sniffed at his lemonade as though he hoped someone had slipped something alcoholic into it while he wasn't looking. "But make no mistake. These are appallingly dangerous men."

"I've seen Charlie Wah in action," I said.

Lau made a tight little P with his lips and blew air behind it. "Charlie Wah thinks he's the last of the old-time mobsters. He affects the whole gestalt: those bodyguards, that haircut, those awful suits."

"Powder blue, the one I saw."

"He dresses like sherbet. He's a pastel rainbow, a complete spectrum of bad taste. He has them made in London, nice piece of reverse snobbery there, by a very good tailor who must go reeling every time a bolt of fabric arrives. They're silk, of course, dyed in Thailand by the inmates of a home for unwed mothers."

"Interesting labor pool."

He looked a little disappointed at my lack of reaction. "It's a good holding pen. Bring a couple dozen Chinese girls through Bangkok, put them up in the home while their papers are cooking, then ship them out."

"Why Bangkok?"

Lau sighed. He was feeling better, but it would be days before he was his old self again, if he still had an old self. "There are two main routes," he said, industriously moving things around on the tabletop. He laid a knife between us. "One is over the Chinese border near Yunnan and then by air into Thailand." He pushed his index finger to the edge of the knife and then hopped over it and skidded onto an unwiped piece of food that apparently represented Bangkok. "In Thailand the CIAs—that's Chinese Illegal Aliens—become Taiwanese or Hong Kongese and fly either to Los Angeles or to New York, sometimes via Taiwan. That's the air route, the most expensive. Fifty thousand dollars each. A hundred arrive on each coast every couple of weeks, about twenty million dollars a month."

The sums were troubling me. "Where does a mainland Chinese get fifty thousand dollars?"

A scowl informed me that I was breaking his flow. "Later. The second route"—he angled the knife about forty-five degrees away from me— "is by sea. Overland across China to Fujian Province, then by fishing boats into the Strait of Taiwan. They're picked up by a freighter and shipped, like computer parts or automobile bumpers, to San Pedro. Three or four miles offshore, they're loaded into small boats and brought the rest of the way in. As you can imagine, a long and uncomfortable trip. Also, no papers are involved. That's tourist class, thirty thousand apiece. A shipment of two hundred makes Charlie Wah six million dollars."

"Who owns the freighters?"

"Dummy companies set up by the Snakes. There's legitimate cargo, too, of course. On a good-sized freighter, two hundred people don't take up very much room. Especially if they're Chinese. Chinese," he said distastefully, "*like* crowds."

"The money," I prompted.

He paused and reached up to pat his pasted hair. "Chinese have very extended families. An entire family, thirty or forty people, will save for years for the down payment to send one young man to America. They're almost all men."

"What about those girls? In the home for—"

"They're going to be prostitutes," he said. "Not that they know it. Come to think of it, I'm not sure the Snakes do. It's just a sideline for Charlie. Charlie has a taste for prostitutes. They're useful in other ways, too."

He looked around absently: one more bright coffee shop, devoid, for the moment, of people who wanted to kill him. A clean, well-lighted place where he could sit with his computer and fax machine and pretend that he was writing and that people were waiting to read what he was writing.

"The men who can't pay," he said at last, "are the more interesting ones, if your interests run to slavery and degradation. They have no papers, no language except whatever Chinese dialects they speak, no money, obviously. They enter a period of indentured servitude, if we're being polite. One year of work, ten thousand dollars off their debt. Of course, there's interest, too. Most of them come tourist class, so that's roughly three years they owe to Charlie Wah and the Snakes."

"Three years doing what?"

He grimaced. "Whatever their masters decree. Restaurants, farms, laundries, garment factories, assembly lines, import warehouses. The Snakes own some of the businesses, but for others they're just a source of cheap transient labor. Say the slave earns fifteen thousand a year, which is standard. That's ten for Charlie, two to send home, and three to live on. Three," he said, watching me with an expression I couldn't read.

I was bone-weary and not paying attention as closely as I should have been. "Doesn't leave much for movies," I said.

He slapped the table flat-handed. "It doesn't leave much for *food*," he said. "These men own one shirt and one pair of trousers. They sleep six to eight in one-room apartments divided into plywood cribs. They buy fifty pounds of rice at a time and boil it in their apartments and flavor it with soy or make it into a gruel they can eat cold. They're afraid to go outside when they're not working, afraid someone from the INS will tap them on the shoulder—'' He stopped himself and gazed over my shoulder, remembering something.

"So," I said, calling him back to the present, "the INS."

He grimaced. "This is how cute Charlie is. This is typical Charlie. Get some poor coolie into the country, soak him for three years' hard labor, and get Tiffle to hand him a phony green card. Then send a phony INS inspector, an English-speaking Chinese, to wherever he's working, got it?'' He was speaking quietly, but he'd picked up a paper napkin and was methodically pulling its corners off.

"The INS guy tells the slave his card is no good. Says he'll be back tomorrow to check it out again, and to have money ready, hint, hint, elbow dig. The slave runs in a panic to Tiffle, who charges him seven hundred and fifty bucks to get the INS inspector pulled from the case and issue a new card. The next day the INS guy shows up anyway and says he's not on the case anymore, but he wants two-fifty not to pass the word to his successor. A thousand bucks," he said, slapping his thigh hard enough with his left hand to spill the lemonade in his right. "One tenth of a year. Pull it three or four times on a few dozen guys, and you've got a nice little extra dividend. More time in the sweatshop for the coolie, less money to eat on, less money sent to mama and the kids in China, another loud suit for Charlie Wah to hang on his fat bloody shoulders.''

"Double play," I said. "Charlie to Tiffle. Tell me about Tiffle."

"Tiffle," Lau snarled, tearing the napkin in half. "He's a fool. He likes Chinese girls, so he went into practice in C-town as a big liberal humanitarian, helping the poor little yellows with the bureaucratic machine. Business setups, immigration law, all that. Well, he shagged a few young ones now and then, but—what is it Shakespeare says about the appetite that feeds on it-self?''

"Something terrific, I'm sure."

Lau ripped the napkin into quarters. "So Charlie hears about him and thinks it might be nice to have a *gwailo* immigration lawyer, the police would never suspect that, and who has access to more Chinese girls than Charlie Wah? All those little unwed mothers. So he sent a few 'immigrants' to Claude Tiffle, and every one of them was a pretty girl, and every one of them had a problem that required Claude to do something just a little more illegal if he wanted to, ah, get paid."

The coffee shop was emptying now, people paying their checks and heading back to work. The noise level had dropped, and our voices were carrying. I'd liked it better full.

Peter Lau put the pieces of napkin on the table in front of him and aligned their edges. "Of course, he was also a prime candidate for disbarment. Charlie set up two or three really dirty deals in a row and then paid the coun-selor a visit."

"How do you know all this?"

"I'm a good reporter," he said mildly. "I found a girl who had quit Tiffle's office—Chinese, of course— and moved to Virginia. I wrote a story using just tiny pieces of what she gave me. That's when the editor of my paper learned that he might have a fire problem."

"Okay," I said.

"But the *point* is that Claude liked it. He *liked* being dirty, and he liked the money that Charlie kept dropping onto his desk, and, of course, he liked the girls."

"How does Charlie deliver the girls?" I was seeing all sorts of possibilities.

"They used to deliver them every Monday, Wednes-day, and Friday. Maybe they still do."

"What else does Tiffle do, exactly? When he's not practicing the two-person bellyflop."

"Phony IDs, real IDs, green cards." Lau glanced

around the restaurant. "Ghost processing, when an il- legal immigrant gets the papers of a real immigrant who's either died or gone back to China through one of the unofficial doors. That's a boom market, dead men's papers. A little money laundering, Chinese into Ameri- can currency, nothing serious, just enough to get him into even worse trouble if Charlie ever decides to open the trap door."

"That's great," I said. "Rampant jerkism."

"Don't think about going up against Claude. He's a fool, but he's almost as mean as Charlie Wah."

I nodded, thinking of ways to go up against old Claude.

Someone tapped me on the shoulder, and I jumped six inches. When I looked up I saw Tran.

"Toilet," he said.

"So go ahead," I said. "You don't need to ask."

"*Toilet*," he said more urgently. "Everybody."

"Oh, my God," Peter Lau said, going pale.

"Come on," I said. He hadn't unpacked his office, so I grabbed two of the cases and Lau's elbow. Tran took the other case and headed for the men's room.

"No," Lau said, standing shakily. "This way." And he led us, in a crouching Groucho Marx run, for the kitchen. Through the windows I could see four Chinese men approaching the coffee shop. They wore the Hol- lywood *mode du jour*, sport coats and jeans. One of them was talking and the other three laughing. The one who was talking was Ying.

The kitchen was large and steamy and densely over- populated. At least fifteen men occupied the room: slic- ing, dicing, washing, drying, frying, boiling, sitting idly and smoking. They gazed at us incuriously, ghosts from another dimension, as we hurried through the room, down a short, dingy corridor, and out the back door.

"Oh, *no*," Peter Lau said, stopping short and going so loose in defeat that I put out an arm to prop him up. "I parked in front."

"Relax," I said. "This has got to be a coincidence." It didn't sound very plausible to me, either.

"No coincidence," Lau snapped. "They came to collect. They have people working here."

"Well, if you'll excuse my saying so, this is a pretty stupid place to hide, then."

"I'm *not* hiding. I want them to know that I'm around, not doing anything. If they go too long without seeing me—"

"Coming into the kitchen, them," Tran said, emerging. I hadn't seen him go back in.

"I *always* park in front," Peter Lau moaned. "Why do I *drink*?"

"If they're in the kitchen, we can make it to the car. It's got to take them a few minutes."

"They'll leave two in front," Lau said hopelessly. "They always do. And they'll bring the headman out here for a talk. Who's not working, who might want to run away."

"Two?" Tran said. He grinned at me.

"Not on your life," I said. "It's broad daylight."

"Anyway, we look," Tran said insistently.

Well, hell. "Do they know your car?"

"I don't know." Lau was green again. "Usually, they sent this one." He turned his head toward Tran.

"Okay. Go around to the other side of the building." I handed Lau the two cases, and Tran piled on the third. "Stay there for ten minutes. If we haven't come to get you, wait another fifteen minutes and then cross the street, nice and slow. Don't look back. Go into a store over there and just watch through the window until you're sure you can get to your car." He was protesting, but I had to leave him to follow Tran.

The restaurant was a one-story cinder-block oblong dropped into the center of a large asphalt parking lot, built before the new Chinese immigrants drove Monterey Park land values up toward the Beverly Hills stratosphere. The back and sides of the building were pink and featureless except for the door we'd come through; ten feet away were the equally featureless sides of the neighboring buildings. The front, which looked onto Garvey Boulevard, was mostly glass and shrubbery, scrubby deep green juniper. The door was off center, closer to the corner Tran and I were about to round.

"Belt," Tran said, pointing at his.

"This is ridiculous," I protested, taking off my belt and hoping Ying was one of the men outside.

"In bushes," he said. "Wait."

I squeezed into the junipers at the corner of the building, and Tran waved at me and then sauntered around the corner. I was wrapping the ends of my belt around my hands when I heard a shout of surprise, and then the sound of running feet.

Tran hurtled around the corner, followed closely by two men, both almost as small as he was. I waited until the one closest to Tran had passed and then stepped out directly behind the second one. In two quick steps I was behind him and looping the belt up over his head and around his neck. I crossed my hands, bringing the belt tight, and dug my feet in, and the man's weight stopped him and snatched at the belt so hard that I would have lost it if I hadn't wrapped it first. He said, "Yuunnng," and his hands went up to the belt, and I saw Tran stop dead and kick out behind him, putting one foot into the midsection of the man behind him.

The man dropped to his knees, and Tran twirled and lifted a boot and punted his victim's head into some imaginary end zone, probably in Hawaii. As the man flopped to the pavement with a wet sigh I could hear ten feet away, the one with my belt around his neck gurgled and went limp, and I aided his forward movement with a shove that bounced his forehead on the blacktop. I kicked him in the ear for good measure, and he lay still.

"Go start the car," I said, retrieving my belt. "Wait for me."

Tran jumped nimbly into the air and landed with both

knees on the kidneys of the one he'd kicked, tearing the man's sport coat up the back seam, and then sprinted for the car. I went to his victim and took a look: Ying. Tran's cousin's face swam into the air in front of me, and I grabbed a handful of Ying's hair and lifted his head and then scrubbed his face back and forth against the asphalt, pushing down with all my strength. He bled rewardingly from forehead, chin, and nose, and the seam down his left cheek opened up very nicely. I realized I was growling as I took a little leap of my own, nothing as graceful as Tran's, and landed on his kidneys with the heels of my Reeboks, hoping he'd be pissing blood for weeks.

The whole thing hadn't taken fifteen seconds. With my heart beating three-quarter time in my ears, I went to the one I'd choked and rolled him over to make sure he was alive. His face was swollen and almost purple, but he was breathing, and I recognized the mild-looking little translator. I took a moment to check his pockets out of habit, found nothing, and, just for the hell of it, I lifted my right foot and dropped on my left knee into his gut. As his breath escaped him with a *whoof*, Alice came around the corner with Tran at the wheel.

He was laughing and pounding the dash, but when he saw the man at my feet, his face darkened.

"Take him," he said through the driver's window.

"Ying's over there," I said. "We can't handle both of them."

"*Him*," Tran said. "Or drive off, me, and leave you here."

"Him it is," I said, grabbing the translator by the back of his pants and hauling him toward the car. Tran leaned over and opened the passenger door, and I tossed the translator into the backseat.

"Around the building," I gasped, as Tran navigated around Ying. "Get Peter."

But Peter wasn't there. While I fought to regain my breath and kept an eye on the little translator, motionless on the backseat, Tran drove sedately across the lot and into the street. Half a block later, he turned to me, grinning fiercely, and raised a fist.

"Turn left," I said. My mind was whirling with possibilities. "Get to the freeway heading south."

"Where we going?"

"We're going to deal ourselves a wild card."

14

Ralph and Grace

"Wo," Dexter Smif said, efficiently blocking the doorway. "You in the wrong 'hood." Then he glanced past me at Tran, and said, "United Nations still in New York." He pushed the door wider, craned his neck forward to give Tran a good look, and nodded. "I be drivin a cab now. Driver got to know where the U.N. is."

"I don't mean to seem unfashionably nervous in a largely minority neighborhood," I said, "but do you think we could come in?"

"*Be* nervous," he said. "This a good place to get your ass chewed." Dexter was impossibly tall and thinner than soap film. He favored uniforms with his name embroidered on the pocket. The one he was wearing was bright orange and said RALPH.

"Ralph," I said forcefully, "we'd like to come inside. Now." The translator had been wrapped in battery cables and stored in the trunk.

He looked down at the name on his pocket. "Fifty cents a letter," he said. "Saves me half a buck. Always thought I looked like a Ralph."

"This is Tran," I said, switching tactics. "He'd like to come in, too."

"T-R-A-N?"

Tran nodded, craning up at Dexter.

"Lucky dude. You a two-buck-shirt man."

"Tell it to *Consumer Reports*," I said, "and get out of the way, would you?"

"No manners at all," Dexter said, stepping aside. Tran and I filed past him into a room that looked like a bordello for dentists.

"Why a cab?" I asked, looking around. The living room was furnished entirely in cut-rate Ikea stuff, leather, black steel, and glass. Literally everything emitted clinical glints of light. "Jesus, I'd hate to think what you do in here."

"All the leather," he said, "make it easy to mop up after. Yeah, new career path. Man can only chore for the city, pick up dead animals for so long. Hey, your cat still dead?"

The first time I'd met Dexter, the city had sent him to pick up an extravagantly deceased cat at the foot of my driveway. "She's been reincarnated," I said, "as a dog."

"All the same to me, by the time I got them, 'cept dog a little heavier to lift. Talk about hard to lift, got a couple of cows, about a week apart, just before I hung up the ole shovel. Cow a week, it was lookin like."

"Tran's Vietnamese," I said, including him in the chat. "He doesn't know from cows."

Dexter gave Tran the eye again. "I know he some kind of sushi. You shave yet?"

"I'll never shave," Tran said, sounding defensive.

"Wo. Two bucks a shirt, no razors. Man can live cheap. You sit on the floor?"

"No," Tran said shortly.

"Shame. Do without furniture, too, you on the way to rich."

"Same you?" Tran asked, taking in Dexter's furniture.

Dexter stopped in mid-flow and made his eyes glimmer at Tran, who took a step back, up against a low table that might have been the educated child of two pieces of scrap iron. Then Dexter laughed. "You should drive a cab," he said fondly to Tran, ignoring me. "Got the right attitude. Fare tries to shovel it at you, you shovel it right back. Hey, a free lesson. Fare say, 'You takin me out of the way,' when you just drivin from Beverly Hills to Santa Monica by way of San Diego. You say, 'Hey, garbageface, get out the fuckin cab.' Less you want to say something bad. You drinking?"

"No," I said, shuddering.

"Does the Pope—" Tran began cheerfully.

"He's drinking," I said.

"Does the Pope what?" Dexter asked, fascinated.

"You don't want to know," I said.

"Pope sounds like a good career path," Dexter said, turning to a perfectly ordinary black cabinet and leaning over to unfold a bewildering number of surfaces, like someone taking apart origami furniture. "Not too many dead cows on the Pope's beat. Somebody hand the Pope a dead cow, he just probably make the sign over it, say somethin in Polish." Open at last, the cabinet gleamed with bottles and glasses.

"The cow," I pointed out, "would still be dead."

"But on the *way*," Dexter said, gesturing skyward with a bottle of Johnnie Walker Black. "On the way to Elsie Heaven with clover everywhere, milkin done on cue by angels in silk gloves. One bull for every cow, just standin around stupid, waitin for the word."

"What word?" I asked.

"Moo," Dexter said pityingly. "What word you think?" He poured two glasses of Johnnie Walker and handed one to Tran. "Want one?" he asked me.

"No."

"Tea? I could make it real weak."

"It'll make my heart race," I said. "You know how I get when my heart races."

"Grace here," Dexter said, nodding toward me,

"only get wrecked on beer. And, hey, thanks for all the cards and letters."

"I didn't have your address."

Dexter started to say something and then laughed again, showing Tran the biggest teeth he'd probably ever seen. "Drink up, little Tran," he said, "and then let's figure out what Grace here wants."

"Wait," I said. "We've brought a friend."

"How many?" Dexter asked two glasses later. Tran was sitting, happy and red-faced from the alcohol, on the couch. The translator was lying on his side on the floor, trussed in jumper cables and belts. He'd still been unconscious when Dexter and I toted him in, and we'd improvised a hood, an old interrogation technique, from a pair of Dexter's boxer shorts. The legs waved over his head like cotton antennae.

I prodded him with a toe.

"Sixteen," he said. Tran had poked him with a two-pronged barbecue fork a minute ago.

"Sixteen Chinese guys," Dexter said, clarifying things.

"Sixteen Chinese guys with guns," I corrected him, "and God knows how many innocent Chinese along for the ride."

"But they Chinese, too," Dexter said. This was what had worried me.

"Chinese shit," Tran said, returning to his main theme.

"You know," Dexter said, rubbing his face with long fingers, "some black folks aren't crazy about Orientals."

I looked at my two allies and went for the hole card. "There's a lot of money here."

"I made out okay last time," Dexter said, although money had had nothing to do with why he'd come in with me. Dexter had a low boredom threshold. He'd been an unwilling soldier in two small but stupid American wars, and while he wouldn't have claimed to be richer for having spent time in Grenada and Panama, he'd retained the skills he picked up in the University of Legal Murder. He demonstrated one of them by popping seven hundred knuckles. "How'm I sposed to tell them apart? I can't tell a boy from a girl as it is."

Tran opened, and then closed, his mouth.

"We'll point," I said. "We'll say, 'Good, Dexter,' and 'Bad, Dexter.' "

"I think I can keep that straight," he said. "Less you talk fast."

"It's going to be easy," I said, "as soon as I work out the plan."

Dexter gave me the big eyes. "No plan?"

"I had one," I said, "until this guy got himself all tangled up in battery cables. Tran here knows where the good Chinese get delivered. Three or four houses in San Pedro." I nudged the fallen warrior with a toe. "Right?" I said. "San Pedro?"

"Umm," the fallen warrior said thoughtfully through Dexter's shorts.

"We got somebody here who'd love to kill you," I said. Tran poked him with the fork again.

"Yeep," he said. "Yes, San Pedro, yes."

"And I thought we'd drop by and really mangle the gears in Charlie Wah's little machine. I'll tell you about Charlie Wah in a minute." The hooded warrior rubbed his legs together, cricketlike, at the mention of Charlie's name. "And I figured that would get Charlie confused, make him lose his way, so that he'd—" I ran out of inspiration and looked at my allies. They looked biracially skeptical.

"Yeah?" Dexter said. "You know, I got a life here—"

"So Charlie would run the wrong way," I said very quickly, "and maybe he'd run into us." Dexter looked at the ceiling. "Charlie's the big bad guy," I added, just to fill the silence.

"Why should I care?" Dexter asked the ceiling. "Bunch of Chinese."

"There's the money. About a million."

"You already said about the money." Dexter sounded hurt. "Money's okay, you know? I mean, I *like* money. So maybe I come in with you for the money, hey, you can get a lot of guys for that kind of money."

"I don't want a lot of guys. I want you."

"Why's that?" He was still addressing the ceiling.

"I need someone at my back," I said. "Someone I can trust."

"You got Junior here," Dexter said, pointing a lengthy finger at Tran.

"Junior," Tran said angrily.

I got angry, too. I'd been sitting on anger for a long time, and when it bloomed, it blossomed all at once, like a time-lapse hibiscus, big and red and blotting out the landscape. "So fuck you," I said, getting up. "Come on, Tran." Tran got up, looking bewildered.

"Hold it," Dexter said. "Did I make a error in tact?"

"You don't even get to keep the money," I said, too mad to care. "Most of it is salt for the mine."

He sat back and waved me back toward my seat. "I never did understand that," he said. "What good is salt in a mine?"

"Dexter," I said, still standing. "I'm in this because of Eleanor."

"Yeah?" Dexter looked at the man on the floor. "What's this got to do with Eleanor?" He'd met Eleanor twice.

"Her brother Horace is looking for someone connected to these guys, but what he's going to find, if he finds anything, is Charlie Wah. I figure, even if I can't find Horace, I can short-circuit Charlie, I can maybe bring Charlie to *me*, before Horace gets killed. Maybe that's all I can do, but it's still something. Maybe it can save Horace."

Tran raised a hand. "These Chinese," he said, looking straight at Dexter, "these good Chinese. They going to be slaves."

"Slaves?" Dexter asked. He regarded Tran and then turned to me. "What you mean, slaves?"

"They're slaves," I said, "in the classical definition. They owe Charlie anywhere from twenty to thirty thousand bucks apiece. With interest. They're going to be worked until they pay it off, ten thousand a year. Three, maybe five, years of slavery."

Dexter got up and poured another Johnnie Walker. Then he tilted the glass in the translator's direction. "Stick another fork in bag-head, here."

"About the ship," I said twenty minutes later to the little translator. We'd established, with a few physical assists from Dexter and Tran, that the current load was coming in by ship. "When will it unload?"

"It's already unloaded," the translator said. He was sitting on Dexter's couch by now, battery cables pinning his arms behind him and my belt around his feet. He still had Dexter's shorts over his head.

"You're lying," I said, watching my plans fall apart.

"You're going to kill me," the translator said.

"No," I said. "But screw me up, and I can probably fix it so Charlie will."

"I went to college here," the translator said piteously. His breath made little puffs inside Dexter's shorts. "Cal State University Northridge. You think I want to work with Charlie? Hey, I'm Chinese, too."

"In the bad old days," Dexter said, "Africans sold Africans to the slavers." He and Tran had new drinks in their hands. "Those Africans the fuckers I hate most."

The translator said, "Oh."

"You ever pretend to be an INS inspector?" I asked him. His English was good enough.

The question took him by surprise. "Who've you been talking to?"

"You don't ask," Tran said. "You answer." He touched one point of the barbecue fork to the man's thigh and pushed it down. The man made a fluttering sound like wind through venetian blinds, and I looked away and saw Dexter staring at Tran with a new expression on his face. It might have been admiration.

"So the boat is empty?" That was Dexter.

"No." The translator shook his head, twisting Dexter's shorts from right to left. "Charlie's aboard. He likes to stay offshore in case anything goes wrong. But the little boats already picked up."

"Tell me about the little boats," I said. "What are they?"

"My leg," the translator moaned.

"That's enough," I said to Tran. He looked up at me as though he were surprised I was still in the room and withdrew the fork. A dark red circle surrounded the hole he'd made in the translator's trousers. "What boats?" I demanded.

"Fishing boats, pleasure boats. They pick up the payload and bring it ashore."

"And they've already done that."

"Like I said, last night."

Okay, forget the houses. "So there's nobody on board now except Charlie."

"One or two guys from Taiwan. Charlie's always got backup, but not much." The translator shook his head, making semaphores with the legs of Dexter's shorts. "Can you undo my hands?"

"No." I looked at Tran and Dexter. "Only one or two?"

"That's it," the translator said.

"Tell me how you get the pigeons off the ship, when the money changes hands, the whole thing."

He sighed. "We bring them into the harbor. The immigrants get off-loaded into the little boats. While the ship gets checked for its registered cargo, the immigrants get driven to the safe houses in San Pedro. They pay the rest of their down payment, and then the businesses come by and pick them up.''

''The businesses,'' Dexter said thickly.

''The people they're going to work for.'' He sounded resigned.

''Slavemasters,'' Dexter said.

''They want to get out of China,'' the translator said. ''Who wouldn't?''

''Back to the down payments,'' I said.

''The down payment is ten K. Let's say they pay five K when they get on the ship. Let's say they pay nothing, or maybe one K for earnest money. Chinese don't like to pay in advance. Then they owe anywhere up to ten thousand when they're safe in America. They pay that in the vans on the way to San Pedro. When they're on American soil, but while they're moving at 35 miles per hour.''

''And they arrive with it intact,'' I said. ''You never grab it while they're still on the ship.''

''We'd have a mutiny. A hundred and seventy-five, two hundred men going crazy on a small ship. No, we wait until they're here, and they're happy to pay.''

''If they haven't got it?'' Dexter asked.

''They've got it.''

''But if they don't?'' I could barely hear him.

''They've *got* it.''

''Fork the asshole,'' Dexter said.

''They get taken back.'' The words came out very fast.

''Yeah,'' Dexter said, ''and you get them back into China with no papers.''

''Thrown overboard,'' Tran suggested. ''On the way back.''

''Somewhere in the middle,'' Dexter said.

There was a long silence. ''Not very often,'' the translator finally said.

''Same as the slaves,'' Dexter said, ''when they got sick.''

"Think about the money," I said to Dexter. "Twenty or twenty-five thousand times two hundred."

"One hundred seventy-two," the translator volunteered.

"I thinkin," Dexter said. "I thinkin about a lot of things."

"What's your name?" I asked the translator.

"Everett."

"Okay, Everett. What's the name of the ship?"

"Please, mama," Everett said. "I'm dead."

"Bet your ass," Dexter said, "less you straight with us."

"Everett," I said, "you haven't got a lot of choices."

"*Caroline B.*," Everett said. Dexter let a breath escape, a whiskey-flavored zephyr. Tran looked down at the fork in his hand and threw it across the room. Then he glanced down at Everett's leg and bolted to his feet, heading for the bathroom.

"Listen, Dexter," I said as the door slammed. "You in?"

"I the guy."

I wiped slick sweat from my face and wiped my hand on my shirt. "Okay. Great. Can you get us someone else?"

"Someone like who?" Tran was gagging in the john.

"Like you."

He regarded me from a distance. "In what respect, like me?"

"Someone fierce and noble."

"I the only noble man I know," he said.

"Besides being noble, he should be dangerous and maybe just a little bit greedy."

The toilet flushed, and Dexter put a long finger into his drink and stirred, waiting.

"Tell him we got a bad white guy, too," I said.

Dexter leaned toward me, licking his finger. "Do tell."

Ten minutes later Tran and I were in the car. Everett

was tied hand and foot again, and stored in the trunk. Tran sat silent in the front seat, as far from me as possible, leaning against the passenger door. He'd fumbled with the door handle getting in.

"Tran," I said, "I want to ask you a question."

"One more?" he said listlessly. "Why not?"

"How many people have you killed?"

After a mile or so I turned to look at him. He was staring through the windshield, and his cheeks were wet. When he felt my eyes on him, he averted his face.

"One," he said.

15

Slow Dance

We hadn't eaten in what seemed like weeks, so we went to a McDonald's and had the meal I'd been aiming for all those bruises ago. Tran dried his cheeks and ate two of everything I ordered, cramming it under his twenty-inch waistline, and I searched my mind for the positive aspects of getting old. One would have sufficed. After he'd gotten up for an ice cream and returned with two, he drove the point home by saying, "You eat like old fart, too."

"You'll be an old fart someday," I said.

"No," he said, attacking the ice cream. If another kid had said it, I might have thought it meant something else.

"You really," I asked, returning to an old theme, "don't think you should call your mother?"

His face went still, and he swallowed before he spoke. "No," he said. "What I'm going to say to her?"

"You can say she's got one son alive."

He went back to the ice cream. "No talking," he said.

I pushed some food around and wondered why I'd wanted it in the first place. I'd finally summoned the will to pick up a french fry when he said, in an elabo-

189

rately casual tone, "How many people you killed?"

I put the french fry back on the plate. "One."

"How?" His ice cream had all his attention.

"Burned him." It's not something I like to dwell on, although I still dream about it.

"*Wah*," he said, giving it an entirely different intonation than he gave Charlie's last name. He was staring at me now. "Very bad."

My turn to change the subject. "Let's go say hi to Mr. Tiffle," I said.

Tiffle's office was a little bungalow set back from Granger Street, which was one-way and wider than a cow path, but not much. Chain link fence surrounded it, keeping the world at a distance from Claude Tiffle's plentiful secrets. Whatever doubt I may have felt about the likelihood of anyone actually having such a name was battered into submission by a comfortingly old-fashioned sign hanging over the gate that said CLAUDE B. TIFFLE ASSOCIATES, ATTORNEYS AT LAW.

"Associates?"

"Oh, sure," Tran said in a tone I was coming to recognize as derision. "Should say 'sweeties.' "

"What did you do here?" The office was dark except for one light in a room at the back of the cottage.

"Deliver money. Sometimes pick up. Two times, I think."

"Front or back?"

"Front."

"What time?"

"Same time like now."

"So," I said, just getting it clear, "you took the money from the houses in San Pedro and brought it here."

"Not always," he said. "Sometimes a car behind us would blink lights. Bright, low, bright, low. Then we pull over and they take the money."

"How did you know it was the right car?"

"Right number of blinks."

The light in Tiffle's bungalow snapped out, and another came on in the front room. "Did you know when you made the pickup whether you'd be dropping it off here?"

"No. Supposed to come here unless we see the car. Mostly, the car."

"Where did it stop you?"

He pondered. "Anywhere."

"It couldn't be anywhere," I said. "Charlie was going to a lot of trouble to avoid having Chinese stopped with the money. He would have pulled you over someplace near wherever he felt safe."

"Charlie on the boat," Tran said.

"Maybe." I thought about the evening. "And maybe our friend Everett is a liar."

Tran mentally ran through some of the trips. "Chinatown," he said. "Always Chinatown."

I was watching the lighted window. No one seemed to be looking at us, but I started Alice and turned on the headlights so as not to appear furtive. Around the corner, I pulled over again. "Did you ever pick up money from the restaurants, like the men we saw today?"

"Not thinking, you," Tran said. "We don't know about that."

"Probably not enough money anyway," I said, attempting to recover a little face. "Not enough to get the cops suspicious if the mules got pulled over."

"Charlie Wah not worried about cops," Tran said. "Worried about other gangs."

"Other *gangs*," I said. "Jesus." A door opened creakily in my mind, and a little light went on, not much of a light, but sometimes it doesn't take much.

"Sure. Other gang takes the money, kills the soldiers. This way they only kill Vietnamese."

"Charlie doesn't care about the soldiers," I argued.

"Soldiers," Tran said patiently, even sympathetically, "don't know that."

"Okay," I said. "I'm stupid. Why the armed guard, then?"

He reached over and shook me gently, as though I were asleep. "So *we* don't take the money," he said.

I thought about it. The more I thought about it, the better I liked it. "You know in English," I asked, " 'good, better, best'?"

"Sure." Tran was openly humoring me now. "In school."

"Say it, then."

"Good, better, best," he repeated, looking puzzled.

I punched him on the arm.

"Good team," I said.

Tran hid a smile by looking at his lap.

"One more place," I said, even though the new place wasn't anything I wanted to explore. "The Jesus lady you told me about." I gunned the car. "Let's go see where she lives."

She lived in Mrs. Summerson's house.

I had known she would, but hope springs eternal. The house sat there at the end of its extensive front yard, looking secluded and spacious, the perfect place to hide thirty or forty CIAs.

I sat at the wheel, trying to put Mrs. Summerson and Charlie Wah into the same room, and failing utterly. Why would Charlie need an ex-missionary? Why bring a *gwailo* into the distribution process? Tiffle I could see: He had his uses. But Mrs. Summerson had been Eleanor's savior; she'd taken care of her when Eleanor was a temporarily abandoned child with limited English. She'd been nervous, I recalled, when we'd asked her about Lo, but still, all those years ago, she'd given Eleanor affection and a home and brought her through the days of Ching-chong Chinaman. Of all the people in the world, outside of her immediate family, and maybe me on a good day, Eleanor loved Esther Summerson most.

And Lo, I thought, adding him to the list.

Eleanor was not going to be happy about this.

"How many times?" I asked.

"Two."

"You delivered or picked up?"

"Picked up."

"Great," I said miserably. "That's marvelous." Alice's clock, undergoing one of its temporary resurrections, ticked at us.

"Gave me cookies, her," Tran said at last.

"I've no doubt."

"We go in?"

"No. I need to think."

"Not good, better, best?" he asked.

"Not nearly." I tried one last time to be wrong. "Listen, Tran, an old lady, tall, thick glasses, white hair cut short, right?"

"In the button," he said. I was going to write a dictionary of idioms someday.

"Well, fuck a duck," I said. "We'll have to talk to her. And when the nice lady you tried to frighten—"

"Eleanor," he said.

"Right, good for you, when Eleanor comes around tonight or tomorrow, you don't tell her about this, okay?"

In the end, I told Eleanor about Mrs. Summerson, after all.

When we got back to Topanga it was past ten, and I phoned her in Venice and asked if she could come take a look at Tran's arm. Then I called Dexter and added "black" to the list of qualifications for the knight in armor he was supposed to be recruiting. When he'd hung up, I dialed Peter Lau, first to make sure that he'd gotten home, and second, to check on what Everett had told me. Everett was trussed hand and foot in my bedroom with one end of Charlie's handy cuffs locked around a leg of the bed. I'd bandaged his thigh.

"Tell me about the timetable for Charlie Wah's shipments," I said when Peter picked up the phone.

" 'S'irregular," he said, sounding as though he either were lying down or should be. "He keeps it that way on purposely. On purpose."

"Then it's flexible?"

"You mean, can he improvise? My stars, no. The last thing he can do. He staggers the arrivals like any intelligent crinimal—scuse, crimmul—would, but the freighter has to talk to San Pedro all the way across the pond, talk, talk, and the arrival date is firm. Maybe they have to line up for a day or two offshore, jus' tote'n float. Better for Charlie. He can pick his day."

"Do you think he's already moved them off the ship?"

"No way to know."

I massaged my shredded ear. "Listen, Peter, have you heard anything about a missionary being involved? Here in Los Angeles, I mean."

"Missionary? What kind of question is that?"

"One that I wish I weren't asking."

"You mean a 'Merican missionary?"

"Have you heard anything?"

"No. Why'n earth would he—" I heard a familiar sound. He was clinking the rings together.

"Peter?"

"I'm thinking. There's something about missionaries. Are you a toll call?"

"Yes."

"Then hold on." He missed the table with the phone, and it took a couple of bounces on the way down. I was rubbing my ear again when the door opened and Eleanor came in, carrying a small shopping bag. She was wearing a nubby red sweater over black bicycle shorts, and she looked like the entrée on a lecher's menu. Bravo, who was sitting with his head on Tran's lap, slapped the floor with his tail and whimpered welcome.

"Bactine," she said, holding up the bag as though that would help me see through it, "and some nice red wine."

"Gaaaahhh," I said, wincing at the idea of wine.

"Kidding about the wine," she whispered. "It's white. Are you talking to someone?"

"No," I said, "I'm hooked up to the radio telescope on Mount Palomar."

"I've got something to tell you after the supernova. *There's* my little patient." She brightened at the sight of Tran.

"Hello, Eleanor," Tran said, slowly and formally. "How are you today?" He sounded like he'd been practicing.

"Tell her," I suggested, "where is the pen of your aunt."

He looked startled. "Pardon?"

"He's just being Simeon," Eleanor soothed. "He does it whenever he can't come up with something better."

Tran stood and raised his hands to his chest, palms together. "Eleanor," he said, "I am sorry."

"For what?"

"For trying to kill you and frighten you." He *had* been practicing.

"That little thing." Eleanor pulled the Bactine from the bag. "Take off that fat man's shirt and sit down, and I'll make you sting."

"Old fart shirt." Tran began to unbutton.

"That's enough of that," said the old fart.

"Of what?" Peter Lau asked.

"Talking to the dog," I said.

"Oh. Had to get my files." He sounded like he'd gotten more than his files. "I knew there was something about missionaries. Back when Charlie Wah was an innocent, pink-cheeked lad, long before the suits and the haircut, he was taken in by missionaries." He swallowed, a long and melodically liquid sound, and ice tinkled gaily. "This is in China, of course. He lived with them, mishnaries, and went to a mishnary school. Quite the little suck-up, too, our Charlie, until he decided that the kingdom of heaven was here on earth and helped a local gang break in and steal everything the school owned. I mean, down to the pencils. Five years later, he and the gang were on Taiwan.''

"I'll be damned," I said. "How could you know all that?"

"Taiwan mag'zines," Peter Lau said impatiently. "Charlie is a businessman as far as Taiwan is concerned, and on Taiwan they write about businessmen the way we do about movie stars. But that's not the *point*."

"And the point . . ."

"The *point* is, Charlie hates mishnaries. Hates them probably even more than he hates p'licemen. You can buy p'licemen, but you can't buy mishnaries."

I watched Eleanor minister to Tran's slender form. Maybe I *should* lose a little weight. "I'm not so sure of that."

"He wouldn't, though, even if he could get a bulk rate. He loathes them. Thinks they're agents of a vast plot to rob Chinese of their birthright."

"Which is what?"

He clobbered the mouthpiece with his hand to conceal a hiccup. "In Charlie's case, it would seem to have been poverty."

"Do you happen to have the name of the missionary who attempted to pervert little Charlie?"

"I do," he said happily. "Charlie tol' all in a interview. Can you imagine interviewing Charlie? 'Whass your favored means of execution, Misser Wah?' An' they call this journalism." Papers rustled, and I watched Eleanor minister to Tran.

"Here we are," he said. He swallowed. "What an evocative name."

I closed my eyes. "What is it?"

"Skinker," he said. "Dr. and Mrs. Finney B. Skinker. I wunner what the 'B' stood for."

"Probably Binky," I said. "Thanks, Peter."

The moment I hung up, Eleanor said, "*What* about missionaries?"

"Just background," I said.

She tossed her hair over her shoulder. "Just horseradish. How did missionaries get into this?"

"Precisely the question I've been asking myself." Tran was staring out the window, apparently rapt at the sight of pitch darkness. The winter fog had slipped in again.

Eleanor gave me a look that I'd long before learned meant *no more nonsense*. "Any particular missionaries?"

"My ear hurts," I said.

She lifted her chin imperiously. It made her neck look impossibly long. Someday I'd have to tell her that it was more alluring than frightening. "Simeon. What has Mrs. Summerson got to do with this?"

"Aaahh," I said, trying to postpone the question. "Listen, do you think Mrs. Summerson was ever married to a man named Finney B. Skinker?"

She stood up, the empty paper bag tumbling from her lap to the floor. "Mrs. Summerson mated for life. That was the phrase she used. I doubt that she mated for life twice. As a Christian, she doesn't believe in reincarnation any more than that little Orlando does. And she certainly never mentioned anyone named Skinker. Sounds like a species of lizard."

"It wasn't Mrs. Summerson, then. I guess you don't want to look at my ear."

"I can see it from here," she said, not quite snapping at me.

I chucked it in. "Tran picked up money from Mrs. Summerson's house," I said. "Twice."

"Nonsense," she said, looking at Tran. Tran, still looking out the window, nodded. "Absolute nonsense," she said again. Then she sat down on the couch, heavily enough to make Tran bounce.

"I'm sure there's a perfectly logical explanation," I said, searching for one.

"Of course there is."

Now we were all looking out the window.

"I lived in that house," she said, a bit tremulously.

"No strange Chinese coming and going."

"Of course not. I lived there. For *years*. I was the only strange Chinese in sight."

"He picked up money," I said. "Tran did, I mean."

"She hasn't got any. She had his insurance, but that was years ago."

"Then she owns the house?" I asked.

"Forever. But she hasn't got anything else."

"Not her money," Tran reminded us, buttoning my shirt. "CIA money."

"She's not smuggling in CIAs," Eleanor said, and then promptly backed up. "And if she is, she's not doing it with a bunch of criminals."

"Not with this bunch of criminals, anyway," I said. "Charlie Wah hates missionaries."

"So there," Eleanor said, and then said, "but Tran picked up from her."

"We'll talk to her," I said. "Maybe tomorrow. Why the wine?"

"I was celebrating." She didn't sound very celebratory. "Horace called Pansy."

"Great. Where is he? Where's Pansy, for that matter?"

"He didn't say where he was, but he's alive. Just said not to worry about anything, the simp. So naturally, we've all stopped worrying. I'm not going to tell you where Pansy is. Suppose these sadists catch you?"

"That's a nice thought. Horace's call certainly cheered you up."

"It did, really it did. But I didn't know about Mrs. Summerson then."

"You still don't," I said.

"No, that's right. And I'm not going to believe anything bad until I absolutely have to." She looked down at her slender hands. The ring I'd given her to wear on the third finger of her left hand was now on the right, where it had been for years, ever since I'd abandoned the best of my potential futures. "Anyway, it wasn't just Horace's call. I got to thinking about you, running around and sticking your big thick neck out, and all because of me. And I realized I've been pretty awful, worrying about everybody except you, and I just thought . . ."

"Thank you," I said.

"I just thought we might get drunk together and listen to some music and laugh a little, and maybe when I got drunk, I could tell you how much I love you for everything you've done."

Tran got up. "Toilet," he said. He was gone.

"This doesn't mean we don't have a zillion problems," Eleanor continued. "God knows we've got a zillion problems."

There was nothing easy for us to say, and she filled the silence with a kiss, breaking me into small pieces inside. I could smell the faint yeasty fragrance of her skin. I rose and put my arms around her and we stood together like slow dancers when the music has stopped.

"I'll get the corkscrew," she said, stepping back, "and you get that boy out of the toilet, and we'll drink for a while. And then, if you don't plan to sleep on the couch again, I'd like to stay here tonight."

"He'll stay in the toilet indefinitely, if you'd like to change the sequence."

"I'm going to need longer than indefinitely," she said. "Women love heroes."

I looked at her good face, her kind face, the face I'd made sad so often. "Eleanor," I said, "there's someone in the bedroom."

She stiffened.

"Not like that," I said. "Come see." I led her across the living room and through the door, and she gazed down at the bundled figure on the bed. "One of Charlie's," I said. "And don't feel sorry for him."

"They know he's missing?" she asked, sounding worried.

"I'm thinking about that. It just means we have to move fast."

The bathroom door opened, and Tran came out.

"Sweetie?" Eleanor said to him. "Guess what. Tonight you get the bed."

16

Snow on the Water

At seven the next morning adrenaline snapped me awake
and I eased myself out from under Eleanor's outstretched arm. Halfway off the couch, I stopped and
looked down at her sleeping face. She lay on her back,
black, straight strands of hair fanning over the smooth
planes of her skin and down toward the secret hollows
of her throat, where it blossomed outward to meet the
fragile wings of her collarbones. I knew if I kissed her
I'd wake her, so I saved the kiss for later and trudged
to the phone to get myself a boat.

Toting the phone outside, I first called Dexter. He
sounded bleary and whiskey-bogged, but he brightened
marginally when I gave him Tiffle's address.

"The white guy?"

"The very man."

"And do what?"

"Watch," I said. "Take notes. I want to know especially about young Chinese women going in and out."

"Follow them?"

"No. Just stay there and keep track. I want descrip-
tions, okay?"

"I the guy," he said again before he hung up.

I needed a boat, and I knew only one boat jock. Before I called him, I tiptoed inside, started some coffee, and went into the living room to kiss the smooth skin of Eleanor's wrist. She emitted a sound that was an entirely new combination of consonants, heavy on *h* and *s*, and I headed back outside, trailing the phone, and called Norman Stillman at home.

I'd worked for Stillman once. He produced the kinds of shows that gave American television a bad name throughout the first, second, and third worlds and used the proceeds from the shows to buy yachts, no less, but he had one redeeming quality: He was greedy.

"Norman," I said, after giving him a moment to pant into the phone while he got his bearings. Norman was rich. Norman got up when Norman wanted to get up. "Norman, this is Simeon Grist. I need a boat."

"The *Queen Mary*," he said grumpily. "She's just sitting there."

"I need it tonight," I said.

"Something in it for me?"

"Um, the grunion," I said. Norman didn't believe in anything he got easily. "They'll make a great show. Why do they run when they're scheduled to run? I mean, how do fish—*fish*, Norman, develop such a keen sense of time? Not to mention—are you listening, Norman— *how do fish run?*"

"Fuck you," Norman Stillman grumbled. "The grunion won't run for weeks."

"You got me, Norman. Okay, so it's not the grunion. How do you feel about slavery?"

"Great," Norman said, sitting up and going *mumph* with the effort. "Always a hot topic. You mean, *white* slavery?"

"Not exactly."

"Aaahh," he said, losing interest. Norman still thought everybody was white.

"And millions of dollars," I added.

"Better," he said. "But I don't know."

"Prostitutes," I said.

"This is exclusive, right?"

"I'll have to tell the cops," I said. "And maybe the radio guys." They could get on the air immediately. Norman's daily show, a national confessional for the sins of the middle class, taped a week in advance of its air date.

"Radio," Norman said scornfully. "Who cares? But no TV, right?"

"The boat."

He figured for a long moment, probably doing subtraction on his bedsheet. "It's not going to get bullet holes in it or anything, is it?"

"Not a chance," I said with wholly spurious conviction. "It's a milk run."

"Pick me up a quart," Norman said, and then wheezed into the phone. "Nobody delivers these days." He wheezed again, and I recognized it as a laugh. I'd never heard Norman make a joke before, and it made me wonder briefly whether I'd misjudged him. Maybe he *was* human.

"I'll need a driver for the boat," I said.

A new wheeze. "A *skipper*, not a driver. Boats got skippers. Gonna cost a thousand. Who pays?"

"If you decide you don't want the story, I do."

"What if you get killed?"

"For Christ's sake, Norman, take a chance." He didn't leap at it. "Would I be doing this if I were going to get killed?"

"You get killed," Norman said, "the thousand'll be on your conscience."

"How do I get the boat?"

He thought about it. "Around two or three, call my girl."

He hung up. I went back inside and kissed Eleanor awake.

For the next four hours Eleanor and I scoured Chinatown looking for Horace while Tran sat home and baby-sat Everett. We checked all of Horace's favorite restaurants, Eleanor using her Cantonese on the owners, and both of us dropping in on his friends. No Horace. One of the friends, a shopkeeper, thought Horace might have narrowly missed running him over on Hill Street the previous night, but when he'd jumped out of the car's way and shouted Horace's name, the driver had accelerated away.

"He was looking for Lo," I said to Eleanor when we left the shop.

"Horace always drives that way," Eleanor said. "All Chinese do. They've usually got a grandmother in the backseat, and all they care about is finding a parking space so the ancestor shouldn't have to walk. Chinese people hit fire hydrants all the time. Anyway, even if it was Horace, what good does that do us now?"

We picked up a sandwich for Dexter, who'd been watching Tiffle's cottage from his big Lincoln.

"People in and out," he said, chewing. "Mostly Orientals, mostly girls. How you doin, Eleanor?"

"*Why* is a better question," Eleanor said. "Sense of family, I suppose."

"They's family," Dexter said comfortably, picking a tomato slice out of the sandwich and dropping it out the window, "and then they's everybody else."

"Keeping score, Dexter?" I asked.

"All in the little black book," he said, waving something at me. It actually *was* a little black book.

"I thought those went out with Hugh Hefner," I said.

Dexter gave me the big eyes. "Somethin happen to Hugh Hefner?"

Back home at three I called Norman's "girl," whose name was Deirdre and who was older than Norman, and was told that the boat and skipper were in place.

"Two little things," I said. I'd always liked Deirdre. Like thousands of low-paid women in Hollywood, she did the work that the men put their names on.

"Only two?"

"I want to be picked up in Santa Monica, not in San Pedro. And the skipper has to know how to find a specific boat in the harbor."

"Where in Santa Monica?" That was one of the things I liked about Deirdre; she didn't say, "Can't do." She said, "Where?"

"Someplace we can wade."

"Skip it," she said. "Too much attention. Get the boat in Marina Del Rey; that's where it docks anyway."

"Where? I mean, do boats have an address?"

Papers got rifled through. "Pier, um, three, slip twenty-nine."

I'd been to Marina Del Rey before, and it was security-happy. "Is someone going to ask me what I'm doing there?"

"You're looking for Pat Snow's boat."

"Pat Snow."

"*Captain* Pat Snow, if you want to sound nautical. What ship are you after?"

I paused. "I don't want you to tell Norman," I said.

"Welllll," Deirdre offered.

"This is dangerous."

"Norman doesn't want to know," she said promptly, "until you bring the boat back. And Captain Snow used to run dope. That's how Norman knows about the boat. Did you see the show? *High Seas*, it was called."

"Loved it," I lied. "Investigative journalism at its best. The boat—pardon me, the ship, I mean—is called *Caroline B*."

"I'll get on the horn with Captain Snow," she said. "Nine o'clock okay?"

"Nine is fine," I said. The line went dead.

The rest of the day was just waiting. Tran and I reblindfolded Everett while Eleanor looked at the fork hole in his thigh and pronounced it nothing to worry about.

"Didn't happen to you," Everett said sulkily.

"Do you get seasick?" I asked him.

"No," he said. Then he said, "Why? I mean, why?"

"High seas," I said. "The *Caroline B*."

We closed the bedroom door on his wails of panic and drank more coffee while the sun fought its way through the afternoon fog. When it got strong enough to warm the skin, we went out onto the roof of the room downstairs and drank more coffee and watched hawks cut slices out of the sky. A few fat and dirty seagulls, disoriented and driven inland by the fog, landed on the deck and cast nervous glances at the hawks.

"Squab with lettuce," Tran said, eyeing them. He began to make little cooing noises, and the birds checked the deck for an attractive bird of the opposite sex.

"I'll fix you a burger," I said.

"Wait," Eleanor said, fascinated. "Can you actually catch one?"

"Stupid, them," Tran said. "Sure."

"Burgers," I said firmly.

"I want to see," Eleanor said.

Tran lay down on the edge of the deck and summoned sounds from his throat that sounded like muffled yodels. His shoulder blades stuck up through my shirt. "No moving," he said to us.

"Still as stones," Eleanor commanded me.

There were four gulls clustered on the deck now, facing each other as though they were waiting for one of them to come up with an interesting conversational gambit. Tran cooed his little yodels, and the birds gradually drifted in his direction, heads bobbing forward and back with every step. I developed an itch in the middle of my back.

Just as I was about to reach back and scratch, one of the seagulls spread its wings and puffed up its breast, and took another step toward Tran. I didn't even see his arm move, just heard an astonished *squawk* and a beating of wings as the birds took off. Three of them, anyway. The fourth flapped its wings frantically, its legs imprisoned in Tran's fist.

"Oh, my gosh," Eleanor said.

The bird in Tran's hand stretched its entire body skyward, wings pumping madly. It squealed and snapped its head down to sink its beak into Tran's wrist. A bead of blood appeared, and the head came up and then down again.

"Let it go," Eleanor said over a sound I didn't recognize as I watched the beak sink into skin again, and then I did recognize it: Tran was laughing.

"Squab," he said, grinning, impervious to the bird's repeated strikes against his wrist.

"Let it go," Eleanor said again, and Tran looked from her to me and opened his hand, and the bird soared skyward, emitting indignant *yawks*. Little globes of blood dotted Tran's brown arm.

"No problem," he said. "Catch two or three."

I got up. "Burgers," I said.

At seven, Dexter called. "Everybody gone. Everybody except the fat guy."

"Tiffle's fat?"

"Make some little country a fine dinner." Dexter said. "And one teensy Chinese snack, real pretty, arrived about two minutes ago. You want me to wait?"

They deliver them like pizza, Lau had said.

"No. Meet us at Topanga and the Pacific Coast Highway. Eight-fifteen, okay?"

"More people than I figured," Captain Pat Snow said, looking at Tran, Dexter, Everett, and me. Captain Snow looked surprised at the fact that Everett was handcuffed, but not as surprised as I was.

Captain Pat Snow was a black woman.

She caught my stare and lifted an affronted eyebrow. She was about thirty-five, with extremely curly black hair fluffing out beneath a dark cap, mocha-colored skin, and a vulnerable-looking pug nose, but there was nothing vulnerable about her hazel eyes. They flayed and filleted me and tossed the waste to the gulls.

"You're younger than I expected," I said lamely.

"Yeah, right," she said. Then she chuckled, but the eyes didn't forgive me any. "Get laddie there on board if you don't want no one to see the cuffs." We obeyed, the boat sagging alarmingly beneath our weight. It was a small cruiser, maybe twenty feet long, with a cabin belowdecks, reached by a small door to the left of the wheel. The decks were littered with automobile tires.

"Nobody going to get killed, right? And I mean him in the handcuffs. You're a big one, aren't you?" she asked Dexter. She was up on the dock now, unwinding the rope that moored the boat to the pier. "Cause I'm not going to be no kind of accessory——"

"Nobody's going to get killed," I assured her, hoping it was true. "We're all going out and we're all coming back."

"Yeah, yeah. Catch." She threw the rope at me, too fast, and Tran stepped in front of me and caught it. Okay, so he had fast hands. Captain Pat Snow stepped back onto the boat and pushed it away from the pier. "This a pickup or a delivery?"

"Maybe neither," I said. "We're going out to look. If we bring anything back, it'll be a person."

"*Caroline B.*, right?" She negotiated the rocking deck toward the wheel.

"That's it."

"Bad ship," she said, turning a key. Engines coughed beneath the deck. "Class B freighter, draws maybe thirty feet, so they got to keep it out a ways. Seen it before."

She did something to the controls, and the boat began to back up through the greasy water. "Why bad?" I asked.

"Folks, right? Delivering folks."

I'd been looking out to sea, but now I turned to her. "How would you know that?"

"Girl's got to keep her eyes open. Hold on a minute."

She glanced left and right, guiding the boat out between fragile-looking hulls. "Out here, probably lots of people know," she said, eyeing the nearer boat. "*Caroline B.* comes in every few months. First they unload her out there, then they bring her up the channel and unload her official."

"Anyway, she's empty now."

"I don't think so," she said.

Everett looked very apprehensive.

"Or maybe we've been lied to," I said, glaring at him.

"No truth in this world," Captain Snow said, twirling the wheel and making the boat spin around. I sat down without planning to. The lights on shore swam away behind us and reemerged on our left, so we were headed south. "You know anything about ships?"

"Nothing at all. They, um, seem to move a lot."

"And you think you're going aboard?"

"We both are," Dexter said, surprising me.

She zipped up her black windbreaker and gave him a skeptical grin. "Hope you can climb a rope." She angled the boat toward the right, in the general direction of the open sea, and the wind was wet and cold. "Shoes?"

"I beg your pardon?"

"High-tops," Dexter said, lifting a large white-clad foot.

"Boots," I said.

"With leather soles," Captain Snow said, sounding irritated. "What size?"

"Um, nine and a half," I said.

She cast me a glance. "What're you, six feet? Little for such a big guy."

"You know what they say bout the size of the foot," Dexter contributed. "Little feet, little dong."

"And you're what?" Captain Snow asked him.

"Twelve."

"In your dreams." She pulled a pack of cigarettes from her dark windbreaker and shook the pack over her mouth. One dropped out, and she caught it between her teeth.

"Wo," Dexter said.

"You and me," she said to me, flipping open an old military Zippo. "We change shoes. I got big feet." She crinkled her eyes at Dexter over the flame. "You got anything to say?"

"Tide fallin'," Dexter observed.

"Norman's a mutant," Captain Snow said, kicking off her shoes, "but Deirdre's okay. Still, even if Deirdre was Our Lady of Fatima, I wouldn't take you out tonight if it wasn't for the money. And the fog." We were well offshore by now, and she pointed a finger toward the southwest. I followed it and saw something that looked like a white sheet lowered from the sky into the water.

"Is that fog?" I asked, leaning against the railing to pull off my boots.

"Thick as linoleum," she said. "The nautical ass-hole's best friend. Cuts off sight and sound. Give me enough fog, and I can steal Catalina." The engines beneath my feet leaped eagerly toward the fog.

"Like when we leave Vietnam," Tran said, leaning into the breeze. "But colder."

"I'll take Simon Legree here downstairs," Dexter said. Twelve or not, he didn't look very happy about being afloat.

"Good idea." I wasn't actually very happy myself. Dexter trotted Everett past Captain Snow and through the little door. A moment later, I heard Everett go "*Whoof*." He'd been pushed onto a bunk.

"He's with them, huh?" Captain Snow said, meaning Everett. She turned the wheel about ten degrees. The sheet of fog yawned before us, its lower edge absolutely sharp against the black water.

"And we're with us," I said, eyeing the white curtain in front of us.

"Getting aboard isn't going to be easy," she said, and the prow of the boat punched a hole in the curtain. I couldn't see anything. The sound of our engines suddenly sounded like something a mile away.

"Back there," she said, "toward the stern, is a grappling hook. It's wrapped in rags to kill the noise." I had to squint to make her out. "I'll throw it, unless your friend there is with the NBA. *Can* you climb a rope?"

"If I have to." It didn't sound like fun.

"Gimme those boots. My feet are freezing. And when I say quiet, be quiet."

"Quiet?" I said. "They're going to hear the engines."

"Lots of engines out here, all night long." Dexter came out of the cabin, wrapped in fog. "You guys throw those tires over the side."

Right. Throw the tires over the side. Tran, Dexter, and I bumped into each other like a bunch of drunks as we pitched the tires over a railing that was much too low for my comfort. The tires had ropes attached to them, and they dangled just inches below the deck level. Like the grapple, they were wrapped in rags.

"You do a lot of this?" I asked, happy to be back behind the wheel. The wind was weaker there.

"Once in a while." She was peering over the wheel, face wet with fog and the cigarette burning itself down between her teeth. "Can't tote dope anymore. The War on Drugs gets real about a year before an election. So it's the occasional stuff off a freighter—furniture, furs, car parts—whatever happens to fall into the water. Problem is, not much stuff falls into the water."

"And if it did," I ventured, "it'd be all wet."

She grinned at me over the coal of the cigarette. "Give the man his weight in fish."

"Still, it must be risky."

"Not so bad. They don't guard them much because we don't take much. And we come in way below them, you know? They're all way up there on the upper decks. Gets *real* cold on a freighter anywhere near the waterline. And then, they're usually drunk."

We motored through the fog, mostly southward as far as I could tell, for almost thirty minutes. Tran curled himself into a ball near the stern and closed his eyes, perhaps viewing private movies of the South China Sea. I watched Captain Snow take her bearings on a small green radar screen, with only occasional glances at the real world. Twenty-eight minutes out, Captain Snow pulled up on a lever I'd come to recognize as the throttle, and the engines died back.

There was nothing but fog. It condensed on our clothes, making little sparkles, and it sat like foam on the dark, oily water. We were running without lights, but Captain Snow seemed to know exactly where we were.

"We *should* be—" she said, sounding puzzled. And then she smiled. "They don't call me deadeye for nothing."

A cliff loomed before us, maybe twenty yards away, maybe twenty feet high. Darker than the fog, darker than the night, it rose from the water like a rock wall. I suddenly heard music.

"Hang on," Captain Snow said, cutting the wheel to put us on a course that would make us sideswipe the ship. "Sit *down*, for Chrissakes." I sat, and the cliff got nearer and nearer, and then our little boat bounced like a walnut shell on the water, and the rags around the tires let out a wet, muffled little squeal.

Even sitting, I fell sideways, toward the ship, and Tran landed on top of me. Dexter rode it out, looking grim. We began to float away from it.

"Grapple," Captain Snow whispered. "Quick."

I extricated myself from beneath Tran and grabbed it. She had it out of my hand before I could even reach up, and I concentrated on the coils of rope below it, making sure they weren't fouled.

"Duck," Captain Snow snapped, and whirled the grapple around her head. It whistled through the air in larger and larger circles as she paid out rope, and then she bent her knees, looked up, and let it go.

The grapple arched up through the fog, trailing rope behind it, hung for a heart-stopping moment at the top of its arc, and then fell. It touched the top of the iron cliff, twisted, and dropped like a stone.

"*Shit*," Dexter hissed. The grapple plummeted to the water between us and the freighter, and hit with a deafening splash.

"Don't move," Captain Snow whispered. "Not a sound."

We all froze, bobbing up and down in the shadow of the freighter's sides, and the music resolved itself into Taiwanese pop, a squeaky-voiced girl singer and an all-string orchestra doing a Chinese version of "Feelings."

We listened to an entire verse before Captain Snow said, "Bring it in."

I was closest to the rope, so I pulled it in, cold and wet, hand over hand. It seemed like I'd brought a mile's worth aboard before the grapple bumped against the side of the boat, and I reached down and grasped it and pulled it onto the deck. My hands were cold enough to be getting numb. I flexed my fingers, thinking about climbing the rope.

Captain Snow took the grapple and held up an index finger. *One more time* is what it said. She did the grapple-twirl arc again and threw it, a lot harder this time, grunting with the effort of tossing the extra weight of the wet rope, and it streaked upward, splashing us all with clammy seawater, turned two or three times at the top of its parabola, and started to come down.

And then it stopped, snagged itself against the side of the freighter with a soft *thump*, and hung there.

"Jesus," Dexter said, blinking fast.

"We don't know yet." Captain Snow put both hands around the rope and tugged. It held. "Grab my legs," she said, and I did. She lifted both feet from the deck. She immediately began to swing toward the ship. I threw both arms around her calves, and our boat drifted toward the freighter until her feet touched down again.

"It's fast," she said, sounding pleased with herself. "You can let go now." I did, and she went back to the wheel. "There's a knife in the center of the rope coil. Cut it if anyone comes to the railing." I picked it up with dead fingers.

We waited again, staring upward. "Feelings" ended and turned into a Chinese duet of "Sounds of Silence." No silhouette appeared above us.

"Okay." Captain Snow wiped her hands on her jeans. "You got fifteen minutes. You guys go up the rope, check things out, and come down again. Anything happens, shots or anything, I'm outta here, you got that?"

Dexter and I nodded.

"And one of you has to jump off."

"Say what?" That was Dexter.

"Can't leave the grapple," she said. "One of you comes down the rope, and the other one gets the grapple free and jumps off, feet first, not too much splash. We'll pull you aboard with the grapple rope."

"Who gives a fuck about the grapple?" Dexter whispered. "Buy you a new one."

"They'll know we were here," I said.

"Be my guest," Dexter said to me. "Water don't look too cold."

"No," Captain Snow said. "You."

"Why's that?" Dexter demanded.

She smiled at him. "He's wearing my shoes. I don't want them to get wet."

"We change, then," Dexter said to me.

"You're *way* too big," Captain Snow said, batting her lashes.

"This a fix," Dexter muttered. Tran made a little whisk-broom sound that could have been a snicker. "Okay, shit," Dexter said. He pulled off his high-tops and then his jacket, shirt, and pants, and stood before us in a pair of baggy boxer shorts covered with something that looked like lipstick imprints. "One *word*," he said, glowering at me. Then he took the rope in his big hands, tugged on it once, and said, "Here goes."

He ascended hand over hand, bare feet bouncing off the steel side of the freighter, while I tucked my hands under my armpits to try to get some feeling into them.

"Up, him," Tran said, as though I didn't know.

"Keep an eye on Everett," I said. I took the sopping rope in my hands and leaped toward the side of the ship, trying to remember how Dexter had done it. *Bounce*, climb, *bounce*, climb, pull the rope toward me, hit the ship with my heels, pull again, arm over arm, don't think about the water below, hit the ship again and throw the next arm up, my hands warming and my heart pumping, and then I was eye to eye with Dexter, and he put his hands under my arms and pulled me over and we collapsed onto a very cold metal deck.

"You owe me," Dexter panted. He looked truly ridiculous.

"Nobody?" I gasped. I was seeing little yellow flares, retinal fireworks from the nervous system.

"Not so far."

The music was louder here. The duo had gone phonetic. *And the people bowed and prayed*, they sang, *to the neon god they'd made*. The deck of the ship was longer than I'd expected, seventy feet or so, and lousy with features: a tower here, a radar dish there, a few inverted lifeboats, a big pile of angular metal in the center with windows at the top of it, probably the place the captain hung out and watched for icebergs or whatever the captain watched out for. There was only a dim light up there, but a door at the bottom of the pile had a brightly illuminated window.

"Thass the main cabin," Dexter said, following my gaze. "Crew gone to be there."

"And the others?" Dexter had at least been on few ships, the ones that had glided over the briny deep to take him to Grenada and Panama.

"They gone to be below. If they still there."

"And where's below?"

He gave me a pitying gaze. "Where you think?"

"I mean, how do we get there?"

"Down the stairs." He waved a hand. The thing I'd been squinting past to see the brightly lighted window turned into a railing surrounding a rectangular hole in the deck. I got up and saw stairs leading down.

"I hate this," I said.

"You gone to stay dry," he said meaningfully.

"How about I give you these shoes, and you go down?"

He put a hand on my back. "How about you take your dainty little feet down them stairs and I stay here and keep a eye out?"

"Okay," I said, "okay. I hope the water's cold."

He hit my butt with a bony knee. I headed for the stairs.

They were steep, and I kept a hand on the rail as I descended. Once down, I was in a metal corridor that was narrower and darker than I would have liked it to be, and the only light I could see came from a single window nine or ten miles in front of me. Keeping my hand against the icy outer hull of the ship, I moved toward it.

The window was in a door, about chin level. I wasn't crazy about the idea of putting my big fat face in front of the window, but there wasn't any choice that I could see. I stepped back, as far from the window as the wall of the corridor would let me, and edged toward the door, hoping the light wouldn't hit my face.

It was milky light, bluish, from cheap fluorescents, and the little window looked onto a very big room. The pane was plastic, scoured with thousands of tiny scratches and smears, and I practically had to put my nose against it before I could see anything. A flicker of motion caught my eye, and I fixed on it and identified it as a television set before I swept the room and saw all the people.

There were lots of them, maybe hundreds, and they all seemed to be men. They sat, packed against one another, watching the Masters of the Shaolin Temple kick the stuffings out of the imperial guard. A fat, bare-stomached guy in baggy black trousers got bounced into a tree, and they all laughed.

Everett was going to hear about this.

I was starting up the stairs when I heard someone on the deck above me. There was a dark space under the stairs, and I was beneath them in about the time it took to unbuckle my belt. I pulled it through the loops in what was beginning to be a practiced gesture, and a foot hit the stairs and stopped. The foot was bare.

"Yo," Dexter whispered.

He was waiting for me at the top of the stairs, rubbing his arms against the cold and looking past me toward the crew's cabin. "Six guys in there," he said. "They dancing to the music."

"I have to look," I said. "See if Charlie's there. Cargo's downstairs."

"Wo, Everett. Look fast. I too old for this shit."

There were indeed three male Chinese couples practicing 1970s disco moves to a Cantonese rendition of "Stayin' Alive." A table was littered with bottles of cognac. None of the six dancers was Charlie, but I recognized one of them from the merry band who had barged into that alley in Chinatown only—what?—two nights before. Working my belt back into place, I ran to the grapple and climbed over, clutching the rope for dear life.

"Remember," I said to Dexter. "Small splash."

With gravity on my side, going down was easier. Hands grasped my pants and guided me on deck, and I turned to see Tran. "Push off," he said. "Quick."

I joined him and Captain Snow in shoving against the side of the tanker, and when we were an arm's length apart she picked up a long gaff, put its business end against the ship, and we all shoved on it. We drifted away, six, then eight, feet, and the rope hanging from the ship's side suddenly began to whip from side to side, and the grapple and Dexter hit the water at about the same time. I hauled in on the rope, scanning the water for Dexter. He surfaced a moment later, spitting water, and grabbed the end of the gaff we held out to him.

Thirty seconds later the engines had been cut in and Dexter was toweling himself dry on a sheet Tran had fetched from the cabin. Then, at a word from Dexter, he went back in and brought Everett.

"You lied to us," I said to him. The freighter was well behind us now, and I didn't have to whisper. "You brought us out here hoping we'd get caught. You wasted our time. You got my friend here wet, and, what's worst of all, you forced him to reveal his taste in underwear."

"They just kisses," Dexter grumbled, buttoning his shirt.

"I thought Charlie was there," Everett said. He couldn't keep his eyes on me; they kept shifting to Dexter.

"You're not taking us seriously," I said. "That's a mistake." I reached down and picked up the knife from its resting place in the coil of rope.

"Wait." Everett ran the tip of his tongue over his lips. "I was wrong."

"You were indeed." I cut the grapple off the rope. "And you were wrong to be wrong. Get his shoulders, Dexter. Tran, hold on to his legs."

The two of them moved into position, and I wound the rope around his waist, making three coils for safety's sake. I was fumbling with the knot when Captain Snow pushed my hands aside and said, "Allow me. You couldn't tie a granny around your granny." She tugged the rope upward until it was beneath his arms, tied something large and complicated over his sternum, tugged it hard enough to make Everett gasp, and went back to the wheel.

"Not over the stern, over the side," she said. "Avoid the propellers."

Everett screamed something that sounded like the gull Tran had caught, and he kept screaming as Dexter and I hoisted him sideways and tossed him into the water. He bounced once, like a skipping stone, and then sank, and I ran to the rope and paid out a few yards' worth and watched him bob up, still screaming, three or four yards behind the boat. He trailed behind us like living chum, fighting to keep his head above water as he zigzagged from one of the churning trails of our wake to the other.

"Not too long," the captain said, working the steel Zippo again. "Hypothermia. Guy's got no fat."

We left him out there for five minutes, until we burst through the fogbank and the lights of shore blinked their welcome. He'd stopped screaming by then, although he hadn't stopped struggling for air. Captain Snow cut the motors and we pulled Everett in, accompanied by a castanet orchestra that I identified as his teeth. When he was flat on his back on the deck, she punched the engines in, hard this time, and the front end of the boat lifted itself out of the water as we surged forward.

"No more bullshit," I said, kneeling next to him.

He shook his head, trying to press his jaws together before he fractured his molars.

"Take him below," I said to Tran. "Warm him up a little." Tran cut the rope and got Everett to his feet, but he stumbled twice before he reached the doorway.

As we pulled into the dock at Marina Del Rey, Captain Snow lighted another cigarette and gave Dexter a grin. "Satisfied with the service?"

"You do bar mitzvahs?" He gave her the grin back with interest, the kind of interest I hadn't seen since Carter was president.

"Your friend here knows how to reach me." She took off the cap and fluffed out the frizzy dark hair, and Tran came out of the cabin propelling a soaking Everett in front of him. "If you want to, I mean. There's a phone on the boat."

"My," Dexter said, making two sweet syllables out of it. "All the comforts."

"Do you mind?" I asked. "We've got to get Everett home before he flatlines."

"On the way," Dexter said. He touched an index finger to the bridge of Captain Snow's vulnerable-looking nose and said, "Permission to go ashore?"

"What if I say no?" Captain Snow said.

Halfway up the dock, in between kicking at Everett's sodden heels to help him along, he turned to me and allowed himself a smirk. "It's the shorts," he said. "Gets 'em every time."

17

Cave Fishing

I'd overstated the case when I described Claude B. Tiffle
to Dexter as a white man. Claude Tiffle had virtually no
color at all. He looked like something that had evolved
underground: eyes as pale and soiled as mushrooms, hair
like alfalfa sprouts, a sparse mustache that looked like a
scraggle of centipede's legs. Fat, wet, white lips it was
easy to imagine him licking, a dirty dimple in his chin
that you could have sharpened a pencil in, and a belly
so beery I expected to hear it slosh when he got up.

Four weary-looking young Chinese women, whom
Dexter had nicknamed Weepy, Bleary, Mopey, and
Snowbell, had reluctantly passed me, like the baton in a
relay no one wants to win, toward the sanctum of Tiffle's office in the back room of the cottage, the one Tran
and I had seen lighted first.

My watch said four P.M. Everett was reclining in Dexter's bathtub, wrapped in an honest-to-god straitjacket
Dexter had proudly pulled from his closet, thereby jus-
tifying all my suspicions about what went on in that
glittering, clinical decor. Tran and Dexter and I had been
watching in turns for most of the day, timing the arrivals
and exits of the staff and getting to know them by sight,

with the odd man out racing to Dexter's apartment to relieve the one keeping Everett company. Although the four women worked from eight-thirty or nine to six, Tiffle himself didn't make his morning appearance until eleven or so, probably enervated by his exertions with Charlie Wah's slave girl of the previous evening.

Tiffle's tardiness, I thought, could be a problem.

Nevertheless, I'd have watched for another full day, making sure that the timetable was right, except that a clock I didn't know how to reset was ticking its way toward the moment when the little boats would take the pilgrims on their last short sail into slavery.

The pilgrims had been on my mind a lot.

"They're peasants," Everett had said defensively the evening before, speaking from the porcelain pocket of Dexter's bathtub. "They've worked like slaves their whole lives."

"They had a choice then," I said. How many of them had served my food, broken their backs in the fields that grew the vegetables I bought, laundered my shirts, inhaled the carcinogenic fumes of the dry-cleaning fluids that allowed me, on rare occasions, to look dapper? How much had I profited from Charlie's game?

"Made they own money then, too," Dexter said, bending low over Everett like he wanted to test his teeth on Everett's throat.

"They wanted to come here," Everett said, kicking his feet, which were about all he could move. "They knew."

"They didn't know they'd get cheated," I said. "They didn't know about the dirty little fake-INS tricks. They didn't know their papers would be shit."

"They *have* to be," Everett squealed, thrashing to get away from Dexter. "Otherwise they'll escape."

"Wrong audience, Jack," Dexter said.

"Chinese are very sneaky," Everett said, as though he were describing a race someone had once told him about. "It costs money to get them here. Ships are expensive, you know."

"What the profit margin?" Dexter asked, straightening.

"Well . . ." Everett began.

Dexter brought his teeth together with a snap. "In dollars. How many? Right now."

Everett looked at me imploringly.

"He's with me, remember?" I said.

"They pay thirty," Everett said. He pursed his lips. "We make ten."

"*How* much?" Dexter demanded.

"Twenty."

"Your eyes," Dexter said meaningfully.

"Twenty-five," Everett said. "Twenty-five."

"So you the big humanitarian, bringing them here and putting them to work for—how many years you say?" he asked me.

"Three," I said, "for starters."

"Your brothers," Dexter said forcefully. "Shit, man, I was you, I'd be ashamed to look Chinese. Three years. You know, they ain't gonna get those years *back*, those years *gone*, asshole."

"That's the way it works," Everett said, looking genuinely puzzled. "I don't make the rules. I just follow orders."

"Shame we ain't got no Jews here," Dexter said. "You could offend everybody."

"When are they going to come off the ship?" I asked.

Everett visibly abandoned hope. He started to make a word, but the breath behind it escaped without shape or meaning. He shook his head.

"I think you still cold," Dexter said. "How about some hot water?"

"I don't know," Everett said immediately.

Dexter put a hand on the tap.

"No, really, honestly, I don't know. Only Charlie knows." He sounded on the verge of tears. "Charlie sets it up with the businesses for the pickup and lets us know about an hour before it's time to move them. Honest.''

"And where's Charlie?''

"Nobody ever knows where Charlie is."

"*Real* hot water," Dexter reminded him, a hand on the tap again.

"But *think* about it," Everett shrilled. "Charlie's the boss. If anything goes wrong, it's Charlie's head. He's not going to tell us anything. Chinese are *sneaky*."

"Charlie's head," I said, "sounds good to me."

"One more time," Dexter said. "When they gonna get moved?''

Everett just squeezed his eyes closed and shook his head, waiting for the hot water.

So at five till four the following day, feeling jumpy, guilty, and seriously sleep-deprived, I left Tran in the driver's seat and rang the bell to Tiffle's little realm.

Once inside I found that the staff member we'd dubbed Weepy sat at the front desk behind a nameplate that said FLORENCE LAM. Bleary, Mopey, and Snowbell seemed to have no fixed places of abode: they passed listlessly back and forth with papers in their hands, guiding me toward Tiffle's lair each time I took a wrong turn, which was as often as possible: I didn't know exactly what my agenda for the conversation was, other than to galvanize Tiffle's greed glands to the point where they'd bounce him out of bed for an early morning meet, but I knew I wanted a look at the inside of the cottage. Snowbell was a knockout, pale and slender beneath a tapered shag of hair that would have prompted Eleanor to stop her in the street and ask who cut it.

"Mr. Skinker," Tiffle said in a fat, damp voice as he rose from his desk and put a hand on his belly, presumably to keep it from flopping down and overturning his desk, "what can I do you for?" He followed his *mot* with a chuckle, one wit to another.

"Actually," I said, shaking hands with a wad of well-chewed gum, "it's *Dr.* Skinker." I was wearing my hair parted on the left, which made it stand up here and there, a pair of horn-rimmed glasses, patched over the nose with adhesive, that I'd found long ago in a parking lot, and a sober, submissive dark suit. Tran had talked me out of the false mustache.

"The good doctor," Tiffle wheezed merrily. "Saw-bones or phud?"

I made a prim *moue*. "Neither. Doctor of Divinity."

"Never enough divinity in the world, wurf, wurf." He held out a Chinese lacquer box and whisked the top off it. "Smoke? No, I guess not. Not in your line, is it? Mind if I do?" He lit one without waiting for an answer, the fat lips hugging it like a living pudding. It didn't take imagination to see why he hadn't gone into criminal law. A shoplifter facing a jury with Tiffle for the defense would have probably gotten the gas chamber. "So anyhoo," he said, spreading the arms of his chair and squeezing himself between them in a cloud of smoke, "what's on your mind?"

"I want to set up a church," I said. "In this community."

He extracted the cigarette from his mouth and regarded it. It was soaking. "Don't you need a bishop or something? Not really a job for a lawyer."

"A church is a business like any other."

His interest was fading. "News to me."

A car backfired in the street, and I turned my nervous jump into a perspicacious chin-scratch. "You may not be aware of the strides our brethren have been making in the Korean community."

"Don't know much about Koreans. Pretty women. Not, I mean, that you—"

I let him flounder until he ran down and then permitted myself a thin ecclesiastical smile. "Very pretty," I said.

"Taller than Chinese," said the connoisseur, lipping the cigarette again and focusing on the adult video loop he probably called his imagination.

"Some of them are exquisite."

"Still," he said, blinking his way back into the room, "a church."

"People come into a community," I said, resisting the impulse to rub my hands together, "seeking brotherhood. They are strangers among strangers."

"Nicely put," Tiffle said dutifully. "Strangers among strangers."

"Miles from home and family, oceans away from old ties. Whom can they trust?" *Whom* might have been overdoing it. "Where can they be sure of meeting people who don't want merely to take advantage of them? Oh, I know about the tongs, but man to man, Mr. Tiffle, we know they're not always committed to the high road."

He nodded, his mouth slightly open, and removed the cigarette. Without looking down, he dried the filter on his tie. The tie was already wet. "Yeah," he said, waiting. "You know, I'm very busy at the—"

"In the house of the Lord, they can relax. When people are relaxed, when they feel safe and secure, they are generous."

The word pacified him. He took a long drag that consumed the cigarette down to the waterline and dropped it into an ashtray. "In the Korean community," I said, pursuing my theme, "membership in the best churches is sought after. It is expensive, and donations are substantial. And in exchange, the pilgrims receive not only spiritual succor, but also, ah, networking opportunities. Once the new arrivals are established, they literally compete to bring in others. It's like—how can I describe it?—like a self-replicating franchise. A very profitable franchise."

"This is interesting," Tiffle acknowledged. "Helping people to get established and all. But what would a lawyer do?" He reached toward the cigarette box again, thought better of it, and contented himself with giving his straining shirt a tug.

I picked up the pace. "A major real estate transaction

is the first step. We need to acquire an existing church. I don't have to tell you how much that might run into. Seven figures, certainly." He lost interest in the shirt and drummed his fingers on the desk. "We would want you to handle the financial details, hold the money, set up escrow. People sometimes misunderstand when clerics attempt to function as businessmen, especially when such large sums are involved."

"You bet," he said, shooting me a look out of his pale little eyes. "Well, sure, I could do that."

"Then, of course, the church will need a board of directors, like any profitable enterprise. Some of them must be Chinese; that would only be right. But the board's chairman should be someone familiar with business law, someone who can advise us on how to put the profits to work in the best interests of the congregation, but without doing—or seeming to do, Mr. Tiffle—anything inappropriate."

He made a sticky little tent of his fingers. "Define inappropriate."

Right. Smartass. I took a breath. "One of the principles of the founder of Christianity was to render unto Caesar that which belongs to Caesar. I would define as inappropriate anything that would bring Caesar's representatives to the door, feeling that they are not being rendered enough."

He gave me a long, doubting look. "Churches aren't taxable."

"Nonreligious financial activity undertaken with church capital sometimes is, though. It traditionally depends on two things: first, how divorced from religion the activity is, and second, how conspicuous it is. Spending the money, I mean."

His nostrils widened. "How much money?"

I sat back and breathed in. "Lots."

"Have you had dinner?"

"I have an engagement, with a missionary, in fact. But it's interesting you should suggest dinner, because if we were to decide to go into business together, I would have to insist on meeting you frequently outside of office hours.'' I raised a hand. ''Once again, the appearance of propriety.''

He went for it. ''Yeah, yeah. Well, early, late, it's the same to me. Except I'm generally tied up from seven to eight in the evening. Personal.''

''Of course,'' I said maliciously. ''A man can't spend all his time at the old grind. Anyway, mornings are better for me.''

''So mornings it is. Tell me again. Why me?''

''Your connections. Your reputation. Your expertise. Mr. Tiffle, I shouldn't say this before we've signed some papers, but you're probably unique.''

''Fine,'' he said, leaning back to a groan of protest from his chair. ''I'd handle the transaction, direct business operations. That it?''

It almost sounded legal. ''And, of course, we'd want your help with the newer immigrants. You deal with hundreds of them. In addition to your regular stipends, there would be an emolument for each Chinese soul— each solvent Chinese soul—you bring to the fold. You could be very, very helpful as we build the flock.'' We exuded oil at each other.

''Yeah,'' he said, yanking at his shirt again. ''I could.''

''I need a shower,'' I said to Tran as I got into the rented car, a gray Flazoolie or something else I'd never heard of. Tran had waited out the meeting in it, half a block away, as arranged.

''Long time,'' he said, sounding nervous. He looked into the rearview mirror.

''Believe me, it seemed a lot longer to me than it did to you.''

''You can get him early?''

''I can get him out of the john if I need him.'' Tran jerked his head around to look behind us again. ''Why do you keep trying to dislocate your neck?''

''Somebody following me.''

''Oh.'' I involuntarily turned in the same direction. ''Who?''

''Chinese. Not there now.''

''Well, balls,'' I said. ''When did you see him?''

''Maybe last night. Today for sure, while you're inside, two times. Not there now.''

''Well, let's get out of Chinatown. You drive, I'll watch.'' I angled the passenger-side mirror so I could see behind us, and Tran picked up Sunset and followed its curves more or less west. Traffic was building, and it was impossible to pick up any single car as suspicious. Absolutely everybody seemed to be Chinese.

''What kind of car?''

''Hyundai. White.''

''Nothing there now.''

''There before.''

''It's time for a new car.''

Ten blocks later I told the smoothie at the rental agency that we needed something with a little more pickup, and he tried to talk us into a Corvette at several hundred dollars a day. We compromised on a little BMW that set Tran's pulse racing, and I let him drive it out.

''You see Weepy?'' he asked as he pulled into traffic.

''Florence Lam,'' I said. Florence was the one who'd opened the office, arriving twenty minutes before the other women. Like Tiffle, and unlike the rest of the staff, Florence Lam didn't go out for lunch; if the circles beneath her eyes were any indication, she was probably too busy. I figured when Tiffle was hungry he just sacrificed a goat in the back room.

''How old Snowbell?'' Tran was sharing the American male experience of ego infusion by automobile.

''Too old for you.''

''Eleanor prettier anyway.''

''Eleanor,'' I said, ''is *definitely* too old for you. Last night, you think you saw the guy outside Tiffle's?''

"Yes."

"And today, he picked you up around Tiffle's."

"I already say so."

"That's interesting."

"Why?"

"Because of what it suggests he doesn't know."

"Pardon?"

"He keeps picking us up at Tiffle's, but never anywhere else. Well,'' I said, "we can either wait for him to make a move, or we can make one ourselves. And if we wait for him, he'll have an agenda. Let's see if we can't take him."

Tran gave the wheel an eager little back-and-forth. "When?"

"Now. Rush hour's good." Even as I said it, my heart sped up. "Damn, I wish Dexter wasn't home."

"Not home. Eating. Dexter always eating."

My blood pressure rose. "Who the hell's watching Everett?"

"Friend, he say."

"Great. A friend. Well, nothing we can do about it now. Where's he eating?"

"House of Breakfast. Olympic Boulevard. Dexter only eat breakfast, but he eat it four times a day."

I checked behind us again. "Let's go interrupt him."

We cruised Tiffle's four times: Tran driving, me sitting on my lungs in the passenger seat so I couldn't be seen through the window. By then Dexter was stationed in his maroon Lincoln on the little dead-end section of Granger Street across Hill. If the tail made a move, he'd have to get across Hill somehow, but I figured he'd manage.

On the fourth pass, Tran said, "Nothing."

I turned to wave Dexter to join us, and we met a block away. "Who's with Everett, anyway?" I demanded.

"Somebody make Everett wish he never learned English. You gone to meet him."

"I can't wait. I need you to follow Florence Lam home."

Dexter made an elaborate show of scratching his head. "Florence Lam."

"Weepy," I clarified.

"I like Snowbell."

"Me, too," Tran said.

"Florence Lam," I said. "And don't let her see you yet."

"You didn't have to say that," Dexter said. "Hurt a man's feelings."

"We'll meet back here at ten and cruise old Granger Street again."

"She got a eye for a man," Dexter said, "she gone to spot me."

18

The Underground Railroad

Esther Summerson's eyes swam supernaturally large and blue through the dusty lenses above me. I was standing on the first step of the porch, looking at her through a fine mesh of nylon, trying to figure out how anything that was likely to happen in the next half hour or so could possibly do anyone any good.

"Yes?" she said. She had the distracted air of someone who is listening to music in her head. The screen door was closed and, I imagined, latched against whatever slavering beast L.A. might decide to deal up. When she'd turned on the porch light from inside it had brought moths, and they swooped and fluttered against the glass, looking for whatever it is moths look for in a light.

"Hello, Mrs. Summerson," I said. I stepped up onto the porch and gave a little wave, hoping to attract some attention. "I'm Eleanor's friend, remember?"

The magnified eyelids came down with an almost audible clank, and when she opened them again she was back in the present and she knew me. "But of course, and how nice," she said, sounding like a missionary again. "It's Mr. Grist. How are the twins?"

"Eating and sleeping," I said, exhausting my fund of baby knowledge. "May I come in?"

She hesitated as though she were translating the words. "Oh. Well, certainly you may. I'm sorry. This seems to be one of my foggy days." She fiddled with the screen door and then held it open.

"I've brought someone along," I said, moving forward, and Tran stepped into view.

Leaning slightly, she peered at him in the half light. She started a smile, but the smile turned into a rictus, and she turned her whole head, birdlike, to look at me, stepped back, and used both hands to slam the inner door. It hit my foot and bounced back against her, knocking her a step backward. I lunged and grabbed her shoulders before she went over backward. Tall as she was, she was even heavier and more solid than I'd expected, and my back creaked alarmingly again.

Her eyes were clamped shut now, and she was shuddering violently. "Go away," she said, mostly breath. She smelled of powder and lavender.

"Where's Lo?"

"You should be ashamed of yourself." She fluttered ineffectually at my hands, gathering strength. "Pretending to be Eleanor's friend. Anyway, you can't get Lo now. None of you can. He's in China, where no one will find him."

"We're going to talk," I said. "Come in, Tran. Close the door."

She made little shooing motions in his direction. "You can't. He can't. I'll call the police."

"You know you won't. How are you going to explain Tran?"

"Please," she said, "I need to sit down. My legs are shaking."

"You know where the living room is, Tran?"

He nodded. "Where she give me cookies."

"Take her there. Let her sit. Keep her in one place."

He took her arm very gently, saying, "Come, please,

Missus.'' She tried to tug herself free and then allowed him to lead her slowly down the hall, talking to herself in Cantonese. I stood, inhaling the aromas of cooking oil and sachet, and waiting for something else, the smell of men: bodies, cigarettes, hair oil, anything that didn't fit into this last, exclusively female, missionary outpost of old China. Pulling my cold little nine-millimeter automatic from my jacket pocket, I searched the house.

The first floor was crowded with heavy furniture and relics of a life of dour and earnest enterprise among the heathen. The walls bristled with photos of rigorously stiff men and women, white and Chinese, the Chinese eyes fixed politely to one side of the camera lens, so as not to stare at the viewer. More groups of solemn Chinese children, like the ones pictured in the living room, assembled portentously in front of the weathered schoolhouse—or another just like it—on the barren plain to have their portraits made. I counted ten of these, all framed and dated, and then stopped counting. Books were everywhere, in both Chinese and English: Bibles, commentaries on the Bible, commentaries on the commentaries, biographies and autobiographies of missionaries, Chinese dictionaries, histories of the Middle Kingdom.

Front room, old-fashioned drawing room, halfbathroom, kitchen with its heavy wok and a mound of half-chopped vegetables, enough only for one, little maid's room with a desk occupying most of it, covered with correspondence in Chinese. A door under the stairwell, the one that should have led to the basement, was locked. The lock was heavy, bright new brass. I put it on hold and went up the stairs to the second floor as quietly as I could, knowing that anyone up there would have heard us come in. Tran and Mrs. Summerson were talking softly but urgently in the living room, all aspirates like wind through trees.

The upstairs was virginal and nostalgic, a doleful museum. The big bedroom contained a single bed heavily flounced in chintz and some very good Chinese rose-wood furniture. On a small bamboo table next to the bed I found a pair of men's silver hairbrushes, perhaps a century old, and in my mind's eye I saw her packing and unpacking them for her husband each time the two of them were transferred or forced to flee. The rest of the house may have been dusty, but the brushes had been polished until the engraved initials *R.D.S.* were almost rubbed away.

Directly above the table in an oval frame hung a hand-tinted photograph of a young woman with lustrous and adventurous pale eyes and a heavy coil of dark brown hair: the young Mrs. Summerson, decades and deaths and continents ago. It was a complicated face, bold and demure at the same time, the face of someone quietly waiting for something momentous to happen.

A long connecting bathroom, unexpectedly cluttered and wet, led to the guest room. The bed sagged in the middle as though it had been folded lengthwise for decades. Everything was musty and coated with a fine fall of dust, weeks and weeks' worth of dust.

When I went down the stairs I was on tiptoe. I found Tran sitting alone in the living room, looking up at the somber Chinese schoolchildren.

I checked the corners of the room, just to make sure. "Where is she?"

"Making tea," he said. "She need tea."

"Why aren't you with her?"

He avoided my gaze. "Want to cry, her."

"And I thought you were dangerous," I said.

Mrs. Summerson was defying popular wisdom by watching the kettle, but when she turned at the sound of my step she was alert and watchful and dry-eyed.

"I need to go downstairs," I said.

Her eyes went to the gun in my hand, and I tucked it into my belt. "I can't open that door," she said.

"Bananas. We both know what's been happening here."

"Do you really think so?" She almost smiled at me. "Be that as it may, I don't have the key. It's lost."

"You're a really terrible liar."

She turned back to the kettle, which had started to hiss steam. "I know," she said, using both hands to lift it to the sink. "I've never been any good at it. But I fooled you before." She sounded proud, like a little girl who's tricked an adult.

"Where's the key?"

For what seemed like a long time, she busied herself with pouring the water into a ceramic teapot and spooning tea from a canister into a little metal infuser. Then she dropped the infuser in, capped the pot carefully, and said, "What's been happening here, then?" She had her back to me. "If you're so smart."

"I don't know all the details, but you—you and Lo, I mean—have been smuggling your old students out of China."

Her spine straightened, but all she did was put the teapot and three cups onto a heavily carved wooden tray. Her hands weren't shaking now. "Aren't you the clever boy," she said. "That must be why they sent you to hunt for Lo."

"They didn't send me. I'll tell you about it in a minute. Where's the key to the basement?"

"I told you, he's in China." She still hadn't turned to face me.

"And I believe you. He's long gone. I just want to see the setup."

"It's quite nice, really. The key is around my neck. Turn your back, please."

"You know I can't do that, Mrs. Summerson."

She rested a hand against the pot, testing its temperature. "What a pity you're such a reptile. Eleanor will be so disappointed to know."

"Call her. She knows what I'm doing."

"Don't be silly. Eleanor wouldn't have anything to do with one of them."

"I'm not. One of them, I mean."

"Then why are you with that boy?" She turned slowly to face me, and when I saw her in profile I was struck by how loosely the heavy clothes fit her. There was no fat left, nothing but bone and muscle and will.

"They made him kill his brother and then they killed his cousin. His girl cousin. They cut her throat. He's on our side now."

The big eyes probed me. "How terrible," she said conversationally. She'd seen worse. "But it's not as simple as sides. There are lives at stake."

"I know," I said. "Horace's is one of them. Look, I can explain it all in a minute. Just give me the key, please, and then we can get down to business."

"Oh, my. I suppose if I don't give it to you, you'll just take it anyway."

"No," I said, suddenly feeling the lack of sleep. "I won't."

She nodded slowly and lifted a hand to pat at her hair. "Then I'll give it to you." She reached around behind her neck and her long fingers located something. She pulled a long, thin gold chain out of her dress and handed it to me. Dangling from its end was a double-serrated brass key. "The light's on the left at the top of the stairs."

"Thanks." I was already moving.

I heard the lid of the teapot being lifted. "Lemon?"

"That would be lovely." The key fit easily into the lock and turned with no resistance at all. The light switch was right where she'd said it would be.

The stairs descended steeply and doglegged to the right. When the room came into view, I stopped and looked at it for a long time. Then I laughed.

It was perfect. Wall-to-wall carpet on both floor and ceiling to absorb sound, a plump couch, and a double bed. Bookshelves sagged beneath a spy's library, crammed with magazines about American life and books and pamphlets in Chinese. A television set and a VCR, equipped with earphones. A treadmill and some dumb-bells to keep the muscles functioning. The bathroom had both a step-in shower and an old claw-footed tub. It was, in all, a lot nicer than my house. Anyone could have lived there indefinitely, deprived only of the sight of sun and sky. And Uncle Lo, I was willing to bet, had been down there with his feet up, watching kung-fu movies on the VCR while Eleanor and I were cunningly cross-examining Mrs. Summerson.

Some papers on the bed caught my eye: Photocopies of old but official-looking documents in Chinese. One of them featured the picture of a young Chinese man who strongly resembled Horace Chan. I scooped them up and went back up the stairs, still laughing.

"Of course he was there," Mrs. Summerson said several minutes later. "He was right down there, waiting for his papers." She was balancing a saucer on her knee and blowing in a genteel fashion at a cup of steaming tea.

"Papers to get him to China?"

She shook her head. "No, but good enough to get him to Canada. The really good papers come from Canada. And then, it's easier to get to China from Canada."

"And these," I said, indicating the photocopies, "belonged to Eleanor's father. He took them from her mother's house." Peter Lau's phrase came back to me. "He was ghost-processing himself, wasn't he? He terrorized Eleanor's family so he could be someone who was dead."

Her eyes widened behind the cloudy lenses, and she hesitated. Tran leaned forward and put a soothing palm on her arm. She smiled gratefully at him. "He needed them desperately," she said. "To get back in, I mean. He would never have taken the children otherwise. He knew he had no time left. There were only so many places he could go, and they had all his papers—I mean everything. It's always safest to have papers with a real Chinese person's name on them. He and Eleanor's father are about the same age, and there's no record of Mr. Chan's death.''

My surprise must have showed.

"Lo," she said with some pride, "is a very smart man. He was an official in those days, but he knew everything had gone wrong with China and he had an eye on the future even then. When men of his age passed away in his district, he burned their death papers. Then he bought the birth and school papers from the family. He created unimpeachable biographies for the dead men and sent the papers off to Beijing with his own photograph. He was probably paying someone to process them. By the time things opened up again, he had any number of valid passports hidden away. Unfortunately, he didn't have them with him when things went wrong this time."

I had a lot of questions, but I settled on one close to home. "Why didn't he buy Mr. Chan's papers?"

"He got too involved with—" She hesitated and blew on her tea again. "With the family," she said at last.

"Oh, good lord," I said, feeling myself blush.

"Eleanor doesn't know," Mrs. Summerson said quickly. "I really think Mrs. Chan was the love of Lo's life. Not that anything is simple with Lo."

Chalk up another one for Mrs. Chan. Tran was standing in front of the picture of the Chinese children, staring at it as though he were about to step into it. He'd withdrawn from the conversation, except to thank Mrs. Summerson for the tea.

"Why didn't he just ask them for the papers?" I said. "They would have given them to him. Why take the twins and make everybody crazy like that?" Nothing was simple with Lo, she'd said, but I wasn't so sure. For the Chans, and maybe for Mrs. Summerson, Lo was a snapshot taken thirty years before. In the thirty years they'd been gazing at the snapshot, a different picture had been developing over decades, hidden from their view. How does anyone know who an old friend will become over time?

"He *couldn't* ask them. He didn't want them to know what he needed. Suppose those men had traced him to the Chans through his notebooks, as he was sure they would, and suppose the Chans had told them about the papers. They can buy Chinese Immigration, you know. If they couldn't, they couldn't stay in business. There might have been men on the lookout for Eleanor's father at every checkpoint in China."

It was so simple, even if Lo was so complicated. "I'll be damned," I said, without thinking. "Sorry."

"I've heard worse in my life," Mrs. Summerson said, "and in many languages. I wish I had some cookies for Tran."

"I okay," Tran said to the picture.

"You should go to New Orleans," Mrs. Summerson said maternally. "You could fish for shrimp."

I went back to basics. "How did Lo usually get back to China?"

"The way he came, on the ship. That's why he wasn't carrying extra papers."

"Okay." I closed my eyes and ran it past. "He came in, he got betrayed, he had to get out, he stole the kids to get to Mr. Chan's papers." She nodded. "I'll be damned," I said again.

"I hope not," Mrs. Summerson said.

"Me, too. Okay, so how your dodge worked, at least most of the time," I suggested, "was that you'd give Lo the name of an old student—"

"No," she said promptly. "The other way around. Lo would find them and talk to them, and if they wanted to come out, he'd write me a letter. We had a code," she confided, sounding very pleased with herself. "He didn't want to use names in case the letters were read, so we made small copies of the class pictures, and he'd work numbers into the letter that told me what year, what row in the picture, and what position in the row, counting from the right. Chinese read from right to left, you know." She laughed unexpectedly. "The first time we did it, I wasn't thinking, and I counted from the left. I was expecting a lovely girl named, oh, what *was* her name? Daisy Wang, that was it, and when the day came I had a great hulking man named Warren Lu. And that was before I'd fixed the basement, so he had to sleep upstairs in the guest room and use my bathroom and everything. Oh, it *was* a mess." The big guileless eyes came back to mine. "You're sure Eleanor knows about this?"

"As I said, call her."

"That's all right. You said you wouldn't take the key by force, and that was good enough for me." She turned and beamed at Tran. "And this boy looks—well, different, lighter in spirit. He let me go off for a little cry when I needed one. A soul saved, even if it was at terrible cost." Tran went scarlet and turned to the little ceramic Christ figure Eleanor had picked up, giving it all his attention.

Mrs. Summerson sipped her tea, the cup looking like a demitasse in her big hands. "Where was I?"

"Mechanics," I said. "Lo let you know who was coming, and then he'd pay the first fifteen thousand—"

"Twenty," she said, "and twenty upon their arrival. I paid him back when he arrived, of course."

"Forty," I said, trying to keep my voice neutral.

"You needn't look like that," Mrs. Summerson said, laughing again. "Lo wasn't cheating me. Ten thousand went to his henchman. Is that the term? Henchman?"

"Henchman," Tran said experimentally, trying it on for size.

"*You* know, the man who told you to come here to pick up the, um, swag." She settled back, looking very pleased with herself. "The one who turned Lo in."

"I don't know anything about that."

Her fingers went to a button on the front of her dress and twisted it. "He's the one who told on Lo. They caught him with much more money than he should have had, and he told them all about our little sideline. They were so angry at Lo. It seems the man who runs it all has something against missionaries. Well, in mitigation, some of them are real sticks. Still, his grudge seems disproportionate. They beat Lo quite severely. He was lucky to escape with his life. And now, I don't know what's going to happen to Doreen."

I passed on Doreen for the moment. "Forty thousand dollars is a lot of money."

"It is, isn't it? Tea?" I shook my head, and she poured for herself. "For the longest time I had no idea where to get it."

"Where *did* you?" It sounded rude, but there wasn't much I could do about it.

"I was just going to tell you," she said reprovingly, "when you interrupted me."

"I'm sorry," I said, wondering when the Dormouse would pop out of the teapot.

"I was, as they say these days, sitting on it all the time. Do you have any *idea* what's happened to California real estate values?"

"I've heard something."

"I paid—*we* paid—fifteen thousand dollars for this house. And we paid most of it in cash, too. Dr. Summerson didn't believe in debt. Usury, you know, is prohibited in the Bible." She ran her fingers through her short, thick hair in a gesture oddly reminiscent of Eleanor. I wondered whether Eleanor had gotten it from her.

"Well, seven or eight years ago people started writing me letters about the house, wanting to sell it for me. I threw the letters away at first—they were from people I didn't even know, and they wrote to me by name, and I thought it was presumptuous." She sipped her tea and made a face. "Cold. But finally," she continued, pouring her cup into the pot and then tilting the pot into her cup, "I began to wonder. If all these absolute strangers were sending me letters about the house, what in the world could it be worth? So I invited one of them here, and I told him that I truly wasn't thinking about selling, but could he make a guess at what I would get for it if I did, and he said four hundred thousand dollars.'' Her eyebrows went up. "We ran whole *schools* in China for ten or twenty thousand dollars a year, including food. Well, it seemed like a sin to let such a vast amount of money just stagnate when there was so much good that could be done with it.'' She leaned toward me confidingly, about to share a secret. "Have you ever heard of a home equity loan?''

"Remotely.''

"It's like magic. The house becomes a big checking account. Now, whenever I want to bring someone out, I simply write a check against the house for forty thousand dollars and deposit it in my checking account. It's as easy as that.'' Her big eyes were brighter than I'd ever seen them.

As easy as that. She must have made many bankers very happy. "How many times have you done it?''

"Four,'' she said promptly. "And this time makes five.'' She put a hand to her mouth. "I'm afraid I fibbed about how many times I've seen Lo.''

"This time,'' I said, remembering the name she'd mentioned. "You mean Doreen?''

All the good feeling left her face, and she looked old and confused. "That's a problem,'' she said, "now that Lo is gone. I really don't know what to do about Doreen.''

"Doreen. Does she have a last name?''

"Doreen Wing. A lovely girl, tiny and *so* smart. She spoke French, too.''

"And the problem?''

"Lo's gone, and Lo's henchman, the one who sent Tran here all those times—''

"Right,'' I said.

"Well, even if the henchman is still in place, this

young man," she fretted, glancing at Tran, "isn't. Whoever replaces him won't know where to find me, where
to send this boy's replacement to get the money. If the
second half of Doreen's payment isn't forthcoming,
they'll put her in some dreadful place. Lord knows what
they'll do to her." She had one hand to her mouth, as
if she'd just said something unspeakable.

"Probably nothing," I said with an assurance I didn't
feel. "Put her to work for a couple of years, unless she
runs away and comes to you."

"She has no idea where I am. Lo brought them to me
after the payment was made."

"You're right," I said, not particularly interested.
"It's a problem."

"It's ghastly. That poor little girl, all alone here with
no one to help her." In Mrs. Summerson's mind, Doreen
Wing was eleven years old and would be until she
showed up, graying, on the doorstep. I was trying to
integrate Doreen into the plan, such as it was, when she
added, "Of course, *none* of them will have anyone to
turn to."

I waited, hoping she didn't mean what I thought she
meant. She just gazed at me, perfectly at ease with the
silence. "None of them," I said neutrally.

"The other two hundred or so," Mrs. Summerson
said. "It *is* two hundred, isn't it?"

"One hundred seventy-two," I said. Everett had been
firm about that.

Tran began to laugh.

"You think this is funny?" I demanded.

"Has to be sad or funny. I choose funny." He thought
about it and laughed again.

"What does he mean?" Mrs Summerson didn't actually sound very confused this time, and I wondered
whether I was being manipulated by a seventy-some-
year-old missionary. Still, I'd wondered about the hundred and seventy-two, too. Over and over. It was the
reason we hadn't simply called the INS about the ship:

that and the fact Charlie hadn't been aboard. I'd been poking at the thought of the hundred and seventy-two like a sun blister I was afraid might be malignant, afraid to go any deeper.

"If we can do anything," I said hopelessly, "we will."

She looked from me to Tran and back again. For a moment I thought she was going to smile. "What do you mean, if you can do anything?"

"We, um, we plan to put a little crimp in their operation."

"Good. Then you can rescue them," Mrs. Summerson said, sipping her tea at last.

"We're not set up," I protested, "to rescue the entire adult population of China."

"Well, surely that's figurative," she said.

"Where could I put them?" I asked, just to slow her down.

"A church," she said. "I have one you could use."

"Swell," I said. "A church."

"Simply deliver them to me. 'Deliver the little children unto me,' as Jesus says in one translation."

"I don't know. I mean, I do know. We can't do it. I mean, what are we going to deliver them *in*?"

"The vans," Tran immediately volunteered. "They go to San Pedro in—"

"Shut up," I snapped. He gave me a Vietnamese snicker. It sounded a lot like an American snicker.

"That's rude," Mrs. Summerson said to me. "I can have the church ready in twenty-four hours."

My resistance gave out. "We'll do what we can."

"Good. And if there's anything *I* can do . . ." she said, sounding doubtful.

"Not really," I said cheerlessly. "Not unless you know when they're coming."

"Well, that's easy," she said promptly. "I have to know, so I can get the money. They're coming tomorrow night."

* * *

Chez Tiffle was dark. The cottage was the same vintage as Mrs. Summerson's, and I was reasonably certain that it also had a nice, big, more or less soundproof basement.

Tran and I had cruised the block twice, trolling for our furtive friend, and on the third pass, Tran said: "Here, him."

I was cramped down in the passenger seat, and as much as I dreaded the encounter, the idea of straightening up had a lot of appeal. "You know the drill."

"Sa*low*ly," Tran said, sounding like his brother. He turned left and then left again. One more left brought us onto Hill, a block from the place where Dexter was waiting in the truncated little stretch of Granger. Tran dimmed the lights once as we approached, and when Dexter pulled out into traffic he was behind the white Hyundai.

"Three blind mice," Tran said, eyeing the rearview mirror.

Traffic was a little lighter than I would have liked it to be. "Watch the stoplights. You want to get a yellow one." The light directly in front of us turned from red to green, and Tran slowed the car by a few miles an hour and looked elaborately around, overacting a man searching for something. We were in the right lane, and cars passed us impatiently on the left. One fat clown shoehorned into a tiny Honda Civic honked at us with a sound like a Velcro sneeze.

"They're both through," I said, looking back nervously. "Slow down a little, would you?"

"Who's driving?" Tran asked, braking anyway. He caught the Sunset light, a good long one, on the yellow, and slowed to a stop. Behind us, Dexter pulled his big tubby Lincoln up so that it almost touched the rear bumper of the white Hyundai.

"Here goes," I said, forming the words around my heart, which had decided to move north and take up residence in my mouth. We'd already disconnected the interior light, so I got out of the car on the passenger side without sending up any skyrockets. Hunched over and feeling like Lon Chaney, I worked my way back past three cars until I was to the left of the Hyundai, and then I pulled out the automatic and stood up, approaching the passenger door.

When I yanked it open and shoved the gun inside, the Chinese man in the driver's seat yelped and whipped his head toward me. Then the yelp turned into a sigh, and he narrowed his eyes and pushed the gun aside.

I stood there, listening to my heart booming in my ears. "Where the hell have you been?" I asked Horace Chan.

PART IV

TIME-BINDING

—

Our tidy notions of time and space quickly break down in the realm of the very small. For example, at the subatomic level it is possible to measure both the velocity of a particle and its position, but it is impossible to measure them simultaneously.

—FRANCES STEIG
The Space-Time Intersection

19

—

The Mild Bunch

One-thirty A.M. In the waxy light of yet another Mc-Donald's, my crew looked pasty and ill-matched. I'd been fantasizing the James Gang and gotten the Musicians of Bremen.

I felt like my battery life had been cut to minutes. Horace and Tran were still bickering. The missing Musketeer, Dexter, had disappeared after we worked the snare that had netted us Horace, saying he'd return with a surprise. I wasn't sure I had energy in reserve for a surprise, but it was always hard to say no to Dexter.

Despite fifteen minutes of concentrated explanation, Horace eyed Tran as though he expected him to sprout fangs and dive for the throat. Tran was, after all, half of the reason he'd abandoned the comforts of home and hearth to stalk the mean and lonely streets of vengeance, or whatever the hell he thought he'd been doing. I let them growl at each other while I listened to my internal clock running down and tried to figure out where we were.

In the sixteenth century, a Jesuit priest named Matteo Ricci showed the Chinese how to create a memory palace. The memory palace, a prototypically Renaissance conceit, was an elaborate imaginary edifice intended to help its owner defeat the erosion of time by providing an organizational principle for the storage of a lifetime of mental baggage. The floor plan of the palace guided its owner from idea to idea, detail to detail, simple to complex: the anteroom might be a museum of first things; branching corridors led to ramifications and possibilities; the inner rooms could be furnished with outcomes. The various stories suited perfectly the Renaissance preoccupation with ordering things from highest to lowest. The memory palace wasn't a new concept in Europe even in the sixteenth century, but it was a dazzler for the Chinese, and Ricci was a persuasive salesman, renowned throughout China for his ability to look once at a list of one hundred Chinese ideograms and recite them, in order, weeks later.

My own memory palace, to the extent that I had one, was a replica of the tumbledown shack I called home. At the moment I was filling its rooms with a jumble of places, times, personalities, cultures, dangers, possibilities, drawbacks, wild cards; and no matter how I arrayed them in the cramped rooms of my memory hovel, the rooms kept filling up with corpses. Some of them people I loved.

If the artifice failed to function, it wasn't for lack of furniture. Tran and Peter Lau, Everett and Mrs. Summerson, had given me more data than I could sort into categories and raised more possibilities than I could entertain. No matter how I tried to order them, I wound up piling everything I couldn't fit behind the couch and mentally jumping up and down on it. Well, that was pretty much the way I cleaned house, too.

Tran got up for yet more ice cream, and Horace lapsed into a pallid sulk. I decided the time was right for a heart-to-heart, took another look at his face, and decided I'd been wrong. Okay, discuss plans.

"This is what we want to do," I said to Horace, who responded with a sullen stare. "Let's take our goals in increasing order of difficulty. One. We want to mess this deal of theirs up in a way that makes it harder for them to do it next time. Got that?''

He nodded without much interest.

"Damn it, we can't get Lo," I said for the third time. "He's in China, remember?"

"I'm Chinese," Horace said meaningfully, "but I speak English."

I retreated. "So we want to screw up the deal. If Tran knows all he says he knows, I think I can do that."

"Yeah?" Horace asked. He put his index fingers under his eyes and rotated them up and down, and I stopped feeling irritated. He was at least as tired as I was.

"Two. We want to put Claude B. Tiffle somewhere dark and small for a long time. If we can do the first, we can do the second."

"Tiffle," Tran spat, materializing with a strawberry ice-cream cone in his hand.

"Old Claude B.," I said. "Three. We want to get Charlie Wah. We want to cross him up so he comes out of wherever he's hiding and runs the wrong way. Into us, preferably." No one said anything. "And that's going to be tough.

"And four," I said, abandoning hope for the discussion, "we want to get out of this alive, in a way that won't endanger your family, Horace, when the assholes sort this out."

I glanced at Horace, and got more reaction than I'd expected. He was staring past me and above me, looking like the crack of doom had just opened in the parking lot.

"Five," Dexter said, dropping a hand onto my shoulder, "we want to free the slaves."

"I was getting to that," I said, and then I looked beyond him and into a face that would have stopped a grizzly in mid-charge. It belonged to a man the color of fresh asphalt who might have been six and a half feet tall and who might have weighed two hundred and ninety pounds, and who might have been the end of civilization as we know it. He wore a pink Bryn Mawr sweatshirt, baggy blue jeans, and a black watch cap rolled low over his eyebrows.

"This here Horton Doody," Dexter said. "He my surprise."

"Horton Doody?" I said involuntarily.

The obsidian marbles Horton Doody used for eyes rolled slowly toward me and fell into a slot that locked them on my face. "Somethin wrong with that?" he growled, bumping the bottom of the aural ocean.

"Horton a knife man," Dexter offered tactfully.

"Wrong?" I said immediately. "What could be wrong? Fine old name, Doody. One of the Philadelphia Doodys?"

The left corner of Horton Doody's mouth twitched upward. He probably thought he was smiling.

"So, Mr. Doody," I said, "you're joining our merry band?" Hope made a belated reentrance, wearing a tutu and gossamer wings.

"Dexter say money in it," Horton Doody rumbled.

"Horton here fond of the green," Dexter advised. "Take a lot of cash to sustain all that flash."

"Whuff," Horton Doody said. I think it was a laugh.

"He already been watchin Everett at a hundred an hour."

"Big job," Horton Doody said, sounding like an entire bowling alley.

"Of course, money ain't everything," Dexter said. "Horton want to free the slaves, too, even if they Orientals."

Something came to mind. "Who's watching Everett?"

"Horton's bigger brother." Dexter said. "He in, too."

"The Doody Brothers?" Horace asked, looking confused. His frame of reference, on rock and roll and practically everything else, had stopped expanding in 1979. "How many more are there?"

"Five," Horton Doody thundered. "I the baby."

"I take it all back," Horace said to me. "You might have the help you need."

"This little Oriental peewee name Tran," Dexter said to Horton Doody. "Big bald Oriental name Horace."

"Horace?" Horton Doody asked. His eyebrows did something complicated under the cap. "Whuff, whuff."

"People who live in glass houses," Horace said, passing a hand self-consciously over his remaining hair.

"And the faggot asked you about his merry band name Simeon. Think he got a big brain. He the one gone suicide us all."

"Whuff," Horton Doody said. He was having a great time.

Dexter looked at each of us in turn. "What a bunch," he said. "Look like somethin in a bum's pockets."

"Count Horace out," I said. "He's going home."

Horace slapped the table. "Goddamn it, Simeon, stop speaking for me."

"But you've got a fam—"

"I know what I've got. And we've got Horton Doody, here."

"He only one man," Tran said. Horton Doody gave him a glance that knocked him back a step.

"Yeah, but he a man we can all hide behind." Dexter said. "And he got brothers."

"Eleanor will kill both of us," I said to Horace.

"Thass Simeon," Dexter told Horton Doody. "Takes on the whole Chinese mafia but scared of his girlfriend."

"Look," I said, the soul of reason, "why don't we all sit down and sort this out? Pull up a couple of chairs, Mr. Doody."

He took it literally. "Name Horton," he said, distributing his weight.

"It's really swell to meet you," I said. "Really, really swell. You have no idea. Tran? Have a seat. Horace?"

"I've got to go the bathroom," Horace said. "I was in that car for hours."

"I'll come with you," Dexter said. "Just a couple of girls."

"That Dexter," Horton Doody said fondly when they were gone. People looked around to see who was moving furniture. "Ack like a African violet. You're cute," he said to Tran, who was working on his ice-cream cone, looking perhaps eleven.

"I can shoot you," Tran said mildly.

"Whuff, whuff," Horton Doody chortled. "You wear high heels yet?"

Things were not going well. To my surprise, Tran smiled at Horton, looking very much like someone with a secret he intends to keep. "Funny, you" was all he said.

"Five of us?" Horton Doody asked me. "And my five bros make ten. That it?"

"That's it. Sixteen of them."

He nodded, apparently thinking about something else. He put both hands on the table, balled them into fists, and gazed at them.

"Two," Tran said helpfully.

The marbles rolled around until they were looking at Tran. Then Doody lifted a fist and moved it, very slowly, until it was almost touching Tran's ear. Tran sat very still, which was more than I could have done. He didn't even flinch when Doody took his ear between two thick fingers.

"Looky," Horton Doody said, and pulled a silver dollar out of Tran's ear.

Tran's eyes went to the dollar and then to Doody's face, and then he broke into a grin that looked like one the Cheshire cat had left behind. "How?" he asked delightedly.

"Come here, honey," Doody said. "Ears like those, you probably a rich man."

Tran pulled his chair over to Horton Doody's, and

when Dexter and Horace returned from the powder room, Tran was well into his first lesson in the fine old art of palming.

"Okay," I said when they were seated. "Let's cut to the chase."

Florence Lam's apartment was a few blocks north of Sunset, a regal old fourplex liberally decorated with angular graffiti. At seven-thirty the next morning, Dexter, Horton, and I were in place. We'd passed a memorable night in a motel about six blocks away, two thin walls away from a Chinese family of thirty or forty, most of whom seemed to be under two years of age and suffering from colic. When I finally went to sleep, I had a second installment of the dream about babies I'd begun at Eleanor's. In this chapter, a second chute opened at the far end of the room and the fattened babies slid down it to make room for the new arrivals. It seemed to me that there was a Chinese restaurant at the end of the chute. The idea woke me up.

I was as ready for action as anyone who's yawning can be when Florence Lam's door opened and she came out backward, fitting a key to the lock, and backed straight into Horton Doody.

"Excuse me," she said automatically. Then she turned around, looked up at Horton, and screamed.

Dexter's hand cut off the scream. He'd slipped behind her and stuck his foot into the open door. Horton simply took a few steps forward, bulldozing both of them back into the apartment, and I followed, feeling like a rowboat behind an ice-breaker.

Up close, Florence Lam was smaller than I remembered, and older. Dark smudges beneath her downturned eyes sullied her fine skin, and her hair was dirty and slightly matted. Florence Lam was neglecting herself.

"Hush," I said, although she'd already choked off the scream. "Nobody's going to hurt you." I closed the door the rest of the way. The apartment was disheveled and grimy. Clothes were tossed onto the couch, and a couple of days' worth of dishes were growing crusts on the small table. She was either seriously sloppy or seriously depressed. "If he takes his hand away, are you going to be quiet?"

She nodded. Dexter experimentally removed his hand.

"I have no money," she said.

"We don't want money. We don't want to hurt you. In fact, we're here to give you a break."

Her eyes widened slightly; she'd recognized me. Then she glanced at Horton Doody, who was still only inches from her. "Can you ask him to move away, please?"

"He don't have to ask me," Doody said, stepping back. He sounded hurt.

"Let's all sit down," I said. "This is your lucky day."

Florence Lam took a chair at the table. Dexter stood with his back to the door, one foot raised and resting against it. I sat on a chair opposite Florence, and Horton occupied the couch. All of it.

"Who are you?" She was using her index fingers to torment the cuticles on her thumbs, but she had her voice under control.

"You don't really want to know," I said. "I need your attention. Are you with me?"

"What choice do I have?"

"Right," I said. "I'm going to operate on two assumptions for the next minute or so. The first is that you share my opinion that your boss is a pustule. The second is that you know what's really going on in that office."

"Like what?" Her eyes were watchful.

"Like many, many broken federal laws. Like ties to organized crime. Like exploitation and extortion, all against Chinese. Like a little prostitution."

She glanced at Doody, who was staring at her like something you might bump into at forty fathoms, and then quickly looked away. "You're not Immigration."

"We're much worse than INS. They have to play by the rules."

She took it in and nodded. Then her lower lip tightened and started to quiver.

"Lady gone to cry," Dexter said lazily.

Florence Lam straightened in her chair. "That's how much you know."

"I'm going to give you some good advice," I said. "But I need a couple of things first. Give me your keys."

Whatever she'd expected, that wasn't it. "My keys?"

"To the office. They're on that ring with the blue F on it."

She took that in with a blink. "Why do you need them?"

"That's something else you don't want to know. May I?" I reached out a hand.

"I need them to open the office."

"You'll have them back in ten minutes."

She looked around the room as though she were saying good-bye to it. "I suppose I have to."

"You have to."

She picked up the key ring, all business now, and sorted out a large brass-colored key. "Front door," she said. "Back door is this one."

I crossed my fingers. "And the basement?"

She looked surprised again. "It's not locked," she said.

"But it does lock, doesn't it?"

"Sure it does. Tiffle loves locks. He's got a lock on everything." She pursed her lips. "Except his fly." Her fingers sorted though the keys and came up with an old-fashioned skeleton key. "This one," she said.

"Got it?" I asked Dexter.

"Oh, please," Dexter said, taking the key ring from her. "Back in a flash." He closed the door very quietly behind him.

"And now?" Florence Lam asked, a little steadier.

"And now the advice. Take a big purse with you to work today. When the others are at lunch, go to the personnel and payroll files and grab everything that's got your name on it. Everything." She hesitated and then nodded, waiting. "Clean out your desk, but don't make it obvious. Leave junk on top of it. Don't go to work tomorrow. Have you got somewhere you can go?"

"For how long?" She was surprisingly calm. Either she'd seen something like this coming, or she intended to go straight to work and tell Tiffle everything.

"For keeps."

"Oh," she said. She swallowed. Her eyes went around the apartment again and her hands went to the purse, and Horton stirred on the couch.

"Uh-uh," he said.

"A cigarette," she said a little sharply. "Do you mind?"

Horton shrugged, and the couch squealed. "Bad for you," he said.

"I'll risk it." She pulled a package of Virginia Slims from the purse and lit up with a silver lighter. When she tilted her head back to exhale she looked younger and prettier. She took another hit and looked around the table for an ashtray, then flicked the ash into a bowl that still had a couple of corn flakes floating in it. "Okay," she said. "I can go—"

"Don't tell us. Don't tell anybody. Just get the hell out of here. You've got skills, you can get a job. You can do something straight, start over."

She passed her fingers over her brow. "Sure," she said. "Start over." Then she coughed, and the cough turned into a sob. She leaned forward, the hand with the cigarette in it pressed against the back of her head, singeing her hair. I took it from between her fingers and let her cry, the sobs breaking apart like soap bubbles in the early light. There's something especially terrible about a woman weeping in the morning.

"There, there, lady," Horton Doody said helplessly.

He shifted his weight as though he intended to get up and comfort her. "You be okay."

"What's he got on you?" I asked her when the sobs had slowed.

"I've signed things," she said, fighting for breath. "We all have. He made us. Federal forms, forged papers, I don't know what."

"Take them with you."

Her head came up, and she wiped at her cheeks with a napkin. "They're locked in his desk. He'd never let me get at them. He's got us all."

"All four of you." Four was just too many.

"Do you think we'd be there if he didn't? Do you know what he *does* to us?"

"I can imagine. Listen, Florence, you can't tell the others. We'll try to get the stuff in his desk, but we can't have all four of you acting crazy. He's stupid, but nobody's that stupid."

"I could call them tonight," she said. It was a question. "That way they won't come back."

I looked at Horton. Horton spread his hands to reveal a soft center.

"You can call them at six in the morning."

"And I can take their papers?"

"Oh, shit," I said. "Just don't get caught."

She reached across the table and took my hand in both of hers and pressed it to her wet cheek. "Thank you," she said.

I sat there feeling fraudulent and uncomfortable as the door opened and Dexter came in. He started to toss me the keys and saw that my hands were occupied.

"Gettin along better, I see," he said. He gave me a knowing smile. "Good thing I ain't Eleanor."

20

Safe Houses

Pressure points.

There were too many of them, I thought, driving south at nine A.M. while Tran caught up on his sleep in the passenger seat. It was almost enough to make me suspicious.

But why shouldn't there be holes in the operation? Charlie had his racket to himself, sewn up with the Snake Triad Black Hats back in Taiwan, and there wasn't much pressure from the White Hat side here in America. Who cared about a bunch of impoverished Chinese? They were an insignificant trickle in the overall illegal immigration picture, nothing like the nonstop cascade over the borders to the South. They provided cheap labor to people who probably contributed to political campaigns. They didn't vote. They may not have had much else, but at least they were safe from the promises of American politicians.

And, as Charlie had said, kill a *gwailo*, and you bring the police. Keep the violence and the exploitation confined to people with yellow skin—or black, I added to myself, or brown—and they'd stay out of your way. It would take something very conspicuous to draw their attention.

The idea I'd been forming for the last three days would provide something very conspicuous. Unless it got us all killed.

Tran dozed most of the way to San Pedro, leaving me lots of time to move mental furniture around as we inched our way southwest on the permanently clogged Harbor Freeway. They're fixing it now, but they're always fixing it. They've been fixing it since it was built, and it still looks like a used-car lot most of the time. I let Tran snooze. I had a couple of big questions to ask him, but they would keep.

San Pedro looks slightly better at dusk than it does in daylight, and slightly worse than it does at night. Unfortunately, I was seeing it in the morning.

I didn't know the street names in San Pedro, and I didn't learn them on that trip. Once we were off the freeway I just prodded Tran awake and let the poured concrete and flat-roofed stucco buildings slide past in the tea-colored air, noting landmarks here and there and listening to Tran tell me where to turn. Finding my way back would be no problem. With luck I'd only have to do it once.

There were four safe houses off the main drags, all within a square mile or two. All were equally anonymous: cheap, run-down one-story houses in what seemed like an endless farm in which cheap one-story houses were the cash crop. They were concealed by their very uniformity, which I supposed was, as Peter Lau might have said, the *point*, and I was looking at the third before I realized what they all had in common: a driveway that curved around the house and disappeared behind it. Ideal.

"Which door did you go to?"

"Front," Tran said, still making Roy Rogers eyes against the light.

"All four houses?"

He was peering through the window now, remembering something. "Yes."

Good, better, best. "Makes sense," I said. "They bring the pilgrims in through the back and keep them in the back. Anyone comes to the front, the CIAs are out of sight. You're not supposed to know about them, so you come to the front."

"Charlie Wah no dope," Tran said grudgingly.

"He's going to feel like one. You always hit the houses in the same order?"

"Always. Quicker that way."

"Same time?"

"Charlie Wah," Tran said, "crazy about time. Number one, seven-oh-four, number two, seven-seventeen, like that."

"But the same times always?"

Tran hesitated, reluctant to deliver bad news. "Sometimes not."

"How much difference?"

"Half hour sometimes, sometimes hour. Always after dark."

"We'll live with it," I said, wishing I had the confidence I was pretending.

"Sure," Tran said, "no big deal."

I looked at him and he was smiling at me.

"Good team," he said.

"Dynamite," I agreed.

"We going to kill them?" he asked.

"No," I said, accelerating toward the last of the houses. Charlie Wah's voice echoed in my ear. "We're going to mess with their heads."

"Listen up," I said to my mismatched gang. We were gathered in the motel room, which I'd booked for another full day. Even the desk clerk couldn't believe it; he'd called in my credit card twice.

Horace, Dexter, and Horton had been crashed on the two narrow beds when Tran and I came in. Now they all sat, tangled in sheets, backs against the wall, waiting for their coffee to cool.

"They're delivering the slaves tonight."

"What time?" It was almost below the range of human hearing, so it had to be Horton.

"Don't know," I said, "but we'll be there first. Let me get through this before you ask questions, or we'll still be sitting here after they've come and gone, okay?"

Skeptical nods all around.

"There are four safe houses, all within a couple of miles in San Pedro. They're in neighborhoods, so shooting should not be anyone's first option. Anyway, from what we've learned so far, there aren't going to be a lot of guards. These people have nowhere to go if we escape, and no one else is competing for their hands."

Eight eyes, different shapes but all dark brown, gazed at me.

"They hit the houses in the same order every time, just to save time and gas. It's a big loop, and when they're finished they can hit the freeway and head back. What they do there, they pick up money. We're going to pick it up instead."

"Money," Horton said, and then sang, "M is for the Many ways we spend it . . ."

"O," Dexter chimed in, "means Only that there's not enough."

Horace caught the spirit. "N," he sang, "is for the No one who will lend it."

I held up a hand, and Tran, who'd been ransacking his brain to translate the next lines from Vietnamese, gave me a grateful smile. "And after we take the money, we're going to take the watchers and move on to the next house. The *minute* we leave, the Doody Brothers are going to pick up the slaves and take them to a church, where people will be waiting for them."

"Pick them up in what?" Horton again.

"In the vans they got delivered in. They'll still be there, right, Tran?"

"Always there before," Tran said.

"Why not do it all at once?" Dexter asked.

"Charlie's not afraid of the cops," I said, "because the cops aren't interested. What *is* Charlie afraid of, Tran?"

"Another gang," Tran said, on cue.

"So we're going to give them another gang. It's going to be a black gang."

Horace looked at me appreciatively.

"They have no sources of information in the black community," I said. "No way to figure out who it might be."

"And this gone to leave Horace's family clear," Dexter said. "But, still, why not do it all at once?"

"Because of Horace. The slaves have crossed an ocean, they've paid money, to get here. Charlie's gang is all they know. They're not going to leave with the Doodys unless the Doodys have a Chinese translator who can tell them what's happening. That's Horace, and we can't let the keepers see him."

"I speak Chinese," Horace volunteered. "Three dialects." He looked positively happy.

"So we pick up all the crooks and all the slaves, and the slaves get delivered to the church," Dexter said. "Then what?"

"Then we salt the mine," I said, knowing it would tick him off. "And I'll tell you about that later."

By eleven-thirty, all but Horace had been assigned chores. Dexter took charge of weapons and technical paraphernalia, and Horton and Tran assumed responsibility for costumes, such as they were. Tran expressed some confusion over my request for fifty used thrift-store dresses with the labels cut out, and he went out shaking his head and muttering in Vietnamese. That left me alone in the motel room with Horace.

My almost-brother-in-law's spurt of enthusiasm was waning, leaving him free to indulge in his penchant for lists.

"One," he said, nursing his Styrofoam cup of coffee, "they're going to be on guard. They know Tran's out there. You belted one of their guys and stole another one."

"Maybe," I said. I didn't think they were that frightened of one little Vietnamese kid; Charlie Wah was too scornful for that. "The one guy who saw anything," I said, "only saw Tran, and I'm sure they've assumed their missing guy is dead—a victim of a little one-on-one revenge." I blew onto the surface of my own cup; coffee in Styrofoam cools more slowly than the Universe. "What's two?"

"That girl, that Florence. You don't know she didn't tell Tiffle everything."

"She doesn't know much except that the sky is going to fall on good old Claude tomorrow morning."

"Tran, then," he said, finally getting down to it.

"Tran's fine." I was becoming very bored with this particular argument. Horace held a grudge by wrapping both arms and legs around it and clinging for dear life.

"He could sell us—"

"Blood is thicker than money." I stuck the tip of my tongue into the coffee and pulled it out fast. "Anyway, they'd kill him on sight, and he knows it."

Horace ran the nails of his free hand over his jeans with a sound that made the hair on my arms stand on end. "I don't know."

I found I was furious. "And I don't know about you."

He looked astonished. "Me?"

"What the hell did you think you were doing?"

His face slammed shut, and for the first time since I'd met him Horace turned into the inscrutable Oriental. He squeezed his cup, making it bulge perilously. "I don't want to talk about it."

"Too bad. I do. You know, I *do* this shit, or something like it, for a living, remember? I'm sure some mathematician could express my death as a probability factor. Well, okay, so I can die. I'm nobody's father, and as much as I love Eleanor, I'm nobody's husband. You're both.''

"Barely," Horace said between his teeth.

"Tell it to the kids," I said, not caring whether it sounded brutal.

"I don't *talk* to the kids," Horace said tightly. "Pansy talks to the kids, Pansy's their window on the world. She explains to them about why Daddy's never home, because he's out selling real estate in the daytime and pumping gas at night, like they can understand. And then, when I get home and they're asleep, she talks to me about how they miss me and how she should get a job like she had before when she was taking pictures and how my mother tells them one thing when she's told them another, and they don't know what to do. Well, *I* don't know what to do, either. My home life feels like a . . . a maze that's all blind alleys.'' He took a gulp of coffee and gasped steam. "Holy Jesus."

I watched him unsympathetically as he fanned his mouth with his free hand. "So let Pansy get a job."

"Right," he said, sowing scorn right and left. "Eight hours a day out of the house. She leaves the room for thirty seconds, the kids cry. My mother moves to Vegas, the kids ask where's Grandma. I'm sure they think God is a Chinese woman of forty-seven, midway between Pansy and my mother. And I'm busting my butt to pay the electric bill.''

"God, that's terrible," I said. "You're jealous of your own wife and mother. And you're a Chinese male chauvinist, to boot.''

"*Jealous*?" He did the thing with the fingernails on his jeans again and then put his hand on my wrist. "You don't know what you're talking about.''

Well, I didn't. I'd never had kids. I blinked, lost for a moment, and he withdrew his hand.

"So maybe a little," he said in a muffled voice.

"Not much," I said soothingly.

"Aaahhh," he said, shaking his head in small swings,

like if he turned it too far it would yank his body after it.

"And your mother—"

"Pansy can deal with her, now," he said. "She sent her home." His eyes came up to me, and he looked like the old Horace again. "That was a big deal for Pansy," he said proudly.

"That makes it your turn, doesn't it?"

"My turn." His tone was noncommittal, but he'd shifted his eyes to his lap.

"Um, that Thai girl," I said, not sure whether he'd hit me.

For a moment I thought he was going to laugh, but he forced the corners of his mouth down and then together, looking like a prince forced to kiss a frog with no princess potential. "I knew I shouldn't have taken you and Lo to that bar," he said.

"Scene of the crime," I ventured.

"Oh, some crime. I flirted with her, I tipped her. I figured it was all just business to her."

I thought it probably had been—jealousy and all— but I didn't want to say so. She'd obviously stoked his ego, and men are such dopes.

"Still," I said, shrugging.

He nodded. "Yeah, yeah. Okay, no more girls."

Mentally I asked the next question and retracted it, then asked it out loud. "She the only one?"

"Are you kidding? How much energy do you think I've got with two jobs?"

"So ease off. You can pay the electric bill on one job."

He thought about it. "Kids are expensive."

"Pansy could save money if you brought home a dollar a day."

He smiled, not at me but at Pansy. "She could, you know. Pansy's Chinese to her toes."

"If you're home more, she could even get a job of her own." I scalded my tongue and gave up on the coffee. Maybe I'd have it with lunch. Or dinner. "Male chauvinism notwithstanding."

I put my hand on his shoulder, and he reached up and patted it awkwardly. "I don't want to turn into one of the guys on National Public Radio," he said.

"You've got miles to go," I said. "Light-years."

He sat back. "Assuming I live through tonight."

That brought me to the problem at hand. I got up and went to the window, looking out as though I expected to see a solution in the street. The window was open, and since the motel had economized on screens, I poured my coffee out through it. It splattered on the asphalt of the parking lot, steaming like the entryway to hell. "Tonight will be okay."

"Listen to you," Horace said. "Talk about male chauvinists. I just don't think it's nailed down. God is in the details, you know."

I turned back to him, feeling my own tension build again. "So find me a nail, Horace. Hell, I'd settle for a thumbtack. The key to something like this is improvisation."

The upside-down-V eyebrows went sardonic. We were buddies again. He sipped, blinked twice, spat it back into the cup. "A little sententious, don't you think?"

"Horace," I said, "you're Eleanor's brother. Even if you think I'm willing to get myself killed, you have to know that your life is sacred to me." I batted my eyelashes at him.

He inflated his cheeks and let the air out with a cynical little pop. "I just hope you know what you're doing. What *we're* doing."

That was easy. "I thought we'd settled that, Horace," I said. I went to him and took the coffee out of his hand and poured it out the window, on top of mine. "I haven't got the faintest idea."

21

A Question of Color

We were in San Pedro by two-thirty. Except for the fact that my mouth tasted like I'd been sucking on a roll of nickels for a week, I was fine. It also helped if I ignored the rate of my heartbeat and the chill that emanated from the sopping patches on the sides of my shirt, courtesy of the two faucets that had been implanted under my arms while I slept.

Horace, Tran, and I were stewing in my latest rented car—a big one with a copious trunk this time—parked around the corner from the first of the safe houses. Unless Charlie's boys ignored the Harbor Freeway, always a strong possibility at rush hour, they had to pass us. Dexter and Horton were halfway up the next street, about fifty yards past the house. The five Doody Brothers, who were all bigger, or at least wider, than Horton, were two blocks away.

Horace, sitting at the wheel, was revealing himself as a nervous chatterer, reviewing, with the expertise of hindsight, all the reasons he should have known something was wrong the moment Uncle Lo showed up. Tran was emanating a prickly force field from the backseat, where he'd curled himself into a concentrated ball of silence, knees against his chin and arms around his ankles. He hadn't said a word since we'd left the motel. Once in a while he'd nod, as though some mental calculation had just come out right. I made monosyllabic responses to Horace's monologue by way of polite punctuation, but I was actually paying more attention to Tran's nods. Each nod, I figured, represented one less way to get killed.

We sat there for hours.

It began to get dark: twenty past six. People were coming home from work, and every car that passed us brought our heads around as though they were drawn by a single wire. Horace had developed an anxious sigh and practiced it so often that the windows were misting up.

"Can you concentrate on inhaling for a few minutes?" I asked. He rolled down the driver's window.

"Soon, I think," Tran said, breaking his vow of silence.

"I thought you were dead," Horace said.

"Later," Tran said.

Lights swept the road. "Heads down," I said. "Here's another one."

Horace and I ducked, leaving only Tran to peer through the smaller window in the rear. "Three lady," Tran said.

Horace sighed.

"Who would have thought," I asked the world at large, "that so many people would live in this stucco nightmare? And who'd have thought they'd want to come home at night?"

"Van," Tran said from the backseat. We ducked again. The van, a big one, a minibus really, went past us at a nice, legal twenty-five miles an hour and turned the corner onto the street with the safe house on it. "One more," Tran said. A second mobile Enormo, twin to the first, followed. "CIAs," Tran said flatly. "Not long now."

One of the walkie-talkies Dexter had procured made

a throat-clearing sound on the seat between Horace and me, and I picked it up. "They comin home," he said. "In the driveway now." He sounded unreasonably calm. "Here's number two."

"You guys set?" I had to say something.

"Horton done pulled four-fifty out of my ear." Horton said, "Whuff."

"You finished getting the labels out of the dresses?"

"Idle hands is the devil's playground. Not a label in the bunch."

"How do you look?"

"The governor of Jamaica ain't gone invite us home to dinner."

"And the Doody Squad?" I asked.

"Tryin to keep awake," said Howard Doody, the eldest of the brothers, from their car. The others were named Harold, Henry, Hector, and Hayward.

"We can all hear each other?"

"No," Howard Doody said. "This your imagination speakin."

"Right. Well, keep the line open," I said.

Tran started to hum. After a few bars I recognized it as "God Rest Ye Merry, Gentlemen." Horace joined in on an off-key counterpoint line lifted from the Modern Jazz Quartet, and I did my best to turn it into a fugue.

"You guys got a future," Dexter said over the walkie-talkie. "Course, you'll only work once a year."

"You know a harmony?" I asked. "We've got an opening in the group."

"We doin Bob Marley. Horton the bass drum." Horton went "Bum, bum, bum," obligingly. It sounded like depth charges.

"Tell Horton," I said, "that he can always get a job in sonar."

"Man say you sound like a bullfrog," Dexter said to Horton. Assorted Doodys laughed.

"Bullest frog *he* ever see," Horton rumbled.

"Coming, them," Tran said. Horace and I did our little dive.

"We think this is it," I said into the phone as the car glided past.

"Ying," Tran said. "One other." We all held our breath, waiting for the second car. After thirty seconds, it hadn't come. "Okay," Tran said.

"They parkin. Here he come, man goin up the walk," Dexter advised us. "Little squirt."

"We'll wait a minute to be sure they're alone. He'll be inside four or five minutes. He has to get the cash, count it, check the CIAs against his list, and make sure that everything adds up."

"Six minutes, maybe seven," Tran corrected me. "First time, him."

"You hear that?" I asked Dexter.

"My ears okay. It's my heart done turned to stone. That's why I such a merciless dude."

Count to fifty. No second car. I tapped Horace on the arm. "We're rolling," I said to the phone.

"Listen to the man," Dexter scoffed. "Rollin."

"Let Horton emerge into the world." The engine caught, and Horace eased the car into the street, lights out. Now that it was actually coming down, I felt light-headed but clear: The game passed seamlessly through my imagination, without a bump or a missed stitch. Tran touched my shoulder lightly and whispered, "Good."

Horace pulled to the curb about thirty feet behind the car that had had Ying in it. There were two parked cars ahead of us, and we were between streetlamps.

"Jesus Christ," Horace said, leaning against the steering wheel for a better view.

Horton Doody, dressed in a flowing robe, was ambling down the sidewalk, looking wider than a king-sized bed. A streetlamp pulled him from the darkness and glinted off the shawl thrown over his shoulders and the colored beads in his braided hair. Since I'd never before seen him with his watch cap off, I didn't know whether the hair was his own or one of Dexter's inspirations.

"He's just going to meander along like that?" Horace asked. "What about a little stealth?"

"It's a question of color," I said. "If they're expecting anything, it's not someone who looks like Horton."

"Nobody expect that," Tran murmured.

"Come on, Horton," I urged. As he approached Ying's car he gave it an incurious glance and slipped the shawl from his shoulders.

"What if the car's locked?" Horace said. He knew, but he couldn't stop babbling.

Horton was wrapping the shawl around his right hand, looking up at the cloudy sky like someone who's just had her hair done. He was still looking at the sky when he reached the passenger door, and he didn't glance down even when he drew back his wrapped fist and punched out the window.

The guy in the car jumped high enough to bump his head on the roof, but Horton had an arm through the window by then and his left hand had come out of the pocket of his robe with a gun that looked big and deadly even from thirty feet away. He yanked the door open and let the driver see the gun pointed at his head, and the man froze. Up the street the light came on in Dexter's car, and he got out and headed for the house.

We were about two minutes in.

Tran and I pulled ski masks over our faces and climbed out of the car, Tran moving quickly toward Horton while I angled toward Dexter and the safe house. Horace remained in the car, watching the play and waiting for us to come out.

Tran had a wide roll of fiber tape and Charlie Wah's trusty handcuffs, and I had my automatic, another roll of tape around my left wrist, a can of spray paint in a holster, and a quiver full of persistent misgivings. As I joined Dexter I saw Horton pull the driver from the car one-handed.

Dexter was wearing something free-flowing and tie-dyed, and he'd teased his hair up into angular spikes that made him look a little like the Statue of Liberty if the Statue of Liberty had been Jamaican. "Hey, mon," he said softly, giving the words a passable island lilt. Behind him, Horton was holding the driver parallel to the ground like a piece of driftwood while Tran wound the tape around his head, sealing both his eyes and his mouth. Then Tran went around to the driver's side and got the keys to open the trunk.

"Waitin the hard part," Dexter said, glancing at his watch.

"About a minute," I whispered. "Hurry *up*, Horton."

Right on cue, Horton tossed the driver into the trunk and floated toward us, his feet hidden by the hem of his robe. Tran shut the trunk, got into the car behind the wheel, and closed the door.

"This my granny's shawl," Horton said. "She going to be plenty pissed."

"Buy her a new one," I said.

"Hell," Dexter said, "tonight's money, you gone be able to buy a new granny."

"Against the house," I said, and the three of us split up, Dexter and me to one side of the door and Horton to the other, six or eight feet away from it. As though he'd been waiting for us, Ying opened the door and came out.

He was walking stiffly, and even in profile his face was scraped and raw. He looked like someone who'd taken a header into a Cuisinart. Dexter and Horton closed on him soundlessly, and Horton's arm had circled his throat before he even made the sidewalk. He made a sound that sounded like *cikkk-cikkk* as Horton lifted him from the ground and shut off his air. In a single fluid motion, Dexter extended a hand, gave Ying a casual little slap on the face, and took his briefcase. Horton toted Ying out of sight around the side of the house, and

Dexter and I retired behind an overgrown bird of paradise and took a look at the haul.

"Mama," Dexter said reverently. The briefcase was stuffed with cash, rubber-banded stacks of fifty- and hundred-dollar bills mostly, plus a few thick wads of brightly colored toy money that I took to be Taiwanese. Folded to one side was a sheet of legal paper. I grabbed it and opened it and then let out a sigh of sheer exasperation.

"It's in Chinese," I said.

"What you expectin? Cyrillic limericks?"

"Well, it means you've got another question for him. He has to read these names out loud. All of them. Anyone who's got a Christian name, I want the Christian name."

He fidgeted, a sign of nerves at last. "Gone slow us up."

"One of them is a woman who knows the lady who's got the church. She can help Horace keep them in line."

"Anything else I don't know about?" He snapped the case shut and took off for the side of the house. I hung back a few steps, not wanting to get too close to Ying, even with the mask in place. I needn't have worried: Ying was totally focused on Horton, who had inserted the tip of his gun barrel into Ying's left nostril. Ying's hands were jammed down inside his pants, elbows straight, and he looked like a man who is trying very hard not to let his bladder go.

"Fuck with us and you're dead," Dexter said softly, flicking Ying's cut cheek with a forefinger to get his attention. "How many passengers inside?"

Ying's hard little eyes rolled toward him. "Thirty-eight."

Dexter had been appointed Grand Inquisitor. "How many of your assholes?"

"Two." It figured: the vans' drivers.

"What kind of metal?"

Ying looked bewildered. "What?"

"Guns, stupid. What kind of guns?"

"Little poppers," Ying said. His eyes found me, registered the mask, and went back to the immediate threat.

Dexter unfolded the paper, held it in front of Ying's face, and lit a Bic. "Read this."

"Names," Ying explained.

"I know they names, you little dink. Read them."

Ying went for an edge. "Who are you looking for?"

Dexter touched the Bic to Ying's unoccupied nostril, and Ying said, "Yiiii," in a shrill voice.

"Hush, now," Dexter said, removing the lighter to a reassuring distance. "Let's see how quiet you can read this."

Ying read it in a shaky whisper. There were Christian names scattered here and there, but nothing that sounded remotely like the one I wanted. When he'd finished, Dexter looked at me and I shook my head.

"Part two," Dexter said. "You gone go back up there and knock on that door again. You do it right, and you might get up tomorrow."

"Any questions?" Horton asked in a voice that made the ground vibrate beneath my feet.

"No questions." The scabbing on his face was rusty and stiff-looking.

"So what you waitin for?"

With Horton and Dexter flanking him, Ying trudged toward the house. When he got to the front door they moved to either side of it, guns upright and backs to the house. Dexter stretched out a leg and gave Ying a little kick by way of a prompt, and Ying knocked. After a moment, someone called out a question from inside. Ying replied in Chinese, and the door opened.

Even after having seen him go through the car window, I wasn't prepared for how fast Horton Doody could move. He shouldered Ying back into Dexter and slipped through the door, hitting the man who had answered it with his chest and sending him sprawling. Dexter curved an arm around Ying's throat and stepped in behind him.

I followed, staring at the dark makeup on my hands.

We were in a short unfurnished hallway. Horton hoisted the fallen man by his belt and carried him into the living room, from which we'd heard a babble of voices when we came through the door. The silence that greeted his entrance was profound.

The room was packed with fatigued-looking Chinese men, mostly in their twenties and thirties, mostly sitting on the floor. They stared at Horton as though Night had just gotten dressed and strolled in.

"Call your buddy," Dexter said to Ying, and Ying emitted a short bark. A man in a white shirt came into the room with a coffee cup in his hand. When he saw Horton, the hand loosened and the cup sagged and then dangled by its handle, pouring coffee over the front of his trousers.

"Come here," Horton said to him, pointing the big gun at the bridge of the man's nose. The man had been one of the laughing pack in the sweatshop. Looking a lot less cheerful now, he threw an uncertain glance around the room as though he hoped his pigeons had turned into a trained army in his absence. Men stared back at him, wide-eyed and empty-handed.

"Now," Horton said, and the man picked his way across the room to Horton's side. "Turn around." Horton made a little circle with the gun, and the man complied. I slipped past Horton and taped the man's hands behind him, looping the tape through his belt for good measure. Then, following the drill, I passed the tape around his head to seal his mouth and eyes. When I'd finished, Horton passed a possessive hand between the man's body and his taped arms. The pigeons watched, silent and openmouthed as I repeated the treatment on the one who'd opened the door, and Dexter wrapped him in a long dark arm, the one that wasn't cutting off Ying's breath.

"Who speaks English?" I asked the room at large, trying to imitate Dexter's island lilt. Nobody answered.

In fact, nobody looked at me, all of them finding the walls and the carpet more interesting than my question. "Okay," I said a bit wildly. "Nobody speaks English, we kill you all."

A face bobbed up. It belonged to a skinny guy with a wispy mustache and a black Marlboro T-shirt, and it looked terrified. "Come here," I snapped. He looked at me, turned to his friends, and then shook his head in tiny, quick swings. Horton snapped his fingers with a sound like a firecracker and pointed imperiously at the floor in front of him. Drawn by a supernatural force, the young man got up and came to us, walking against the wind. I put my hand on his arm, and he started violently, eyes still fixed on Horton's face.

"It's okay," I said, realizing belatedly that most of them had never seen a black man before. "You're going to be fine." I wrapped my fingers gently around his arm. "Here's what I want you to say. Tell them we're here to set them free from the Snakes. Tell them to hold tight for one minute, and they'll be all right."

"No," he said, a totem of disbelief.

"What the *fuck*?" Dexter asked the ceiling, hugging Ying and the guy who'd answered the door, and looking like the middle man in a trio about to start dancing the hora.

"Yes," I told the Marlboro man. "If they stay here they'll belong to the Snakes. If they wait a minute, we'll get them out of here and keep them safe from the Snakes and the Immigration Service. We'll take care of them."

Dexter muttered monosyllables, and Horton emitted subsonic chuckles. The Chinese man stared at the floor.

Horton stopped chuckling. "You want to get dead?" he asked.

The Marlboro man took one terrified look at Horton and let loose a brief burst of Mandarin. Any uncertainty he might have felt about delivering the message had vanished at the sound of Horton's voice: he sounded positively Messianic.

When he'd finished, people looked at each other. No one moved.

"Good enough," I said. "Hang on."

"We gotta *go*," Dexter hissed. "Drive time." He still had his arms around two Chinese throats.

I grabbed the Marlboro man's arm and tried for a reassuring smile. "Sit still, hear?"

We closed the front door behind us, and I took Dexter's henchman, as Mrs. Summerson would have called him, in my grasp, and used my free hand to spray-paint RASTA POWER across the door. I saw Horace sprinting around the corner toward the car with the Doodys in it, and we turned Ying and the two henchmen in the direction of the car Ying had arrived in. As we neared it, Tran got out and popped the trunk, and one of the guards joined the driver in the trunk, with an assist from Horton. I hauled the other one to my car, and Horace opened the trunk. After it had been slammed down, I made a run to Dexter's car, grabbed fifteen or twenty dresses, and went back in to distribute them among the bedrooms with all the other stuff the pilgrims had hauled along to the New World. By the time I'd climbed into my rented whatever, Horton and Dexter had taken off with Ying between them, and Tran had followed in Ying's car.

"Okay," I said over the walkie-talkies as I started the car. "That was the hard one."

And I thought I was right until the door at the second safe house opened, and I found myself staring over Dexter's shoulder at the terrified face of Peter Lau.

22

Taking Wing

Lau gaped at Dexter, who had Ying in front of him, with the air of someone whose final earthly expectation has been proved wrong. As Dexter raised his gun over Ying's shoulder, someone put one eye around the door, and Horton Doody lifted a leg, hiked up his skirts, and tried to put a foot through the door.

It was a heavy, old-fashioned oak door. It attained maximum velocity instantly and slammed against the skull behind it with Louisville Slugger results. The head disappeared, and the door bounced back, cracked Peter Lau on the shoulder and knocked him toward us, and then bounced back and hit the falling warrior on his way down. Dexter passed Ying to me like a discarded partner in a reel and shoved his gun at Peter's open mouth.

"*No*," I whispered. "Take Ying, and leave him to me." By then, Horton was through the door and reaching around it to do further damage to the guy who'd hidden behind Peter and whatever surprise Peter had been intended to provoke, and Dexter grabbed Ying again and carried him forward. I took Peter's arm and said, "Shut up and do what I say."

"Bu-bu-bu-but," Lau said.

"You're okay," I said. "This is Simeon." His arm was so boneless that I grabbed a handful of jacket and yanked him along behind me, toward the living room.

The next thing I knew, someone was shooting.

The shots made muffled little snapping sounds, and I heard a *smack* and Horton went, "Whuff," and this time he wasn't laughing. He took a step back into the hallway, releasing the man he'd carried in with him and kicking him behind the knee. The man fell, and Ying turned quickly and lashed out with a foot at Dexter. Dexter blocked it with an upraised knee and shoved Ying into the living room, and Horton's semi went off like the world's biggest deck of cards being shuffled. He leaned forward and grabbed his thigh.

A woman screamed.

I let go of Peter and stiff-armed the fallen man, slamming his head sideways, and then grabbed his left arm, lifting and twisting it until the joint went *pop* and it was dislocated. He moaned and rolled over onto it, trying to stifle the pain, and I was up and running toward the doorway that led to the living room, my gun out with a bullet in the chamber. Peter stayed in the hallway, saying something that sounded like a Chinese prayer.

Ying and the man Horton had been holding were hanging on to Dexter like dogs trying to bring down a bear, Ying's hand pulling back and then driving four straight fingers up and under Dexter's ribcage. Dexter gargled. Pilgrims hugged the floor, two deep in some places. Something flashed across the room and a man ducked behind a couch, but not so quickly that I didn't see the automatic in his hand. I fired twice at the ceiling and then dodged left, hoping he'd come up and take a shot in the direction of the sound, but I tripped over a body and went down on my hip and elbow, and my gun went off again, involuntarily this time, and the woman screamed once more.

A crack and a whimper drew my attention, and I saw the guard who'd been flailing at Dexter go down, his face broken and bleeding from the barrel of Dexter's gun. Ying pulled himself free from Dexter's grasp and fled into the hallway, stumbling over the man Horton had dropped before he disappeared from sight.

But now fingers were scrabbling at my gun and I turned back to stare into a pair of terrified eyes belonging to a kid of eighteen or nineteen. The moment I looked at him, he froze solid. Something made a huffing noise from the doorway, and there was Horton, gun in his left, making a motion with his right that needed no translation anywhere in the world: *Get down*. The pilgrims dug holes in each other to get closer to the carpet, and Horton emptied the gun into the couch, blowing big gaps into the fabric and scattering white stuffing into the air like popcorn. He stitched the couch methodically, left to right and back again, and then repeated the entire pattern for good measure. When he stopped, the air rang with reverberation and reeked of cordite, and no one was moving.

The woman was halfway across the room, lying on top of a man. She had short graying hair and wore a shapeless gray dress, and she was as still as stone.

I got up, checked my gun, and stepped over the bodies to get to the couch. Feeling altogether too large to miss at that range, I edged along its length and then lunged around its far corner. The unexpected guard was a huddled mass of cloth and blood, tucked into a ball that hadn't been small enough.

"He's finished," I said to Horton, who was standing in the doorway and leaning forward to examine his right thigh. A deep red stain was spreading over the front of his robe. "This ain't gone clean," he said.

"Out of here," Dexter said. People were beginning to stir.

"Just a minute." I went to the woman and knelt by her. When I touched her, her head came up and dark eyes bored into mine. "Doreen?" I asked.

She paled. "No," she said in English.

I put my mouth to her ear. "Mrs. Summerson," I whispered.

"No," she said again, not buying it.

"You were in her school," I said. "1941. Third row, eighth from the left. Come on, she needs your help."

She looked around the room, thinking it over, and then extended a hand in a ladylike fashion so I could help her up. "Ask if anyone's hurt," I said when she was standing.

She said something musical and interrogative and got no answer. Most people lay absolutely still.

"Ask them all to get up," I said. "Tell them no one will harm them."

What she said this time had a current of command in it, and people began to disentangle themselves and get to their feet. Dexter used the time to dust himself off and go into the back of the house. Men backed away from him, but no one made a play of any kind. No one was bleeding, although some of them were feeling themselves for wounds, unable to believe their luck had held.

"Roundin third," Dexter announced, coming back into the room with a briefcase and tossing me a reproachful look. "How you doin?" he asked Horton.

"Muscle," Horton grunted. "I seen worse in high school."

"Doreen," I said, "there will be men here in two minutes to take all of you to Mrs. Summerson. One of them will speak Chinese. Mrs. Summerson is his family's friend. Tell these people to go with him. Got it?"

She nodded, looking dazed, and I glanced at Dexter. We'd had shots, and there was no time to solicit recruits. As we rounded the corner, I saw Peter Lau cowering in a corner, and stopped cold.

Tran was standing there, drawn inside by the gunfire, and he was folding a knife. Ying lay facedown in the center of a dark lake of his own making.

"Two," Tran said to me in the softest voice I'd ever heard.

Even Horton kept quiet.

"I told them they were all Vietnamese," Peter Lau said as we drove toward the third safe house, trailing Dexter's car. The surviving guard had been thrown into its trunk, and the two dead ones were wrapped in blankets and plastic bags in my backseat. By now the Doody Bus Co., abetted by Horace and Doreen Wing, was picking up the second houseful of slaves. "They saw your little stiletto freak, but they didn't see you." He swallowed several pints of saliva. "I figured nothing would happen. I figured no one was crazy enough to try to bust Charlie." He rested his head against the window. "I figured they'd let me go home."

"How'd they get you?"

"Someone in the restaurant, I guess."

"And you don't think they mentioned me?" I wasn't really thinking about me; I was thinking about the Chans.

"I don't know." He was sitting with his hands clasped protectively between his thighs. "Maybe, maybe not. The slaves hate Charlie. They might answer only the questions they were asked. If they're worried about Vietnamese, maybe they didn't ask the right questions. You know, 'Who else was in the restaurant before our man got taken?' 'Peter Lau.' 'Was he with anyone from the Vietnamese gang?' 'Yes.' They only asked *me* about Vietnamese."

"Right," I said.

"But now," he said, "they'll come after me."

I rounded the corner leading to the third safe house and watched Dexter and Horton's car pull to the curb. "We've got people behind us," I said, "picking up the slaves. They'll be delivered to a church. Listen, Peter, are you one hundred percent sure I can trust you?"

"Do you think," he asked wistfully, "I need one more person who wants to kill me?"

"Okay. We'll deliver you to the same church, like you got picked up in the sweep, and you can get home from there. They come back to you, you were delivered blindfolded. It was a black church, somewhere in South Central maybe, but you don't know where. The gang that took you were all black."

"You think that'll wash?"

Dexter and Horton were getting out of their car.

"If it doesn't," I said, "I've got things more important than you to worry about."

The third and fourth safe houses went like Japanese clockwork, with the substitution of one of the henchmen from the first house knocking on the door instead of Ying. We hit the standard two watchers and two briefcases full of cash, flung the standard dresses around the bedrooms, and painted the standard slogans on the wall. At the fourth house, I said nothing, as we'd arranged, and Dexter and Horton, talking blacker than I'd imagined they could, managed to let one of the guards get free, so there'd be someone to report back to Charlie. He'd scaled the fence of a neighboring house as effortlessly as someone who'd just discovered the antigravity principle, and we let him go.

By then the pigeons were mounting up, and Tran had to grab the second van at the last house and join the Doody Brothers Transport Co. By the time we were through, we had six of Charlie's guys, taped wrists to ankles and blindfolded, divided between the trunks and Dexter's backseat.

We took surface streets to L.A., heading north on Western for most of the trip and driving like a caravan of school safety patrols on the way home from work. It took more than an hour, which was what I wanted. By the time we hit Wilshire, around eight-thirty, I guessed Charlie Wah would be getting anxious about his missing collectors and their little briefcases. He was going to be a lot more anxious in the morning.

At Wilshire and Crenshaw we pulled off onto a side street. I consolidated the money into two very full briefcases, and Dexter swung east, heading for his apartment and an appointment with a junkie doctor whose shaking hands were about to be cured by a glare from Horton. The bullet was still in Horton's thigh, which spared him an exit wound but meant that there was some potentially messy medical work ahead.

"Shit," Horton had said, "for this much money, he could of shot me in the head."

By the time we had the cases snapped shut, five vans were stacked up behind us, filled to overflowing with rescuees, and I found Horace trying out his Mandarin on them. It sounded rusty even to me, but the guys seemed calm, or maybe just glazed. As Peter Lau had said, they had nothing to lose.

The church, a big one in a Hispanic neighborhood that was starting to go Korean, was lighted up like Christmas, and the moment Mrs. Summerson opened the door, Doreen Wing began to cry. I didn't know what it was—relief that she wasn't going to be killed, delight at seeing Mrs. Summerson, shock at her teacher's age, or sheer exhaustion—but Mrs. Summerson wrapped her big arms around Doreen and patted her with her big blunt hands and talked to her in a Chinese dialect that Horace didn't understand until Doreen's sobs subsided into hiccups.

"And is this all?" Mrs. Summerson asked, looking at the other one hundred and seventy-one pilgrims being herded forward by large Doodys. We were still on the front porch, being dive-bombed by moths.

I rejected several intemperate replies. "It's all there were."

"Haven't you done well," Mrs. Summerson said brightly. "Please, come in, come in." And she extended her arms to all of them, running through dialect after dialect until they were all smiling and nodding at her.

We congregated in the chapel, the Chinese taking seats in the pews while Mrs. Summerson and Doreen talked a mile a minute to them, and I waited for a break in the flow and took her arm.

"We need someplace to talk," I said.

"The pastor's office is open." She linked her arm through mine, and we set off toward a door at the rear of the chapel. I had one of the briefcases in my free hand.

"Here are their names," I said, handing her the manifests. We'd found one in each of the briefcases. "That should make the papers easier."

She leaned against the pastor's gray steel desk, a big strong woman in a shapeless brown dress. She didn't seem vague anymore. "The papers are no problem. I'm getting buses to take the babies to Las Vegas tomorrow, out of harm's way. The papers will arrive in a few days. They'll like Las Vegas, more, I'm afraid, than they should. I just hope they don't lose all their money."

"They're not going to get all their money," I said.

The big eyes widened when I opened the briefcase and began to count. "One hundred and eighty thousand dollars," I said. "Forty each for the four you brought out and twenty for the advance payment on Doreen." I tidied the piles I'd made and started counting again. It took a long time, and her eyes stayed on my face, which was impressive. I'd have been staring at the cash.

"This is one hundred and seventy-two thousand, a thousand each for the folks in the living room. They can use it to get started, if you can keep them from losing it in Las Vegas."

"I'll do my best. What happens to the rest of it?"

"It's going in a good cause," I said. I stood up, toting the briefcase. It felt a lot lighter. "May I use the phone?"

"Right there," she said, pointing to a black four-pound behemoth with a dial. "Do you need privacy?"

"For your sake, maybe I do."

"Well," she said, going to the door, "come in when you've finished. We're making tea."

"I will," I replied, resisting the impulse to roll my eyes toward heaven and flipping through the pages of my phone book for the right number.

"Jeez, yeah?" Claude B. Tiffle grunted, and I found myself hoping I'd just contributed to coitus interruptus.

"This is Dr. Skinker," I said through my nose.

"Froom," Tiffle said, either cutting through the phlegm or operating under the assumption it was a word. "Little late, huh?"

"I told you we'd have to meet at unusual hours."

He made a *poot-poot* sound, gathering his wits. "You mean now?"

"No. Tomorrow morning at eight."

He breathed disgruntlement into the phone. "Is this important?"

"In God's scheme, no. In terms of your future, yes, indeed."

"What's going to happen?"

"Earnest money," I said. "For the purchase of the church."

He cleared his throat. "How much?"

"Six figures." It was the truth. "You'll be there?"

"Yeah, okay." He was alert now. "Eight, right?"

"Eight."

"Where?"

I swallowed. "Your office."

"Glad to be of service," he said.

"No happier than I," I said, hanging up.

"One million twenty-four thousand dollars," I said. "That's eight thousand and change per pilgrim, roughly, minus the money I gave to Mrs. Summerson." Dexter's mutant coffee table was awash with cash, and four brief-cases lay open and empty on the floor. "And about fif-teen thousand in Taiwanese. Make it a million forty all together."

"I in the wrong line," Dexter said.

He'd traded in his robes for a pair of jeans and a lime-green shirt that identified him as a two-dollar-a-shirt man named Paul. Tran was asleep on the leather couch, and Horton was out cold in Dexter's bedroom. The doctor had come and gone, a frail, frizzy-haired white man with yellowish skin who smelled like a chemical dump. Two of the Doodys, after checking on the slumbering Horton and making clucking noises, had gone out to watch the prisoners in the car, and the other three had taken off to put the two bodies on ice, I didn't know—and didn't want to know—where. Everett still had possession of Dexter's bathtub.

"Fifty each," I said to Horace, fanning myself with a wad of bills. "And another fifty for each of Horton's brothers. That'll leave about half a million."

"Lot of salt," Dexter said, eyeing the green.

"We're looking," I reminded him, "to attract attention."

"Quarter of a million gone to catch the eye, too."

"Half has a nice ring to it."

"You want a ring, go to Zale's. You can pick up a real flasher for three or four bills."

"Dexter," I said, glad that Horton was off marauding in the Land of Nod, "you're pocketing fifty thousand for one night's work."

"What am I going to do with fifty thousand dollars?" Horace asked querulously.

"You could give me some," Dexter said. "All donations gratefully received."

"You make a down payment on a house for Pansy," I said. "Give the kids a yard to play in."

"I'd have to cut the grass," Horace said.

"Astroturf," Dexter suggested, giving up on further riches. "What time is it?"

"You're wearing a wristwatch," I pointed out.

"Man with fifty thou in his jeans don't look at his own watch. Get some style."

"I've got fifty, too," I said, counting it out. "We all do. I guess we'll just have to keep checking for sunrise."

"Ain't no good to be rich if everybody else rich, too," Dexter said, checking his watch. "After two. Let's get some poor folk over here and lord it over them."

"Here's yours," I said, pushing money at Dexter. "Don't spend it all on implements of torture."

"Peewee asleep," Dexter observed. "Let's give him twenty and split the rest, act silently superior all night."

"Ha," Tran said without opening his eyes. "You silent. Ha."

"Must of heard the money," Dexter said.

"Here," I said to Horace. He looked down at the banknotes like they were cabbage. "Your turn for trunk patrol," I told him. "Take some coffee to the Doodys."

Horace got stiffly to his feet, grumbling. He left the money on the table and went out to check on our human baggage.

"Pizza," Dexter said, solving his snobbery problem. "Order up some pizza, sneer at the delivery boy."

"Anchovies," Tran said, rolling over to face the back of the couch.

"Man eat fish on everything," Dexter said. "Fish cookies, fish ice cream."

"Good for brain," Tran said. "Try sometime."

"You could always stiff Horton," I said to Dexter.

"Not a wise career path," Dexter said. "What you want on your pizza?"

"Sausage." I yawned and stretched the joints of an aging man. "Three hours, more or less. We'd better give ourselves forty minutes to get there."

Dexter, at the phone, said, "Thirty's plenty. We just gone sit there a couple of hours anyway."

"We go in in the dark," I said for what seemed like the hundredth time.

"We go in in the dark," Dexter mimicked. "Hello, that Domino's?" He waited. "You can't be closed, man, we hungry."

"Denny's open," Tran said without turning his head. "Get breakfast."

"A hundred bucks," Dexter said to the phone. "And that's the tip."

"You'll be broke in a week," I said.

"Damn straight," Dexter said to the phone. "Four big ones, one with sausage, one with everything, one with—"

"Anchovies," Tran said stubbornly.

"—little fish all over it, and one with anything you want. Think that'll do for Horace?" he asked me.

"Horace won't eat."

"He could go home," Dexter said. "Extra little fish, hear? Pour the little fuckers all over it."

"He could, couldn't he?" I asked.

"Could what?" Horace asked, coming in. "They're alive. Nobody wants coffee."

"You could go home," I said.

"Not likely," Horace said. "Not when I'm having so much fun."

"Could of fooled me," Dexter said.

"That's because I'm hungry," Horace said. "My blood sugar is low."

"Horace won't eat," Dexter said in his white man's voice.

"Shame it's so late." Horace picked up his money and fanned it idly. "Nobody delivers now."

"They do to the rich and famous," Dexter said.

23

Salting the Mine

At 4:55 A.M. Chinatown looked like a closed department store. The streets were dark and empty; even the Christmas lights had been given a rest. Two Chinese men in paramilitary uniforms strolled Hill Street. They were laughing.

"Foot patrol," Horace the Expert said smugly from the driver's seat. "Neighborhood association. They do the whole circuit in forty-five minutes and then start over."

"Do they go up Granger?"

"Nah. Only the main streets and the shopping alleys. The merchants pay them."

"Our resident fount of wisdom," I said.

"I had lots of time to figure it out." He loved knowing more about anything, anything at all, than anyone else did.

"Speaking of time," I said automatically.

"Almost five. We're right on top of it."

He pulled over at Hill and Granger and I got out. The night had grown sharply colder and the sky was low with fog and pale with city light. Two homeless men sprawled in a patch of weeds, partly covered by yesterday's news.

The metal gate opened with a faint rusty protest. There was a streetlamp directly in front of the house, something I should have noticed before but hadn't, and I followed my lengthening shadow up the walk toward the dark bungalow, hoping that Tiffle wasn't shagging some silky immigrant on his desk. He was going to need his strength before the day was over.

I punched up 11-14 on the alarm keypad to the right of the door. Tiffle's birthday, Florence Lam had said, another piece of evidence that his brain worked on alternating current. Dexter's duplicate key turned without so much as a snag, and the light from the streetlamp illuminated Florence's desk, convincingly messy and busy-looking. I pushed the door as far closed as I could without the latch clicking into place and switched on my flashlight. Moving quickly but deliberately, I searched the rooms, including the basement.

The basement was entirely satisfactory. It extended beneath the entire house, it had a rough wooden floor, and there were no windows. Metal filing cases stood against two of the four walls; the others were occupied by a massive old gravity furnace and the stairs I had come down. The door at the top of the stairs opened out, as I'd hoped it would. The skeleton key worked just fine.

Tiffle's desk was a steel hymn to paranoia. Not only did the three drawers lock, but an iron rod had been passed through their handles and locked to the desk frame at top and bottom. It might as well have had a neon sign on top of it saying SEARCH HERE. I was looking for the keys—not that I needed them, but as a way to pass the time—when I heard the first car door slam shut outside.

Five o'clock in the button, as Tran would say.

I had my hand in the inside pocket of Tiffle's suit jacket, which was hanging behind the door, and as I pulled it out my fingers snagged on something. "I'll be damned," I said, pulling out a little key ring with four double-serrated keys dangling from it. "Thank you, Claude." As I slipped one of the keys into the lock at the top of the iron rod, the first car pulled away and I heard footsteps on the front porch. The second car door slammed and the front door to the cottage opened almost simultaneously.

"Surprise," Dexter said from the front room. "Where the balloons and whistles?"

"How many you got?" I called.

"Four. Rest with Tran and two Doodys."

"They all inside?" The first lock turned easily.

"No, you dinkus, I left them on the step."

"You know where they go." The lower lock resisted, and I chose another key.

"Yeah, yeah, yeah." Shoes scuffled across the floor and then down the steps to the basement, and I heard the door close. A moment later the front door opened to a confusion of soft voices, one of them a deep Doody rumble.

"Here your jimmy," Dexter said, coming into the office. He was toting a crowbar.

"Don't need it. The man thoughtfully left his keys."

"Guy got to be in serious minus territory." He leaned forward and studied the desk. "More locks than the mint, and he leaves the keys here." The lower lock turned, and the metal rod slipped loose and clattered to the floor. "Good thing we ain't bein sneaky."

"Dexter, why don't you go help Tran or something?" I flipped through the remaining keys.

"You the one needs help. Try the one with the nail polish on it."

I did, and it fit smoothly into the top drawer and turned. "See?" Dexter said. "Good thing you got friends."

"You're breathing on my neck." I pulled the drawer open.

"I doin it free, too. Cap'n Snow would pay good cash

for a little of that. What's in the box, you think?"

"Opening it," I said patiently, "will be my very next act."

"Lordy," Dexter said. It was full of money: five stacks, apparently all hundreds, each three inches thick. "A little dividend," Dexter said. "One each."

I hesitated and then said, "Why not?" and scooped the money out of the box and handed it to him. "A sideline, maybe, something Charlie Wah didn't know about."

"Or insurance," Dexter said, stuffing money into his pockets. "Getaway stash."

I put the box on the desk and rifled though the rest of the drawer's contents. A manila envelope contained thirty or forty green cards, genuine to my unpracticed eye, and four Canadian passports. The spaces for the photos were blank.

"Hot shit," Dexter said over my shoulder. "Hello, Uncle Sam."

"Downstairs, them," Tran said, coming into the room. "Talk too much."

"Let's hope they keep it up," I said, fishing out a cardboard stationery box that had been shoved to the back of the drawer. "Oh, well, Claude, you wicked dog." The box was packed with Polaroids of naked Chinese girls, taken right there in the office. They were all young and all unsmiling, but other than that they ran the gamut from plain to beautiful, fat to thin. They had been posed obscenely, and breasts pushed themselves at the camera like swollen bruises, sex organs gaped like wounds.

"Cops gone love that," Dexter said.

"Bleary," Tran said, picking one out with thin fingers. "Here Mopey."

"Find Weepy and Snowbell," I said, handing him the box. "Keep them."

"I'll keep Snowbell," Dexter offered. "Just kidding,'' he said, his free hand upraised, when I turned to look at him.

An economy-sized box of twenty-four Trojan condoms rounded out Claude's private museum. Tran passed me the box of Polaroids, keeping four, and I closed the first drawer and went to work on the second.

"They all untaped?" I asked as I worked.

" 'Cept they hands and they eyes," Dexter said.

"Good," I said. "Where are the cases?"

"Hall," Tran said. "You want?"

"Not yet." The second drawer was full of papers: deeds, quit claims, contracts, business partnerships, immigration forms. I flipped through them, looking for signatures and finding *Florence Lam* neatly written at the bottom of seven. Folding them lengthwise, I put them on the floor. Then I thought again and pulled out all the papers with women's signatures. "What time is it?"

"Five-forty-two," Dexter said. "Gone be light soon."

"Get the Doodys to untape their wrists and eyes, and then nail the door shut."

"Yes, Massa," Dexter said. He straightened up and threw an arm around Tran's shoulders. "Come on, peewee, the Doodys got work to do."

"Ho, ho," I said to the third drawer. It was empty except for a small stack of photographs bound by a rubber band. Charlie Wah's face gazed paternally up at me from the first one.

He hadn't known he was being photographed. He'd been caught coming up the walk, with Granger Street fuzzy and indistinct behind him. He figured prominently in five others: one talking to Ying, two walking down Hill Street with his bodybuilders, one at the wheel of a car, and one, barely recognizable, in a restaurant somewhere. Each of the pictures bore a little electronic date in the lower right corner. Tiffle had been busier than Charlie knew.

Just for the hell of it, I got up and went into the front

room, listening to the blur of voices from the basement. Rolling a piece of CLAUDE B. TIFFLE ASSOCIATES letterhead into Florence Lam's typewriter, I typed CHARLIE WAH, and then SNAKE TRIAD, TAIWAN. I looked at it for a moment and then realized what I'd forgotten to ask Everett. I couldn't ask him now, so I pulled my little phone book out of my pocket and dialed.

"Whassit?" Peter Lau asked blearily.

"Peter. Simeon. Sorry to wake you."

"Jesus," Lau said. "My head."

"Listen, I need Charlie Wah's real name."

Bedsprings creaked. "Why?"

"I want to send him a letter."

"No, you don't."

"Just give me the name, Peter."

"Wah Yung-Fat. Spelled like it sounds, but no 'o' in 'Yung.' "

WAH YUNG, I typed. "Hyphen between Yung and Fat?"

"Yes. What time is it?"

-FAT, I typed. "Time for Charlie Wah to start worrying," I said. "Keep your radio on the news stations."

I hung up and carried the paper into the office, where I folded it tightly and slipped it under the rubber band around the photos. Then I closed the drawer, got up again, and trudged into the hallway to get the cases.

I put five or six thousand into Tiffle's little box and closed it, then spread the rest of it, more than half a million dollars, over the surface of his desk. It looked impressive. By now nails were being driven into the door at the head of the basement stairs, and then the banging stopped and Dexter ambled in, the hammer still in his hand.

"Wo," he said, glimmering at the money. "Enough salt for Colonel Sanders."

"It'll make a nice picture, don't you think?" I locked the desk and tossed Tiffle's keys on top of the money.

"Less the cops snatch it."

"There'll be too many of them. They'll be watching each other. You got the list?"

"LAPD, INS, U.S. Marshals," he recited. "Chinatown Association, Chinese Legal Aid Society, ACLU, *Times*, the radio and TV guys. Start dialin at seven. Give 'em the salt, the slicks downstairs, and the ol' *Caroline B*."

"Don't forget the safe houses," I said. "We haven't got any real slaves for them, but we've got four houses full of stuff."

Dexter snapped his fingers. "The dresses," he said, his face lighting up.

"You're a deeply intelligent man, Dexter." I scooped up the documents Florence Lam and the others had signed and put them into one of the briefcases.

"I the bee's knees," Dexter said. "Toss that." I flipped the case at him, and he caught it one-handed. "You throw like a white girl," he said. "A very *young* white girl."

"See you later."

"You gone sit here, huh? They can't get out."

"Just in case. No point in taking a short cut now."

"We had more like you," Dexter said in mock admiration, "we wouldn't be sniffin around after the Japanese."

Tran came in behind Dexter. "Getting light," he said. I tossed him the second case. "Beat it."

"You forgot to say we sposed to put a egg in our shoe," Dexter said.

"If an egg in your shoe," Tran said to him, "you eat it."

"Hey," Dexter said, brightening, "time for breakfast."

I sat there as the room gradually filled with light, bringing the green of the money out of the gloom like the colors of an underwater reef, and thought about the pilgrims and their long passage and the years of labor they would pass in dingy workplaces and crowded rooms, all to live in a country that didn't want them, that would send them home if it got a chance, but that they thought of as a rich mine, the Gold Mountain where they could trade their hours and days and years and skills for the money they folded meticulously each week into envelopes and sent home to the land of empty stomachs and waiting women. And I thought about Tiffle and his greedy acrobatics with phony green cards and false INS inspectors and the girls he'd invaded on his couch, and wished he were going to take a harder fall.

At seven-ten, while Dexter was making his anonymous phone calls about a cellarful of illegal immigrants, half a million dollars in cash, and a waiting ship, I went out into the dull day and relocked the door behind me. Horace was parked on the short cul-de-sac of Granger on the other side of Hill, and I slid into the car next to him and watched the police and the federals arrive around seven-thirty, followed by men and women with cameras and microphones, and Horace leaned over and punched me on the shoulder when, at eight on the dot, Tiffle sleepwalked right into them.

We drove aimlessly for an hour, listening, and at nine we made the news: a thirty-second story about a Chinatown lawyer, some Chinese prisoners in the basement, and half a million bucks. At nine-thirty I reclaimed Alice from her parking spot, followed Horace while he returned the rental, and dropped him at home, where he could start being nicer to Pansy.

By ten-fifteen, Dexter and I were sitting in Captain Snow's little boat, bobbing up and down in the fog and keeping an eye on the *Caroline B*. Or, rather, I was keeping an eye on the *Caroline B*. Dexter had a fishing pole in one arm and Captain Pat Snow in the other, and both of them were looking down at the water.

Some people are said to have postcoital tristesse. Astronauts talk about postorbital letdown. I'd managed to pull off most of something that, two days earlier, I'd privately given no chance of working, and I felt like cold fried eggs. The discontent was so strong as to be physical, a queasy, hollow core in the center of my abdomen that wasn't caused by the rocking of the boat. The only thing that could relieve it, I realized, would be the sight of Charlie Wah coming across the water, on his way to the wrong place.

After forty-five minutes I was sure he wouldn't come. After an hour, I *knew* he wouldn't come. At eleven-thirty, Dexter caught a fish, and Captain Snow cooed appreciatively and helped him take it off the hook.

At eleven-forty-eight, a big black-and-white cruiser emerged from the fog. There were lots of men in uniform on its deck, and there wasn't much question where they were going. Still, we waited until they went aboard, and then Captain Snow made the engines hum and we headed for Marina Del Rey. I left Dexter on the boat and took a long walk up the dock to my car.

On the way home, I realized I wasn't going there. The Pacific lay gray and cold to my left as I passed the Topanga turnoff and headed toward Alaska. There was a longer news story on the radio around twelve-thirty, and by now they'd gotten around to the houses, which the announcer dubbed "rest stops on the slave highway." Apparently someone had seen a little capital in it, because a couple of politicians served up outraged, over-written sound bites about exploitation and human misery. One of them, an Orange County admirer of Louis the Fourteenth, yapped shrilly about the need to control immigration more effectively and protect American jobs, just like there were millions of Americans eager to work sixty-hour weeks for three thousand a year, net.

Nothing about the *Caroline B.* yet, and nothing about Charlie.

Maybe the parts of it I'd pulled off hadn't been the right parts. Maybe I should have let the INS get the pilgrims and concentrated on Charlie, taking the long view: There'd be fewer slaves for a while. On the other hand, as Everett had said, *they want to come.* So maybe there weren't any easy answers.

I hate it when there aren't any easy answers.

By the time I hit Rincon, we'd made the one o'clock news, the national news out of New York. The dresses had been announced to the media, and the report was rife with implications that there were forty or fifty female slaves, presumably naked, rattling around the streets of Los Angeles. Never underestimate the power of cash and sex and the media fascination with the word "slave." I grinned for a moment at the image of Norman Stillman trying frantically to reach me, and then hoped that the phone lines between Taiwan and Charlie Wah's left ear, wherever it might be, were about to catch fire.

Charlie. Just his name was enough to bring me back down to earth. I watched a bunch of freezing surfers pretend to have fun as I ate a couple of greasy fried clams on a pier somewhere near Santa Barbara. The thought of Charlie and his pastel suits and his prostitutes finished off whatever remnant of my appetite the grease on the clams hadn't already quelled. I hurled the rest of them, one at a time, at the heads of the surfers, and gulls swooped down and picked them out of the air.

Charlie was going to skate. He might have a few bad hours with the Snake overlords, and his trip back to Taiwan probably wouldn't be a pleasure cruise on the Love Boat, but he'd still be able to afford his terrible clothes. He'd still be able to play with other people's lives, making and breaking promises and watching the thick blood flow whenever he got bored. Nobody was going to practice the Death of a Thousand Cuts on him in retribution for the two Vietnamese kids in the sweatshop.

Since the clams were all gone I balled up the paper sack they'd come in and pitched it into the gray air. A fat gull caught it and dropped it and squawked at me indignantly. I squawked back and headed toward Alice.

Fog had ghosted its way in from the sea. It pressed itself against the slopes of the mountains and thickened maliciously as I drove south, cutting visibility to a hundred feet or so, and I saw one, then two, accidents, all crumpled metal and flashing lights, and I slowed to a crawl, fixing my eyes on the taillights of a truck in front of me and letting it run interference. I figured it would mash anything in front of us flat, so that I could just ride over it. Smart.

Mr. Smart Guy. Charlie, free as a seagull with millions in the bank. Eleanor's family, never able to be sure that they wouldn't get tied to this somehow and waiting for the knock on the door. Two men dead. Millions of Mainland Chinese lining up to put their money into Charlie's sticky hand and head for what they thought would be freedom, poorer by ten thousand dollars and one last hope.

The truck driver gave up around four and turned into a seaside motel that announced itself in a smear of pink light as THE LAST WAVE. Deprived of my scout, I slowed even more and watched the world grow dark. Above the glow of Alice's instrument lights, Uncle Lo smiled at me from wherever he was, safe on a dead man's papers. I switched off the news and found some rock and roll, loud and mindlessly busy, and daydreamed about the next time I'd meet Lo. Like the truck driver, he'd guided me into the fog and then disappeared. I couldn't seem to remember a time when it wasn't foggy.

I punched up the news again at six-thirty as I turned into Topanga Canyon, and got a story about the Feds busting a ship in San Pedro, the *Caroline B.*, operating on a warrant based on an anonymous tip. Nine people, all Taiwanese nationals, taken into custody, no names. Part of an international ring smuggling Mainland Chinese into the country. The word "slaves" was used four times. In a related story, the good folks living next to the safe houses had suddenly realized there'd been something strange going on and stepped forward eagerly to tell lurid tales of broken-spirited young women being herded in and out. It made me feel good enough to stop at the Fernwood Market and grab a six-pack.

It was close to seven and already completely dark, the night black and fog-muffled, when I climbed out of Alice and scaled the driveway. I whistled for Bravo, but he was probably off disrupting the agendas of the local coyotes. Ready for a shower and sixteen hours' sleep, I felt my way to the door and opened it and then stepped inside and switched on the light.

The first thing I saw, sitting on the stool in front of my computer, was Mrs. Summerson, looking dazed and large and empty and frail. The second thing I saw was Charlie Wah.

24

Velocity and Position

"Looking bad, Charlie," I said, and he was. His eyes were puffy and skittish, and his hair was pressed flat on one side as though he'd slept sitting up. The suit of the day, a stomach-curdling shade of lemon yellow, was wrinkled and bunched, and something sagged heavily in his pocket, dragging the jacket further out of shape. His necktie was at a lopsided half-mast, and he'd apparently missed his step coming up the driveway because one yellow knee was smeared with dirt. Still, the little gun in his hand was clean and bright and well maintained and absolutely steady.

"You live like a pig," he said. He was standing beyond Mrs. Summerson, in front of the living room's one south-facing window.

"Well," I said, "we can't all afford to dress like Life Savers. I guess you weren't on the boat."

The gun came forward an inch or two, and my abdominal muscles went into involuntary aerobics. He saw it, and he smiled, but then he replayed what I'd said. "The boat?"

"The good ship *Caroline B.*, your floating hotel. She's now the property of Uncle Sam."

The smile congealed on his face, and his gaze suddenly went right through me, fixed on the distance as he started a whole new set of calculations. A sound from the bedroom drew his glance, and one of the steroid junkies, the one with the single eyebrow running across his head, came out, toting my spare gun. He pointed it at my midsection, and Charlie relaxed his, still distracted by all the shuffling realities in his head.

"Here's Bluto," I said to Mrs. Summerson. "Have you met Pluto?" She didn't stir, just looked at the floor as though she were trying to see through it.

"What have you done to her?" I asked Charlie Wah.

"A little lesson in mortality," Charlie said absently. Then he was back with us, giving me a glare that would have blistered paint. "The old have a low pain threshold. I wonder how high yours is."

"It's subterranean." I wasn't much liking the conversation's drift.

"That will simplify matters." The gun came up again, and he said something to the bodybuilder. Bluto tucked the gun in the back of his pants and came toward me, gesturing for me to lift my arms. He patted me down quickly and thoroughly, relieving me of the automatic and the wad of money I'd counted out for myself at Dexter's. The gun went into his pants pocket and the money into Charlie's free hand.

"How much?" he asked, hefting it.

"Fifty," I said.

He wrinkled his nose. "Cab fare. Still, it's reassuring to know that you kept some. I suppose each of your associates has a similar amount?"

"Suppose anything you like."

He said something, and Bluto punched me. I didn't even see it coming, just watched Bluto's face change suddenly and then my head exploded and I was lying on my back on the floor with my ears ringing and the room rippling in front of me like I was looking at it over a radiator.

"I suppose each of your associates has a similar amount?" Charlie Wah repeated, word for word.

"Yes," I said, not trying to get up. I was damned if I was going to let him see me stagger.

"Two hundred fifty thousand dollars," he said. "Add that to the two-eighty you left with Mrs. Jesus here, and we're over half a million. What in the world prompted you to leave half a million in Tiffle's office?"

"A love of symmetry," I said. He'd heard the half million on the news, but he didn't know about the money for the pilgrims.

He shook his head. "Let's get things straight," he said flatly. "You've cost me immeasurably. I've lost money, respect, and now a ship. There's nothing that I won't do to you." He reached down and flicked his forefinger forcefully against my right eye, which I barely closed in time, and when I got it open again he was shape-shifting through my tears. "Anything you can think of that hurts, I can think of too. And, unlike you, I can do it." He glanced at Mrs. Summerson, big and mute and absent on her chair. "I can even enjoy it."

"Charlie," I said, "you're getting personal."

"I suppose I am," he said, without much interest. "Certainly, if I cause you unnecessary pain, it will be for my own satisfaction. But there are business reasons, too. I need to recoup as much of my money as I can, and I have to annihilate the men who disrupted my transaction and cost me my ship. Anything less will not be understood by my associates."

I watched him sweat.

"I was on the telephone most of the night," he said in an aggrieved tone. "In Taiwan they actually took seriously the idea that some blacks were trying to move in on us. They were expecting some sort of proposition this morning: a partnership, perhaps. But then we got the news about Tiffle, and it all fell into place."

Blacks. The one we'd let go had apparently called Taiwan.

"Still, you might have gotten away with it if you hadn't handed so much to the police, just to inconvenience Tiffle. I don't understand how you could mount an operation so complicated, so elaborate, and then do something so revealing."

He wanted me to talk. "My memory palace was full."

"Was it?" he said dismissively. "Well, we're going to help you to clean it out." He gestured to Bluto, who went into the bedroom and came back out carrying a coil of rope. Bluto surveyed the room briefly and then threw one end of the rope over one of the beams below the ceiling, the beam from which the hermit who built the shack had hanged himself some thirty years earlier, when he realized they were paving Old Topanga Canyon Boulevard a mile below. The man had prized his solitude.

Bluto took both ends of the rope in his hands and hoisted himself on it, bringing his legs up and parallel to the floor just to show off.

"He weighs more than you do," Charlie Wah observed. "Too much muscle."

"It's a strong beam," I said, my voice sounding thin and far away.

"Get up. Take off your shirt."

"Take off your own shirt. It might help the suit."

The gun tilted down to point at my midsection. "What's going to happen to you on the beam won't be pleasant, but it'll hurt less than being shot in the gut."

I got up and took off my shirt. The buttons seemed to be smaller than I remembered.

"Over there," Charlie Wah said, wiggling the gun toward Bluto. "Don't do anything you're not told to do, or I promise you really exquisite pain. Is that what they say? Exquisite pain?"

"For Christ's sake, Charlie," I said. "Get a dictionary." The shirt landed at my ankles. Feeling as naked as a shelled shrimp, I took the long walk to Bluto.

"Hands out," Charlie Wah said. "Wrists together."

Bluto was an expert; it took him only a few seconds to wrap one end of the rope around my wrists. He knotted it off tightly enough to make the veins on the backs of my hands pop out, and then he backed off and began taking in the other end of the rope, hand over hand. He pulled effortlessly until I was dangling by my wrists, barely able to reach the floor on tiptoe. When I was stretched to capacity, he tied the rope's end to the leg of the wood-burning stove and stood back to admire his handiwork.

"This is a good trick," Charlie Wah said. "We use it on first-time runaways, people who try to welsh on their contracts. There are very few second-time runaways." He reached into the sagging pocket and pulled out a shiny little ballpeen hammer. "It also has the advantage of being consistent with the natural causes you are probably going to die from in a little while," he said, advancing on me, "unless you are very, very cooperative." We both listened to the lie, and he smiled apologetically. "A drunken fall from your sun deck." He stopped in mock dismay. "Stupid me, I've forgotten something," he said. He pointed behind him and snapped his fingers, and I saw a black medical bag at Mrs. Summerson's feet.

Bluto scurried to the bag and opened it. He withdrew a corked bottle of vodka and a hypodermic needle large enough to use on a horse. For a moment I thought I was going to vomit. Compared to the needle, the ballpeen hammer looked like the hand of friendship.

The cork popped as Bluto drew it out. "Not too much at first," Charlie Wah said. "We want him coherent."

The long needle probed the vodka, and I watched the level fall as Bluto drew back the plunger. It took about a quarter of the bottle. Looking beyond him, I saw Mrs. Summerson's magnified eyes fixed on the hypodermic. So someone was home, after all.

"Good," Charlie Wah said. "Hurry up."

Bluto came toward me with the needle in both hands,

and I hoisted myself on the rope and swung my legs at him, trying to get the needle. He avoided me easily and swung wide to the right, going behind me. He moved very quietly. I lifted my feet again and swiveled on the rope to keep him in sight, and Charlie Wah threw an arm around my waist and pulled down with most of his weight. The beam groaned but held, and I lost sight of Bluto.

Something struck my right shoulder like a fist and immediately became the center of a circle of fire. Heat coursed up and down my arm and I resisted the compulsion to try to swing away, frozen by the image of the needle breaking off inside me. I felt a tugging sensation, and Bluto stepped away and into view, examining the empty hypodermic. Charlie said something sharp in Chinese, and Bluto handed him my spare gun. Charlie glanced at it and dropped it into his jacket pocket.

Then I was drunk.

It happened almost instantly: a brightening of the colors in the room and a high singing in my ears. Charlie Wah's wretched suit glowed like the world's last lemon drop. Bluto was back at the bottle, tilting it to get the rest of the liquid within reach of the needle.

"No," I said automatically. My tongue was thick enough to choke on.

"I agree," Charlie Wah said. Was he weaving or was I? "Not yet, anyway. We don't want it to act as an anesthetic." He reached out and tapped my shoulder lightly with the hammer. "I want the names and addresses of the four people who helped you. We'll start with the black ones."

"Martin Quimby and Klaus Fuchs," I said, pulling names out of the air. And then I remembered Tran and added, "And George Smiley."

Charlie tilted his head and regarded me. "Too easy," he said. "Let's see if you stick to it." Then he drew back his arm and swung the hammer directly at my chest.

I actually heard the rib break. A tide of hot red pain swept over me, starting at the broken rib and spreading through my body until it filled even my toes and fingers with a sticky, unholy heat. I gasped for breath, and the pain started again, a spark at first, then expanding outward like a ball of flame, pulsing ahead of the deeper pain that propelled it, and I was screaming. When the scream was exhausted, I grabbed air again and the seed of pain exploded once more, and this time I stifled the scream and hung there, trying to take in sips of air.

"You learn fast," Charlie Wah said approvingly. "Some fools scream over and over again. We actually lost one to a heart attack. What are their names?"

I hung there, gaping at him like a fish. Their names, whatever they had been, had been washed from my mind. I closed my eyes, and the room began to spin wildly, and I forced them open again, trying to anchor the universe with the weight of Charlie Wah's yellow suit.

"We'll break one on the left side this time," he said, raising the hammer.

"Dexter Smif. Horton Doody. Howard Doody," I said. He'd never find them.

He gave the hammer a little heft and looked deeply into my eyes. "Even you couldn't make up those names," he said at last. He thought for a moment. "Smif?"

"That's the way he pronounces it. I don't know what it says in the phone book."

"Addresses, please."

"I don't know their addresses." The hammer came up. "They're in my computer," I said, the words tripping over each other in my eagerness to get them out before the hammer fell again.

Charlie Wah leaned toward me and gave the broken rib a little tap with the hammer, and I heard my voice scale upward again and snap like a dry wishbone, and then I was hanging there, coughing and sobbing.

"Is that all?" he said with exaggerated patience.

"Yes."

"It wasn't," Charlie Wah said, stepping back. "The little one who didn't really look very black was the Vietnamese we should have killed?"

"Tran," I said. "I don't know where he is."

"You do, you know, but we'll get to that later. Each of them has fifty thousand dollars?"

There were words there, floating right in front of me, and I grabbed them. "Unless they've spent it."

Charlie Wah's face creased in merriment. "The Vietnamese will never spend it," he said. "But who knows about black people?"

"Yeah," I said, wishing I could double up.

"Which would you prefer," he asked conversationally, "another broken rib or another shot?"

"What do you want from me now?"

He looked at Bluto. "Enjoyment."

"You'd better hurry," I said, using as little air as possible, "before Dexter and Horton spend your money."

"A shot, I think," Charlie Wah said. "Then we'll see about the rib."

Bluto toddled toward us with the syringe. "Don't do anything active," Charlie Wah cautioned me. "That rib is a very dirty break."

The fire in the arm again, and then my head swam violently, as though some giant baby had picked up the dollhouse and given it a twirl, and then the pain screaming from the rib miraculously subsided to a roar. I closed my eyes in relief, and when I opened them I was looking at two Charlie Wahs, overlapping each other.

".... too drunk," I heard myself saying.

"Too drunk for what?" Charlie Wah asked politely.

"Computer," I said. The last syllable was very difficult. I suddenly found I couldn't hold my head upright, and my chin bumped my chest.

"You have a point," Charlie Wah said. He backed

away from me and wiggled a finger for Bluto. "Cut him down."

Bluto came toward me in a series of waves, and I had to close my eyes again to keep from vomiting. I felt his hands pass professionally over my ribs, and then the rope slackened, and I went down on my seat, the rib compressing another vast ball of pain into a seed and then exploding it, and my body jerked open again. When I opened my eyes I was flat on my back.

Bluto had a knife now and he was sawing at the rope around my wrists, not being overly careful about not cutting me, and Charlie Wah was standing in front of Mrs. Summerson with his gun loosely trained on us. Then the ropes parted and I took my eyes off Charlie and off Mrs. Summerson and looked anywhere else in the world as she very slowly stood and picked up the heavy stool as though it were a Q-Tip and brought it down on Charlie Wah's head.

Bluto turned at the sound as Charlie crumpled, dropping his gun, and I grabbed the handle of the knife and turned it against the nerve-rich web of skin between Bluto's thumb and index finger. He jerked back to me, letting loose a scream and reflexively jerking his hand back, and I snatched the knife and drove it into the muscle of his calf, feeling it hit bone and slip aside, and he went down on top of me. Charlie was beginning to stir as I pushed Bluto off, the rib sending out concentric circles of pain, and I got to my feet at the same time Charlie's fingers touched the gun and launched myself at the light switch, flipped it off, and backed away.

In the sudden darkness, my legs hit the stool Mrs. Summerson had dropped and I went down on my side, the side away from the broken rib. I hooked an ankle under the stool and kicked it away from me, and when it landed a flame blossomed in the dark. Charlie had shot at it.

The *boom* from the gun ricocheted back and forth for what seemed like half an hour as I dragged myself toward the couch. The floor was heaving like a ship's deck beneath me and I was fighting down the greasy clams that were trying to climb back up my throat. I was drunker than I'd ever been in my life.

Then the darkness blistered in front of my eyes and pushed itself toward me, and I almost drowned in it. I gulped air to remain conscious, and someone moved, and Charlie fired two shots, and I heard one of them smack into flesh and there was a deep groan from Bluto as I turned my head and vomited and then vaulted for the couch, for where the couch had to be.

As I landed, Mrs. Summerson started to scream. Charlie snapped off something in Chinese and the screaming stopped, and then there was silence. A tardy bird sang outside, and my mind seized on the notes and turned them into a loop, a bird's drinking song, high-pitched and monotonous. The darkness started to blister and swell again, but I found the will to push it away and listen.

There should have been a moon. The fog had sealed it off so completely that it might have been circling another planet. Someone breathed: Charlie, I guessed. Near where I had last seen him, anyway. Someone else coughed, a deep ugly sound with fluid in it: Bluto, probably, still on the floor. I pressed the tip of my tongue against the top of my mouth, an old radio trick for eliminating breathing noises, and slowly drew air around it. The rib pinged brightly, and the pinging increased as I leaned over the back of the couch and put my right arm down behind it.

"I hear you," Charlie announced. I froze, bending down over the broken rib, and the couch rippled and heaved beneath me. I had to put my other hand, the one bleeding from Bluto's knife, onto the couch to keep from losing my balance, and Charlie fired again at the noise, once this time, and the bullet slapped into the leather to my left. Dust tickled my nose.

"There's nowhere you can go," he announced. "This is the only door out."

Keep talking, I willed. I'd gotten both arms all the way down, and my fingers brushed the carpet. Just the carpet. I'd have to move down the couch.

It was a creaky couch.

"We can work this out," Charlie said, sounding confident. "I've got the money. Hey, you can *have* the money. What's fifty thousand? Little change," he continued, getting the idiom wrong. "Nothing to die for."

A scuttling sound from the kitchen and then an enormously loud clatter in the living room, and Charlie fired again, and I scooted down the couch, trailing my fingers on the carpet and hit cold metal with both hands. My skin, wet with sweat, squealed against the leather, and Charlie pumped two blind shots into the couch. More dust, invisible clouds of it, billowed out, and I fought to breathe through my mouth again.

"FYI," Charlie said gaily, "I've got your gun, too. Lots of bullets left."

His shoes squeaked. Bluto moaned weakly on the floor. I wrapped my fingers around the metal and the effort pushed the breath out of me, and I inhaled dust through my nose. Another deafening clatter. Mrs. Summerson was throwing frying pans.

Charlie didn't fire this time. He didn't say anything, either. Over Bluto's labored breathing I heard something soft, like a knife through silk, and I realized Charlie was sliding over the carpet. There was only one place he could be going. I fought to locate it in the swirling dark.

Another clatter, Fibber McGee's whole closet this time, but by the time it ended both semiautomatics were in my hands and I'd lifted them free of the couch. Prickly dust crowded my nostrils and the night swam in slow, undulating waves all around me. Fumbling at the guns' safeties, I aimed at the spot Charlie had to be heading for, and—sneezed.

It's impossible to sneeze with your eyes open, so I

didn't actually see the light snap on, but I yanked back on both triggers and felt the guns jumping, jumping and roaring more times than I'd expected. I opened my eyes in time to see Charlie slowly sliding down the wall beneath the light switch as bloody holes appeared in his suit, awful red on awful yellow. He fired once at the ceiling and lay back, his head propped up against the wall. His eyes were wide and confused.

I sneezed and vomited simultaneously, a new and mind-altering experience, and the broken rib kicked in to make it truly memorable. When I was back in the room again, I saw Mrs. Summerson staring down at Bluto with my last frying pan in her hand. He was clearly dead.

"Murderer," Mrs. Summerson said, and it took me a long, pain-slowed and alcohol-befuddled moment to realize that she meant Charlie, and not me. She slowly brought the blue eyes up to mine.

"Are you all right?" she asked.

"No," I said. My bleeding hand slipped off the back of the couch, and I tried unsuccessfully to shift my knees to take my weight. "Get the money out of Charlie's pocket and call this number, would you?" I said. I gave her Dexter's, twice. Then the room upended itself for the last time, and my face hit the floor.

25
—
Dimmer Sum

The Empress Pavilion was jammed as always, but we'd come early enough to get a table.

Mrs. Summerson sat possessively next to Doreen, who had inadvertently brought Charlie to me. She and Mrs. Summerson had gotten the pilgrims settled in at the church and gone back to Mrs. Summerson's house for a long catch-up chat. They'd been there, undoubtedly sipping tea, when Charlie and his boys dropped in, using the address Lo's henchman had volunteered. Dexter had found Doreen bound and gagged in my bedroom when he'd come to pick up Charlie and Bluto.

By now, the other pilgrims had already been dispatched to Las Vegas.

Eleanor had claimed the chair to my right, between me and Mrs. Summerson. Across the table, Horace was spooning out something mysterious for Pansy, who passed it on to the twins. The twins were being good enough to convince me, momentarily at least, that they'd been worth all the fuss. Tran, looking brown and healthy, sat next to Pansy.

The three wild cards were seated opposite Eleanor and me: Hammond, Sonia, and Orlando. We'd been halfway out the door when Hammond had called and asked if I was free for lunch, and some perverse instinct had prompted me to invite them to join us.

"Nice place," Hammond said, every inch the good sport. He loathed Chinese food as much as I loathed television evangelists.

"Ooooh, *dim sum*," Sonia said, eyeing the waiters and their carts. "Keep an eye on me, Al, or I'm likely to outweigh you."

Hammond patted her hand, lowered his head at me, and charged. "Been a lot going on lately with the Chinese."

"Boy, hasn't there been?" I asked brightly. "It's all you hear about." The story had been everywhere, and Stillman's show—with me furnishing background, off-camera through a voice filter—had actually broken news off the TV pages. The cops had located dozens of Charlie's earlier slaves in Los Angeles, although surprisingly few of them seemed to be women destined for sordid lives of sexual servitude.

Hammond had no way of knowing about the four bodies Dexter, Captain Snow, and some Doodys had dropped into the sea, heavily weighted, about six miles offshore. Nor did he know about Everett, whom the Doodys had placed aboard an eastbound train after pounding his parents' phone number and address out of him and threatening their lives if Everett ever came back to L.A.

"Nothing to do with your little hypothetical problem," Hammond said.

"That was just uncles," Eleanor said, the picture of innocence. In justice, she didn't know about the bodies, either. I was going to tell her eventually, probably the next time we made love. Like maybe in an hour.

On the other hand, maybe we'd just make love.

"I spent decades doing the Lord's work among the Chinese," Mrs. Summerson volunteered, "as a missionary. Misery among those fine people is an everyday commonplace. It doesn't even make the news.''

Hammond registered the fact that she was a missionary with a heavy blink.

''Same Vietnamese,'' Tran said, serene and secure in the knowledge that he'd given thirty thousand dollars to his mother and had already bought a ticket to New Orleans, where he planned to buy a shrimp boat. ''Always trouble.''

I grabbed a breath to interrupt him and winced. Beneath my turtleneck, I was taped from navel to gullet like a mummy who got the curse wrong and aimed it at himself.

''You're Vietnamese?'' Hammond asked, looking not at Tran but at me.

''He's sweet,'' Sonia said, beaming at Tran. ''Look at his adorable little face.''

''Look this,'' Tran said. He glanced down, pulled a quarter out of his salad fork, and spun it across his fingertips.

''Magic,'' Orlando said impatiently, ''is just a trick against time.'' He was apparently peeved that we hadn't shown up with a seventeen-year-old girl in tow. Sonia hit him with an elbow.

''Say again,'' Tran said, lifting his eyebrows.

''We've all been sitting here at the table,'' Orlando said, ''so we know you didn't slide that quarter under your salad fork. We've all had experience with salad forks, so we know they don't have quarters inside them, because no salad fork in the past has ever had a quarter in it. You contradict time when you pull the quarter out of the salad fork, which is why it's entertaining.''

Eleanor leaned in and rested her chin on her hand. ''Do you still think time travels in one direction only?'' she asked Orlando.

He shrugged impatiently. ''Maybe it's all here at the same time: past, present, future. We can all look at the past. You do it every time you look at a star. The light you see started traveling toward us years ago, maybe millions of years ago. There isn't even any way to know whether the star is still there. It might have exploded when dinosaurs hatched eggs in Montana. It might flicker out tomorrow night, as far as we're concerned, but its death actually happened, in earth time, while some *Tyrannosaurus rex* was eating a little mammal. Back when mammals were nothing to worry about.''

"Bringing it closer to home," I offered, "there isn't any way to be certain that a person you think you know is still there, either.''

"Your time, his time," Orlando mumbled. "They're not the same.''

"I've been thinking," Eleanor told him, "about time. Since the last time I saw you, I mean. I've decided I'm no fan.''

"I'm sure that time is bereft," Orlando said crankily.

"It changes us in ways it shouldn't," she continued. "It separates us, it makes us strangers to the people we're supposed to love. It buries the past and obscures the future. It dulls and yellows the world around us. Eventually, it kills us, but it doesn't even let us off that easily. First it turns us into something we don't want to be: frail, ailing, dishonest with ourselves and mistrusting of others. And then, when we're hurting, it slows down to give us leisure to wish for what we were.''

"Oh, please." Orlando sounded disdainful. "If you want to think about it in personal terms.''

Eleanor slipped something into my hand, something with sharp edges. "I think about everything in personal terms," she said. "I'm a person. I think time is a cheat. It encourages us to make bets we can't win and then snickers nastily when we try to go back and bet again. What it doesn't tell us, what we can't know when we're young, is that all bets are for keeps.''

The thing in my hand was a postcard, a brightly colored picture of some rosy-cheeked Asian people standing around with some animals that might have been yaks. "But still," Eleanor continued, "what strikes me is that most of the ways we measure time are beautiful. Old pocket watches. Medieval water clocks, dividing the day and night into so many splashes of water. Sundials. Aztec calendars carved into wheels of stone. Time counted in music, three or four beats to the measure. Stonehenge. Did you know that the ancient Chinese used incense clocks? They took a metal plate and cut a design into it, a single complicated groove, and they filled the groove with different kinds of incense, one for each two-hour period. Then they lit one end. People could wake up and know what time it was by the perfume they smelled."

"Dr. Summerson gave me an incense clock," Mrs. Summerson said wistfully. "Sung Dynasty."

I turned the postcard over and stared down at it.

It was postmarked China.

"We never know what time it is," Orlando insisted. "My time and your time—"

"Hush," Sonia said. And, miraculously, he did.

It was a normal, junky, third-world postcard, printed on cheap, fiber-flecked paper that had been soiled by many hands. *Hello children*, it said, in rigidly rectangular English script, a script with years of missionary-school practice behind it. *I ask your forgiveness.*

Eleanor leaned over and kissed me on the ear as I read the signature. It said *Lo.*

I folded the card in half and looked up, catching Hammond in the act of giving me Force Ten Cop Suspicion.

"Do we have time for all six courses?" I asked.

__JAMES ELLROY

"Echoes the Best of Wambaugh"
New York Sunday News

BROWN'S REQUIEM   78741-5/$4.99 US/ $5.99 Can
Join ex-cop and sometimes P.I. Fritz Brown beneath the
golden glitter of Tinsel Town...where arson, pay-offs, and
porn are all part of the game.

CLANDESTINE   81141-3/$4.99 US/$5.99 Can
Nominated for an Edgar Award for Best Original
Paperback Mystery Novel. A compelling thriller about an
ambitious L.A. patrolman caught up in the sex and sleaze
of smog city where murder is the dark side of love.

KILLER ON THE ROAD   89934-5/$4.99 US/$5.99 Can
Enter the horrifying world of a killer whose bloody trail of
carnage baffles police from coast to coast and whose only
pleasure is to kill...and kill again.

Featuring Lloyd Hopkins

BLOOD ON THE MOON   69851-X/$4.99 US/$5.99 Can
Lloyd Hopkins is an L.A. cop. Hard, driven, brilliant, he's
the man they call in when a murder case looks bad.

BECAUSE THE NIGHT   70063-8/$4.99 US/$5.99 Can
Detective Sergeant Lloyd Hopkins had a hunch that there
was a connection between three bloody bodies and one
missing cop...a hunch that would take him to the dark
heart of madness...and beyond.

FAST-PACED MYSTERIES
BY J.A. JANCE

Featuring J.P. Beaumont

UNTIL PROVEN GUILTY	89638-9/$4.99 US/$5.99 CAN
INJUSTICE FOR ALL	89641-9/$4.50 US/$5.50 CAN
TRIAL BY FURY	75138-0/$4.99 US/$5.99 CAN
TAKING THE FIFTH	75139-9/$4.99 US/$5.99 CAN
IMPROBABLE CAUSE	75412-6/$4.99 US/$5.99 CAN
A MORE PERFECT UNION	75413-4/$4.99 US/$5.99 CAN
DISMISSED WITH PREJUDICE	
	75547-5/$4.99 US/$5.99 CAN
MINOR IN POSSESSION	75546-7/$4.99 US/$5.99 CAN
PAYMENT IN KIND	75836-9/$4.99 US/$5.99 CAN
WITHOUT DUE PROCESS	75837-7/$4.99 US/$5.99 CAN
FAILURE TO APPEAR	75839-3/$5.50 US/$6.50 CAN

Featuring Joanna Brady

DESERT HEAT	76545-4/$4.99 US/$5.99 CAN

Coming Soon

TOMBSTONE COURAGE	76546-2/$5.99 US/$6.99 CAN